AMERICAN COUSINS

Adele Archer

AMERICAN COUSINS
(Book 2 in the International Relations Saga)
By Adele Archer

Copyright © Adele Archer 2016

All rights reserved. No part of this publication may be reproduced, distributed, or transmitted in any form or by any means, including photocopying, recording, or other electronic or mechanical methods, without the prior written permission of the author, except in the case of brief quotations embodied in critical reviews and certain other non-commercial uses permitted by copyright law.

Acknowledgements

With thanks to Amy, for selflessly offering and giving your invaluable help when I needed it most. Also thanks to Gareth for your graphics wizardry.

Also by this Author

International Relations

TABLE OF CONTENTS

1. ENGAGEMENT AND…ENGAGEMENT
2. MISSING IN ACTION
3. BACK FOR GOOD?
4. PRENUPTIAL AGREEMENTS
5. THE GATHERING
6. CRISIS AT CHRISTMAS
7. BEARER OF GLAD TIDINGS
8. GLADER TIDINGS?
9. LOVE AND MARRIAGE
10. YOU TOO SHALL GO TO THE BALL
11. PLEASED TO MEET YOU
12. A FAMILY AFFAIR
13. DO ME A FAVOUR
14. THE FABRICATED FRIEND
15. SUSPICIOUS MINDS
16. KEEP YOUR FRIENDS CLOSE
17. TROUBLE AND STRIFE
18. THE GREEN-EYED MONSTER
19. PREVENTING THE UNPREVENTABLE
20. IN THE AFTERMATH
21. WHAT TO DO, WHAT TO DO
22. I WISH I MAY, I WISH I MIGHT
23. PERSONA NON GRATA
24. SWEET REVENGE
25. NIGHT OF NIGHTMARES
26. KEEPING A DISTANCE
27. CRASH AND BURN
28. NEED YOU LIKE A HOLE IN THE HEAD
29. LOVE YOU TO DEATH
30. GONE
31. HAPPY ANNIVERSARY
32. DANCING IN THE DARK
33. TO DO OR NOT TO DO
34. DEAL BREAKER
35. BACK
36. CRYING FOR HELP
37. IN HINDSIGHT
38. PART OF THE PAST
39. THE LAST GENTLEMAN CALLER
40. HERO
41. THE TRUTH WILL OUT
42. IT'S A GIFT
43. WHAT BECOMES OF THE BROKEN HEARTED

AMERICAN COUSINS
Adele Archer

ENGAGEMENT AND...ENGAGEMENT

Summer had been nothing to write home about, typical of England in truth. There had been a two-week hot spell in June followed by endless rain. When the weather was poor, Dee experienced pangs of guilt – not that she could control it of course. Her fiancé had moved from America to England just to be with her, and she couldn't help feeling she owed him better weather. In fact, whenever London wasn't perfect in any way, Dee suffered shame over it. Be it a rise in crime, bad service in a restaurant, or just the constant bloody pissing-it-down-rain; Dee blamed herself. She desperately needed the U.K. to be this idyllic little island of yesteryear (typically post 2nd World War would've been optimal) for her foreign partner; dry-stone-walled English country lanes, polite and affable countrymen, friendly public houses and every door left on the latch because it was such a safe country to live in. It had to be just right because Milo needed to love it the way she loved it; to think of this place as home.

But the United Kingdom evolved just as the rest of the world evolved. Richmond, that leafy suburb of London that she called home, had its faults just like any place on the planet - but Dee didn't want to be anywhere else. Still, September had surprised everyone with a freak Indian summer they could all enjoy, or would have enjoyed if a certain someone hadn't decided it was time to emerge into the world.

Sitting by Dee's hospital bed, Milo dozed peacefully in a squeaky polyurethane-covered armchair. His head was resting on folded arms while Dee slept fitfully. Their six months as an official, bona fide couple had not been plain sailing; he was away in the States on business more than either of them were comfortable with and Dee didn't jet off with him because of her irrational fear of his parents (well, actually no - that was quite rational, they despised her) and her advancing pregnancy. However, when they were together they were as happy as clams. All too soon the brief break from proceedings was over and Dee woke up with a start.

"...Ow...ow-ow-ow..." she groaned. That intense, driving pain had returned to her pelvic bone again. It was a little like menstrual pain - times a thousand.

"It's okay, I'm here." Milo gripped her hand and felt hers clamp down on his tightly. Dee was beginning to groan in an octave that was steadily growing higher and higher in pitch. It soon would only be audible to dogs. "Remember your breathing, just try to relax into it..." he advised her.

"*Relax into it?* Are you crazy? I feel like I'm trying to pass a bowling ball here!" Dee ranted in a panicky voice. "Where's the gas and air?" she said with an uncharacteristic wildness in her voice.

"Here." Milo hurriedly passed her the tubing and turned it on at the canister. Dee began drawing on the mouthpiece frantically. "No, not like that - slow and steady breaths like the midwife said."

"This is unbearable...I'd rather die than feel like this!" Dee removed the mouthpiece from between her clamped teeth just long enough to tell him. The gas and air just made her feel dizzy; it simply confused the pain rather than lessened it.

"Don't say that. It will just be a few more hours and then the pain will be over - and you'll be holding our new baby in your arms to show for all of this."

"A few more hours?! I can't go on a few more hours!" The trouble was, they were fairly early on in proceedings. Dee had been in the early stages of labour for about ten hours. They were knowledgeably informed that the baby's head was engaged but Dee had only dilated a couple of centimetres, so an end wasn't quite in sight.

"Just calm down..." Wrong thing to say.

"*You* calm down! You couldn't do this! And it's all your fault anyway! I didn't ask to have another baby, y'know!"

Milo bit his tongue, reminding himself how lucky he was not to be in her position experiencing this. Still her acidity struck home a bit. "...Well, no. But you *were* as excited about this as me. If you weren't in so much pain-"

"Just do something to help me!" she howled. Milo opened his mouth but couldn't formulate anything to say. Luckily the midwife came in at that moment with her broad, cheerful grin that Dee loathed.

"Goodness me, what a fuss - I could hear you from down the hall," she clucked and rolled her eyes. Milo shoved the gas and air back into Dee's mouth because he saw from her face she was about to explode. "Would you like to try the birthing pool again? You really ought to get up and walk about at least - a bit of gravity would do wonders."

"No I don't!" Dee shouted, yanking the mouthpiece out. "I can barely move without triggering another contraction! I've done all that you asked and you promised me it would help, but it didn't!" she growled menacingly.

"Can't you give her something for the pain?" Milo asked hopefully.

"I've brought in some Pethidine but it's really the last dose I can give."

"Well stop jabbering and hurry up and give it to me then!" Dee snapped. The midwife shook her head with a well-used sigh, bringing the syringe over on a little cardboard tray.

"How are you holding up, Mr Phillips?" she asked. It was 7 o'clock in the morning and they had been awake much of the night after Milo had rushed Dee in at about 3am in a panic. This was hard for him; he hadn't been present at Andrew's birth so felt at a bit of a loss. He did all the things he had read about; rubbing her back, offering encouragement, helping her with breathing techniques but at the end of the day, he was helpless.

"...I'm okay - a bit tired...I just can't get comfortable on this chair-"

"*YOU* can't get comfortable?!" Dee's rage was triggered off once more. "Oh, you poor bastard! You should go home to bed and leave me to it!"

"She doesn't mean it," the midwife advised him calmly with a small arch of an eyebrow.

"Yes I do! I *do* bloody mean it!"

"Why don't you go off and get yourself a coffee? Dee will sleep for a bit after this." The midwife was already injecting the medication into Dee's thigh.

Milo sighed dejectedly and rose to his feet. "...I think I will..." And extricating himself from his fiancée's angry grip, he left Dee cursing the midwife some more.

*

In spite of the early hour, Milo was surprised to find the waiting room full of familiar faces. Forrest and his two cousins, Ginny and Felix had arrived. And of their own volition, Jerry and Elliott had put in an appearance too. Milo glanced at them sourly where they sat in rose-pink-coloured chairs and went to get himself a dull-tasting plastic cup of coffee from the machine.

"Morning, guys. I didn't expect to see you here Felix - I thought you were leaving today?" Milo scoured the machine menu for the simplest coffee he could find. It was too early for a fancy latte, mochaccino or a cappuccino. Even from a machine.

"I am, but I wanted to see the baby before I disappear." Felix was leaving for Paris later that day to work on a musical for the best part of six months.

Milo smiled at him gratefully. "Thanks, man. I hope it comes soon for you."

"How is she?" Forrest wheeled himself over. He and his cousins had received a garbled text in the middle of the night and felt it right to be with Milo as soon as morning came.

"Terrible..." Milo rubbed his tired eyes. "She's in so much pain and I just don't know what to do."

"Can't they do an epidural or something?" Felix was leaning against the side of the coffee machine, wishing he was allowed to smoke.

"The obstetrician and the midwife want to hold off on that if they can, it makes it harder to push."

"Seems barbaric to me." Felix made a face.

Ginny carefully scanned the machine options once Milo had retrieved his drink. She rubbed his arm. "Having a baby hurts, there's just no getting around that," she said soothingly.

"Well, I wouldn't go saying that to Dee if I were you. She'd probably stove your head in," Milo sighed again. "She's just so *angry*..."

Elliott laughed from across the room. "Yes, she was just the same when she had Angel."

Jerry glanced up from his newspaper with a scowl. "Perhaps if you spent more time in there with her instead of swanning around drinking coffee, she'd be less afraid and therefore, less angry," he said with a casual drawl.

"Jerry-" Elliott began witheringly.

Milo's brow knitted and his mouth hardened into a thin line. "Dee and I have been here all night and I've barely left that room! And why are you here? You wouldn't even speak to her for months!" he growled. It had actually taken Elliott about two weeks to make contact again after the big announcement but Jerry had kept his silence for two whole months. Still, Dee hadn't seemed to bear a grudge.

"We're family, and family fall out sometimes. Dee and I are close enough that we understand each other," he remarked blandly.

Felix sighed a weary sigh. "Stop being such a tool, Jerry. Milo is her family now."

"We are all going to have to learn to get along, Jerry," Forrest agreed pragmatically, wheeling himself across the room to mollify his cousin. However, Jerry and Milo did not agree - they neither needed nor wanted to get along. Milo saw no need for these disapproving half brothers (who didn't even know they were half brothers anyway) and would be glad if they stayed out of his and Dee's lives for good. He could dream.

*

At around 1:45pm, the business end of proceedings had finally come into being. Dee quite literally screamed as she pushed down hard; perspiration streaming down her forehead, clenching Milo's hand until he thought the bones would be crushed.

"I can see the head crowning!" the midwife cried exultantly. "This will all be over soon."

"Get it out!" Dee howled in complete and all-consuming agony. Weren't second babies supposed to be easier? This was going no better than the last time.

"Babe, look at me - you can do this," Milo told her encouragingly.

"I can't, I can't...I'm so tired..." her fearful eyes were the size of saucers. "I just want it to stop - I can't take this pain anymore..."

"I know, darling - but it won't be much longer. Just one final effort," he assured her, pressing his forehead against hers.

"Promise me I don't ever have to do this again...this is our last baby, okay...?" she insisted frantically.

Milo paused momentarily. "...Okay..."

"I need you to push really hard Dee, the hardest you can!" the midwife declared and the contraction was so strong and continuous, Dee could do nothing else. Between little pants, she pushed down with her abdominal muscles and any other muscles available - bearing down with all her might. "I can just get my hand around the head! Big push now!"

Dee pushed again, eyes clenched tight, teeth gritted, growling with the intensity of the pain. And then she felt a pulling, a wrench and a sliding sensation as the midwife said, "stop pushing now!"

"Oh my God..." Milo was laughing and crying all at once.

"You can open your eyes Dee, it's over...your baby boy is here." The midwife was proudly displaying a mucky, purplish creature. She carried the silent thing away to do something that neither could see, there was a loud wail and she was bringing him back wrapped in a towel.

"...It's a boy?" Dee asked in a daze as the baby was placed in her arms. He squinted up at her with his little dark blue eyes, completely bald and grizzling grouchily. Both Dee and Milo were crying now and her husband-to-be kissed her gratefully.

"He's beautiful...thank you so much Dee, you're amazing," he said. The three were all now wrapped up in a little huddle.

"...I'm sorry I was such a cow..." Dee snivelled and he laughed, still holding them both as though fearful they would disappear. But Milo wouldn't, he was an *actual* father again.

"I'm used to that," Milo joked. If he had been looking for the accepting, silent type, he had chosen the wrong girl.

"Shut up..."

That was the day Finley Lance Phillips emerged into the world.

MISSING IN ACTION

December was bland and colourless. The deciduous trees were lifeless and ugly, their gnarled branches stabbing up at the permanently murky grey sky. Even the evergreens were an uninspiring bottle green and the whole town somehow seemed to wear a wishy-washy hue. Much like Dee's mood of late. Motherhood (at least the early stages) was something that Dee had never really excelled at. She spent her days in a permanent state of angst - being in charge of something so small and helpless was frightening if you stopped and thought about it. And taking care of that very small and helpless thing alone was undoubtedly much worse. Dee felt herself becoming increasingly isolated; she knew nobody else with a new baby (having very few girlfriends) and being a new mum separated her from the life she had before. She felt distanced from Bruce and Patrice and even the coffee shop. The advent of Christmas was the only light at the end of the tunnel; it was a beacon she forced herself to focus on.

Dee Campbell guided her two-and-a-half-year-old daughter, Angel along the bustling pavement on George Street. She hauled her three-month-old son, Finley in a heavy baby car seat by her side, battering it against her leg, bump-bump-bump as she went. Struggling with the two children, one skipping and the other bawling, Dee staggered into The Lanes towards 'Bookish', the coffee shop she owned in Richmond.

"You didn't have to come in today." Evan Townsend opened the shop door to greet her, a little bell tinkling above their heads. Dee loved the sound of that bell. He had caught sight of Dee on the street from where he sat idly behind the cash register. Evan, the ex-owner, was indispensable. He managed the shop so proficiently that Dee need never set foot in the store again. And she had never felt more dispensable in her life. "We're not busy."

Dee wondered if she ought to be worried about that too but she was too tired to let it get to her right now. "...I know, I just needed to see that the outside world really existed..." she muttered weakly as Angel ran off to her favourite Wendy house in the play corner of the shop. The little girl's hair had grown into a sandy bob, the colour of her late father's and it fell into little ringlets about her shoulders yet the top was poker-straight. She was like her father facially too; a permanent reminder of him, but then she could easily have been Milo's as well. Dee placed down the car seat beside her usual table in the window and unclipped Finn. She fished him out and cradled the little boy whose wailing subsided to a half-hearted blubbering.

"When is that fiancé of yours coming back to wipe that miserable frown off your gob?" Evan enquired as he poured her a steaming cup of filter coffee from the jug before she need ask.

"...Before Christmas, but what would I know?" Dee grumbled, flopping down on a soft, rust-coloured leather chair. Evan placed their coffee down on the table and joined her.

"Is everything alright with you two?"

Dee bristled and her lifeless eyes flashed at the threat of doubt in her future husband. "Yes, we're fine, he's just away on business more than we'd like, that's all," she replied coolly.

Evan scrutinised her silently for a minute. "So how long has he been gone this time?"

"Nearly six weeks - he rings me every day. I just wish I could see him more often," said Dee distantly. She loosened her shocking pink scarf and slipped out of her parka. Dee tried not to feel irritated under Evan's earnest stare constantly searching for some chink in her resolve.

"It must be hard with two kids though - Finn being such a young baby and all." Evan cooed over the child.

"I've got Mrs Dawson's help," Dee said gratefully. The children's nanny had been invaluable and Dee would quite truthfully not have coped otherwise. To have her partner constantly at her side was the one thing she craved. "Bruce been in?" she murmured absently.

"Yes, asking for a job as usual," Evan groaned.

"Can we give him a job yet?" Dee asked hopefully, her outlook beginning to brighten.

"Not if you want to pay him what he earns already at the hotel. I'll look at the books again in the New Year and reconsider it. Although, I'm sure we'll regret it if we do. The only difference will be that we'll have to *pay* him to sit around and drink coffee," Evan said with a level gaze. Dee had never been given cause to overturn his decisions. Evan was always right in these matters.

"And are the accounts okay? Should I be concerned that we aren't busy?" She glanced around the shop and saw only two tables occupied by two other couples.

"Oh no, I was rushed off my feet at breakfast time with the morning people and the commuters. This is just that funny lull-time of the day. Things are going well, I promise you. I'd say so if they weren't."

Dee sipped gingerly at her scorching coffee. "So how is Mia?"

"She's looking forward to Christmas." He smiled warmly at the thought of his eleven-year-old daughter. Those deceptively serious green eyes glimmered behind his rectangular glasses and he scraped a hand through his receding mid-brown hair.

"I'm glad you decided to spend it at mine," she said.

"I'm glad you invited us. I hope you haven't taken on too much, inviting so many guests." Evan twisted his mouth. "Let's just hope Milo is there to join us..."

Dee opened her mouth to protest but realised she had no defence. Milo may be home but maybe he wouldn't. It was not lost on her that the best part of December had passed and Christmas would arrive in just a couple of days.

"And the wedding is still on for April?" Evan continued.

"My God, did I inadvertently walk into Jerry and Elliott's office?" Dee looked about her sardonically. The frosty atmosphere between the brothers had warmed somewhat in the eight months since her decision to marry Milo. At least Elliott had come to accept the fact, whilst Jerry had now relented enough to trade insults with her. So all in all, things were back to normal.

"I'm just worried about you, Dee," Evan said mildly. "You're not your usual off-the-wall, vaguely irritating self...do you think you might have postnatal depression?"

"No, I don't think that!"

"There's nothing to be ashamed of if you did - it's normal to have the baby-blues, but for some people it turns into-"

"I'm fine!" she asserted curtly. "Look, I'm a bit down, naturally, because I have a new baby and my fiancé isn't in the country at the moment. But we're just as much in love as we ever were so...yes, the wedding is still on. And everything will settle down soon." But Dee was gloomy. She longed for him. The daily phone calls took the edge off her loneliness, but the moment the receiver went down and his voice disappeared all the way back to the States she missed him all over again. Only half of their nearly nine months as an official couple had been spent together. Of course, Milo had been an adoring father to the children and a loving, attentive partner to her. But business called him away far more than either of them had expected.

The problem was that their periods together were interrupted so regularly, the moment they became accustomed to living with one another and family life, he was off again. So they went on in a perpetual honeymoon state, but with that came the pitfalls of doubt and insecurity.

"Okay, I'm just asking." Evan held up his hands in surrender, it was pointless trying to make this woman open up if she didn't want to. "...And did you decide on your new surname yet?"

"Yeah, I think so. I'm going to call myself Phillips. I'm fed up with the double-barrelled thing. People are always disappointed to find out I'm not actually posh...or very common," she explained.

"Oh, here she is. Working hard as usual," said Cameron Quinn as he slumped down at their table uninvited. Funnily enough, Dee hadn't heard the bell tinkle at his entrance into the shop.

Dee covered her surprise quickly with a mock-unaffected air. "Talking of working, why aren't you ever at that damn University? Did they suspend you for inappropriate behaviour with female students again?" She turned on her own brand of charm. Dee had had plenty of practice adeptly fielding the constant insults from her ex and one-time college teacher.

"Hmm, that's very amusing. Hello Finley, isn't he like his father? That's if Milo actually *is* his father," he sneered rather unattractively.

"Well, he could hardly be anyone else's," Dee said impassively, staring at the brown foam-scum gathering around one edge of her coffee cup.

"...I wouldn't stake my life on it." Cameron had been ever mindful of the impending birth. Perhaps he hoped the baby was a figment of her imagination. "I'm sure you put it about a bit. So how is Lance-Mk-II?"

"Milo is fine, thank you. He'll be back before Christmas." Dee's composure wavered a little on that touchy subject.

"How nice, so now you only need worry about what women Milo has been hooking up with while he's been away – maybe that Amber girl from the New Year Ball. That 'going to the States on business' rouse is absolutely infallible," Cameron suggested mockingly.

"I wish you'd sort out the intelligibility of your abuse. Who exactly in my relationship is it that's cheating? One minute you're accusing me of infidelity and then it's Milo. Admit it, you've just come in here to vent your random, illogical venom - again," Dee sighed, regaining complete control. It was terribly easy to get the better of Cameron since he was the only one who had any real feelings left from their brief time together.

Evan put down his cup with a deliberate clatter. "Cameron, why don't you just emigrate? Or failing that, get the fuck out of our shop!" he glowered. Evan virtually never swore, but Cameron could drive the meekest of people to curse far worse than that.

"*Our* shop? You're just a hired help now, Evan. Dee only keeps you on because she's too stupid and lazy to run this place herself," Cameron commented.

"You see, Evan? Now I'm stupid and lazy. Tomorrow I'll be a conniving, scheming harlot and the day after that I'll be a simpering victim. Shoddy," Dee advised - tinkling her teaspoon distractedly on the side of her mug. Cameron irritated her intensely of course, but he couldn't be allowed to know that. Evan laughed out loud. The only positive aspect of Cameron's repeated unwanted company was that it unfailingly brought out Dee's smart-mouth; the Dee Evan had first met.

"Cameron!" Angel bounded over from the completely wrecked play corner (the devastation her doing) and enveloped Cameron in a hug. He was too regular a visitor for Dee's daughter to forget about him as Dee had hoped.

Cameron stroked Angel's sandy fringe from her eyes. "Hello sweetheart." He smiled with genuine warmth and Dee was forced to avert her eyes or she may just throw up.

"Mummy, Cameron come over and play soon?" she asked hopefully.

"...We'll talk about it, honey," Dee grimaced. Her daughter still displayed genuine feelings for this man that Dee had come to loath.

"Yes, you talk about it and let me know when you have a window in your diary," Cameron interjected knowingly and rose to his feet. "Well, it's been lovely seeing you all. I'll be in touch, Dee," he said and ambled cockily from the shop.

Evan frowned. "You ought to do something about him, like hire a hitman," he said under his breath before Angel wandered off again. Evan had become fiercely loyal to his boss in the short time he had come to know her. Partly because she wasn't much like a boss at all.

"Seriously Evan, what can I do? He lives around here and I can hardly force him to move," Dee replied sullenly. But, thanks to Cameron's stirring, her mind was starting to conjure up all the unlikely possibilities of what her fiancé may or may not be getting up to. She kissed the top of her adorable baby's head who continued to whine intermittently.

*

That evening Mrs Dawson bustled around the kitchen in a cleaning frenzy. No surface was safe from her trusty spray and cloth. She had become a regular at the house most mornings and evenings. She had a talent for feeding, bathing and dressing dirty children, conjuring up delicious meals, dispensing of used dishes and keeping an entire house spotless and toy-free.

Val Dawson's short grey hair was motionless, sprayed in place and flawless, much like her ever-painted face. She wore her remarkably unwrinkled, if slightly frumpy clothes neatly over her wiry frame. Val was always well turned out. She had taken the place (in domestic terms at least) of Dee's mother, assisting the struggling woman with the complexities of juggling two children, a business and the upkeep of a large Victorian house.

"Thanks, Val. Finn's finally dropped off," Dee said gratefully, after gingerly creeping down the stairs and into the kitchen. But Finley was actually becoming quite a decent sleeper, unlike his sister who had required complete silence from the moment she fell into slumber. Val could whizz a vacuum around in the same room as sleeping Finn without disturbing him.

Val returned her magic cleaning devices to the cupboard under the sink. "Oh good," she smiled pleasantly. "Like I say, if you can express some milk for me and freeze it, I can take him off your hands for a few hours tomorrow. You look like you need a good sleep. When is Mr Phillips coming back?" While Val and Dee had long been on first name terms, she was always formal in reference to Milo. There was something about Milo that brought out subservience in people and Dee couldn't understand why.

"Before Christmas," Dee murmured blankly for the third time today. If she said it enough, she may start to believe it. "He should be calling me tonight with his flight details. You get off home and I'll see you in the morning. I couldn't have coped without you today," Dee said absently, she had her mind on her shabby if comfy sofa in the room she called the 'cubbyhole', longing to slump down and stare vacantly at the TV. She felt remotely guilty about having enough money to buy help. There were billions of mothers out there who managed single-handedly and Dee knew hardship well enough to be vigilant against complacency. She was extremely lucky and she had to keep reminding herself of the fact.

"You'd cope alone if you had to," Mrs Dawson assured Dee, as if reading her mind. She wiped her over-worked and wrinkled hands upon her apron and untied it. "Right, I'll see you tomorrow." Val gave Dee a kindly if slightly condescending pat on the arm and left the house.

Dee slunk out of the kitchen, across the newly-polished wooden floorboards into the cubbyhole and flopped down on the sofa. The remote control was soon glued to her hand and Dee mindlessly channel-hopped, restlessly waiting for that same time of night when the telephone would ring. No sooner than she had taken her mind off the impending and momentous time of the day, the phone rang. "Hello? This is the lady of the house speaking."

"Hi, honey," a rich and welcome voice greeted her with a little chuckle.

Dee felt instantly relieved. "Hi, you," she said, her dormant heart warmed.

"What are you doing?" Milo asked in that familiar, drawling American voice.

"The children are asleep and I've just sat down and scanned every channel on TV and I can safely say I have a hundred channels of crap to watch," she closed her eyes, imagining his presence beside her, not just his voice.

"I can't wait to see you guys," he said softly.

"When *are* you going to see us guys?" Dee asked hopefully. "It's nearly Christmas."

There was a minimal yet significant delay before he answered. "Um, that's where I'm having problems," he began gravely. "We're having terrible snow storms in the New York area and a lot of flights are being cancelled."

"Oh no," Dee groaned. She had heard about the snow on the news but had put it from her mind. Surely a spot of frozen rain could not stop their joyful reunion. "But Milo, you are richer than God. Can't you charter your own jet again?"

"Babe, I promise you I'm doing my best. If there is any possibility of any plane being allowed to take off for England, I'll be on it. But I'm not going to get myself killed just for the sake of Christmas."

"…You won't be home for Christmas, will you?" Dee felt her eyes pool up with tears. "Angel will be devastated and people are starting to ask questions because you're never here."

"What people? What questions?"

"People think we're having…difficulties," she admitted in a wavering voice.

"Well, you tell those people we are just fine," he replied with an affronted tone. "Dee, I'm doing everything in my power to get home. You know I want to be with you for Christmas too," Milo assured her.

Dee was too upset to answer at first. Just then she was startled by a rattle at the door as if a key were turning in the lock. "Oh, hang on a minute, Milo. I think Mrs Dawson is back. She must have forgotten something." Dee rose to her feet and wandered out into the hall.

The front door opened slowly and there before her was Milo with a mobile phone in his hand and a mischievous smirk on his face.

"You little…" Dee gaped and slowly padded towards him in her bare feet. She stopped before her partner with her hands on her hips. "Do you think that was funny? How many times am I going to have to remind you that

Americans can't do 'funny'?" Dee was very nearly angry with him.

"Oh come on," he grinned, kicking the door shut behind him. "I couldn't resist, I was aiming to keep it up for half an hour but you started doing that tearful thing and I was too excited about seeing you." Milo stepped closer. "Your hair has grown," he noticed, gently smoothing a piece of her bobbed hair, now long enough to scrape into a small pony-tail, between his fingers. "Aren't you going to kiss me?" he murmured, moving into her personal space.

"You don't deserve a kiss," Dee grumbled weakly but he was already pressing her against the wall. Their eager mouths met and Dee wrapped her arms about him, strangely nervous. The butterflies in her stomach took flight and although he was the father of her child and soon to be her husband, he still made her feel jittery like a new boyfriend might. He let her go and Dee wiped the last of the tears from her eyes.

"I don't think we look like a couple having difficulties," he said. "So you say the children are asleep?" Milo furtively undid the top button of her white, fitted shirt.

Dee groaned. "Honey, I wish you'd told me you were coming back tonight. I need to wash my hair and the baby has been sick on me a million times."

"I don't care, you look great to me," he ran a finger across her cheek. "It's been so long since we've seen each other. Let me look at you." Milo gazed at her adoringly.

Dee squirmed under his scrutiny. "Don't Milo, I look horrible. I'm going to have a shower."

"Alright, I'll just look in on the children if that's okay and I'll catch you up." Milo kissed her again and reluctantly set her free. Dee ran an affectionate hand across his back as she passed by. Climbing the stairs, Dee smiled to herself all the way to the top. He was home.

BACK FOR GOOD?

Dee attempted to calm herself down as the powerful spray of water jets buffeted her body. She was finding it impossible to even catch her breath. Milo was here; she could hear him bustling about on the landing, no doubt waking the children. Dee tried to dampen down the feelings of excitement building inside her. Why did she feel so terribly nervous? This was the man she was to spend the rest of her life with but he instilled such a sense of trepidation in her. In a good way.

"I'm sorry, I accidentally woke Angel. She gave me a big hug and went straight back to sleep, she's just adorable. And Finley looks so different already," Milo remarked with barely contained enthusiasm as he came into their en-suite bathroom. "I hate being away from you guys."

"We aren't exactly enjoying it either," Dee replied pointedly, scraping her wet hair back.

"Can I join you?" As Milo opened the sliding shower doors, he was already stripping off his sweater and jeans, his longing for Dee evident as he joined her.

"Sure," she said almost sheepishly. "...So, how have you been?"

For a moment he stood there with a silent smirk on his face, appraising her with his deep brown eyes. "No talk now, I want you. I haven't had sex in a month..."

After they were done, if she ever had any doubts about their future, those concerns dissolved whilst his naked skin touched hers. Things had become slightly over-zealous, as they always did when they had been apart too long, and both were breathless.

"I wish you wouldn't go away anymore, Milo," she said in what was almost a whisper. He held her so close she could only see a patch of his chest. "...I just miss you all the time."

Milo held her at arm's length and smiled. "...Are you looking at my hair? It's gone insanely curly again, hasn't it? Where do you keep the hair dryer these days?" he asked, pulling away. Milo detested his wavy hair and insisted on drying it as straight as it would go. He was always so immaculately turned out, he made Dee feel untidy.

Dee rolled her eyes, a little bit bemused, as he climbed from the shower. "God, you're such a girl. I've seen you with wet hair a million times and I like it. I just wanted to look at you because I feel like I don't see you very often. Don't run away," she said but he was already halfway across the bathroom. He was laughing to himself until the sound of Finley crying burst their bubble-like mood of contentment.

"I blame you for that..." Dee groaned with a weary sigh.

*

Milo was lying on the bed naked, languidly reading a women's magazine when Dee returned half an hour later. He was so relaxed and at ease there, Dee thought, as she scrutinised him momentarily. Obviously he did not share her awkwardness at the newness of their situation.

"Hi." Milo didn't really look up but held out a hand to her and Dee sat beside him in her white towelling robe. He absently loosened the belt and pushed it off her tense shoulders so that they were both nude again. It was as if he wanted to erase the time elapsed between their lovemaking and the half hour spent feeding Finn. But he nonchalantly went about the business of browsing his magazine again. "There's a real life story in this magazine about a fifty-five-year-old woman who had a fling with her daughter's husband and had his baby. I'm sure they make these things up," Milo said distractedly before he became aware of the quizzical look in her eyes. "...Are you still up half the night with Finley?"

"No, only about twice a night these days. He gets hungry more or less every four hours," Dee explained.

"Is the breastfeeding going okay?"

"Yeah," she replied distantly. Dee was still feeling a little self-conscious around him because the 'New Boyfriend Syndrome' always took a few days to wear off when he had been away for a while. Sitting here naked was slightly off-putting too.

"Isn't our son amazing?" Milo mused contentedly. "He's just perfect, tiny little fingers and toes, that cute button nose. He's going to be really good looking; I just know it. He already is..."

His bottomless enthusiasm and inane casualness began to grate on her nerves. "You've just missed a month and a half of our son's life," she advised slightly tersely.

Milo physically blanched. "But I-"

"And that's a month and a half you'll never get back," Dee continued, but seeing his expression began to feel rather sorry for her spurned partner. She held his hand tighter and stroked it. "These early moments of a baby's life are gone so quickly that you have to cherish every single day. They aren't tiny for very long."

Milo sat up, chagrined. "Do you think I enjoy being away from Finley? Do you think I like missing all his first moments when I missed so much of Andrew's life?" he said, injured. "Andrew is never coming back; he's dead. So every day I thank my lucky stars that I met you and got this second chance to be a father to Angel and Finn."

"Then why aren't you ever here?"

"Because my business is in America, Dee, you know that!" he argued.

"But I don't know why you have to be there all the time!" she snapped hotly. "What, there's nobody else on your team who can make decisions? You have to be there in person daily or your business will go under? You're in Real Estate, Milo, you aren't the President. If you have to work this hard, you can't be doing very well!"

"I'm good at what do! I care about what I do!"

"And what about us, do you care about us?"

Milo virtually exploded. "The moment I get a chance, I'm on a plane coming back to you guys! I spend my goddamn life in the air!"

"Well, lucky us! And just think of all the frequent-flyer points!"

"You and the kids could be with me every single day if you wanted to be! Why won't you ever come back to New York with me? Your store practically runs itself and yet you refuse to come to America!" he glowered.

"I have a three-and-a-half-month-old baby who needs to settle into our home surroundings, I need to be here!"

"What, in case Cameron happens to drop by?"

"What the hell is that supposed to mean?" Dee jumped off the bed. "I've got two kids under three and a coffee shop to run, d'you think I've got time to see that wanker behind your back?" She was simply livid, even if arguing naked was a little disconcerting. "Is that why you spend so much time over in the States? Because it gives you the opportunity to meet up with Amber?"

Milo had the look of a man who was desperately confused. His rapturous homecoming was turning sour. "I love you. I gave all that up for you. You know that. You don't *really* believe I'd see other women, do you...?"

"...No, of course I don't," Dee muttered wearily and sat back down on the bed, utterly deflated. "I just had these dreams of raising this baby together and it isn't happening - I just want you home for good. If I didn't love you and I had feelings for someone else, I'd be pleased you were always away. But I do love you and I would never-" she began tearfully, wiping her face with the back of her hand, unable to finish.

"I know that, I didn't mean what I said about Cameron." Milo took her hands with such a pitiful look on his face that Dee wished she had never picked this fight - she had spoiled tonight and she knew it.

"I know you're making all the sacrifices in this relationship. I know I'm asking a lot of you to leave your home-country...but I thought it was what you wanted."

"It is what I want," Milo reiterated vehemently. "...Is this us having problems now? Because if we are, I want to fix them," he assured her.

"So do I. But I'm just too tired to get into that tonight. I really need some sleep. I'll be up again with Finley in a few hours and fighting in the nude isn't as much fun as it's cracked up to be," Dee mumbled weakly.

He smiled again at last. "No, it's not..."

"Do you want me to get you something to eat first?"

"No, I ate on the plane," Milo lied. She looked dog-tired and he wasn't hungry anymore. He had been too edgy on the plane to eat and he knew she would be insistent he had a meal if he told the truth. "Go to sleep, baby, you're shattered. And I'm pretty tired too."

*

Try as he might, Milo's head was too crowded to doze off. He craved to continue their conversation but Dee had nestled into the crook of his arm and quickly fallen into a deep sleep. He would also be rather partial to some more intimacy but she was exhausted, and he understood that.

Milo had barely been able to sit still on his flight from America. Just to know he was coming home to England, coming home to his fiancée and children; this was a huge milestone for him. There was no longer the tiresome problem of persuading Dee to give him the time of day. Last year he had continually faced the stumbling-block of Dee's resentment toward him, and even when she did succumb to him she would always run away again. Now he was able to unlock the front door to their house with his own key and caress Dee and hold his kids whenever he wanted to. It was a domestic world he had not actually realised he had longed to be a part of and sometimes he could hardly believe his good fortune. Still, even this domestic bliss was not always perfect. Milo was beginning to realise that Dee was struggling and he needed to find a compromise. He was determined to do that in the morning.

*

Milo cradled his baby son, gently resting the boy over his shoulder whilst he sat at the kitchen table reading yesterday's paper. Finley Lance Phillips's features greatly resembled Milo's. Milo trusted Dee enough never to question his parentage but the child was the spit of him, so there was no doubt in his mind anyway. The fine hair on Finley's head curled like his father's, but was the extraordinary pale blonde of his mother's and his eyes were the same luminous turquoise. He was an even mixture of both parents.

Dee sat opposite him, laboriously feeding Angel a bowl of porridge. It was two days before Christmas and the house was dressed with tasteful yuletide decorations. Now that her fiancé was home, everything was in place for the big day. She watched how carefully Milo handled the baby with an obvious glow of contentment and pride about him. Dee had never seen him so happy. He wasn't one for great speeches about his feelings on a daily basis but he showed his pleasure at his new situation in every gesture. Just the look of satisfaction he wore on his face said it all.

Mrs Dawson busied herself about the kitchen making a cooked breakfast. She seemed to have an inhuman sense of culinary timing and was never overwhelmed, never flustered. "It's nice to see you back, Mr Phillips," she said genuinely.

"Thank you, Mrs Dawson," Milo replied, his eyes twinkling as he smiled furtively at Dee.

"Honey, I've got some wedding invite samples and I need your opinion." Dee reached into a large envelope in the middle of the farmhouse table and pulled out the handmade paper samples.

"Oh Dee, I don't know about these things. I am a man, you know," Milo reminded her warily.

"Yes, but you're a man of breeding and money and taste, whereas I am a girl of comprehensive schools and council estates, so I think your opinion is more sophisticated than mine," Dee asserted.

Milo laughed in the way that only Dee could make him laugh. "Let me see, then...I like the ones with gold leaf on, I guess."

Dee wrinkled her nose. "Oh, I thought they were garish, I didn't really think much of them..."

"Whatever." Milo rubbed at his eyes, mildly exasperated. He removed his hand to watch Mrs Dawson wander out of the kitchen with a knowing smile on her face. "...Dee, let's just get married," he told her abruptly.

"Um, we are. That's what these invites and place card samples are in aid of," Dee said with a baffled shrug. "We're all set for April, aren't we?"

"No, I mean let's get married now, before I go back again...I was thinking of New Year's Eve?"

Dee watched him in silence for a moment. "You want to get married in....eight days' time? Are you mad? How on earth can we arrange that?" She shook her head.

"There's nothing that can't be arranged if you can afford it. New Year's Eve falls on a Saturday this year so it's perfect for a wedding and it's a normal day of business."

"Yes, but in eight days' time! I thought we agreed on April?" Dee felt strangely panicked. Surely he must be jesting with her. "What's the big hurry?"

"I think I'd feel more secure if we were married before I went away again, and I think you would too," Milo explained as though this was the most sensible suggestion in the world.

"Is this about last night?" Dee groaned. "Look, I wish I'd never started it. I'm totally committed to you with or without that piece of paper; there's no need for our wedding to be a rush-job."

"But it isn't just a piece of paper, is it?" Milo arched a shrewd eyebrow. "I'm sick of calling you my fiancée or girlfriend because that sounds so inconsequential. We've just had a baby and we're planning to spend the rest of our lives together but nobody believes were actually going to go through with it."

Dee sighed. "...I do know how you feel, I keep wanting to tell people you're my husband, but then I realise I can't..." Dee was almost swayed for a moment. "But Finn will only have just turned four months and it's too much to deal with. I've got everything booked up for Easter time." She had felt rather proud of herself for booking the very Saturday they had initially chosen up at Orleans House. Now she was supposed to start again?

"Dee, you really must start taking advantage of being wealthy. We'll hire a wedding-planner like we should have in the first place. This is all too much hassle for you as a new mom," Milo insisted brusquely. "I'll make a few phone calls later to see if I can find somebody who can take it all on. Let's just see what happens, okay?"

"...I suppose," she said weakly. "But where could we get married at this short notice? Maybe I could try Orleans House again or Ham House..." Dee began making notes on the back of an envelope. She had never planned on a church wedding anyway but even a civil wedding would definitely prove very difficult to arrange at this late stage.

"Dee, somebody else is going to take care of all those decisions for you, remember?"

"But we've not given our guests any notice. What about your parents and family in America-?"

"...Hi guys," Elliott announced rather apprehensively. Mrs Dawson stood behind him looking somewhat guilty for letting him in. Dee and Milo stared at him wordlessly for a moment.

"Hello Elliott," Dee greeted him in a slightly strangulated voice. They had met for the odd coffee but he rarely came to the house since Milo had moved in.

"I'm sorry it's a bit early, but I was passing. How are you, Milo? I didn't know you were back."

"Evidently not," Milo replied, forgetting his manners. "...I'm fine, thank you, Elliott...right, I think I'll go for a walk and buy today's newspaper at the store. I'll take Finn, he could do with some fresh air." He stood up awkwardly.

"Don't go on my account, Milo." Elliott uneasily rubbed the back of his neck with the flat of his hand.

"I'm not." Milo stood a good four inches above his estranged cousin. "Are you coming girly-girl?" He grinned at Angel.

"Yes, Daddy!" Angel excitedly leapt from her chair.

"If you're very good, I might get you some candy," he said warmly, leading the little girl through to the hall by the hand.

"Sweets!" Dee called after him as tolerantly as she could.

Milo ignored her but there was a begrudging smile creeping onto his mouth. With his sleeping son in his arms, he left them to it. "Come on - let's get Finn into the pram and your shoes and coat on, then."

"Americans, what will you do?" Dee commented dryly as Elliott gingerly stepped closer.

Elliott seated himself at the table and seemed to take a steadying breath. "All set for Christmas?"

"Pretty much, we've got Forrest, Felix, Ginny and the children, Bruce, Patrice and Evan and his daughter over for the day. You and Jerry would be more than welcome too," she added as an afterthought.

"...Oh, that's very kind. We were thinking of popping in for an hour or so to see Angel," he said with a smile as Mrs Dawson set a cup of filter coffee down before him. "Thanks, Mrs Dawson. So what's all this?" Elliott asked as he noticed the numerous invites on the table.

"Oh, sample invites for the wedding. The trouble is, Milo has just sprung on me that he wants to get married sooner than April. In fact, he wants to get married on New Year's Eve, if you'll believe that. I mean, who gets married at New Year's?" Dee grumbled. "And you try finding a venue for eight days' time. I think he's kidding himself."

Elliott surveyed Dee's scribbled envelope-list of National Trust Houses for civil ceremonies and looked up. "I have a venue...I always thought you might ask us in the first place. You could get married in our hotel," he offered in a small voice.

25

Dee watched him suspiciously for a time. "Get married at your hotel? Oh yeah, Jerry would absolutely *love* that," she laughed incredulously.

"I'm sure I could persuade Jerry if he thought it might help fix your relationship with him. You could get married in the afternoon and all the guests could go on to our New Year's Eve Ball in the evening," he shrugged as though his solution was not preposterous (which it was).

"...But Elliott, why would you do that for us? You don't even *like* Milo," she reasoned.

"Well, he's the man you've chosen to marry and you're evidently serious about him so I don't want it to drive a wedge between us," he explained stoically. "Jerry and I hate that we don't get to see as much of you as we used to. I know you think we just want access to Angel but the fact is, well, you're the closest thing we ever had to a sister. We do miss you, Dee."

"But you're both so cold to Milo. He tries his best to get along with you for my sake but it's not easy when he's always met with unpleasantness. I'm going to be Milo's wife and that means my loyalties will always lie with him. I don't understand why you can't be friends again; he *is* your...cousin-"

"I do my best to be civil and Jerry is getting better. But I just wish you wouldn't let Angel call him *Daddy*, it seems so unfair to Lance."

"Angel chose to call him Daddy, we had nothing to do with it...and he loves her like his own. Don't you think it's good that Angel has a father-figure in her life?" she asked. "I used to be a little uncomfortable with it at first but she adores him, and I promise we will tell her all about Lance when she's old enough to understand."

"Well, I'm glad we agree on that."

"And what about Finley? Is he going to grow up thinking his uncle Elliott and uncle Jerry worship his sister and want nothing to do with him?"

"Of course not, he's your son and we love you - so we love him too. I told you that at the christening. Finley's a beautiful boy and when he's older, I'd love to take him out for the day when we take out Angel."

Dee frowned, unconvinced. "That being said, I think I'll have to decline your venue offer. It's very kind of you but it wouldn't be fair on Milo. You make him feel uncomfortable."

"Well, think of this as us trying to build bridges. The whole day will be on us, our wedding gift to you," Elliott implored her. "Where else are you going to get a venue as good as ours at such short notice?" He smiled because he had her there.

Dee shifted reticently in her seat. "...It's really sweet of you to offer, Elliott. Won't you have too much on your plate with the Ball? And do you really think you can get Jerry on board?"

"I know I can, he talks about how much he misses you all the time. We can cope with another event on top of the Ball," Elliott insisted blandly, pushing back his chair. "Well, I'd better go before Milo gets back."

Dee watched him with a measured gaze. "No, you stay for breakfast, Elliott. Prove to me you can spend an entire hour in the same room as my fiancé, and I might just take you up on your offer." She said it as though she was doing *him* the favour. Elliott narrowed his eyes before rolling them and promptly sat down again.

PRENUPTUAL AGREEMENTS

The quarrel (even though Milo would insist it was just a friendly debate) continued on into its fifteenth minute. Dee could prove that as she had been glancing at her watch irritably through each of them. "Just because something is offered, doesn't mean we have to accept it," he rattled on as they strolled hand-in-hand down George Street. The tall American wore Finley in a baby-sling strapped to his front and the child nestled there in between the opening of Milo's wool coat. He was turning into the archetypal new man. Dee guided Angel along beside her with her free hand as they caught up on some last minute Christmas shopping that afternoon. In spite of the *discussion*, there was something so truly perfect about being out and about as a family that Dee knew she would never grow complacent and take it for granted. She had lost too much.

"This may be our one chance to be reconciled with them," Dee reminded him for the umpteenth time. "If we turn them down and throw the offer back in their faces, they will be horribly offended."

Irked now, Milo shrugged. "So? I'm not having our wedding day used as a vehicle to please them. We don't even know Jerry will agree yet and we're wasting time when we should be checking out other venues."

"Or your *wedding planner* should be," Dee huffed. "Elliott said he will call me tonight with a definite offer," she insisted adamantly. "Anyway, what's wrong with their hotel? That's where you and I met. Isn't it good enough for you?"

"It's fine but there are other equally nice hotels and beautiful buildings in Richmond. I just don't trust those two," he muttered grimly.

"If you just told them you were their half brother, I think-" Dee began but was put off by his warning glance.

"I will decide if and when I tell them that," he glared.

"Which means you'll never tell them. You never got to make it up with Lance because he died before you got the chance - don't make the same mistake with Jerry and Elliott. God, if I found out I had a half brother out there, I'd be-"

"Alright Dee, I've just got home! Can I at least enjoy Christmas with my family before I start making huge, life-changing revelations?" Milo turned to her outside a shop front.

Dee was spurned. "...Okay, I only wanted..."

"You only want to help, I know," Milo said gently and touched her scarf, trying to catch her eyes beneath her woolly beret which she had pulled down low, "and I'll make everything right when I think the time is appropriate. And *if* they make a definite offer, we'll get married at their hotel on New Year's Eve...if that's what you really want," he said softly and kissed her.

"Thank you." Dee smiled up at him impishly.

"I just want to be married to you. I don't care where we do it." And he grinned as Angel squeezed between them to join in on the affection.

"Oh, how adorable," Cameron Quinn said, standing before them. He had been watching from further up the street and a malevolent disposition had come over him. Cameron rarely saw them together, but when he did, his total humiliation and frustration welled up in him and spilled out like a maniacal rage. But he hid his spite under a smarmy film, a tissue of civility just to get close enough to her to share it. "It just warms the cockles of my heart to see such a perfect family out together. And you never know, one of these children might even be Milo's."

"Cameron, when did you turn into such a knob?" Dee asked casually, far more casual than she felt.

"What exactly are you driving at?" Milo narrowed his eyes.

"Oh don't worry, I'm not suggesting Finley is mine, but you were away an awful lot so who knows who else Dee had on the side?" he said with a look of complete innocence. "Don't look so worried, I'm not here to upset your happy little apple cart. I'm even keeping an eye on Dee for you while you're in the States." Cameron slyly winked at her.

Dee wondered if kicking an intensely irritating man in the family jewels was classed as assault. Milo stepped closer to Cameron with a threatening glare. "If I were you, I'd find a new town to live in, Cameron. Believe me; you don't want to run into me again..." Milo rumbled menacingly.

"God, he does that butch thing so well, doesn't he?" Cameron laughed. "Anyway, I'll drop in on you soon, Dee. Bye Angel darling." He gave her arm a pat with a sickly familiarity and indolently ambled away.

Dee's shoulders sagged as she awaited the inevitable. Milo turned to her with a face like thunder. And although she was innocent, Dee just knew she would stammer and stutter and come across as though she were guilty of some figment of Cameron's warped imagination.

"What did he mean by that? Has he been over to the house?" Milo glowered with a look of malice. Milo really was a gentle giant, but he was unaware that when his face took on that set, he could be rather intimidating.

"*No!* He comes into the store to wind me up sometimes, but that's all," Dee shuffled her feet nervously, her cold hands jammed in her pockets.

"And you never thought to tell me that? If he's been to the house and you haven't told me-"

"You'll what? You'll do nothing because you're never here!" she fumed. How dare he? The audacity of the man; to spend half his life in another country and then proceed to accuse *her*! "Give me my child! Give me Finley right now!" she shouted belligerently, causing some unwanted attention in the street.

To say Milo was unnerved was an understatement. Perhaps he hadn't expected her to react quite so explosively. "...I'm sorry, I'm sorry, alright?" He took her elbow before she completely lost it.

"You don't trust me and you never will!" Dee vainly struggled to wrench her arm from his grip.

"I just get jealous, okay? I want to be with you and I hardly ever get to be...and Cameron sniffing around makes me feel insecure," he conceded. "Don't you ever feel like that...?"

She sighed. "...Yes," Dee muttered reluctantly, her hostile temperament dissolving as rapidly as it had arrived. They were silent for a while, watching the other for some kind of signal. Angel paced around awkwardly. Her mummy and daddy shouting at each other in the street was no fun.

"I've not even been home for twenty-four hours and we've already fought twice...shall we get a coffee?" he asked hopefully. "We need to talk."

"...Alright," Dee said wearily and let him slip his hand back into hers. The family took a right and sloped, not especially energetically, into The Lanes, off George Street. They silently passed the antique shops and coffee-houses to trudge towards Dee's shop.

*

Evan knew well enough by their stony expressions to leave Dee and Milo alone. He placed two foaming cappuccinos before them and fled. Angel headed straight for the play corner to escape the tense atmosphere between her parents, whilst Finley was forced to linger.

Milo gazed glumly at Dee while she inconspicuously breastfed the baby. "...You aren't having second thoughts about marrying me, are you...?" he wondered grimly.

Dee rolled her eyes with an exasperated sigh. "No, Milo. All couples quarrel."

"We fight an awful lot," Milo reminded her, "and you sound very final sometimes."

"Look, I just want you to trust me."

"I do, I know you're faithful to me. It's just Cameron gets under my skin and I don't trust *him*," he explained. "Because I'm away so much, I can't help worrying about it."

"And there's the problem, you're away too much." Dee waved a derisive hand in the air.

"We speak on the phone every night," he reasoned as though that made all the difference.

"Which is great, it's my favourite part of the day." Dee reached across to lovingly grasp his hand. "...But it's not enough."

Milo's shoulders slumped. "I know, it's not enough for me either," he said dejectedly. "Does Cameron come in here much?" he asked with feigned nonchalance.

"Maybe once a week, I don't know."

"But never to the house?"

"Not as yet, no."

"Doesn't he strike you as a little unbalanced? I mean, he was always creepy from what I could see - that leering way he was looking at you just now...he's just the kind of guy who would follow his ex around and-"

"But I already have my very own stalker." Dee squeezed his knee with an affectionate smirk. But Milo was not amused.

"It's not funny. Guys like that murder their ex-girlfriends, don't you see he's been spurned and it's driven him a bit crazy? How can you want someone like that around your daughter? I'm telling you - it's not safe."

"Cameron is just a dick, he's not *mad*!" She very nearly laughed. Her fiancé could be terribly over-dramatic sometimes. "Look, unless he emigrates, he will be around until he gets bored of goading me. He *will* get bored, though. He's just been hurt and he's being a bit pathetic. You'll have to learn to live with that for now," Dee insisted logically. "The problem is, you're letting Cameron get to you, whereas I'm not that bothered by him. Look, I want to spend the rest of my life with you, but it's got to be *with* you, Milo, not thousands of miles apart."

"I'm going to fix that," he determined.

"Babe, I think moving the wedding forward isn't a great idea. It's too much to arrange over Christmas and we need to fix the *being apart* thing first."

"Dee, it's important to me that we're married *now*. I know I'll feel so much happier," Milo professed so seriously that she was certain he actually believed it. "When I get back to America, I'm going to promote somebody to make my decisions when I'm in England. Then I'll work from home and Chancery Lane virtually full-time," Milo said decisively. "Once Cameron sees we're married and we're serious...and that I'm home, he'll back off," he asserted more to himself than anything. As always, Milo viewed the world in black and white. Every problem had a simple fix if he threw enough money at it. "I'll speak to my parents and the rest of my family tonight."

"This isn't going to be easy."

"Well, that's the wedding planner's concern. You can spend tomorrow getting your wedding dress sorted out."

"But I wanted to spend the day with you and the children," Dee grumbled disappointedly.

"We've got the whole of Christmas alone together," Milo breezed importantly, "or we would have if you hadn't invited half the world over for Christmas Day," he said with a mock-accusing look in his eyes. He grinned knowingly as Dee's mobile sounded with a text message.

"Oh, it's from Elliott. It seems Jerry has agreed...so the hotel is booked for New Year's Eve," Dee grimaced. So the biggest obstacle had been overcome already.

Milo wrinkled his nose, unimpressed. "Is this what you really want...? It feels kind of weird. Didn't you marry Lance there?"

"No, I've already told you - we had a garden party wedding at Jerry's house. I actually think this is really fitting because that's where you and I met. And letting Elliott and Jerry host our big day could be the bridge that rebuilds our family," Dee said with a big, romantic grin on her face. "Besides, you're not in a position to be picky, Mr I-have-to-get-married-this-second-or-I-might-die." And the more Dee thought about the setting, the more she began to feel excited. Maybe this change of plan would kill two birds with one stone. At last Dee could marry the love of her life and father of her son and maybe it would bring Elliott and Jerry on side too. Anyway, there was no going back now.

THE GATHERING

Christmas Eve was an odd one. It was the kind of day Dee detested; a day in which she had endless errands and appointments. She had been summoned to the hotel first thing that morning on Elliott's instructions to go over the plans. Dee met Ginny and Bruce there; her maid of honour and her personal assistant (Bruce would have been a bridesmaid too if he had only he looked better in a dress). Angel, Paddy and Melody had tagged along too for a fitting of their miniature bridesmaid dresses and Finn was here by default. Dee rarely went anywhere without him.

Dee had become rather fond of Ginny over the last eight months, they often met for coffee or lunch and it was so refreshing to at last meet another like-minded female with children. The wedding party had been hurriedly introduced to Rhoda, the hotel wedding-coordinator (another of Elliott and Jerry's generous gifts to the bride). Rhoda would take over the entire arrangements, so all Dee had to do was say 'yes' or 'no' to the options she was given.

"Okay, now there's a long day ahead of you." Elliott paced brusquely from the elegant Georgian reception room which Dee had instantly decided was the place she would become Milo's wife. It was in this very room she had first laid eyes on him at Lance's wake, when he had proceeded to insult her on that momentous day. Happy times. Yes, there were some rather mixed emotions attached to this hotel but Dee had no doubts she wanted to make her vows to Milo right here.

"He's very manly when he's being important, isn't he?" Bruce whispered under his breath and both Dee and Ginny smirked.

"Bruce, are you sure you aren't supposed to be at work today?" Elliott glowered, aware of the unheard mockery even if he hadn't exactly caught the gist of it.

"You gave me the day off, remember? I'm Dee's personal assistant-stroke-advisor," Bruce chirped. "She couldn't possibly be expected to make all these decisions without me."

"Hmm...now Rhoda will take you to one of the conference rooms where you can decide on your flowers, invites and things. The dressmaker is due in an hour for your dress fittings. So, I'll let you get on." Elliott stopped before them in the foyer, clasping his hands together behind his back, totally professional and focused.

"Thanks Elliott," Dee said genuinely and touched his hand. This seemed to break his concentration and he smiled, transformed into her old friend again.

"It's the least I could do," he said softly as Jerry drifted over to join the group.

"Oh Jerry, I want to thank you too," Dee said before he could construct a belittling comment. She enveloped him in a hug and he seemed stunned for a moment, and then returned the embrace. "This means a lot to me."

"I err...well yes, you're our sister so...it's our pleasure," he spluttered.

"Yes Jerry, it is pretty big of you both," Ginny interjected, holding the sleeping Finley in her arms.

Jerry turned to face her, his eyes narrowed as if studying the beautiful raven-haired and olive-skinned woman for a moment. "...Ginny, it's nice to see you." He awkwardly placed a hand on his cousin's arm. "I'm sorry I didn't get to talk to you at Lance's funeral...I wasn't myself," he admitted guiltily.

"No, I understand. I missed you at the christening too. You were only there for about five minutes and then you were gone." Ginny concealed the mirth from her expression but somehow she was enjoying seeing him squirm.

"...Yes, well...I had important business to attend to and I couldn't break my commitments."

"It seems the last time we actually spoke was when we were about ten, running around the Phillips's pool half-naked. Well, maybe we can catch up at Dee's on Christmas Day - I understand you'll be dropping in?" Ginny tilted her head to one side with an impish flutter of her lashes. Jerry stared at her, wearing a mystified, gormless expression that only a man could.

"Yes, I'll be there. Y-your daughters are beautiful... just like their mother..." Jerry stammered.

"Oh, thank you," Ginny answered gratefully, knocked off her guard momentarily.

"Hello Finley," Jerry gingerly touched the tiny child's hair. He had never been particularly affectionate towards Milo's son but he couldn't resist ruffling his sweet little curls. He suits you," Jerry said under his breath so that only Ginny could hear and met her eyes briefly. "Angel, don't forget to come and see me in my office before you go, I have a present for you." Jerry kissed his niece. "Elliott, I need to discuss something with you." He took his arm and led his brother away.

"...Yikes," Dee blinked.

"Oh my God! Jerry Stark was blatantly checking you out!" Bruce squawked at Ginny.

"Don't be silly," Ginny blushed, "he's my cousin." To be precise, he was her adoptive mother's sister's nephew. Or something like that.

"I feel like I just walked in on my parents having sex..." Dee said in a mock-mortified voice and Bruce burst into laughter.

"Oh, you're as bad as each other, you two," Ginny growled but inside she was smiling.

"Shall we get on?" Rhoda asked meekly, interrupting the proceedings. She wearily rubbed her temples, flattening out her bobbed brown hair and straightening her glasses. The three sniggering adults and prancing children followed her to the conference room. Rhoda had the feeling she would earn every penny of this particular assignment.

"God, I haven't seen Jerry flirt like that in...ever!"

"I *know*!" Bruce enthused but pulled up short. "Now wait guys, I got up so early today so I didn't get a chance to grab a coffee. Hey Rhoda, hey Miss! Can we have a coffee first?"

As Ginny followed behind, she was aware this wedding was going to be one big hoot with these two jokers and she felt honoured to be involved. Christmas was sounding more and more appealing. If only she could wipe the stupid smirk off her face.

*

Christmas morning did not arrive with snow. When the curtains were drawn back to welcome the day, the streets were not white; no red-breasted robins sat chattering on the gatepost and no men in tall Victorian hats strolled by greeting women in full skirts and bonnets. Dee sighed. However, the sun shone pleasantly, the sky was an almost polarised blue and all-in-all it was not a bad day. Dee pottered about the kitchen not achieving very much at all, apart from boiling a kettle and jamming two thick slices of bread in a toaster. This was not the traditional Christmas breakfast of a family-size tin of chocolates, Dee had no appetite for that just yet.

She had so much to do that she could not think where to start, so Dee decided not to start at all until help arrived. Finley was plastered to her front in a baby-sling, fast asleep and Angel sat at the farmhouse table concentrating on her current felt-tip masterpiece.

"Mummy, we open presents now?" Angel asked hopefully.

"No, I told you, we can open a few after Daddy gets up and we've all had breakfast."

"I want toast and milk," Angel ordered, returning to her picture.

Dee rolled her eyes. "That's what I'm doing." She thickly buttered the toast, adding a large helping of honey and dutifully placed it in front of her daughter with a glass of milk. Dee absently stroked her now four-month old baby's incredibly soft curls whilst considering her own breakfast options before Milo wandered into the kitchen.

"Merry Christmas, family," he chirped brightly. "Let's enjoy the peace before the world and his wife arrive." Milo sat down at the table beside Angel, blowing raspberries into the laughing child's neck. He rubbed the sleep from his eyes, still in his pyjama trousers and little else. "So, exactly how many people are coming over?"

"...Err, six adults and three children..." Dee mumbled under her breath.

"So that makes thirteen of us?"

"Yes, and that's if Jerry and Elliott don't drop in. You don't really mind do you? I just wanted a big family Christmas and I wasn't even certain you'd be home."

"Ye of little faith. No, I suppose I don't mind really," Milo shrugged mildly. "And what's the itinerary today?"

"Well, Patrice and Bruce are coming over early to help with Christmas dinner preparations and then I have to meet Jerry and Elliott mid-morning at the hotel to visit the place where we scattered Lance's ashes..." Dee said grimly. "You're welcome to come. He was your brother too."

"I think I'll pass...I wondered what the flowers were for..." Milo said distantly, gazing at the white lilies on the counter. Although he was always understanding and said nothing, he sometimes felt rather uneasy about never matching up to the great Lance Stark. Dee still grieved for her dead husband and sometimes that was hard for Milo to come to terms with. In fact, he was far more jealous of Lance than he ever had been of Cameron.

"It's just something the guys want to do as an annual thing at Christmas and they waited until Boxing Day last year so I could come with them...I felt bad about it," she said regretfully, thinking about last Christmas spent in blissful limbo with Milo. "Is there anything you need to do or anywhere you have to be to remember Andrew?" Dee asked.

"No..." Milo dealt with his own loss in a totally different way. He would hide away in the study for a few hours and pour over old photo albums alone. Christmas was a happy time, but for this bereaved couple, there was much sadness attached to the day.

Dee sighed. "Well, if you need some time alone or you and Forrest want to go off by yourselves, you just do whatever you need to for as long as you want," she insisted. Dee knew Milo's grief was still very fresh. Andrew had not even been dead for a year and sometimes Milo suffered some very bad days. He would be grouchy and despondent and Dee knew better than to get in his way on those occasions.

Both were silent for a while as the grim conversation permeated the atmosphere of the joyous day. Dee quietly padded over and kissed the top of her fiancé's head and he snaked an arm around her.

"...I really love you, you know," he responded softly. Then the doorbell sounded, making Dee jump.

"Oh, that'll be Bruce and Patrice," she concluded. "I didn't mean for them to come over this early but without Mrs Dawson here, I'm going to need all the help I can get!"

*

Cooking was in progress. Bruce and Patrice bickered dangerously over the food preparations. Patrice was the real culinary expert and foodie, but Bruce had to have his say. Evan attempted in vain to put in his own two-pennies-worth on the rights and wrongs of cooking the bird. Deciding that too many cooks did indeed spoil the broth, Forrest, Felix and Ginny casually circulated the house, drinking champagne and over-filling themselves with nibbles. The children, Mia, Melody and Paddy played rather nicely even though Mia was five years older than the six-year-old twin girls. Angel had been enjoying the noise and bustle of active children about the place until she was hurried out of the house by her mother to meet her uncles for a reason too complex to explain to a child.

Milo observed the house that he had come to call home, gradually besieged by family and Dee's friends. He held his son and quietly took in the raucous atmosphere with mixed feelings. Andrew should be here. There would have been no change in the outcome of his situation; Milo knew for certain that he and Dee would have ended up together even if Andrew had never drowned. His son would have so enjoyed the company of all four of the girls and doted over his baby brother. It was unfair. Unceasingly unfair.

"Hi, you were miles away." Forrest finally gained his brother's attention where he stood in the kitchen doorway.

"Mm...? Oh sorry, Forrest," Milo answered distantly.

"What time will Dee be back?"

"I don't know; she's visiting her dead ex-husband. They may need time to catch up," he said blandly.

Forrest frowned. "...Christmas is kind of a tough time for you two, huh?"

he observed. "Were you thinking about Andrew?"

"It's hard not to."

"He would have really enjoyed all this, all these new and crazy people. I just bet he's watching us now with a big grin on his face," Forrest mused.

"...Huh." Milo wrinkled his nose derisively. Dead was dead as far as he was concerned. Black was black and white was white. Heaven was just a fictional place created by people like Forrest to make death more palatable. Milo knew better, which was why there was no comfort available to him.

Forrest raised a knowing eyebrow. "You don't resent the fact that Dee has to pay her respects to him now and then, do you?"

"Of course not," Milo replied unconvincingly.

"Can I hold my nephew?" he asked and Milo placed the small, curly blonde-haired child down on his brother's lap where he sat in the wheelchair. Finn's bright blue eyes blinked and his little head wobbled precariously on his neck.

"Don't take it personally if he cries, I think he's due a feed soon." As Milo wondered where in the world his fiancée was, a key turned in the latch and both men looked up to see Dee and Angel return from the hotel.

"Hey guys, is everybody here?" Dee asked weakly. Her eyes were bloodshot, and patchy red blotches were only now beginning to recede from her face. Angel scurried off to follow the noise of children playing in the lounge, glad to escape the depressed faces.

"Everybody's here but you." Forrest smiled warmly.

"Forrest, sorry about the short notice, we're really grateful that you're still able to marry us at New Year's." Dee paced over and kissed his cheek.

"It's no trouble at all, I'm just honoured you still want me for the job," he responded.

"Are you okay with Finn?" she asked.

"Sure, I'll bring him back when he cries." Forrest grinned. "I can promise you that." He lovingly held his nephew in his lap and awkwardly wheeled himself with alternate hands into the lounge.

"Are you alright?" Milo asked tentatively.

"Yeah, I'm glad it's done...how about you? Do you want some time out?" Dee gently took his hands.

Milo narrowed his eyes. "Time out for what?" he said.

"You know what," Dee told him bluntly.

"Not everybody has to grieve as extravagantly as you," Milo sniffed.

Dee knew from that comment that he was indeed suffering and Milo dealt with his loss in such a guarded way, sometimes it spilled out as inappropriate anger. "What do you mean by that?" She tried to bite her tongue.

"I don't need showy displays to alert people to the fact that I haven't forgotten my child is dead."

"Showy displays?" Dee seethed, flashed an exasperated hand at him and stormed upstairs.

"...Dee," Milo groaned and chased her up, catching her just before she reached the top of the second flight. "I'm sorry." He sat her down beside him on the top step.

"Why did you say that? We just wanted to pay our respects. I have the right to visit Lance's trees." Dee often referred to the ring of trees on the hotel grounds where she and Lance had resolved to be together, as 'Lance's trees'. It was the only place thinkable to scatter his ashes. "What sort of person would I be if I ignored that chapter of my life?"

"I know, but I guess I still feel jealous of Lance sometimes. It's ridiculous, but I do," he admitted, slipping his hand in hers.

"He's dead," Dee reasoned.

"...And if he wasn't?"

"You can't think like that...I probably never would have met you if he hadn't died. Anyway, Lance and I were divorcing, so who knows what would have happened in the unlikely event that I'd met you? I truly believe what happened between you and I was fate," she assured him.

"What if I don't believe in fate? What if the course of your life is dictated by your own decisions?"

"I didn't get to decide whether or not Lance died, just like you didn't get to decide about Andrew's fate on that boat trip," Dee told him. "...I love you, Milo. Lance was no angel but the fact that I need to remember him doesn't detract from how I feel about you."

Milo gulped awkwardly. "Did you- did you love him more than me? Just a little bit?"

"No, I didn't," she told him adamantly.

"...I'm sorry. You have every right to mourn your loss. He was my brother, I should understand." Milo carried a strong sense of guilt about that. "I'm just very aware that people are looking for some kind of reaction from me over Andrew. I guess I'm too private a man for that."

"You can grieve however you want to, I just thought you might want some time with Forrest," Dee explained pragmatically.

"I can't share anything with him, we don't have that kind of relationship," Milo insisted.

"Why can't you? I find him so easy to confide in. He's such an approachable kind of man."

"Dee, I took away his legs!" Milo threw up his hands. "Every time I look at him I'm reminded of how I robbed him of his life. I've even robbed him of a woman to love and any chance of children! I've spent my life thinking only of myself and I still manage to walk away with you, with a family."

"Forrest is happy with his lot."

"Of course he says that. He's too nice a guy to blame anyone...but *I* know. And I can't expect him to understand my loss," he said. By now, a tear was tracking its way down his cheek. "The only person who understands is you..."

Dee held him for a long time as he wept bitterly at the top of the stairs. Head in hands, he rocked to and fro, crying for the serious little boy with the sandy hair who should be turning nine in a month. Andrew should be here; here with his new family, but Andrew was gone. Dee realised her mistake. She had been so tied up in her own grief that she had neglected to be a part of his. Milo was as understanding as he was capable of being about Lance, his emotions about his dead brother were mixed up with his own grief and a misplaced kind of jealousy.

CRISIS AT CHRISTMAS

In spite of the grim events of the morning, Christmas afternoon was going rather well. Bruce, Patrice and Evan had made a superb job of roasting the large goose and creating every other type of culinary delight one would expect on this festive occasion. Dee had been completely banished from her own kitchen which she was rather pleased about. At around three thirty, dinner was coming to a close as the gathering devoured the marvellous food placed before them at the huge mahogany table in the dining room. The four children sat together at one end of the table, snickering and playing with their food.

The atmosphere between Dee and Milo had somehow become electric after their harrowing morning. It was always like this once they had quarrelled and made up. She was almost glad that Patrice's seating plan had separated them, or the pair would have spent the entire meal playing footsie or gazing stupidly at each other. Sometimes it seemed a trifle odd to still be so heart-stoppingly in love with a man who was soon to be her husband forever more and was already the father of her son.

Dee had found herself seated next to Felix instead, with her sleeping son in her lap. She felt oddly tongue-tied around him. It was a shame really because at last year's New Year Ball and at Andrew's funeral, it appeared that they had become fast friends. But Felix was away an awful lot for a man who professed to live in London - he had only just come back from working in Paris, so Dee hadn't seen him but for a brief 'hello' when she had given birth to Finn. Dee was dreadful like that; if a person wasn't constantly in her life, she found it difficult to maintain a friendship with them (hence finding it so hard to become completely comfortable in her relationship with Milo). Still, Felix always seemed very affable on the occasions she did see him, so Dee thought it was about time she got to know Milo's talented cousin properly. "...So, you're back from Paris earlier than expected?"

As though he had been worrying about the same thing, Felix said tentatively, "...Oh, these productions always throw the 'six-month' figure at you, but it rarely takes much longer than three if you know what you're doing."

"Well, it's nice to have you back..." Dee cleared her throat nervously. Why was she so incredibly bad at small talk?

"Thanks...and thanks for inviting me for Christmas."

"My pleasure."

Felix scratched his temple thoughtfully. "Does he always stare at you like that?"

"Um..." Dee was about to pretend she didn't know what Felix was talking about but decided she couldn't deny what was plainly obvious to everyone, Milo couldn't keep his eyes off her. "Only if he hasn't seen me in a while."

"And are you looking forward to becoming part of our friendly and, may I add, extremely attractive family?" he smirked.

"I am, I am," she smiled back. The tension seemed to be ebbing away now which was a relief. Dee had been confused as to why they were so friendly once, only to be awkward around one another now. "And how do your extremely attractive family usually celebrate Christmas?"

"Well, after the usual ritual goat-slaughtering at midnight on Christmas Eve and the ceremonial rattling of dried monkey paws after Christmas lunch, we like to relax in front of the TV mostly," he mused and Dee laughed. She had forgotten how amusing she found him.

"Sounds more or less like what I have planned," Dee shrugged blandly.

"Lucky I brought my robe and cowl then," he sniffed. Dee decided he spoke with a little bit of a nasal mew, like a cat. His nearly black eyes were often narrowed as he spoke and he would bare his teeth a lot in a Cheshire-type grin. Felix the cat.

"You'd have looked pretty damn foolish if you hadn't. Any plans for marriage yourself? You seeing anyone?" she pried.

"Me? No, I'm a raving celibate monk!" he carried on, on a roll now. Then he sat thoughtfully for a moment. "So how is it that I've hardly spoken to you since that day at the funeral?" There had been the big marriage announcement at the restaurant and a couple of brief 'hellos' here and there, but really nothing much to suggest she had truly connected with Milo's cousin.

Dee sighed. "...I don't know, even though you guys are in London and so am I, we're not exactly neighbours. And when the baby was born, which would have been a good opportunity for me to get to know you and Ginny better, you were abroad," she attempted to explain succinctly. "Ginny was around...and she's my bridesmaid so I got to know her better than you."

"So what you're really trying to say is, *'Felix, you're dead to me'*?"

Dee burst out laughing. "Well yes," she joked. "No honestly, I know you have that club in the West End and as soon as Finn is a bit older, I was thinking of asking Milo to take me there to see you play."

Felix gave her a quizzical grin. "...Really?"

"Of course." Dee was about to assure him that she would come to know him and Ginny not only as friends but as family, when Forrest tapped a glass with a fork.

"A few words from the hostess!" Forrest said, the couple of glasses of red having gone to his head.

Dee blushed before hurriedly pulling herself together, placing her baby on her hip as she stood. "Guys, having you all here to share Christmas with us is just amazing. I'm a little orphan girl so, like it or not, I think of you all as my surrogate family," she began a little diffidently but received an 'awww'. "Patrice, Bruce and Evan worked so hard to produce this fabulous meal, and I feel really guilty because I swanned about doing nothing. But then I provided the venue, so that's the least they could do," Dee continued, grateful there was a little titter of laughter. "I just want to finish by saying, make yourselves comfortable because my home is your home - so you really ought to help out more with the mortgage. Anyway, eat, drink and be merry!" She raised her glass and the guests gave a little cheer and followed suit.

"So what's with the rush-job wedding?" Bruce felt now was a good time to ask the big man since he had been drinking. Dee looked up from where she was cooing over her son in her lap. She glanced at Milo and he smiled.

Milo cleared his throat. "Well, if you had a fiancée as perfect as this, wouldn't you want to marry her before she got away?"

"You think she might get away before April?" Felix smiled, rocking back and forth in his chair, his nervous energy ever present.

"Well, you never know. There are a lot of younger, better looking guys out there." Milo stared across the table at Dee. He had been watching her all afternoon, watching her chat to everyone, and every time she walked by, he would lightly brush his hand against her arm or back.

"Honey," Dee grumbled, giving him a withering look.

"Well, I think a New Year's wedding is a fabulous idea," Ginny interjected. "Quite frankly, I'm sick of calling Dee your girlfriend when she's clearly more than that."

"Our point exactly," Milo agreed.

"Right, can we get on with what we came for, presents?" Bruce stood up, rubbing his hands together. The others laughed and after the children tore from the room, the group trooped out in single file to the guest lounge.

On his way out, Felix whispered, "terrible speech." He wandered after the others. Dee raised her eyebrows and shook her head with a smile.

"Don't say things like that," Dee hissed reprovingly at her fiancé as he ventured over.

Milo shrugged, taking the baby from her. "I was only joking." He stole a kiss, barely able to keep his hands off his soon-to-be-wife.

"I don't want people thinking I'm predatory, moving from one man to the next. I'm painfully aware that you're going to be my second husband but this time it's going to be for keeps," she told him archly as the door chime sounded.

Milo sighed audibly. "Just when I was beginning to enjoy myself," he groaned.

"Be nice, okay?" Dee gravely padded to the front door to greet her brothers-in-law for the second time that day.

*

Including all the children, there were fifteen people in Dee's house on the Vineyard. As afternoon faded into evening, the children were busily tearing into their presents and the adults soon followed suit. Dee had ensured that nobody went home disappointed and lavished every one of her guests with gifts. She sat contentedly upon her partner's lap since most seats were taken even in this spacious room.

Milo eyed Dee dubiously as the expensive presents continued to be unwrapped.

"Don't say a word," she warned the most fastidiously frugal businessman she knew. Although he was always very generous with his family, he wasn't rich for nothing.

Jerry and Elliott sat drinking red wine on the crowded sofa. Angel bounced around on her uncle Elliott's lap and it felt good to be part of such a large gathering on Christmas day after two years of quiet and mournful celebrations. One Christmas Lance was sick and dying, the next he was not there at all.

"You know, I never thought I'd say this, but they kind of look good together," Elliott observed, noticing Dee and Milo whispering and giggling on the opposite sofa.

"Oh Jesus, not you too," Jerry growled.

"All I'm saying is, I don't think we were right about Milo just playing games with her. He'd have left by now if Dee meant nothing to him," Elliott pointed out pragmatically. "You can clearly see Milo's besotted with Dee. He adores his baby and he's really great with Angel."

"How wrong we were about him," Jerry said cuttingly.

"Hi guys, can I get you anything?" Ginny ventured over with a smile. The venue was Dee's house but everyone was keen to chip in with hosting duties.

"No, why don't you join us?" Jerry smiled for the first time this afternoon. Elliott knew well enough to be somewhere else.

"I'll help Angel open some more presents," he said and Ginny replaced him beside Jerry.

"This is really good for family dynamics. I'm glad you came over," Ginny assured him.

"So am I. Were you this pretty when we were kids?" Jerry shook his head incredulously, perhaps slightly mellowed after half a bottle of wine to himself.

"I was a fairly gawky, unattractive child, actually. You've improved with age too."

"We used to have fun holidays, didn't we? I remember looking forward to summer every year. I couldn't wait to get to America or for you guys to come visit us," Jerry reminisced.

"I don't know. I always felt kind of left out being the only girl. You used to pull my pigtails so I didn't like you much," Ginny admitted with a chuckle.

"Really? I'm much nicer now," Jerry smirked.

"Are you, Jerry? Because you haven't been terribly pleasant to our family over the last few years," Ginny reminded him. "Milo was the one who stole Lance's first fiancée. Forrest, Felix and I never did anything to hurt you but you wouldn't even speak to us at Lance's funeral."

"...I know. I dealt with my brother's death very badly. I was very angry with everyone back then," Jerry confessed ashamedly.

"I understand," she said reasonably. "Who knows how I would behave if I ever lost Felix?" Ginny gave Jerry the benefit of the doubt. She was like that.

"...So, do you think they're for real?" Jerry jerked his head in the direction of Dee and Milo.

"I know they are," Ginny insisted. "Milo could be very selfish in the past, but he's different now he's met Dee. If you were around more, you'd see they're really good for each other. Milo worships the ground Dee walks on and he's a great father to those kids."

"So everybody keeps telling me," Jerry rolled his eyes.

"It's really great that you're holding the wedding at your hotel. It's going to be a wonderful day."

"When it's all over, I would love to take you out to dinner," Jerry said, unusually unabashed.

"Is that allowed?" Ginny laughed.

"I'm not really your cousin, am I?" Jerry reminded her.

"...Well...I think I would really like that too..."

Milo watched Jerry and Ginny's animated conversation from across the room. "I'm not sure I like the idea of Jerry Stark banging my cousin." He pulled a face.

"Milo! Jerry's a pretty good catch, actually," Dee reasoned, still sitting comfortably on his lap.

Milo laughed out loud then noticed her expression. "Oh, I'm sorry, you were serious."

*

Dee gingerly placed Finley down in his cot for the night and quietly padded from the room. She switched on the light to the master bedroom and began to fold and tidy away her haul of presents. As an orphan, having her beloved house filled with the sound of people she loved and cared for made her smile to herself with contentment. Dee had been so determined that this house she had worked so hard on and invested so much love into, remain her home. Although she had offered Milo the choice of where to live, in all honesty she would not have been able to stand moving after a childhood of frequent upheaval.

A figure at the door startled her and Dee inadvertently gasped. "Jesus, Milo, you frightened me."

"I'm going out of my mind down there..."

"Look, I know I invited a lot people. I'm sorry, I should have consulted you but I really thought you might not make it home for Christmas-"

"That's not what I'm talking about." Milo was watching her strangely and closed the door behind him, blocking it with his back. "I can't stop looking at you. You brush by me and I can barely keep a lid on it. I just want to throw you down on the couch and take you...but with all these people around all I can do is stare at you like an idiot."

"Oh," Dee laughed, flattered if a little embarrassed. He was already walking towards her and roughly pushing her down on the bed. "...What if they notice we're missing...is Angel alright downstairs?" she mumbled between kisses.

"She's fine...everything's fine" Milo whispered, becoming instantly excited as he adjusted her clothes. Milo's lust for her was too explosive to wait anymore.

Afterwards, Dee lay with her future husband on the bed, quietly lacing their fingers together, gently grooming each other the way monkeys did. They were fully clothed but rumpled and would need to neaten up their dishevelled appearance before they returned to the party.

"Milo, you and me – what we have...is this always going to be what you want?"

Milo languidly rolled from his back to his side to face her. "I don't know what you mean."

"Well, you've had a lot of girlfriends before you ever met me...and you've never really been in an ordinary relationship like this..."

"I still don't follow," he admitted blankly.

Dee tried to formulate where she was going with this in her mind. "...You're a very *physical* person. I wouldn't want to think in the future you'd fine this mundane-"

"Oh Jesus," Milo groaned, exasperated. "So you think just one woman can't satisfy me? You know, I remember having a marathon conversation very like this with a pregnant woman matching your description in a hotel bar about ten months ago. Are we having another *'should we be together?'* talk?" Milo raised an incredulous eyebrow. "Don't I tell you often enough how much I adore you?"

"Mm, but that's what nags at me," Dee confided, trying to proceed cautiously now because he was easy to upset despite his gruff exterior. "People are always telling me, *'Milo adores you. Milo worships you. Milo's obsessed with you.'* And that's flattering, but all those feelings are fleeting."

"I'm going to marry you in six days, I don't have to, but I'm going to. What we have now is what I've been searching for my whole life. I didn't know it was what I wanted until I met you, but I assure you this is what I want now. If you think I'd ever tire of you, you're wrong. You're the most exciting person I ever met. I love you and I love our children and I love our life together." Milo stroked her face with a serious edge in his eyes. "I know having a new baby is hard on you and if I come on too strong, it's only because I'm madly in love with you. You just have to tell me to back off..."

Dee's insecurities were instantly quashed. "Oh no, I don't want you to back off."

"Good, but I can if you want me to. So now that's settled...how long do you want to wait before we think about having another baby?"

"You are kidding, right?" Dee sat up, eyeing him sceptically.

"No. I'm getting pretty good at this family-man thing," Milo stated matter-of-factly.

"You said in the delivery suite that I wouldn't have to go through that again."

Milo screwed up his eyes as though trying to remember something from twenty years ago. "...Oh...yeah, but...I just said that because you were in pain. I didn't think you really meant it."

"Oh, I meant it. I'm not having any more kids, Milo. This is my dream family," Dee informed him flatly. She flattened out her crumpled clothes and rose from the bed. "We'd better be getting back downstairs or people will guess what we've been up to."

Milo appraised her silently for a moment. "…Oh…well it's your call of course. Just let me know if you ever change your mind…"

"I won't." Dee pulled him unceremoniously up from the bed. He watched her carefully, attempting to hide his disappointment. She knew what this was about, of course. His child had been tragically taken from him and although Finn had gone some way to healing that wound, Milo could never be truly contented. Not unless Andrew came back from the dead. Her husband was still somewhat broken and there was a lot more healing to do. Countless new babies were not going to be the answer.

*

As the evening was coming to a close, the gathering became more inebriated and more jovial. It was one of the best Christmases any of them could remember for some time. There was something about mixing people who would never normally choose to be friends that sometimes led to successful dynamics. Dee was rather pleased with herself, not that she had done a great deal.

"I can't believe it, really? Are you serious?" Bruce hopped and jiggled about so vigorously, Dee was wondering whether he actually needed the toilet.

"Of course I am. I'll expect you in the shop at 9am the second of January," Dee stated with a deliberate calmness.

"She's giving me a job in the coffee shop on my current salary! Do you believe that, Patrice?" Bruce squealed with excitement.

"Mm, I believe it." Patrice eyed Dee suspiciously.

"Thank you, Dee. You won't regret it! Happy Christmas, everybody!" Bruce fled from the room to announce the news to his ex-bosses.

"Is this another of your pathetically obvious attempts to give us money, Dee?" Patrice asked. "You don't actually need Bruce in that coffee shop, do you?"

"…Okay, we don't desperately *need* staff although our part-time girl is leaving and Evan is getting busier and busier - and I can hardly ever be there because Finn is so young," Dee stressed vehemently. "Anyway, you never let me help you guys out! You can refuse to accept my money if you want, but let me do this for Bruce. He hates working at that hotel and I can afford to employ him," she protested.

"You're never going to be a proper business woman when you do things like this. Don't ever expect to make a profit from that store," Patrice grumbled, but a reluctant smile was already creeping onto his face.

"Well, if we go under, I'll make sure Jerry and Elliott give Bruce his job back. I have friends in high places." She looped her arm through Patrice's and as they strolled through to the lounge, they were surprised to find Milo chatting with Jerry, Elliott and Ginny. Bruce was nowhere to be seen. When they came closer, Dee and Patrice realised there was actually a low-level disagreement ensuing.

"Look, I never *asked* Angel to call me 'Daddy'. I look a little like her father so she just took it upon herself," Milo shrugged casually, hands in pockets but Dee knew by that steely glint in his eyes, something malevolent was boiling inside him.

"And *you* took it upon yourself not to correct her," Jerry retorted.

"Why should I? The poor kid needed a father and I wanted to be her dad. Don't you think she's suffered enough?" Milo said with an irritating reasonableness.

Elliott and Ginny shifted uncomfortably where they stood, both on the verge of interjecting but never actually doing so.

"And on the subject, I think now that Dee and I are getting married, I should be allowed to adopt her," Milo continued.

"Is this some kind of joke? Shall we all just pretend Lance never existed at all?" Jerry gaped.

Milo turned to Dee sharply. "I thought you'd already spoken to them about this?"

"I never got around to it," Dee gulped. Milo had been banging on about it and she had reluctantly agreed, but had been putting off the actual 'talk'.

"Is this what you want, Dee?" Elliott asked finally, his eyes searching hers.

"Yes," Dee replied helplessly. "I wasn't sure at first...but I think it would be good for Angel. She loves Milo."

"We're not trying to re-write history. We have every intention of telling her who her real father is when she's old enough to understand," Milo insisted, "but I'm alive and I'm here. I don't want her to feel she isn't a part of this family. I love that little girl and she loves me. I want to be her father officially."

"Milo, maybe wounds are still a little raw for all this adoption talk," Ginny began tentatively. "Perhaps give these guys some more time to grieve for their brother."

"Why the big interest in Angel anyway? You never had much input into your own son's life before he died," Jerry reminded him cruelly. "Besides, you have your own new baby now so there's no need to go on with the pretence of being a father to Lance's kid. You're barely related to her at all!" he sneered.

"He's her uncle, just like you!" Dee exploded finally and Milo glared at her warningly. "...I mean, s-second cousin..."

"What is she talking about?" Elliott glanced from Milo to Dee suspiciously.

"Nothing," Milo answered and kept his baleful eyes fixed on Dee's, pinning her to the spot.

"Milo, this is ridiculous!" Dee threw her arms up in exasperation.

"Dee, just leave it," he growled.

"What's going on?" Jerry's resolve began to crumble. Something was afoot and he wouldn't leave this house until he knew exactly what it was.

Dee took a deliberate breath, gritted her teeth and took the plunge. "Milo is your half brother..."

THE BEARER OF GLAD TIDINGS

The atmosphere was thick, stifling and all Dee's doing. All eyes were cast her way and she had no option but to plough on. Dee was rather partial to the idea of turning on her heel and leaving the brothers to it.

"Dee!" Milo stared at her with daggers.

Dee decided then to ignore him since it was too late. "Your father had an affair with Milo's mother before any of you were born. Erwin was his father too. Milo's your half brother, Lance's too - obviously..."

"Milo, is this true?" Ginny gaped, completely dumbfounded.

"...Yeah," Milo conceded weakly with a lacklustre roll of his eyes.

"This is bullshit!" Jerry finally responded with a not entirely unexpected outburst.

"Why do you think he looks so much like Lance?" Dee took Jerry's arm gently but he shook her off.

"Does Forrest know?" Ginny murmured.

"Actually, no. I would have liked to have had this conversation with him first," Milo stared disdainfully at Dee. "But Dee evidently didn't deem his feelings to be important-"

"Honey," Dee said plaintively but realised too late she had gone too far.

"I told you it was my decision if and when I was going to tell anybody about this. I asked you to leave it alone but you couldn't keep your mouth shut!" Milo rebuked her and stalked from the room, leaving the others to an awkward silence.

*

The frivolous atmosphere of the festive day had long gone. Shut away in her cubbyhole that only she and her daughter ever really frequented, Dee gazed mindlessly at the TV, flicking with a restless agitation from channel to channel. She only had herself to blame, of course. She had opened up her big mouth and let out a secret that was never hers to tell. It wasn't even an accident. Dee had been so tired of all the slurs and smears on her future husband's character that a malicious anger had built up within her and triggered the need to blurt out the truth that had been buried for so long. A huge quarrel had ensued with accusations from all sides and the opposing parties had stormed off in varying directions. Dee had escaped here in floods of tears that had passed in time and now she felt numb, deflated.

"Oh, here you are. So this is your little hidey-hole, is it?" Felix crept into her private, darkened world and looked around at the walls lined with shelves of books before joining her on the rustic sofa. "What you watching?"

"I really couldn't tell you." Dee chewed on her nails.

"Let's find something to watch then. Is this where you keep your movie collection?" Felix guessed accurately as he got down on his knees to open a cupboard housing DVDs on neatly stacked shelves. He proceeded to peruse Dee's collection. "Are these all yours? You've got a lot of the same films that I have - all the Frank Sinatra's and Doris Day's. And here's 'On the Town', 'Young at Heart', 'Calamity Jane'. Oh, you've got 'Rear Window' and 'The Rope'."

"...Mm, I really like Jimmy Stewart."

"Me too," Felix said thoughtfully, looking up and then glancing back at the shelves again, "my God, this is getting spooky. I think I've met the female version of me...I'm not sure about the Jackie Chan stuff, but still." He flicked through her collection with a clack-clack-clack. Dee wondered at his odd indifference to personal space and wouldn't have been surprised if he started on her bookshelves next. Dee was glad that at least *he* was enjoying himself.

"This has been the worst Christmas ever..." Dee moped glumly.

"Yeah, and that was *before* the fist-fight," he teased absently.

Dee scratched her head. "So, what's going on out there?"

"What? Oh, Jerry got a taxi but Elliott is still here. Bruce and Patrice went home and so did Evan..." Felix continued to scour Dee's movies.

"Is Forrest okay? I thought you'd be consoling *him*." In fact, Dee was surprised Felix was in here with her at all. She had always been reliably informed he was Forrest's best friend - she couldn't yet call herself a close acquaintance of Felix's.

"I was but Ginny seemed to be doing a better job so I thought I'd see how you are." For a man who had recently discovered the truth about his cousin's parentage, Felix seemed rather relaxed. "He's pretty shocked, we all are."

"You don't look it."

Felix perched on his haunches and mused quietly for a moment. "...Well, now I know Milo is actually a Stark...it makes a lot of sense. In fact, it would explain a lot. He was always very different from Forrest, sort of unlovable. Starks tend to be slightly bitter – not that *all* Phillipses are fun to be with."

"Well, if he was unlovable and bitter, it was only because he'd found out at an early age that his uncle was actually his father," Dee said curtly whilst narrowing her eyes.

"Wow, it's nice to see that you are still championing Milo's cause even when he's not speaking to you. You know, he doesn't need defending – not from *me*." Felix smiled with his hands up in the air as a sign of surrender.

Dee realised she had misread Felix. She had been misreading him for months. Dee surveyed him pensively. A famous composer and musician in Jazz circles, Felix was not traditionally handsome. He was rather small, in fact not a great deal taller than Dee and his limbs were almost emaciated. Felix had the look of a man who had partied too hard in his youth, drank too much, smoked too many and went to bed too late far too often. But he had a nice face. There was a glint in those dark brown eyes and a lopsided grin on his unshaven face that was likeable. His short, black wavy hair complimented his olive skin. Some might call him cute, not Dee, but some might. "I'm on Milo's side, remember?" he said plaintively. "I only want the best for him. I persuaded him to get together with you, didn't I?"

"So the fable goes. I'm sorry. I'm just mad at myself," Dee conceded. "I betrayed a confidence. Do you think he'll be able to forgive me?"

"What, Saint Dee of Richmond? Are we talking about she who can do no wrong?" Felix laughed heartily. "My God, don't you know he would never jeopardise his relationship with you?" He continued to chuckle, so much so that Dee was niggled by it.

"What's so funny?"

"I don't think you realise what the rest of us have to endure," he advised her. "Milo is besotted with you; he hangs on your every word. He stares at you like he's never going to see you again. All we ever hear from his mouth is, '*Dee this, Dee that*' and it's me you ought to feel bad for - listening to him harping on about his amazing fiancée all the time."

"I'm sure you're exaggerating..." Dee squirmed. Milo seemed pretty casual around her but evidently he sang her praises to every other poor soul.

"No I'm not, but it's sweet." Felix returned to sit beside her on the couch. "I'm glad he's happy at last."

Dee sighed. "I need a new wedding venue. Do you think McDonald's would oblige? If we just buy a few hundred happy meals, people wouldn't feel cheated, would they?"

Felix laughed. "I don't think they do parties at McDonald's anymore," he said jocularly. "Come on, cheer up. This is nothing Milo can't sort out. Are you feeling any better?"

"A bit, thanks. It was nice of you to check on me." At least she was smiling now. "I think I might hide in here for a while until things calm down or Finley wakes up. Do you want to watch 'It's a Wonderful Life'?"

"It wouldn't be Christmas if we didn't," he agreed readily.

"You know, you're the most affable famous person I've never heard of," Dee joked and raised a wry smile from her fiancé's cousin. And from that evening on, they *really did* become firm friends.

*

It was his first cigarette in many months and Milo had to admit it was one of the best he had ever savoured. Sitting at the desk in the study, Milo stared out into the night that Christmas evening. He was thinking how that scenario had gone exactly how he had always imagined it would. Well, he never *had* envisaged being welcomed with open arms into the Stark family. Somehow he felt a strange affinity with Angel who really did not belong fully in either family. Milo had one foot in each camp too.

"Hi, can I talk to you?" Elliott appeared at the study door.

"If you must," Milo spun around in the plush black office chair.

"I thought you'd quit smoking." Elliott diffidently came in and sat on a matching leather recliner.

"I did," Milo inhaled even deeper since he would probably never get to smoke another one.

"So, you're my brother, huh?" Elliott asked eventually.

"Half brother, yes," Milo replied. "Look, I never meant for you guys find out like this."

"How long have you known?"

"Since I was about ten or eleven, I overheard my mother discussing it with my father - Austin, I mean," Milo sighed and decided it was time to explain. "It happened when your mother and father were newly engaged. Erwin often visited Austin in the States and on one of those occasions he had a brief fling with my mother. My mother told Erwin he'd got her pregnant but he didn't want a part of it, not with his new wife at home in England. Austin knew I wasn't his but he never discussed it with me. I realised there was a reason he had always been so cold towards me, but he gave me a roof over my head and paid for my schooling. I guess he decided that was his only duty to his brother's bastard son."

"You've known all that since you were a boy and you never said anything to anyone?" Elliott shook his head.

"Not until I met Dee, no. And she couldn't even keep it a secret for one single year," he smiled.

"Don't be too hard on her. Rightly or wrongly, she did what she did for you," Elliott said softly. "Dee's very upset about blurting it out."

"I know. I'm not really mad at Dee. I've been promising her for a long time that I was going to tell you guys when, in honesty, I don't think I was ever going to get around to it."

"Why not, Milo?" Elliott was still grappling with this news.

"What was the point? What good would it have done?" He swivelled from side to side in his chair. "By the time we were all grown up I had such a bad relationship with you guys, I didn't see how learning I was your big brother was going to help."

"How come we were allowed to spend every summer together when Austin knew the truth? How come Erwin and Austin still got on?"

"I suppose they patched it up for appearances sake."

"Now it makes sense, they say you changed when you were around that age...and that was when you found out," Elliott mused.

"When I changed? When I began going off the rails, you mean?" Milo frowned. "When everything you believe to be true turns out to be a lie, when you stop belonging...you can't help but change a little."

"It must have been awful for you," Elliott conceded. "So one year I lose a brother and the next year I gain another one..." he reflected thoughtfully.

"Not much of a trade, was it? I guess Dee and I are going to need to find a new venue for our wedding in the morning," Milo stated flatly.

"Why would you think that? It's not your fault my father slept with your mother. We can't help who we are," Elliott remarked plainly. "If I've got any say in it, you're still getting married at our hotel...if you want to-"

"But have you got any say in it? Jerry has just been given the worst news imaginable and he sure isn't going to want to do me any favours."

"Jerry will get over this, maybe things will even improve now that we know. You are our brother after all."

Milo laughed. "I don't know how I managed to upset everybody so much all these years. I wish I hadn't quarrelled with Lance over that property or stolen his fiancée. I wish I'd told him who I was and we'd resolved things before he died," Milo said grimly. "And I know I've just gone on to upset you and Jerry. I should have waited after Lance died before I started anything with Dee - but have you ever wanted somebody so much, you just couldn't help yourself?"

"Sort of," he admitted. "I think we might have taken it better...it's just you started sleeping together within four months of Lance's death."

"I realise it was too soon but was out of my control. You might even say it was love at first sight – which might be seen as tacky at her husband's funeral, I know. I couldn't stop it. I regret a lot of things, but I can't regret what happened with Dee. She's what I live for," he said so flippantly that Elliott was quite certain he actually meant it.

"Dee seems really content since she found you. You're a good father to those kids and we can talk about adopting Angel at a later date," Elliott affirmed. "I want Dee to be happy and you make her happy so you're going to get married in our hotel. That's all there is to it."

"Thanks," Milo said, looking up at the clock, noticing it was nearly ten. "Has everybody gone?"

"Well, after the tension, Bruce, Patrice and Evan took off. Jerry's gone home but Forrest, Felix and Ginny are still here. I understand they are staying overnight."

"That's right. Look, I'm glad we had this chat," he admitted. "I need to talk to Forrest." That thought had been nagging at Milo since the truth had come out. "I expect the news has upset him as much as you guys."

"Okay. I'll call you in the morning to confirm the wedding details." Elliott stood up to leave. "It'll be fine. We'll talk some more when things have blown over. I guess I'd like to know more about my older brother."

*

Tossing and turning in the darkness, Dee knew there was little chance of any sleep until Milo came to bed. She had watched the movie and managed to enjoy a fairly pleasant evening with Felix under the circumstances before he went to find Forrest and Ginny. She was sick to her stomach for opening her big mouth and had cried so much, her head ached. Dee was just beginning to doze off due to sheer exhaustion when a crack of light coming through the half-closed door disturbed her and Milo crept in.

"Are you awake?" he whispered.

"...Yeah, are you okay?" Dee sat up and snapped on the lamp.

"I'm okay." Milo sat on the bed.

"I'm really sorry." Dee felt the tears spring up in her eyes again. "I've ruined everything."

"It's fine. This secret was going to have to come out one day and it's better that everyone knows," he insisted, slipping a hand into hers. "I'm sorry I spoke to you like that in front of everybody. I feel utterly horrible about it." Milo actually seemed more concerned about that right now and Felix's words came back to her. Sometimes Dee found it hard to conceive that Milo was still so infatuated with her after all this time. This level of adoration was never truly apparent to her but she was constantly surprised by other people's take on their relationship. She still found it hard to take on board that Milo deemed himself lucky to have her.

"Don't be stupid, I deserved all I got," Dee decided sheepishly.

"You were right, I was never going to admit the truth and I'm glad it's out in the open." Milo undressed and climbed into bed beside her. He moved closer into the warmth Dee had created under the covers. "I've had a long talk with Forrest and he's a little upset but that's to be expected. I've had a lot longer to get used to this than any of my brothers."

"I'm sorry," Dee repeated. Now the news was out, Dee did not understand why she had been so desperate for the world to know the details of Milo's parentage. What difference did it make? Jerry and Elliott would not miraculously change their opinion of Milo after years of detesting him.

"Honey, I'm not mad at you," Milo assured her with a comforting hug. "To be honest, it's a weight off my shoulders. Elliott even says we can still get married at the hotel."

"Are you serious?" Dee gaped. Considering Milo had completely sprung the new wedding arrangements on her, Dee would actually be heartbroken if she could not marry this man on New Year's Eve anymore.

"Yes, he actually seems okay with it. I'm surprised he took it so well."

"That's great. I really hope this whole thing calms down and you can all get used to being a family," Dee said wearily. "I was so sure you'd never forgive me."

"There's nothing to forgive." Milo shrugged. "You did it for me. You were just trying to defend me like you always do. I've never had someone who was always in my corner before. I love you for it."

"I love you too." Dee snuggled in closer so she was completely enveloped in him.

"Did you leave milk for me in the refrigerator? I'll get up with the baby tonight."

Dee opened her weary eyes which had begun to close with drowsiness. "Again? You got up last night."

"And you've been coping on your own for weeks. I'm pulling my weight whilst I'm home," Milo insisted and would broach no argument. Dee didn't bother to ask *when* he was leaving again exactly, because the thought was too unpalatable.

*

There were many sore heads on Boxing Day morning. Dee's wasn't one of them since breastfeeding prevented her from getting drunk. The Phillipses and Kellermans sat around the kitchen table (there was something homelier about this this room than the dining room – it was the heart of the house) moping and groaning about how awful hangovers were once one was past the age of thirty. Now that Dee was firmly in her thirties too, she was in agreement - if only she could have a drink to prove the theory. Felix, Ginny and Forrest had been the last to bed, Felix the last of all. On the odd occasion she woken up to turn over, Dee had heard him rattling around the house. He must have been up until the early hours.

Despite Dee's protestations, Val Dawson had insisted in coming in for two or three hours to help out with the morning chores whilst Dee had house-guests. Mrs Dawson had asserted that her husband would be 'driving her up the wall' by Boxing Day morning so Dee let her have her way. While Valerie was cooking a full English, Felix (who had never much liked being waited on) cooked something else more to his taste and contentedly shared the hob space and work surfaces with the nanny.

Forrest quietly stroked and fussed over little Finley. Last night had been disturbing, but now he was fully in possession of all the facts, it was as though he had always known. They were alike in looks, but his elder brother had been too different, too removed. Forrest had often wondered if he himself had been adopted because he was so unlike Milo. But then he was unlike his arrogant and loveless parents too. Then his painful thoughts were interrupted.

"Are you okay?" Dee whispered under her breath, Angel jerking around rather off-puttingly on her lap.

"I'm fine." Forrest faked a warm smile.

"I'm sorry." Dee had been waiting for a good opportunity to apologise, but instead stole the only one at hand. "I wish I'd never said anything."

"It's alright. I'm glad I'm not in the dark anymore. Milo is still my brother, no matter who his father was. Nothing has changed," he assured her but inside he was saddened. Forrest had always told himself that many siblings were estranged and did not understand each other. There had been a seven-year gap between their ages and Forrest had always attributed the gulf to that. But in actual fact, Milo was only his half brother. He was as closely related by blood to Lance, Jerry and Elliott as he was to Forrest.

"Just as long as you know I didn't mean to hurt anyone. It's been tearing Milo apart for years and I couldn't stand to see him bear it alone any longer," Dee explained. "If you need to talk to me about it, I'm always here." She touched his arm gently and rose from her chair. Angel scooted off and began tearing around the kitchen like a mad thing as Dee went to join Felix where he stood at the hob, fixing French toast. "Ooh, eggy-bread, can I have some?"

Felix rolled his eyes over at her disparagingly. "You English have to cheapen everything."

"French toast just doesn't sum up what it is," Dee reasoned blandly. "...Is he really okay?" she said softly, jerking her head in the direction of Forrest.

"Well, the news has really thrown him but he'll be alright. They're still brothers," Felix said reasonably. Then it was clear he was finished with that topic. "Last night was fun, wasn't it?"

"It was alright." Dee shrugged nonchalantly but couldn't sustain her blasé routine and began to snigger. "No, it was fun. I mean, last night was pretty horrible on the whole but at least you and I are BFFs now." She was smirking again.

"Good, because I was starting to think you didn't like me very much," Felix confided with a wry smile, checking the underside of his egg-laden bread with a spatula.

"Well, stop going off being famous in Paris or New York or wherever. Otherwise, you *really will* be dead to me," Dee told him in no uncertain terms. "For a while there, I used to worry you might have decided in hindsight that I was a bit weird..."

"Weird? Oh no, amusing maybe," Felix insisted vehemently. "I happen to think you're really witty and we share the same kind of humour. How could I possibly find somebody weird who I've shared such an amazing duet with? That sort of thing forms a lifelong bond, it does," He arched a mocking eyebrow, hinting at Dee's forced karaoke experience almost one year ago.

"Don't remind me, I'm still mentally scarred by that." Dee could hardly forget that New Year's Eve night when she and Milo were desperately attempting to ignore and shun each other even though they had actually fallen desperately in love. "Anyway, I'm glad I've broken the ice with you again...it's important to me that I get along with Milo's family."

"Then you'll be glad to hear that Forrest, Ginny and I are considering moving from Chelsea to Richmond just to be near you," he fluttered his lashes at her. "Milo is looking for a property for us right now."

"All of you together in one house?" Dee cocked her head to one side like a spaniel.

"Yeah, but it's got to be a *really big* house so I can get away from my annoying twin sister and her even more annoying kids whenever I want to."

"Up on Millionaires Row? Richmond Green or Richmond Hill?" she questioned.

Felix shrugged. "Somewhere like that. We want to be able to look down our noses at you, that's the main thing." he joked.

"Don't you want to live by yourself at some point? What if you meet a woman and want to start a serious relationship?"

"Then I'd move out. But right now I don't want to live on my own," Felix remarked casually. "I spend half my life on my own in hotel rooms when I'm travelling for work."

"Well, that will be really great - all our family together in one place," she enthused. "Two slices please, in your own time." Dee gave an impish little grin, punched him lightly on the arm then returned to her other guests. She stopped behind Milo and wrapped her arms about his neck. Dee gently kissed the top of his head and Milo visibly relaxed in her embrace.

Felix watched from the corner of his eye. As his initial predictions had told him, Dee was down-to-earth and straightforward. Felix respected that. Also, he hadn't failed to notice that she was sort of pretty in an understated kind of way; savvy, funny and really very likeable. Even now Felix was still mystified that his normally superficial and shallow cousin had hooked up with someone so grounded. It was just a pity Dee didn't have a sister. Oh well.

Then with the simple ringing of a doorbell, the relaxed Boxing Day morning took a strange and unexpected turn for the worse.

GLADER TIDINGS?

By the furrowed brows and complete absence of anything resembling a smile, everybody knew that Jerry and Elliott were not here on a social call as they seated themselves at the kitchen table. Perhaps Jerry was still angry and smarting from last night. Still, Dee couldn't help but worry that his expression was grave rather than cross.

"...I'm sorry but we need to speak to Dee alone," Jerry began hesitantly.

"Jerry, we're having breakfast." Dee sat on Milo's lap as suddenly there was no place to sit with all these people here.

Elliott sighed. "Jerry, they're all going to find out soon enough - maybe it's best they hear it from us..." He too was wearing a pained expression on his face and this was making Dee extremely uncomfortable. There was a prickling sensation running up the back of her neck and she just had this feeling...

"Well, the children have already been fed and watered so I'll just take them out for some fresh air," Val said decisively.

Jerry glanced up and gratefully said, "...thank you - I think that would be best..."

Once Val had departed with the small people Milo cleared his throat brusquely. "If you've decided you don't want us to get married at your hotel anymore, you could have just sent us a text..."

"No, it's not that. That offer still stands - you're still welcome to get married with us...but after I tell you what's happened, you may not want to," Jerry said uncomfortably. "We were called into work very early this morning...because the police were there..."

"Oh...?" Dee glanced uncertainly at Milo.

"I don't know if any of you guys read about the body of a woman that was discovered in the woods just outside town by a jogger and his dog a few days ago...?" Elliott added diffidently.

"Oh yes, I heard about that," Felix said casually, still eating his breakfast of French toast. He was the only person at the table who hadn't instinctively put down his knife and fork at their arrival.

Dee swallowed, her throat was so dry she could actually hear the gulp in her ears. "No, I hadn't heard…what has that got to do with you guys…?" Dee rarely read a newspaper or sat down to watch the news. It was invariably depressing.

Elliott seemed to look to Jerry for reassurance, then said, "…the body has been identified as Kate Taylor."

"Who's Kate Taylor?" Felix said between chews without looking up.

"…The secretary," Milo concluded before either of his half brothers could. He stared directly into his fiancée's face which had suddenly drained of blood and gone awfully grey in colour.

Felix raised his eyes finally and screwed up his face. "What secretary?"

"…Oh no…" Dee had raised her hands up and involuntarily placed them over her mouth.

Ginny glared at her brother who she felt was being incredibly dense, if not insensitive, and said, "…that's the secretary Lance had an affair with - the one who was blackmailing him?"

Jerry met her eyes briefly. "Yes."

"…Wait, so…was she ever classed as a missing person?" Forrest shook his head in confusion.

"No, she was supposed to have emigrated," Dee replied, removing her hands to reveal that her mouth was now just a thin line. "Now it seems she hadn't left the country at all…"

"But she must have been gone about…what, just under two years? Why haven't any family members or friends reported that she hadn't been in contact?" Forrest asked with his usual blunt logic.

"It appears Kate wasn't a very popular lady. She was an only child and her parents had disowned her years before. The few friends that she had had been so badly treated by her once she came into- *all that money…* they wrote her off too." Elliott splayed his fingers out before him on the table pensively.

"So the police popped by to tell you all about it on Boxing Day morning?" Felix had returned to finishing off the final remnants of his food. Dee watched how he cut each morsel of bread intricately and put it into his mouth. She didn't know how he could stomach it, hers lay untouched.

"It seems murder investigations don't pause for public holidays," Jerry responded flatly.

"So it was definitely murder…?" Dee said before she had processed the thought enough to realise how stupid she sounded.

"Well yes, unless she battered herself to death then buried her own body in the woods," Jerry hadn't meant to reply so harshly to the person here who would have been affected by this the most.

"Why have the cops come to you guys first?" Ginny hugged herself and rubbed her arms, suddenly feeling unnaturally cold.

Jerry sighed and rubbed his tired eyes. He quite clearly hadn't slept after last night's heated argument – and probably wouldn't sleep for days now this had happened. "Because the prime suspect is my brother...and he's dead. So I guess the next stop was us..."

*

Dee honestly hadn't meant to hare from the room like that. She managed to hold in the contents of her stomach until she reached the downstairs toilet. When she recovered herself, sluiced her mouth with mouthwash and splashed water on her face, Dee unlocked the door and found her troubled-looking partner waiting outside for her in the passageway. Milo didn't say anything, just placed his arm around her shoulder and gently guided her back to kitchen. Felix, Forrest and Ginny seemed to have made themselves scarce but she knew they hadn't left the house as she hadn't heard the distinctive sound of the front door. Milo carefully sat her down at the table and seated himself beside her, his arm comfortingly around her waist. She was shivering, he could feel it.

Elliott and Jerry greeted her with pitying eyes whilst Milo picked up a glass of water and encouraged her to drink it.

"Dee, I'm sorry we didn't break the news to you more gently but there just isn't a nice way to say-" But Jerry couldn't finish.

"Are the police coming to see *me*...?" Dee kept her eyes focused on the china teapot in the middle of the table and took deep, even breaths. She could quite easily throw up again.

Elliott reached across and placed a hand on hers. "They want to interview anyone who ever worked at or had any connection with the hotel. And you fit the bill, I'm afraid. The Detective Constables are interviewing the rest of our staff now – Bruce and Patrice were horrified at being called in. We said we'd pick you up and bring you to the hotel - we thought the news would be better coming from us."

"Why the Richmond staff? Why not the West End branch? That's where she worked." Dee desperately needed to make sense of this. Lance surely had nothing to do with this atrocity and there had to be some evidence to prove his innocence – if only they could find it.

"Yes, but when Lance took over the Richmond branch for that short time-" Elliott glanced uneasily at Jerry who had nearly been ousted by his late brother all those years ago, "...he brought his own secretary with him. Even after he returned to his own branch, Kate would often show up at our hotel throwing her weight around with the poor staff. She wasn't very well liked...and don't forget her remains were found just outside Richmond..."

Just the word *'remains'* made Dee physically heave again. Luckily there was nothing left inside her. She hadn't been aware she was so weak-stomached. Dee was conjuring up awful images in her mind's eye. A broken, battered body unceremoniously tipped into a shallow grave, freshly-dislodged earth hurriedly shovelled over her lifeless face in the dark and near-silent woods. Lance standing there, breathing hard, wiping his dirty hands on his jeans.

Milo rubbed his hand in circles in the small of her back. "Deep breaths..." He was deeply worried; for Dee to react that way meant that she must actually believe-

Dee managed to compose herself again. "...But what will I tell the detectives? I don't *know* anything - you wouldn't *tell* me anything..."

"Then they shouldn't need to talk to you for very long," Elliott insisted soothingly. "You just tell them the complete truth, Dee."

Milo raised his concerned eyes from his fiancée bleakly. "Why is Lance the prime suspect? You said she was widely disliked..."

"Well, because...because-" Jerry blustered.

"Milo knows everything I do, guys. We keep no secrets from each other." Dee sipped gingerly at the water again and Milo ignored Jerry's bitter, accusing stare.

Elliott exhaled audibly. "...The police know about the embezzlement and they know about the blackmail." His late brother had rightly suspected he was soon to be disowned and cut off financially by his father, so had slowly and secretly siphoned off money from the business into another offshore account. Kate Taylor had discovered this indiscretion amongst accounting paperwork and used it to extort money from her hopelessly despairing boss, money and sex. "We told them everything we know but it seems they had already uncovered most of it. They know he bought her a flat and a car and God knows what else...and that they had been sleeping together at her apartment for months - against Lance's wishes," he added for Dee's benefit, glancing at her momentarily. "They knew she had him over a barrel and that he was desperate..."

"Not desperate enough to kill her, surely!" Dee blurted out. So that was it? The secretary showed up dead and her ex-husband and father of her daughter was being secretly judged and convicted by all of them? Even by her?

Thankfully, Milo was keeping calm for the both of them. "And there's nobody else in the frame? It sounds as though towards the end she trod on a lot of people. There's no disgruntled ex-boyfriend or lover?"

Jerry glanced at Elliott. "...The police had spoken to an ex-best friend before us...and they seemed to be hinting that there was some other mystery lover in the picture. But they were quizzing *us* about who that could be so they obviously don't know who he is."

Dee suddenly brightened. "So Lance could be innocent!"

Elliott chewed nervously on his lip. "They wouldn't give us any details...but they seemed to be inferring that it could have been a professional killing. And Lance had that kind of money." He shrugged. "Whoever did it went to great, and probably very expensive, lengths to cover it up. Some woman bearing Kate Taylor's description flew to Australia on her passport, spent money on Kate Taylor's bank and credit cards...then promptly disappeared into thin air. But the real Kate Taylor would already have been dead by then."

Dee's voice was strangulated when she next spoke. "...Do they suspect any of us? Do they suspect *me*? *I* had motive too."

"Dee, I really don't think so. I imagine Jerry and I are certainly going to be in trouble for keeping the embezzlement secret once Lance had admitted it, but they don't suspect us of anything sinister. And they seem to believe you were completely in the dark up until after Kate went missing," Elliott explained.

"Look, we'd better head back to the hotel; we assured them we'd be bringing you back with us shortly." Jerry scraped his chair as he rose to his feet.

"I'm coming with you," Milo asserted as he helped Dee shakily to her feet. As all four headed from the kitchen, they found the others loitering in the hall. It was obvious their semi-secret conversation had been overheard.

"...Jerry," Ginny began tentatively. "How are you going to be affected by this? Are you guys in a lot of trouble...?"

"I don't suppose it's going to be incredibly good for business, if that's what you mean," he sniffed derisively.

"You make sure you tell the police *everything* you know. I know you want to be loyal to your brother's memory - but this crime can't hurt Lance anymore, he's dead. But you're alive...and it can hurt you," Ginny assured him.

Jerry narrowed his eyes. "So you want me to sell my brother down the river to save my own skin?"

"If you tell the truth, you have nothing to be afraid of," she began again more bravely. Jerry studied her for a moment then gave her a curt nod. The four trooped from the house in silence.

Ginny, Forrest and Felix awkwardly milled around about the hall for a moment, contemplating packing their things and going home.

Felix shoved his hands in his pockets and twisted his mouth thoughtfully. "They sure do exciting Christmases around here - I hope they invite us next year," he said with that incorrigible schoolboy impudence he had about him.

Forrest glowered at him with a slow shake of his head. "Do you ever take anything seriously? What is the matter with you?

*

The house was oddly silent when Dee returned from being subjected to over an hour-long interview at the hotel. The Detective Constables, a man and a woman, had been remarkably nice under the circumstances. Dee had told them everything she had known at the time and everything she had become aware of after Lance's death. She was as helpful as she knew how to be and kept back nothing. Honesty was the best policy from now on; somebody was dead and Dee had to know the truth about how that woman had died. Even if the truth was unspeakable.

The house-guests had apparently all gone back to Chelsea, judging by the deathly silence, and Milo read the note the nanny had left on the completely clean and tidied kitchen table. Mrs Dawson had obviously cleared away the chaos of breakfast they had left behind in their haste.

"She says she took the kids to her house for a couple of hours and she'll bring them back a little later," Milo simplified the note for his soon-to-be wife. "Go and sit down in the lounge. I'll make you a coffee - you must be exhausted." He had been treating her like a fragile china doll since this morning; as though she may fall apart at any given moment. But Dee didn't feel as though she would fall apart anymore, not since the vomiting episode, and certainly not after talking to the police. She felt a great deal better now that she wasn't in the dark anymore.

Settling herself neatly on the sofa, Dee looked up to visually appraise him when he entered the lounge with two mugs of coffee. "...What?"

"Nothing...you've been so brilliant today. I don't think I could have handled that without you," she admitted. He gave a gruff shrug but she knew he was secretly pleased about her recognition of the fact. Milo loved to play the 'great protector' to his new family. She watched him pensively as he sat beside her, placing the mugs on the cluttered coffee table. "...I think we should postpone the wedding - put it back until April again. There's too much crap going on and it will spoil what is supposed to be a lovely day."

Milo rubbed his chin circumspectly. "But I *really* want you to be my wife before I go back."

"But you're not going *soon*, are you?" Dee suddenly felt very fragile again.

"Sooner than I'd like - just to sort things out in the States so I can be here more permanently," he said assuredly, sensing her fear. "Come back to New York with me this time. I'm not comfortable leaving you here alone with the children after what has happened today."

"I don't think the police would agree to that just yet..." Dee sighed. "I just feel so weird about getting married when there's a murder investigation involving my ex-husband going on. This is all too much for poor Jerry and Elliott to cope with on top of everything else."

"I think us getting married at their hotel in five days sends a message to everyone that we're all still united as a family. How does it look if we turn our backs on them now? Their business is going to be badly affected by this, I promise you. Our wedding says that *you* still respect and trust them...and stand by them." Milo didn't honestly know if he felt that way at all. He just *really* wanted to get married quickly and another venue at the eleventh hour seemed impossible now.

"Do you really think so?" Dee was always very easily swayed when her loyalty was under question. Milo nodded sincerely and Dee had to agree with his sentiments. "You're such a good man, if Jerry only knew that..."

"They're my half brothers." Milo laid it on a little more thickly.

"Why is it so important to you that we're married right away?"

Milo contemplated that momentarily. "I'm not sure...you're the most important person in my life and getting married makes that a fact. I know it shouldn't matter, but it does to me." he admitted urbanely. Well, at least that part was true. He didn't honestly give a fig about the venue.

"It's probably the dominant American blood in you which makes you so corny, Milo. But I love you anyway." Dee grinned, slipping her small hand in his. Milo raised an eyebrow - he always meant what he said about loving her, every word. Dee was just so English and still mildly suspicious of his adoration; she never fully took him seriously.

LOVE AND MARRIAGE

The morning of New Year's Eve was grey with the odd heavy shower of rain, perfect English wedding weather. Dee stared sightlessly from the kitchen window, standing in her usual morning attire of a towelling robe and slippers while Mrs Dawson bustled about making everybody a light breakfast. The day before the wedding, Dee had spent the majority of the day in a robe too. Bruce's brain-child for the 'hen day' was a luxury day of being pampered and preened at the beauty spa. Only two actual hens were in tow since Dee's friends were mainly men. Dee and Ginny enjoyed being amongst the boys; Bruce, Patrice and Evan. Although Dee had just been through a fairly traumatic ordeal (which wasn't exactly over) and had not exactly been looking forward to her hen-day, prancing about in a big white towelling robe and towelling slippers had gone some way in cheering her up. Milo, Forrest and Felix had spent the night at Jerry and Elliott's hotel after a day of golfing and whatever else men did - Dee only hoped they hadn't partied too hard later.

"Lucky the entire affair is set indoors!" Mrs Dawson chirped, laughing heartily about the current downpour while she confidently scrambled eggs and toasted bagels.

"It could just as easily have rained in April," Ginny interjected from where she sat with her daughters and Dee's children at the table. Bruce read a newspaper, Patrice expertly scraped the contents of a grapefruit onto his spoon and the wedding morning progressed rather quietly.

"Dee, you haven't said much this morning." Bruce glanced from the headlines of the local paper – 'the body in the woods' story putting him off the thought of breakfast a little. He still hadn't quite gotten over being questioned by *real* police about the secretary's death. His best friend turned from where she gazed listlessly out into the street. "You're not having second thoughts are you?"

"No, of course not," she frowned. "...You don't think *he* is, do you?"

"I highly doubt that," Ginny said forthrightly.

"Come and sit down, Dee. Breakfast is ready." Mrs Dawson placed the plates before her eager audience and proceeded to open a large bottle of champagne.

"A champagne breakfast! Oh thanks, Mrs D," Bruce enthused, folding up the paper, rubbing his hands together and promptly forgetting the murder of a woman he only vaguely knew.

"Not *more* champagne, I'm sure a breastfeeding woman isn't supposed to consume champers as regularly as this." Dee wrinkled her nose and joined the others at the kitchen table.

"It's not every day you get married. Plus, it's wedding tradition," Mrs Dawson insisted.

Dee sighed. "Sorry Val, I'm not very hungry either."

"You eat up, you have a big day ahead of you and you'll need all your strength." Valerie Dawson wasn't taking no for an answer.

"Don't remind me." Dee rubbed her eyes and stroked Finley's soft hair where he sat in a high-chair.

"You could do a better job of looking more excited," Patrice said disapprovingly.

"I'm excited about being married, honestly. It's just this whole big ceremony, everyone looking at me. It's my own fault, Milo would have been happy with a small affair but I insisted we make a big fuss to show people we were proud to be together."

"And you were right. This is a very big deal and it needs to be a lavish occasion. It's the greatest day of your life so a big celebration is in order," Ginny explained.

"Mm, what time did the wedding planner say we had to be at the hotel?" Dee turned her attention to Bruce, the wedding assistant extraordinaire. She tried to attach happy memories to that place, and not those of a possible crime-scene.

"Rhoda said she wanted us there at ten. Evan is bringing Mia about the same time," Bruce confirmed. Dee was glad she had chosen all four girls to be bridesmaids in the end. They would look adorable – and Mia would set an example as the sensible one.

"If that woman tells me how to handle children one more time, I'll strangle her," Ginny, the lead bridesmaid, growled. So she had *four* girls to take care of, but she had been organising children for six years! And what she didn't know about little girls wasn't worth knowing.

"I wonder how much Jerry and Elliott pay that woman, because I could do her job with one hand tied behind my back," Patrice assured them derisively.

"It's too hot in here...I feel sick-" Dee jumped up from the table with a scrape of her chair and darted out into the hall. She hurried upstairs and fled to the bathroom. Deciding there wasn't a great deal more air in there than in the kitchen (though it was undoubtedly cooler), she opened a window and took a few gasps. Dee sat down on the edge of her roll-top bath and attempted to take deep breaths to ease the nausea.

Ginny soon found her friend taking a lungful of air and staring with fixed concentration at the floor. "That's right…deep breaths, slow and steady…"

It didn't take too long before Dee felt remarkably improved. "…Sorry, thought I might need to up-chuck, but I don't." She smiled weakly at Milo's cousin.

"I'm glad to hear that!" Ginny laughed, but she was mostly just relieved. "Don't worry, you just got in a panic."

"Yes, probably…" Dee began to feel relief as the nausea ebbed away. "Thanks for checking on me…" She merely felt embarrassment now.

"So what do you think brought that on?" Ginny enquired anxiously.

"…Look…I know what you're thinking, but I'm not having second thoughts. I'd have already had those by now." Dee quickly put Ginny's mind at rest. "…But this thing with Lance has really *got* to me."

"Of course it has - the whole situation is appalling," Ginny reasoned. "Whether he did it or not…you can't let it consume you, Dee. You're not responsible for what Lance may or may not have done."

"But the father of my daughter-"

"And she's not to blame either. You know, we may *never* get the resolution to this that we're all looking for. Unless the police find something to tie this to Lance, you may never know what really happened. If it was a professional killing, there probably *won't* be any concrete evidence. And the prime suspect is dead so he isn't going to confess…"

"…But Ginny, none of it makes sense. Kate Taylor died of multiple internal injuries – it sounds as though she was beaten to death. Hitmen don't kill their victims like that, there would be too many bodily fluids left behind, too much evidence. You would expect a cold-blooded execution, wouldn't you? A bullet to the head? Whoever killed her was personally involved, *angry*," Dee stressed. The floodgates had been opened and she had to talk about it now.

Ginny had been attempting to steer her away from the subject, but now even her curiosity had been piqued. "You think Lance actually killed her himself…?"

"No! I don't know…but somebody did…" Dee didn't want that to be the case, somehow a professional killing was marginally more palatable even if Lance had arranged it. "Lance was dying, when he had only days to live and was still lucid...why didn't he tell one of us what he'd done? Wouldn't a man on his deathbed feel some kind of remorse? He had nothing left to lose, they couldn't lock him up...so why didn't he *tell* me?"

Ginny was forced to think about that in greater detail than she was comfortable with. "I don't know much about human psychology...but what you're saying seems very sensible." She rubbed at her temples to try to alleviate a stress-headache that was threatening. "Did you mention this to the police?"

"Yes. And they listened. I get the feeling that had occurred to them too. They asked me about everything we talked about in the days leading up to his death."

"Dee, you're right to want to talk about this to make sense of it...but this is your wedding day. Shouldn't we put it aside just for today?"

Dee scratched her head. "I have no choice but to think about it today. Lance loved me enough to want to marry me once. But then he had an affair with another woman, and I know he and his brothers kept insisting it was blackmail, but what if it wasn't entirely? I forced myself to accept that explanation when he was sick, but secretly, I've always thought he must have wanted her...even if it was just a little bit. Who gets blackmailed into having an affair-?"

Ginny conceded a grimace reluctantly. "I don't think you'll ever truly know what was going on in his mind."

"I kind of lied about the cold feet...no, I don't mean I don't want to marry Milo. I love him to bits. I just wish we had stuck with our original April plans. I've only been widowed for eighteen months - this wedding all seems so rushed."

"January, April, what's the diff?" Ginny smiled warmly. "Lance betrayed you, then he died. You can't help that you fell in love with someone else. Human beings aren't supposed to be solitary creatures and you found Milo and that has to be a good thing," Ginny advised wisely. "They make you take vows about *in sickness and in health* but they don't mention what happens after death. What were you supposed to do? Wear black for the rest of your life and hibernate? As I understand it, you were going to divorce Lance anyway."

The overwhelming anxiety Dee had been feeling eased just through the act of being able to discuss this pent-up angst. "Apart from my kids, Milo is the best thing that has ever happened to me."

"You belong together. And you've gone too far down this road to let the past ruin your future. Milo is the father of your son. Angel has come to see him as a father too. You've made commitments and promises more binding than any wedding ceremony already," Ginny reminded her. "What's more, he adores you - you've changed his life. Just shut this 'murder business' in a box for today and try to enjoy your wedding."

"I will," Dee promised adamantly. "Ginny, I'm not very good at telling people what they mean to me but since it's a special occasion...well, I'm really glad Milo had a cousin like you. I've never had a proper girl-friend before. Well, I'm not going to get all soppy and sentimental but I'll just say I'm really glad we've become friends," Dee finished awkwardly. "And not just because you're a girl."

"I feel exactly the same way. Who knew I'd actually get along with one of Milo's girlfriends?" Ginny concluded. "So, let's eat something, throw on some clothes and think about moseying over to the hotel."

*

The Georgian reception room was alive by twelve thirty that morning. Perhaps a hundred guests had gathered together and were sitting in rows of period mahogany chairs in one of the regalest reception rooms in The Erwin Stark Hotel. A string quartet played gentle, classical music in the corner. The harp, a cello and two violins created a restful backdrop to the wedding proceedings. The ceremony was to be a fairly informal occasion in spite of its grand setting and Milo proved to be a good host. He met and greeted family and friends with his trusty best man, Felix. When the appointed time loomed closer, he gingerly journeyed to the top of the room where the marriage was to be performed.

When Felix turned to speak to his cousin, he noticed that the genial host role had slipped. Milo now seemed rather grey in pallor and his eyes darted about nervously. "Are you alright?"

"You do think she'll turn up?" He squirmed uncomfortably in his charcoal grey morning suit, loosening his cream cravat.

"Are you kidding me?" Felix cocked his head to one side to gauge if Milo was indeed pulling his leg. Then he realised Milo was totally serious. "Of course I do, one hundred percent. You guys are set in stone, this is just a formality," Felix insisted adamantly.

Milo looked out into the congregation, spotting good friends and not-so-good family members; namely his parents glaring resentfully at him. Behind them sat Dee's best friends, Bruce and Patrice, laughing raucously. Rhoda the wedding planner paced about anxiously, barking orders down the microphone of her headset but nobody was entirely sure to whom. His eyes came to rest on his four-month old son in the capable hands of Mrs Dawson. Milo contemplated his children, *his* children. Angel was his blood and the love he had come to feel for her was as strong as that of any father, as strong as the love he had for his both his sons. Surely Dee could never turn her back on this mismatched family of theirs, could she? Twelve forty-five had been and gone and Milo could only pray Dee was just fashionably late. Then the string quartet broke into 'The Wedding March' and Milo sighed with relief.

Beautiful Dee Campbell strolled in on the arms of both Jerry and Elliott Stark. Elliott was a given but her decision to pick Jerry as the other man to give her away seemed a strange one, but not to Dee. Jerry had taken a punt on her, given Dee her first official job, and taken her under his wing. Like a father, he had given her confidence when she was poor and virtually alone in the world. Like a father, he had rebuked the questionable decisions that she made. Dee certainly could not choose between Jerry and Elliott, who had always been in her corner, so it had to be both. Dee wore a beautiful gown; ivory silk inset with beading on the bodice, the skirt was full and brushed the floor gently as she walked. She wore an ivory sash of organza about her shoulders and her pale blonde hair was twisted up in a chignon from the nape of her neck and swept aside from her face. Her stunning head bridesmaid, Ginny, was followed by four smaller bridesmaids; Mia, Paddy, Melody and Angel in their matching red silk dresses.

Milo's breath caught in his throat, just the way it had when he first approached Dee in this very room over eighteen months ago. He had expected her to be beautiful, of course, but not the vision she turned out to be today. She caught him watching her float up the aisle with that secret smile on his lips, his gorgeous brown eyes glittering with admiration and a little bit of mischief.

When she finally reached his side and the music petered out, under his breath he said, "You showed up then?"

Dee shrugged. "I couldn't get out of the bathroom window."

"You're the most beautiful bride I've ever seen," he said quite seriously.

"Oh come on - I mean, thanks...you too," Dee stuttered. "Beautiful in a manly way, I mean...and a *groom*, that is," she continued to yammer and Milo looked as though he might kiss her until Forrest wheeled himself over to greet them in full clergyman garb.

"Cut it out you two, I've got a job to do," Forrest whispered with a smirk. He cleared his throat and began the service.

The sentiments were probably wonderful but Dee and Milo didn't really hear them. Although Forrest was slightly nervous and a little awkward and his voice wavered because this was his brother's wedding, they didn't notice. They were giving each other not-so-discreet grins because this was it; the moment they had been waiting for. At last they would be official. The ceremony flew by and Milo and Dee eagerly answered their 'I dos' in the right places and exchanged rings. The only section of the wedding that actually caused them any concern was the part where anyone present had the right to object to their marriage taking place. But the room was quiet, no ex-boyfriends or girlfriends reared their ugly heads to spoil the day. So they were married in the very room where their paths first crossed on that scorching June day a year-and-a-half ago.

*

After the register had been signed and copious photographs had been taken (Dee hadn't known which direction to look in or which lens to smile at), Dee grabbed the opportunity to take a quick break from proceedings to psych herself up for the rest of the day. Getting hitched was the easy part; it was the mingling she dreaded. Elliott came to check on her in his office which he'd encouraged her to take a breather in.

"You okay?" He found her swivelling in circles on his office-chair behind his desk. She looked very small and childlike even in her wedding dress.

"Yeah...there are a lot of people out there. All looking at *me*." Although she may sometimes come across as a bit of an extrovert, in truth, being the centre of attention was actually terrifying for her.

"...Mm, sometimes it's better just to get your head down and get through it." He sat down in a chair opposite hers. He wasn't much of a socialite himself. "But you're happy though, right?"

"Oh yes, very. I just needed five minutes to regroup." Dee had to keep reminding herself that she was actually married again. "...Elliott, I know it's pointless me saying this now but, I've felt so guilty about putting you guys through the extra pressure of a wedding when you've got so much on your plate."

"I know, and you gave us a million chances to back out but we didn't want to. You're my sister and I wanted to throw you the wedding you deserved," he explained stoically.

"...Yes, but with the Ball later and everything..."

Elliott sighed. "Between you and me...we probably would have been forced to cancel the Ball if your wedding guests hadn't been staying here. A fair few of our Christmas hotel guests have left early..."

"Why? Because of the murder? That had nothing to do with you guys or this hotel. Neither Lance nor Kate Taylor even worked here!" Dee was outraged.

"But they did for a short while...and Kate Taylor's body wasn't found too far from here. Plus, there has been this ominous police presence while they carried out all their interviews – it's created a miserable atmosphere." He scratched his head. "So you've done us a favour really, the place is full when it wouldn't have been."

Dee chewed anxiously on her lower lip. "...Y'know, I was never very comfortable after I was first told about the affair that Kate had conveniently disappeared off the face of the earth...but you guys said-"

"Dee, we were totally honest with you. Kate had shown up at our hotel shouting her mouth off that she was quitting the hotel and emigrating to Australia to start her own business. I heard her say it with my own ears...the smugness alone was unforgettable..."

"So whoever killed Kate used her own plans for emigration to cover up what they'd done..." Dee considered circumspectly.

"So it seems...and went as far as to involve somebody else. A woman posing as her entered Australia with her passport and her credit cards before disappearing into thin air..."

"But that suggests that you're sure the killer was a man. Maybe she was killed by her girl-friend or...Kate was a very unpopular woman, she shamelessly used everybody close to her," Dee insisted but Elliott screwed up his nose derisively and turned his head away, staring mournfully from his window. "...Elliott, you do believe Lance is innocent, don't you-?"

He was silent for just a little too long. "I want you to do something for me, Dee. I want you to hurry up and push this adoption thing through." Elliott suddenly pinned her to the spot with his eyes. "I think it would be better for everybody if Angel grew up as a Phillips, not a Stark."

Dee was stunned at this request. "You can't honestly mean that. Lance was your brother; don't you want to clear his name?"

Elliott gave an exasperated sigh. "Wake up, Dee! Who else would want Kate Taylor dead more than Lance? Disgruntled ex-best-friends don't murder people! But the victims of blackmail...? Lance would have lost everything and gone to prison had his secretary breathed a word of what she knew. She was extorting huge amounts of money from him, making him sleep with her to keep his secret - he was desperate!" He rubbed his eyes, exhausted from the sheer worry of it all, she could tell by the dark circles under his eyes he wasn't sleeping. "Do you want Angel to grow up with that hanging over her head? Her father a murderer? Jerry, you and I - we can't escape this; we'll all be tarred by this. But I think if there is any way of keeping the truth of her real parentage from Angel, then we should-"

"I'm not going to do that, Elliott." Dee's mouth was a hard, thin line. "I'm not going to lie to my child for the rest of her life. I know Lance was far from being an angel but-"

"Whatever his excuse, he cheated on you, Dee. Did any of us really know

Lance that well? Who knows what else he was capable of?" Elliott had always assured her of his late brother's remorse up until now.

    Dee looked away dismissively. "I refuse to believe Lance was capable of murder until it's proved otherwise..." she said. "...We'd better be getting back..."

YOU TOO SHALL GO TO THE BALL

Sitting centre stage at the top table at their wedding lunch, Dee and Milo held hands and chatted, their eyes fixed on the other, mooning over each other like newlyweds should. Dee gazed admiringly at her platinum wedding ring nestling beside her engagement ring. It was official, they were husband and wife. And Dee was adamant that being married definitely seemed to agree with her.

"Are you nervous about your speech?" Dee asked, tracing a pattern on his palm.

"Nah," Milo insisted but then his face cracked into a grimace. "...Actually I am a little bit. What about you? Are you still going to say something?"

"I think so. At least you've written yours, I have no idea what I'm going to say yet."

"Well, that's your own fault for being so cocky. You aren't even expected to speak, let alone ad-lib," he scoffed. Before they could tease each other more, Felix was loudly tapping his glass with a piece of silver cutlery.

"Can I have your attention please?" Felix stood up and seemed to be more at ease with the crowd's attention than Forrest had been, he was a born performer. His speech was exactly as Dee expected; terribly witty, slightly derogatory of his recently-married cousin but always geared towards receiving a laugh. The congregation just lapped him up and the more he got into his stride, the more nervous her husband became. Milo was paler in pallor now, he sat on his clammy palms in an attempt to dry them on his seat; it wasn't going to be easy to follow a man who was so experienced at entertaining a crowd in-between his musical numbers.

Milo needn't have worried. His speech wasn't half as funny as Felix's (the groom wasn't supposed to be), but he received his share of laughs. What he did best was to play on the audience's heartstrings. He followed tradition, thanked who he was supposed to thank and spoke of the people who could not be there - notably those who had sadly passed away before their time. Dee was brought to tears by his heartfelt words of adoration. Never had a man loved a woman quite so much and Milo was incredibly adept at getting that across. He meant every word and even his harshest critics were forced to think again about his motives.

Dee completed the speeches with a little impromptu rambling of her own. She relied on her natural sense of childish and quirky humour which was pleasing to an audience of people mainly supportive of her (it was odd to think there were a handful of people here who didn't wish the couple well at all). But Dee didn't let that unnerve her. Between the quips, she made it politely clear to her critics that she and Milo were in it for the long haul. And the tremulous applause that greeted the three speakers was exactly as Dee had hoped.

*

After the wedding meal, the guests wandered around and mingled back in the Georgian reception room, catching up with old family members and friends. Dee was rather proud of her poise and repose once she had carried out her hosting duties amongst people she'd never met before. She was congratulated and kissed on the cheek so often, her face ached from keeping that fixed-smile...*fixed*. Dee stood with her daughter propped on her hip whilst Milo cradled Finley in his arms.

"Are you happy, Mrs Phillips?" he asked her brightly, just people-watching.

"Mrs Phillips, I like the sound of that...yes, I'm very happy," she replied.

"Does it feel weird being married again?"

"...Yeah, considering we've been living together for nine months and we have children together, it feels kind of strange. But it feels right at the same time." Milo watched her lift her pretty chin to regard him, a vision in her stunning wedding dress. Before they could talk more, Agatha Phillips came to join them. Dee grimaced, realising this was the first time she was actually going to meet her mother-in-law face-to-face.

"It was nice of you to give your father and I a passing mention in your speech," Agatha chided Milo the moment she arrived. Dee sighed, how could she have expected anything less?

"It was as much a mention as you deserve, mother. You've hardly been supportive of Dee and I and you've had absolutely no input into the wedding, so what would we be thanking you for?" Milo frowned.

"You may not be thanking me now, Milo, but one day you will. One day you will realise I was the only person who actually told you the truth. It's never going to work out between you, you're totally mismatched socially and financially. I just hoped you would come to the same conclusion before you went through with this debacle..." Agatha seemed to have no compunction to be civil in Dee's presence at all.

"Agatha, this is your grandson, Finley. He was born four months ago and neither you nor your husband have ever met him. I guess it was a bit of a struggle to scrape the flight money together. But anyway, here he is." Impoliteness always brought out Dee's smart mouth. Agatha eyed her scathingly.

"We've been very busy which was why we haven't been to England up until now. I'm well aware I have a new grandson and I look forward to getting to know him," she said coldly, giving the child a cursory glance, and Dee a distinctly baleful look. "That does not change the fact that you're a very conniving woman and you're going to drag my son down with you."

"Drag him down to where?" Dee twisted her face in mock-confusion.

"Milo does not belong with you - he wasn't raised for this. You may have got your claws into Lance, but that does not mean Milo is obligated to step in and be a father to his cousin's daughter."

"I think you mean his *half brother's* daughter." Dee arched an eyebrow and Agatha's green-brown eyes suddenly flashed with malice.

"Dee, drop it," Milo sighed and his shoulders slumped because he knew his new bride was unstoppable when in this vengeful mood.

Dee continued regardless. "The whole thing is common knowledge. I would have thought you shared a common bond with me. You had a relationship with your husband's brother and so did I. The only difference is, your husband was *alive* at the time and what *I* did is no secret." Dee stroked Angel's sandy hair from her eyes and strolled away casually, leaving Milo to deal with the fallout.

*

Seated at one of the round guest tables, distantly fingering the ivory linen tablecloth, Dee sat with her very best friend Bruce and Angel plonked on her lap. Angel was ruthlessly dissecting a bunch of white gerberas, dropping their leaves in an unattended glass of champagne.

"I mean, they were lovely speeches, all very moving," Bruce intoned. "It's just all three of you seemed to be having to explain yourselves. All I'm saying is, you don't have to explain yourself to anyone. Your relationship with Milo is a wonderful, wholesome thing and doesn't need to be justified."

Dee wasn't listening. She stared absently into the middle distance. "...I can't believe I've just shouted my big mouth off again," she groaned, watching Angel mournfully. "I know I should have made more of an effort to get my in-laws to like me but that woman just pushed all the right buttons. I'm sure she tried to bait me on purpose so I'd fall out with Milo. I ought to have risen above it but-"

"Dee." Milo suddenly seated himself beside her and caught her wrist with an ambiguous look about him. This time he was without his son. Dee quickly spotted Finn was in the arms of Elliott across the room where he chatted with Forrest.

"...Oh honey, I'm sorry...but your mother just brought out the worst in me," Dee grimaced. "I'll apologise...well, no, I won't apologise exactly but I'll smooth things over," she jabbered on nervously. "I don't mean to disrespect your parents and you know I wouldn't intentionally try to hurt you."

"...It's alright. She already knew everybody was in-the-know about my parentage. I called her after Christmas because I knew your first meeting was going to go something like that. Can we talk by ourselves?" There was a strange urgency about him.

"...Um, yeah...Bruce, could you find Mrs Dawson and ask her to take care of Angel for a while?" Dee put Angel down and gave her a kiss. "You've been a good girl for Mummy today. Mrs Dawson will look after you while Mummy and Daddy have a chat."

"Okay Mummy." Angel smiled brightly as Bruce obligingly took the child away.

"Come on." Milo took Dee's hand briskly and rose to his feet. She followed suit.

"Are you alright? You're mad at me, aren't you?" Dee sighed. "I don't blame you but I really would have been nice if she'd have been nice to me. I should have been a grown-up, your mother is an unpleasant woman but she's still your mother and I of all people should know that family is more important than anything," she wittered on, not even noticing Milo had taken her into the lift and was pressing a button.

"...What, my mother? Jesus, Dee, I don't care about that old witch. The only person I care about is you and I won't let her speak to you like that again...even if that means we don't see her anymore." He seemed agitated and distant somehow.

"Oh, right...is everything okay? Where are we going?"

"To the marital suite," he replied distractedly.

"Okay, good idea...I want to get out of this dress," Dee agreed but chanced to glance back at his anxious expression. She realised this wasn't just a ruse to get her alone (if it were, he would have made a very obvious quip about *getting her out of that dress*). "For Christ's sakes Milo, will you tell me what's wrong if it's not about your mother?"

"I spotted Cameron lurking about the hotel..." he stated blankly.

"...Oh...are you sure?"

"I'm sure. I tried to catch up with him but he disappeared."

"Well...so what? We're married now so he can't spoil anything. Weddings are public ceremonies so you can't legally stop somebody attending. If you think about it, he's a little pathetic and we should just feel pity for him," Dee insisted, resting her back against the wood-panelled wall of the elevator.

"...Do you think you chose the right man?"

"...Hmm, now you mention it, I think I should have hooked up with Cameron, never had my son and never spent the last nine months of my life being the happiest I've ever been! Get a grip, Milo, there was no competition!"

"Sorry, I just get so crazy and irrational when I think about Cameron," Milo sighed.

"Didn't we already *do* this? We met, you were mean, I got mad, we made up, then we were friends, then we had *the thing*-"

"You're hilarious." Milo narrowed his eyes.

"And I'm *yours*!" Dee clasped his hands.

"...Yes you are, aren't you? And I've got a piece of paper to prove it." He smiled as the elevator doors opened.

The sight of the hotel room brought an unexpected smile to both their faces. The beautiful four-poster bed was littered with red rose petals. Some comedian had been there before them and decorated with white toilet paper, draping an entire roll around the wooden bed posts.

"I can't imagine who would have done a thing like that." Milo rolled his eyes knowingly.

"Me either, it's a real mystery," Dee said, sniggering. "Right, I'm going to get changed. This is the second time I've done this, so I don't feel the need to spend the entire day in my wedding dress-" Dee turned to face him suddenly. "Oh, I didn't mean- today has been wonderful and the fact that I've been married before doesn't detract from it. You've been married before too so you know what I mean, don't you...?"

"I'm sorry, what? You mentioned something about taking off your clothes and I didn't listen to the rest," Milo joked pleasantly and placed his arms about her waist.

She smirked. "And he's back. Oh honey, it's great, isn't it? Actually being married *to each other*?" Dee suddenly hugged him tight. "Now, can you unfasten this contraption so we can get back to the party?" She turned her back on him and he unbuttoned the delicate silk-covered buttons down her back. He slipped his hands inside the dress.

"I think this is the part where we're supposed to consummate the marriage..." he whispered seductively in her ear.

Dee rolled her eyes. "...But everyone will wonder where we've got to." She watched him sliding the dress off her shoulders.

"They know exactly where we've got to. It's expected. This is the only time we have because we'll probably be too tired or drunk after the Ball. You want this marriage to be legal, don't you?" There was a wicked little smirk about his lips.

"Oh yes, I definitely want us to be legal," she said quite seriously, with widened, childish eyes. "...I never made love in a bed of red roses before."

"Ah, that's because you haven't been married to *me* before," he advised her matter-of-factly. "...You know, Dee? By the time we're old and grey, you won't be able to say you haven't seen or done anything." Milo knitted his fingers with hers.

"Good, I want to experience everything with you." She turned around and looked up into his big brown eyes. "But more than anything, I'm just looking forward to growing old with you...well, y'know, you're already kind of old but-"

Milo gave her that good natured glare. "...You're a real charmer, you know that?"

"It's a gift," Dee told him simply.

With that, he pushed her down on the bed, breaking through the toilet paper streamers, both landing amongst the red rose petals.

*

By the time evening came around, Dee was very glad she and Milo had snuck away early to share some romantic time together but also to rest her eyes for a short while. Now she felt refreshed and ready to start all over again, which was fortunate since the Ball was to begin in just over an hour. Dee had taken a cat-nap with her new husband, shared a shower with her new husband, and then her new husband called Mrs Dawson and asked her to bring the children up to their suite. Most of the guests would have retired to their own rooms for a brief break from proceedings anyway; freshening up and changing for the big night. The newlyweds had spent nearly two hours with the kids, just being an official family unit for the first time. Dee had fed and changed Finley on the bed whilst Milo played a one-sided game of snap with Angel on the sofa. To avoid a strop, Milo reluctantly resorted to letting the little girl win more often than not. The children were soon to be whisked away for the night so Dee and Milo made the most of their company since the wedding had kept them apart for much of the day.

Dee was now in a fluffy towelling robe, cooing down at Finley on the bed, his tiny fingers curled around hers as she encouraged him to attempt to sit. "What a clever boy, yes you are, yes you are," Dee almost sang to him.

Milo looked up and smiled at the sight of his wife and son interacting so beautifully. Again he longed for Andrew to be there with them, as he did every day. In his imagination he had a fond image that Andrew would have come to stay with them for good if he had lived, though in reality this would probably never have happened. Renee would not have allowed it, but these were his dreams and he could fantasise whatever he wished.

"Snap, Daddy!" Angel called out excitedly, beating him fair and square.

"Good girl, you beat me," Milo said, impressed. He poured much of his energies into this little girl since Andrew's death. All the love and attention Andrew had never received even when alive; this was now focused on Angel. Angel was Milo's now, and the older she grew, the more she took on the look of him, they even had a similar temperament; insatiably happy one moment and prone to broodiness and moods the next. So it was decided pretty much between the pair that they were father and daughter, no matter who had a problem with it.

A sharp knock at the door broke their idyllic and quiet family time as Mrs Dawson poked her iron-grey-haired head around the door. "If you're ready, I'll take the children home."

"Yes," Dee said reluctantly and stood up with the baby. Angel bounded over and Dee scooped her up in a hug. "Be a good girl for Mrs Dawson tonight and we'll see you in the morning. I love you so much, sweetheart," she said tearfully, still hormonal, still emotional from the rigors of being a new mother. She detested leaving them and never got used to it.

"B-bye, Mummy," Angel said with a firm hug. *Somebody* had to be the brave one. Dee and Milo kissed their children goodbye and soon they were gone. It was to be Dee's first night without Finley and she was to find it difficult.

Milo held his soppy wife tight. "Come on, cheer up. It's time to get ready for the Ball."

*

The Erwin Stark New Year Ball was as awe-inspiring and magical as ever; if not even more so this year. As the glitter ball slowly spun in the centre of the room, its mirrored glass reflecting squares of light around the room, Dee was seated beside her new husband at a large round table. They were joined by Forrest, Felix, Ginny, Bruce, Patrice, Evan, Jerry and Elliott. However, Jerry and Elliott barely sat still for five minutes at a stretch because they insisted on fussing over the night's arrangements and interfering with perfectly capable staff when it really wasn't necessary. Still, the table of ten was a light-hearted and happy one on the whole.

"You needn't worry about me not wanting to re-consummate the marriage this evening." Dee turned to face Milo with a hushed voice. "You look really hot in that tux."

"You're drunk," he replied with a smirk, it was the first time she had been in a year. "But I do like you in that red dress; I'd like you even better out of it."

"Ah well, if you play your cards right tonight, you may get lucky."

"Will you two cut it out? You're putting me off my dessert." Bruce wrinkled his nose.

"Have we done the big surprise yet?" Ginny clapped her hands.

"Ginny!" Felix let his head fall back in sheer disbelief.

"What big surprise?" Dee pricked up her ears in excitement. "Is it for me?"

"Ginny, surely it's obvious we hadn't done the big surprise yet," Milo scolded.

Ginny desperately flailed for something to say. "...I'm sorry but nobody tells me anything and I am supposed to be the head bridesmaid," she complained. "I would have thought you couldn't have kept it from her any longer."

"What surprise is this? I don't know about it," said Bruce, almost affronted.

Milo rubbed his eyes, seemingly unsure. "Only Ginny, Felix and Forrest were in on it."

"Come on Milo, tell me. What is it?" Dee tugged at his sleeve in anticipation.

He sighed. "...Well honey, this is my wedding present to you. I'm sorry I couldn't tell you before and I hope I haven't been too presumptuous..." Milo pulled his phone from inside his tux jacket and dialled a number. He put the phone to his ear. "Hi...yeah, shall we do this now?" Milo waited for a reply. "Okay, come on over," he said and ended his call. Dee watched him with a strange nervousness creeping up on her.

From behind her, Dee could hear the sound of heels and then a hand on her shoulder. Dee looked up at a young woman with short, wavy, virtually black hair. She was pretty in a girl-next-door kind of way and her dark brown eyes glittered with genuine warmth. Those eyes almost seemed to well up as though she were so happy she was moved to tears. Even though the mysterious woman was a stranger, she seemed terribly familiar somehow.

"Hi Dee, my name's Cassie Grant," she said in an antipodean accent. "I'm your cousin."

PLEASED TO MEET YOU

It was funny how a table that had just moments ago been virtually full of people was now almost deserted. The others had run for the hills when Dee's secret relative had arrived. Dee's ashen face must have been a picture; so much so that Milo had decided the women simply must be left alone.

"But I don't understand…I don't *have* any cousins…" Dee gaped at the woman sitting beside her at the empty table. "…My mother and father were both only children - I thought…"

"No - my dad, Gordon, was your mother's brother," Cassie explained diffidently. "But your mother had a falling out with *my* mother before you were born - before *I* was born. My mother was an Australian student at Edinburgh University - my parents emigrated to Australia and didn't patch things up with your parents before they left." Cassie was nervously fingering the stem of her champagne glass. Perhaps the family resemblance was all in Dee's head, but Dee could barely stop gawping at her. Cassie reminded Dee of her mother, a dark version of her mother.

"And nobody tried to sort things out? In all that time?"

"It was a huge quarrel. Your mother didn't think my mother was good enough for her brother," Cassie advised grimly. "Ten years later my father wrote to your mother to try to heal the rift but she never replied…and he thought she wasn't interested. He didn't know that she was actually dead. He certainly didn't know about *you*…" she sighed. "We only came back to the U.K. five years ago after my mother died…and that's when he found out about the car crash…and that your parents had a daughter who survived…we've been looking for you all this time."

"…*God*." Dee wrung her clammy hands before her on the table. Alone, all that time she had been alone and hadn't known there was a family out there.

"And here you are, just a few miles down the road all this time…"

"Why, where are you living?" Dee looked up.

"Wimbledon!" At last Cassie smiled and her face lit up the room with her big Australasian grin.

"You're kidding!" Dee clasped her hands without thinking but Cassie beamed even harder and it seemed such a natural thing to do. This was Dee's family - a real blood-relative! "What have you been doing here for the last five years?"

"I'm a tennis coach," Cassie laughed. "Wimbledon seemed to be a good place to gravitate to. I used to be a junior on the Australian circuit but it never came to anything so now I coach."

"A tennis player? Oh my God, if I could have chosen any sporting career, that's exactly what I would have chosen to do," Dee enthused excitedly.

"Ooh, do you play tennis?"

"...No..." Dee shook her gormless head.

Cassie blinked. "...Oh...well, come and have a free lesson whenever you like."

"And what about your father - Gordon?" This had to be the best present Dee had ever received, her dream of real relatives being in existence had actually come true.

"Well, my dad hasn't been very well or he would have been here too...he just got out of hospital actually; his second heart attack in two years..." She lowered her beautiful brown eyes.

"Oh, I'm so sorry...he will be alright won't he?" Then Dee began to experience an unexpected kind of fear of losing an uncle she did not even know.

"He's just recovering from major heart surgery but the surgeons were really pleased with the results. And we think this time he's going to be okay. And now he knows that *you* are alive and well..." Cassie began to dab at her eyes emotionally. "I'm so sorry, but you should have seen his face when Milo contacted us...I've never seen him so happy. I promised I would bring you to meet him as soon as possible. You will, won't you?" she asked almost fearfully.

"Of course, of course," Dee felt tears beginning to pool in her eyes also. They were still holding hands. "You don't understand what this means to me...I guess that's why Milo decided to look into it. How did he find you anyway?"

"I don't know how exactly, he hired a private detective, made some calls, did some digging...I guess these things are easier when you have resources," Cassie mused. "And here's us beating our heads against a brick wall for five years with no leads, no clues...after your grandmother died and you went into care for a short time, the trail seemed to go cold. You just seemed to vanish." Cassie gave a sullen sigh. "Your husband is a pretty amazing guy; he's a bit intimidating, but he's still pretty amazing," Cassie insisted.

"He really is...a lot of people find him a little imposing at first, but he really isn't like that. I wish he'd told me earlier; you could have come to the wedding."

"Oh, I was there. But we decided you had too much on your case this morning to receive this kind of news. Milo thought it would throw you so we decided to wait until tonight," she said with an air of intrigue in her voice. "I was the crazy lady at the back taking millions of pictures; I can't wait to show my dad those."

"God, if only I'd known...when my grandmother died, there was nobody, and all along-" There was that catch in her voice, that little waiver she had been trying to avoid. Tears began to spill down her face. Tears she had been holding in for years.

"Oh honey, it's okay, we've found each other now." Cassie scraped her chair closer and put her arms around Dee. Both women had an inkling that from then on, they would be inseparable.

*

Dee eventually found her husband at the bar, perched on a stool nursing a whiskey. He looked up tentatively as she joined him, climbing up on a barstool beside him.

She surveyed him quietly for a minute. "...I knew there had to be a good reason for marrying you," she smirked.

"Did I do good?" Milo sipped his drink.

"You did great..." Dee slipped her hand into his and did not speak again until he looked at her. "...I don't think you realise what a wonderful thing it is that you've done for me," she said seriously.

"It was just a few phone calls." Milo shrugged his shoulders. "I'm surprised nobody ever checked it out before."

"My grandmother told me her son, my dad, was an only child. And she said my mother had a brother who was dead. I didn't think to challenge that," Dee explained. "Why would she lie to me?"

"Perhaps she didn't lie. Maybe she didn't know any better. Perhaps that's what your mother told her and your father just corroborated it..." he said simply. "I just got to thinking; it's kind of unusual to be entirely alone in the world. I just felt there *had* to be some family somewhere, no matter how distant. So I thought I'd do a little digging, I didn't want to say anything to get your hopes up if there was nobody. But anybody could have done what I did."

"But they didn't, nobody ever thought to do something like that for me...nobody but you. I'll be grateful to you for the rest of my life..." Dee said, suddenly quite serious. "...Why are you so kind to me?"

"I'd do anything to make you happy," Milo replied as though it was the most obvious notion in the world. "I know you say you *are* happy, but deep down I see there is this hidden sadness in you, an empty void in you that I just wanted to fill. After nine months together, I realised that *I* couldn't fill it on my own. It's just a tiny thing in comparison to what you've done for me...when I lost Andrew and I had nothing; you saved me..."

"Oh no, I did that for entirely selfish reasons - I was in love with you. But even if you hadn't managed to find any of my relatives...that void *was* filled by you, Milo. You've turned my life around...if anything, you saved *me*..."

"Then it's agreed, we saved each other." Milo smirked his incorrigible little smirk. "Now, since I've done such a nice thing, do you think I deserve a reward...?"

Dee narrowed her eyes and grinned all at once. "...Like what?"

"Can I have a cigar? Just one...I know you're the boss but it *is* my wedding day and I'm absolutely craving a smoke," he said sheepishly.

"Well, so long as it's just one," Dee said begrudgingly.

"Great." Milo pulled a cigar from his pocket. "A friend of my dad's gave it to me and I just couldn't say no." He lit the cigar, put it in his mouth and inhaled deeply with pleasure. "That is amazing. It's lucky I love you so much...because I couldn't have given up for anyone but you."

"Hmm, isn't it a wonderful thing to know the great Milo Phillips has to ask his wife if he can have a smoke? Enjoy that, honey; it's your last one." Dee kissed his forehead and climbed down from the stool. "Love you," she called back, walking away with a smile.

"Love you too...ball and chain," Milo commented dryly and smiled a satisfied smile.

*

Dee would be the first to admit she was slightly inebriated as she slumped down beside Forrest where he sat alone, perhaps looking a little melancholy in his wheelchair at an empty table. "Hey Brother-in-Law!" But her drunkenness had caused her to miss the signals; his doleful eyes and distant stare.

Forrest sipped his beverage and flashed a weak smile. "...How do you like your new cousin?"

"Oh Forrest, she's amazing. I'm not just saying that because she's one of my only living relatives, but I feel like I've always known Cassie. She's kind, she's funny and don't you think she's beautiful?"

"Well yes, there is a distinct family resemblance. She's a bit like a dark...*you*," he said. "So, Milo saves the day again, huh?"

"Well, yes...it was a really sweet thing to do..." Dee shifted uncomfortably in her seat, sensing an underlying resentment beneath that unhappy, forced smile of his.

"Mm," Forrest replied. "He's very good at throwing money at problems to fix them."

"...I don't think money comes into it. Milo sat down and thought about something he could do to really make me happy; he took the time to understand what I really yearned for - without me even having to tell him," Dee explained with deliberate condescension then thought better of it. "Forrest, is everything alright?"

Forrest sighed. "I'm sorry, it's been an eventful day," he said as he grasped her hand and seemed to come to his senses, "Milo worships you and just saw an opportunity to show it. I apologise, Dee. I'm really tired...and I've had a couple of drinks." He grinned sheepishly.

"And the rest!" Dee punched his arm, grateful that normal service was resumed. "You've had a pretty stressful day. I don't envy your job at all. I'm sorry if we pressured you into conducting our service when maybe you just wanted to enjoy the day like everybody else..."

"No, I was honoured, really I was. It isn't that, Dee...today has just made me realise that I'm tired of being alone..." he confided softly and a little bit awkwardly.

"Forrest, you'll meet the girl for you when the time is right," Dee assured him adamantly.

"I'm thirty-six," he grumbled.

"People take longer to settle down these days. Milo was forty-two when he met the girl of his dreams, yours truly." Dee flashed her eyes.

"But the difference being, Milo can and always could have anyone he wanted. I'm just his disabled and annoyingly saintly brother; the runt of the litter. It's not like I want Milo's life - I don't want the level of superficial female attention he used to have. All I want is to meet someone who I can share my life with, but who would want me like this?"

"Oh give it a rest, you're a babe - all you Phillipses and Starks are! I bet you a thousand pounds that you'll be seeing someone special by the end of the coming year." Dee forced him to take her hand and make the bet. He gave a lopsided smile and tentatively shook her hand.

"Hi, can I join you both? You're Milo's brother, right? Forrest?" Cassie Grant suddenly appeared and seated herself at their table. "Can I just say; your service was the most moving thing I've ever heard. I was nearly in tears. No, I'm lying - I *was* in tears," she assured him emphatically with those big brown eyes only on him and that endearing accent. Forrest was stunned into silence.

"...Err, thank you...really? But I was so nervous..." He watched as she nodded her head enthusiastically and he cleared his throat, awkwardly shaking her hand. "...So, you're the prodigal cousin, Cassie Grant? Dee has been singing your praises just now. You don't know what this means to her...and I'm very glad to meet you."

"Easy money," Dee muttered under her breath with an impudent smirk. "I wonder if I double my money for winning the bet a year early?"

"I'm sorry?" Cassie glanced up at her new cousin innocently.

"Nothing, nothing. Now I hope you don't mind if I leave you two to get acquainted, I must mingle...I am the bride after all..." With the scrape of her chair, Dee stood up and left them to it.

"What did she mean by that?" Cassie gave a confused and slightly embarrassed smile at the handsome clergyman she had been left alone with.

"...Oh, I don't know...I've given up trying to make sense of the workings of your strange cousin's mind. Still, she's the sweetest sister-in-law I could ask for."

"Yes, she's even better than I had been imagining."

*

Dee closed her eyes, blissful in the arms of her husband on the dancefloor as the fifties style big band played Gershwin's 'The Man I Love'. As a favour to the newly-married couple, the famous jazz pianist, Felix Kellerman, lead the band on piano and many of the party-goers watched in awe. Felix was amazingly talented - even Dee realised that, and she was no expert.

"He's really good," Dee commented to her husband. She had only once heard Felix play live before; at the last New Year's Ball. She was reminded why he was so highly rated amongst people in the know.

"...Mm, but don't tell him that. His head is big enough as it is."

"You know...this has to be up there as one of my top two favourite weddings I've ever had." She stroked his chest.

"Now that's just below the belt, Campbell." Milo frowned good-naturedly.

"My name is Phillips." Dee stopped and mulled something over momentarily. "...I really, *really* love you, Milo...and this is one of the happiest days of my life. I'm not the most verbally expressive person in the world, but if I don't tell you this enough, never forget that I-" Dee stalled and struggled for an appropriate term of her affection for him. "...Oh crap, every sentiment in the English language has been so overused that nothing really sums up how I feel about you..."

Milo watched her carefully. She was a slightly under the influence of a certain alcoholic substance but he had learned that his new wife never said anything for the sake of making conversation. Dee found emotional displays fairly difficult so he knew she was serious when she floundered to find the words to express her love for him. "...Then show me," he said softly.

A sweet little smile crossed her face and she leaned in to kiss him. This was nothing unusual. They kissed all the time, but it was such a heartfelt kiss that they both reacted. He cupped her face in his hands. Neither was big on huge public displays of affection but both kissed with a sense of need, urgency; wanting more.

"Let the girl up for air, for God's sake."

Milo and Dee abruptly broke apart to find Cameron was their unwanted guest.

"What the hell are you doing here?" Milo was unusually unnerved by Cameron's appearance.

"Cameron, this is our wedding day, you showing up here is in poor taste." Dee narrowed her eyes with a vague hint of threat in her voice.

"Why is that? This is a New Year's Ball, anyone who can afford it can buy a ticket," he said blandly.

"I saw you hanging around earlier today, you were trying to crash our wedding," Milo accused him.

"Well, get on with it, Cameron. What have you got to say to us that's so important? We're married now so you're wasting your breath, but go on - spit it out." Dee folded her arms and slipped into the nonchalant mode which always seemed to disarm Cameron so well in the past.

Cameron stared at her, that glib exterior slipping away as she knew it would. "We had a life together, Dee...we could have been a family, you, me and Angel - I loved that little girl like she was my own. Then *he* came along and took everything I ever wanted away from me..."

"...I love him," Dee shrugged.

"He's just a Lance look-alike. You're kidding yourself into thinking you have your old life back but it's just a fake re-enactment. And Lance was never worth your attention in the first place. Lance cheated on you. He stole money and he slept with another woman to cover it up. Now they're saying he probably killed that secretary! But you forgave him everything because he fooled you into thinking he did it for you, for your family. Can't you see I would never have betrayed you like that? No amount of money or blackmail could have tempted me...and you want to recreate that relationship with *this guy*?" Cameron clasped her wrist.

"...Cameron..." Dee flinched.

"Take your hand off her," Milo said darkly.

Cameron ignored him. "*This* Lance is even more worthless than the last one. You've got yourself trapped into this marriage because you had his baby, but I can still take you away from all this, you and the children. You don't have to be stuck with this mistake."

"Take your hand off her, I won't tell you again," Milo repeated himself with even more malevolence but Cameron perhaps did not register the danger or was too desperate to care. Dee witnessed that familiar anxiety in his eyes and it made her want to cry. What had she done to this once intelligent, likeable man?

"I'm miserable without you, I've tried seeing other women but it just doesn't feel right..."

Dee's eyes misted over. This was awful; to see Cameron reduced to this filled her with self-loathing. She should never had led him to believe there was any future in their relationship, she ought to have seen he was far more involved than she was. "...What could I do, Cameron? I had to move on...I didn't love you," she explained ruefully. Milo noticed Dee was becoming upset by the whole scene and her emotional display disturbed him. "It's been nearly two years...you've got to move on too..."

"You don't mean that. You used to love me and I know that hasn't changed," Cameron told her desperately. He grasped her other wrist so that both her hands were caught in his, he gripped her so tightly that red welts began to form on her skin around his fingers.

"I don't love you, Cameron...I'm sorry...but you're hurting me. Let me go..." Dee's voice broke and this triggered something in Milo. He struck out with his fist and connected with Cameron's jaw. Cameron wheeled back from the force and landed on his back on the dancefloor.

"Milo!" Dee heard a scream rip painfully from her own throat. "You didn't have to hit him!" She covered her face with her hands and the music ground to a sudden halt and so did all the other revellers on the dancefloor.

The humiliation had only just begun. Jerry and Elliott arrived on the scene and held Milo back as though he may finish the job and kill Cameron. But Milo was standing motionless and staring at Dee. He seemed rather stunned, as if he was startled at the outcome of his own aggression. Bruce and Patrice had joined the commotion and did the decent thing, carefully helping Cameron up off the floor. He was bleeding heavily from his mouth.

"Okay everybody, go about your business," Felix began in his jocular manner on the mic. "Haven't you ever seen a punch-up at a wedding before? In my country, it's mandatory." He had been in England so long;

Felix had adopted some of the lingo and much of the sarcasm. He was in his element up on stage and was obviously accustomed to dealing with rowdy crowds. Felix began to play skilfully and the band struck up again. The onlookers soon dispersed and returned to the merriment of the Ball.

Ginny had resumed her lead bridesmaid duties and arrived to place a placating arm around Dee's shoulders. She was crying and totally unable to curb it.

"Alright, let's get these two jokers out of here," said Jerry with his Manager's head on.

"It's okay, Milo, Cameron is an asshole. You just have to learn to ignore him," Elliott advised, patting his new half brother's shoulder.

Felix had left the band to play and came down to survey the damage. "You alright, Milo?" he asked his deadly silent cousin.

"Let's get him to my office," Elliott said in a hushed voice to Felix who nodded in agreement. Milo stared hopefully at Dee as they led him away but her face was still buried in her hands. Bruce and Patrice sat the dazed and confused Cameron down at a table and set about patching up his pummelled face with napkins. Ginny and Jerry took the distraught Dee from the dancefloor and out to the balcony to get some air.

Forrest and Cassie looked on from the edge of the dance area. Forrest turned to her grimly and said, "Welcome to the family."

A FAMILY AFFAIR

Elliott rifled inside his tuxedo jacket pocket and fished out a new packet of cigarettes. He undid the cellophane wrapping with nervous fingers and offered the open box to Milo. Sitting in a swivel chair at Elliott's desk, Milo accepted his second sinful cigarette of the day. Elliott, a heavy smoker himself, lit his half brother's cigarette then set about lighting his own.

"Thank you for managing to take the guest's attention off the incident, Felix," Elliott began at last. Felix shrugged in reply and Elliott continued, "...You really don't need to get so irate about Cameron, Milo, he's really not a threat. Dee worships you," he assured him. Milo said nothing for a time and seemed deeply disturbed by what he had done, or more correctly, disturbed by Dee's reaction to it.

"So, what exactly did Cameron say?" Felix helped himself to a glass of whiskey from Elliott's drinks cabinet.

Milo sighed. "...He just professed his undying love to my wife...and then talked about taking her and my kids away from me..." It was the first time he had spoken since the incident with Cameron had begun. "He was gripping Dee's wrists so tightly that he was hurting her and I asked him twice to takes his hands off her...but he wouldn't," he explained blankly.

"Look, I understand. Of course you're protective of your wife, but Cameron has no sway over Dee. I knew Dee back in the days when she had never even heard of you, and she was never really interested in Cameron the first time around, let alone now. He was just an opportunist who preyed on her whenever she was at her lowest ebb. You don't need to be jealous, it's you she's in love with," Elliott reasoned. "I was never really in favour of your relationship with Dee at first, but the more I saw you together, the more I realised how you two made sense."

"...Elliott, I'm sorry about causing a scene but-"

"It's fine. It's my fault for not ensuring Cameron was banned from the premises today...let's say no more about it," Elliott stubbed out his cigarette. "Between you and me, I've always wanted to punch Cameron myself, so I'm glad my brother did it for me. I'd better go and check on proceedings," he smiled and opened the door to his office. "And I'll make sure security kick Cameron out of the hotel."

"Thanks Elliott." Milo gave a grim smile as Elliott left.

"Jesus, he's changed his tune," Felix remarked. "It's a pity Jerry hasn't embraced you as his new *brother* the way Elliott has...but it must be weird. I mean, you've always known the Stark boys were your brothers and you've never been able to say anything. They must be totally thrown by the whole thing..."

"Did you see the way Dee looked at me? She was absolutely mortified that I'd hit him...but I only did it for her..."

"Don't beat yourself up over it. Any normal guy would have done the same. Once Dee calms down, she will understand your position," Felix insisted.

"Do you think she still has feelings for Cameron? She seemed genuinely concerned for him..." Milo shook his head.

"Now stop right there, you're not being rational. Elliott is right, Cameron is no threat to you," Felix told him adamantly and as he did so, the girl in question came into the room.

"...Hi," she announced herself sheepishly, her eyes red and her face blotchy from crying. "Felix, could I speak to my husband alone please?"

"Of course." Felix paced over, gave her a hug and whispered. "Don't be too hard on him. I'm here if you need to talk."

Dee nodded and watched him leave. She turned to her husband, sitting behind Elliott's desk as if this were his office. Milo tapped ash into a crystal ashtray and watched tentatively as Dee came around to sit on the desk beside him.

"You shouldn't have hit him, Milo," Dee told him again in no uncertain terms.

"...He was hurting you..."

"I could have dealt with it."

"He was talking about taking my wife and kids away, he was making you cry," Milo defended himself.

"Don't you understand? I feel terrible about what I did to him! Don't you ever feel sick with guilt about all the women you've let down?"

"No," he answered casually.

"Well maybe you should! It isn't Cameron's fault that he got in too deep. I'm to blame, I let a relationship happen that I knew full well wasn't going anywhere."

"What is all this concern for a man who's been making our lives hell for months? Why don't you show any concern for me?"

"Because you *punched* a pathetic man who was already down on his luck!" Dee threw up her hands, exasperated.

"So? I was defending you, defending my honour! You should be proud of me!" Milo argued in response.

"What's wrong with you? There's just no defence for violence! Did you think it would make me think more of you? Do you think it made you the big man? I'm not the least bit proud of what you did!"

"I warned him twice but he wouldn't let you go and before I knew what I was doing-" Milo trailed off. "...Do you still love him? Is that why you're so angry with me?" he asked dejectedly.

"No! I have never been in love with Cameron in my life. When will you ever trust me? I married *you*...why would I risk it all for a man like that?"

He shook his head uncomprehendingly. "...I feel like I'm living in the shadow of my brother; like Cameron says, I'm just a cheap imitation of Lance. How can I ever hope to compete with the big love of your life?"

"Because you are the *bigger* love of my life..." Dee said wearily, checked herself then stopped talking. But the comment hadn't got past her husband.

"...Are you saying – Dee, why couldn't you just tell me that before...?" he asked with pained fatigue, but unable to keep a glimmer of surprised pleasure creeping over his face.

"...Okay, end of conversation, I don't want to talk about it anymore," Dee stammered awkwardly and went to stand up but he caught her hand.

"All this time I've been feeling like the booby prize and you - you should have said..." he asserted. "There's nothing to be ashamed of...it's not a crime to love your present husband more than the former."

"No, it's like me dying and you meeting somebody else and loving her more than me."

"That could never happen. You and I belong together...and even if Lance hadn't died, I would have met you one day. And I'd have taken you from him...if you hadn't already left him..."

"...I don't want to discuss this anymore," Dee said tersely, stood up and walked to the door. Milo, on the other hand, *did* want to discuss it but decided by the glowering look on her face to leave it for another time. "Come on, it's nearly midnight, let's get back to the Ball."

Milo checked his watch, eleven forty-five. "...Alright," he said softly and came to join her at the office door. "Do you forgive me for spoiling our wedding day?"

"You didn't spoil it, you didn't ask for this to happen," she said from under furtive, hooded eyes. "...This time last year, I thought I'd completely blown it and you didn't want me anymore. And this year we're married. I can't ask for more than that. But you can put that cigarette out right now. You've just decked somebody at our party - there's no reward for that."

Milo laughed. He ducked his head down enough to reach her lips which were over a foot lower in height than his. Dee readily responded, needing to be reassured with a kiss right now.

*

A couple of days had passed after the wedding and Dee found herself in the passenger seat of Milo's car. She checked her hair in the mirror and Milo smiled to himself. She was anxious to look her best but he couldn't fathom why it should matter.

"I'm sorry there isn't going to be a honeymoon for a while. You're not disappointed are you?" Dee placed a gentle hand on his arm.

"No, I understand Finley is a little too young for us to go on a proper vacation without him. We'll do it in a few months when you feel happy to leave him." Milo would have preferred to have the traditional honeymoon alone together now but he would never force Dee to do something so against her principles. "I need to get back to New York anyway to sort out my predecessor."

"I don't want to think about that," Dee grumbled.

"It's just for a few weeks and after that I will only need to take very short trips every now and then," he promised.

"Mm," Dee replied, unconvinced. "It's nice of you to drive me to Cassie's but you didn't have to."

"It's okay, I knew you'd be nervous about meeting your uncle so I thought I should drive," he said pleasantly and pulled up outside a detached house on a leafy lane in Wimbledon. "Well, here we are. Off you go." Milo turned to look at her but Dee seemed to be making no effort to climb out of the car.

"...Yeah, I'm just-" Dee lifted her hands to make a gesture to explain her lack of movement but couldn't even do that. She dropped her hands and sighed.

"It's alright. He's a really nice guy, actually. I promise you'll like him," Milo assured her.

"...I'm sure he is but it isn't that. I just always expected to be by myself, I resigned myself to it. In fact, it's all that kept me going. Then I found Lance but when that all went wrong, I resolved it was best never to let anyone get too close again...and then you came along," she concluded anxiously.

"And you let me in and you're happier for it. They're your family, so you can't run away from this."

"But my uncle is sick - heart conditions don't just go away. How do I break my resolve when I know he's probably not going to be around for very long?"

"You have to let people get close to you. You have to allow yourself to love people. Andrew's gone but I wouldn't trade the time I had with him for the world - no matter how much it hurts." Milo stroked the hair from her eyes. "You fell in love with me and let me become your family and now look how happy we are," he reminded Dee and wrapped her in his arms. She took comfort in the very feel of him, in the familiar aroma of his sweatshirt. Dee just wanted to stay there all day.

"Thanks Milo, I love you," Dee said, gave him a parting kiss and climbed from the car.

"Call me when you want to be picked up, I'll go get a coffee," he called after her. She glanced back at him meekly in the Aston Martin and watched him pull away. Dee turned back to the task in hand, took a deep breath and slowly walked up the drive.

Cassie welcomed Dee warmly into the neat little suburban house. It was tastefully decorated in neutral colours and Dee assumed that either her tennis coach cousin was doing okay for herself or her uncle was fairly comfortable. It was an ordinary house and these were ordinary people in an ordinary salary bracket, but she was glad that they were not impoverished as she had been.

"I'm sorry you guys didn't get to have a honeymoon," Cassie commented as she showed her through to the kitchen and cheerily put the kettle on.

"Oh, it's okay. We'll take a break alone together when Finn has finished breast feeding, maybe when he's six or seven months old. It's not right for a baby that young to be without his mother for so long," Dee insisted, looking about the kitchen, furnished in a New England white-wood style. "Anyway, we've done alright for a couple with a new baby. We had the wedding night to ourselves and saw the kids in the morning for a couple of hours, I fed Finley then my nanny let us have the rest of the afternoon alone together. I'm very lucky really."

"Not that I knew you before you married Milo – or your first husband for that matter, but it's nice to see that you're still so grounded," Cassie said in a thoughtful voice.

Dee awkwardly shifted her weight from foot to foot. "Well...luckily Milo has really embraced our low-key lifestyle," she smirked. Dee sat down at the table and placed before her a couple of large photo albums she had brought along. "Have you lived here since you came from Australia? It's very nice."

"Yes, my dad bought it for us as soon as we arrived after my mother died..."

"Well, here she is at last," said a man in the kitchen doorway. Dee looked up to see a man in his late fifties or early sixties. He was of average height and build but carried rather a distended abdomen. His once sandy hair was now heavily peppered with white and grey, but receded only a little at the temples. The man sported square, gold-rimmed glasses, was clean shaven and emitted the most genuine friendliness Dee had ever experienced. "Here's my Dee," Gordon Grant beamed. Then he sunk down into a carver chair at the table, put his head in his hands and wept.

Dee was frozen to the spot. She hadn't mentally prepared herself for a grown man crying. But soon she was comforting her uncle. "It's okay, we're all together now," Dee heard herself saying. There were warm tears trickling down her own face before she even submitted to the fact that she was about to cry.

"I've let you down, I've let you down," he sobbed bitterly. "You've been alone since you were a child and I could have taken care of you..."

"Dad, don't do this to yourself," Cassie soothed and set down a tray of tea things and freshly baked scones on the table.

"Please don't be upset on my account – I had my grandmother for a few years...and when she died, I was more-or-less old enough to take care of myself. My life is so much better now...so you don't have to worry anymore, I'm really happy," Dee promised him.

Gordon looked up rather more brightly. "Here you are comforting me when I should be comforting you." He spoke in a mixed-up accent, a pleasing blend of Scottish with a little trace of an Australian intonation that was easy on the ear. "I didn't expect to see you so soon after your wedding."

"I couldn't wait any longer to meet you. I wish you'd been there," Dee admitted.

"I'm afraid I wasn't up to it. Your husband did invite me but...well..." he sighed. "Still, I saw the photos and I must say you're a good looking couple. I like your new husband. I could tell from the instant I met him, he was very genuine."

"Yes, he really is," Dee agreed. If it wasn't for Milo, this would not be happening.

"He doesn't speak more than he needs to, your fella – but I respect that in a guy," Gordon laughed and Dee found herself laughing along with him. He was exactly the type of man she had always imagined that her dream father would be, ever ready with a jovial quip or a sardonic comment. "You've found yourself a decent one there. It's obvious he thinks the world of you."

"I'm very lucky," Dee conceded.

He placed a warm hand above hers. "You're the image of your mother, did you know that?"

"...I only have a couple of photos...but I can see that we're alike."

"It's only that pale blonde hair that you've inherited from Alan..." he mused. "He was a very handsome and intelligent man, your dad. But they were both intellectually brilliant in their way – that's why Becky was so taken with him. I bet you're a chip off the old block, ey?" Gordon gave her a familiar poke in the ribs.

"...No, not really...underachiever, that's me." Dee grimaced.

"More like your uncle, then," he chuckled before his face changed to a graver set. "I'll be honest with you, Dee, my sister and I weren't close towards the end – she didn't like my wife. They just could not be in the same room as one another. Becky felt my wife, Sarah, was far too opinionated," he said uneasily with a brief, almost apologetic, glance at Cassie, "and your mother had a bit of a fiery temper and a smart mouth – she always had to have the last word."

"I wondered where I got that from," Dee sighed.

Gordon sadly gave a sigh of his own. "We stopped talking to Becky completely one Christmas after a big row," he reminisced ruefully. "We emigrated to Australia soon after and nobody informed me about the car accident years later. I have a feeling your grandmother, Alan's mother, didn't even know I existed – she certainly didn't know my contact details if she did. It was only when I returned to Edinburgh that I found out what had happened to your mum and dad – and that a child had survived. So we came down and bought a house in Wimbledon since your grandmother had lived nearby...but your trail went cold."

"You did your best..."

"You must miss them very much." Gordon wiped the last of the moisture from his eyes.

She twisted her mouth. "...I miss the idea of them. I was very young and I don't remember much about them, if I'm honest. Their faces are just a blur in my memory." Dee looked up to see them staring at her thoughtfully. "...People sometimes think that's strange because I was six but I remember so little. I remember being very sad and I felt pushed from pillar to post but-"

"I understand – I suppose a small child needs to forget just to be able to cope." Gordon laced his sun-wrinkled fingers together. "But we're all here now. I know you and my gorgeous girl Cassandra will be the best of friends." He smiled lovingly at his daughter.

"...I'm so glad I met you both, Uncle Gordon...can I call you that?"

"I really hoped you would." Gordon held both their hands. "I just wish we could have known you sooner." The man just didn't seem to be able to get past that.

"There were some hard times at the beginning, of course...but I'm mostly happy with my lot in life. Had I gone to live in Australia with you, I would never have met Lance or Milo and my two kids wouldn't exist." Dee dabbed at her eyes because she knew how upset her uncle was over this. But had she never set foot in that hotel, her life would have been a different life, she would be a different Dee.

"Of course and I'm glad you've had some happiness in your adult life. As soon as we knew of your existence, uppermost in our minds was the need to find you...I just thank God your husband did a better job of finding us than we did of finding you." The tears began to well up in his eyes again.

"It's going to be alright from now on. We're all together now," Dee asserted, taking the role of the strong one in the family. She had been the strong one all her life. "...Uncle Gordon, I just need to know – how sick are you...?" she gulped uncertainly.

Gordon smiled his warm and generous smile, a smile he shared with his daughter. "Those surgeons reckon they have done a pretty good job on my tired old heart. I want to spend the rest of my years making my daughter, my niece and her children happy. Believe me, right now, I don't feel like dying." He gave her a nudge and Dee laughed.

"I'm glad to hear it."

"So, why didn't you bring those children of yours to see me?" Gordon put on a mock-affronted look.

"I wanted to meet you on my own first and get all the crying out of the way...but I was hoping you and Cassie would come and stay with us for a few days really soon. I want my kids to get to know you both properly. You can be Auntie Cassie and Grandpa Gordon...I've never been able to offer them a real family before." Not from her side of the family anyway. Dee fought to stabilise the feelings of sheer euphoria and hope building up within her. Her hopes had been shattered so many times before.

Gordon laughed a hearty laugh. "I'll just go and pack my bags."

DO ME A FAVOUR

The house was busier and more chaotic than Dee had intended that particular Friday evening. Bruce and Patrice had shown up with Evan on their way back from work a week after the wedding. Bruce and Evan bickered an awful lot as Bruce wasn't terribly good at subservience as far as Evan's 'coffee shop authority' was concerned. However, the pair actually got along very well when they weren't rubbing each other up the wrong way.

"So, who's up for a Jackie Chan evening?" Bruce demanded, sitting on the carpet in the cubbyhole. Evan sat by Patrice who was concentrating on a women's magazine where he lounged on the oversized sofa.

"Oh, not again!" Evan groaned. "I wouldn't have thought a *you* would be into that kind of thing. What about a Jimmy Stewart evening? Dee has a lot of Jimmy Stewart movies," he suggested as an alternative.

"Yes, but there aren't any good martial arts scenes in those." Bruce helped himself to another glass of red wine from the bottle that sat on the coffee table. Dee smiled and loitered with a sleeping baby in her arms in the doorway but kept a watchful eye on the empty hall. She was waiting for Milo to descend the stairs with suitcases for his flight to America tonight. Angel was tearing up and down the hallway in her pyjamas and bed-socks doing skids on the shiny wooden floorboards. Dee also listened out for Felix who was making a phone call to his agent in the guest lounge. Felix was here for the purpose of driving Milo to Heathrow Airport. It was easier for Milo to fly first class than to organise a private flight. "Can you believe Dee actually has a famous person for a relative who hangs around her house?" Bruce enthused whilst tipping the contents of the wine glass into his mouth.

"Bruce, you spent the whole of Christmas Day with him and you had never even heard of Felix Kellerman before I told you who he was." Patrice gave him a withering look over the top of the magazine.

"So? You hadn't heard of him either!"

"Actually I had," Patrice reminded him, eyes back on the article, "and it was *Dee* who hadn't heard of him..."

"Well, I'm not the one getting all *'crazed fan'* about it." Dee turned her attention back to her room-full of male friends. "He isn't in a boy-band, you know Bruce. Felix is a classically trained jazz musician-composer. You don't even *like* jazz," she reminded him sourly.

"But he's been on TV and everything - apparently," Bruce confided sagely.

"Yes, but probably on some artsy show that you wouldn't be seen dead watching," Evan scoffed. "I wouldn't have thought his work was exactly up *your* street, Bruce."

"Oh shut up, like *I* don't enough class to appreciate classical music! Or jazz-" Bruce began belligerently but trailed off when Felix returned to the room.

"Felix, how come you got landed with the job of taking Milo to the airport?" Dee had wanted to ask that question since Felix had arrived but hadn't found the opportunity until now. "He could have booked his usual driver."

"My sentiments exactly, but he wants to *'talk business'.*" Felix made speech marks with his fingers and pulled a bemused face.

"Oh...well if you don't fancy driving back to Chelsea, you can always come here and crash for the night since Richmond is closer," Dee proposed with a shrug.

"...Oh thanks, that's really sweet...but I have to get back." Felix visibly brightened, seeming pleasantly surprised that she had asked. The sound of Milo stomping down the stairs made Dee bounce on the balls of her feet and walk out into the hall, pulling the cubbyhole door almost closed behind her.

"You all set?" Dee said with a forced cheery disposition, Angel barging past her to perform another world-class skid.

"Yep, but I have a little room in one of my suitcases to sneak you guys in." Milo dumped his luggage by the door.

Dee gave a sluggish smile. "How long will you be gone?"

"No longer than six weeks," he estimated with a thoughtful glance up to his left.

"...God, that's forever," Dee grumbled, slumping back against the front door frame. "Does it really take six weeks to find someone to stand in for you?"

"There's a lot to sort out, baby. But if it gets too much, you can just scoop up the kids and get on a plane. You don't even have to give me any notice; just come. I'll charter you a jet the moment you say the word," he said hopefully.

"...We'll see," Dee replied, staring at Finn cradled in her arms.

"Okay...so, I've left Angel's adoption documents on the table in the kitchen. I've signed everything I need to and you just have to sign your sections. Get the papers to my legal team as soon as you can. They'll sort out the rest," Milo said quietly so Angel wouldn't hear. He wanted all the loose ends of his family life tied up before he left.

"Alright," Dee agreed, still a little uncertainly. "...Will you write me love letters? I mean *real* letters that you write by hand and put in the post...I'll write you too."

"Oh *God*," Milo groaned. "I'm planning to call you every night. And wouldn't emails be more sensible than snail-mail?" He had become more adept than he could ever have imagined at expressing his feelings for her verbally, but to write it in words was a fairly new concept for him (whichever type of mail she requested).

"Please, it would mean a lot to me...I've never had a love letter that came in the post before. You can email me as well..." Dee was acutely aware that this relationship was more like a first love; like the initial few months of a terribly intense affair between young and inexperienced lovers when emotions were high and raw, certainly not a partnership between two jaded marriage veterans.

"...Okay, but some parts will be romantic, and some parts will just be filthy," he grinned and pressed up against her. Dee carefully moved Finley aside so he wouldn't be crushed.

"I can live with that..." Dee let her head rest against his chest. Tears stood in her eyes and her voice wavered. "...I don't want you to go..."

Milo sighed, resting his chin on the top of her head. "...Now don't get me started..."

"Like you ever get upset the way I do about us being separated."

"Are you serious? I've been crying like a girl ever since we got together."

"I'm sorry about tonight, I didn't know Bruce, Patrice and Evan were coming over and they didn't know you were leaving this evening. We could have had a few hours alone together if I'd been more organised and made sure the kids were in bed earlier..." Dee said apologetically.

"It's okay. I'd much rather you weren't all by yourself tonight." Milo kissed her forehead.

"I wish you could stay a few more days..." Her face cracked and the waterworks started even though she had been steeling herself not to cry again.

"But Dee, you knew I was only coming back for Christmas and New Year...and to get married."

"I know...but we were just starting to get used to being together again." In fact, this last visit, she had finally started to feel one hundred percent comfortable around him. Getting married had really sealed something within her. Milo was entirely hers now.

"Look, after this last trip, I will be home so much more. I'll just be making the odd flight back to the U.S., but only for a few days at a time."

"I was thinking you could open an office in Richmond and then we could meet up for lunch together sometimes...it's just a thought," Dee shrugged, wiping her eyes with the back of her sleeve.

"That's crossed my mind too. We'll see if it's viable when I come home," he whispered, ducking his head a little to make it easier to kiss her. She was so very small. "...Honey, I'm sorry...I really have to go or I'll miss my flight," Milo sighed.

"I know. I love you so much." Dee placed her free arm around his neck for a brief, awkward, baby-sandwich hug.

"I love you more than anything...I'm going to find being without you and the children really hard. It gets harder every time I go away." Milo stroked her hair and they kissed softly again for a short while before Felix came out of the cubbyhole into the hall.

"I'm sorry...but um...tick-tock, Milo," he reminded him gently, pointing at his watch.

Milo reluctantly pulled away from his new bride. "...Okay...love you, babe." He placed one last kiss on her mouth, brushed a stray piece of wet hair from her tearstained face and opened the front door. "Bye little man." Milo kissed his sleeping son's downy head. "Bye baby-girl, I'll be back soon," Milo called Angel with a wry grin. She performed a show-stopping slide into his legs and hugged them tight.

"Bye Daddy! Pwesent, yes?"

"Absolutely!" Milo hugged and kissed his soon-to-be daughter and gave Dee a final circumspect glance.

Soon the two men headed down to the Felix's car with a couple of cases. Dee sorrowfully waved them goodbye and closed the door once the car had turned the corner, out of sight.

*

Felix skilfully lit a cigarette whilst steering into the lane heading out towards the M4 motorway. He wasn't especially in the mood for a night-time jaunt out to the airport. "So what did your last chauffeur die of?"

"Insubordination." Milo rubbed his tired eyes with his thumb and forefinger. He had found that parting more difficult than ever before. Why couldn't she just quit being so stubborn and come with him? That way, they and the children would never have to spend a single day apart.

"Huh...now, what is this *business* we have to talk about?" Felix began again almost immediately. "I don't recall ever doing business with you before..."

"...Oh, that." Milo cleared his throat decisively. "I just wanted to ask you for a small favour. I need you to keep an eye on Dee for me."

"...Keep an eye on her? Keep an eye on her how?" Felix narrowed his eyes as he methodically handled his racing-green Lotus.

"It's no big deal. I'd just like you to be around to make sure she's okay," Milo shrugged nonchalantly.

"How do you mean, *'okay'*? What do you mean, *'be around'*?"

"God, you're insufferable sometimes. If you must be so suspicious about everything...more precisely, I just want you to be around in case Cameron shows up at the house or the store to harass her again. I need to know Dee's safe. Basically, all I'm asking is that you to keep me informed of what's going on," Milo explained blandly.

"Oh, *that's* all you're asking, is it? You just want me to spy on your wife?" Felix raised his eyebrows and shook his head.

"It's not spying! You'd simply be looking out for her!" Milo snapped.

"Don't you trust Dee or something?"

"Oh, I trust Dee alright, it's Cameron I'm concerned about. If he knows I'm out of the country for a while, do you honestly believe he'd keep his distance? You saw what happened at the wedding."

"But as far as I'm aware, Cameron hasn't shown up at the house since you and Dee got together."

"But he *has* shown up at the store and I just get the feeling that, since the wedding, he's upped the ante." Milo had such a serious look on his face that Felix knew this request was not in any way half-hearted.

"So, you want me to keep tabs on your wife," Felix repeated, only using different wording. "I think you're confusing me with someone who doesn't have a life."

"Felix, I know you're busy, but there is nobody else I can ask to do this for me. I've always felt I could trust you more than the others..."

"Yeah, yeah, great soft-soaping tactics but this is *me* you're talking to." Felix rolled his eyes over at his cousin.

"No, I'm serious. You were the one who persuaded me I should go for it with Dee when nobody else thought I was worthy of her and I've never forgotten that."

"But Milo, I live in Chelsea and it will be really awkward for me to keep an eye on things in Richmond," Felix whined. He could gradually feel himself being worn down already.

"Not for much longer. A fabulous property up on Richmond Hill has come my way and my company now owns it. As soon as I saw it, I knew it would be the perfect place for you, Forrest, Ginny and the kids. You guys have been talking about moving closer to us and the house is enormous. You would all have more privacy than you could ever need. It's my gift to you guys and you can move in whenever you want," Milo said in his most pleasant voice.

"Milo, I don't expect you to buy us a mansion just so I'll do this thing for you," Felix spoke darkly, suspecting a bribe.

"The house has nothing to do with this issue with Dee and Cameron. Forrest and I have been discussing getting you guys a place nearer us for weeks. And I'm not going to take money from my *own family*. I just want to do a nice thing for the people I care about and who have stuck by me," he shrugged as though mildly offended.

Felix shifted uncomfortably in the driving seat. "...Look, I really want to help you out, man, but...I don't actually *know* Dee as well as I should..."

"Don't you like her?" Milo arched an eyebrow.

"Now don't do that. You know I think Dee is cool and I feel, since Christmas, we're on track to be really good friends. But I just don't happen to think we've fully *established* that friendship yet," Felix explained plaintively.

"Then start establishing it."

Felix groaned. "Why me? She's already best-buds with Ginny - why not ask *her*?"

Milo shook his head dismissively. "No, you're the only one I can trust. Ginny or Forrest would make a big deal of it and make out like I'm being underhanded."

"You mean they'd turn you down because you *are* being underhanded!" Felix remarked irritably. "...Look, I'll meet you halfway. Call Dee when you get back to New York tonight and tell her that you've asked me to check in on her and the kids a few times while you're away. Just tell her you're a bit worried about her being alone since Cameron has been acting up. That way, it's all above board."

"No, I'm not doing that." Milo waved a disparaging hand at his cousin. "Dee's still cross that I punched Cameron at the wedding. If he came to the house or the store to harass her, she wouldn't tell me about it in a million years; not after what I did. If she thinks I've put you up to this, she won't trust *you* either. I need you to gain her confidence so that she'll feel comfortable confiding in you. This way, if Cameron shows up at the house, you'll either be there to see it or she'll probably tell you about it. And then you can tell me."

"Then what will *you* do?" Felix asked doubtfully.

"I don't know yet, but I can't spend six weeks in the States without knowing what's going on with my wife and kids. You know I'm only asking you to do this because I love her."

"It doesn't sound like a particularly *healthy* kind of love...you really ought to trust her. Besides, it's going to be pretty deceitful of me to keep showing up out of the blue, gain her confidence and then report back to you. What kind of friend would I be?"

"The kind of friend Dee needs but doesn't realise it yet...you'd be protecting her."

"Protecting her? She's surrounded by *men* half the time; Patrice and Bruce, Evan, her brothers-in law!" Felix grumbled. "What the hell use would one little me be?"

Milo sighed and decided to try a different tack. "...Look, I wouldn't ask you to do this if I wasn't really anxious about it. There was something about Cameron at the wedding that made me think he was a *danger* to Dee. I don't think he's completely balanced anymore and I'm concerned about her and the children being alone. It's really not much to ask of you - it's just for a few weeks because I'll be back for good soon. If you move into the new house as soon as possible, start dropping in for coffee at the store and show up at our house now and then, you'll just be accelerating a friendship that would already be established if you weren't abroad all the time. You're my cousin and you're her family now, there's nothing more important to Dee than family," Milo assured him reasonably. "...So, will you do it? You know I'd do the same for you," he coaxed with his persuasive, big-brown-eyed stare.

"...Oh, alright!" Felix reluctantly agreed. "But if Dee starts to think I'm some kind of sad, friendless loser, the deal is off!"

THE FABRICATED FRIEND

It was the perfect job. Bruce Yates was in his element working at the coffee shop; if 'working' was the right terminology to use. If chatting and loafing around drinking coffee were classed as work, he laboured extremely hard. Dee sat with him at one of the unused coffee tables with her baby strapped safely to her front in a sling. Angel was attending pre-school which she did for two hours every week day morning now. Dee poured diligently over a letter she penned in black, spidery writing. It had been years since she had written a real letter – with a pen. Her writing was scruffy and slightly illegible so she was regretting it now.

"*'My darling; there are things I want to do with you that I could never have considered doing with anyone else, every part of my body and my being longs for the feel of your naked, sweat-glistening skin against mine. I ache for you. My body tingles and awakens with just the mere thought of-'* whoa there! This is strong stuff!" Bruce cited aloud. Dee eventually raised her eyes with a slow-witted comprehension of the familiarity of those words.

"Bruce!" She snatched Milo's love letter from Bruce's clutches. "There *are* limits, you know!"

But Bruce ignored her. "I mean; the things he wants to *do* to you made my eyes water! I didn't realise you married people were so racy."

"Don't. Read. My. Personal. Letters!" Dee intoned angrily and shoved the letter hurriedly back between the pages of her current paperback chic-lit where Bruce had pilfered them from in the first place. "Not unless I ask you to..."

"Milo sounds like an amorous kind of guy...is he good in bed?"

Dee eyed him cautiously then her face cracked into a sly smirk. "...Well...since you ask, yes." All of a sudden, she seemed to be in the mood for talking. "I wasn't the most *physical* person in the world before - but since I met him, it's like he's woken something in me that was lying dormant..." Dee admitted coyly. "Even though we've been together for nine months, my stomach still flips sometimes when he walks into the room. I'm always excited to see him and we haven't even *begun* to be complacent about each other. I guess that's because we don't get to spend enough time together. Still, I feel lucky that he loves *me*."

"Rubbish," Bruce chided. "He's the lucky one."

"Well, whatever, I'm just glad he's my husband. He only left two days ago and already he sent me a love letter. He must have written it and posted it from Heathrow that night." Dee studied the postmark on the envelope when she had fished it out, confirming her suspicions.

"I'm really glad for you. It must be great to be in that exciting part of a relationship..."

"Yeah, it is," she mused, then checked herself due to the sudden change in atmosphere. "...Oh...but you and Patrice have been together for years...and that honeymoon phase isn't supposed to last forever. You're alright, aren't you...?"

"...I dunno'," Bruce sighed, shaking his head with one lacklustre movement.

"I've always envied what you and Patrice had...is everything okay between you?"

"I'm not sure," he sighed. "...I don't think Patrice feels the same about me." The jovial disposition he normally displayed had deserted him.

"Don't be stupid. Patrice adores you." Dee shook her head uncomprehendingly.

"Past tense, Dee, he did. I think these days Patrice wonders what he saw in me. I think I embarrass him."

"No, he thinks you're hysterical. You're the funniest guy I know, everybody wants to be with someone who makes them laugh," Dee insisted vehemently.

"...Hmm, he doesn't seem to be laughing anymore," Bruce said with an air of finality.

Dee simply refused to believe this. If Bruce and Patrice's relationship was in trouble, nothing was safe or certain. "You're just going through a rough patch; this happens to everybody. Have you told him how you feel? I bet he'd be mortified if he knew you felt this way. Maybe he's got too much on at work. Ever since he became bar manager at the hotel, he's been under a lot of pressure."

"He loves his job; he thrives on the pressure. I really think it's me..." Bruce caught her eye in such a way that Dee was forced to listen and stop interjecting with encouraging comments. "You know how it is - it happened with Lance. You were love's young dream and then you saw him for what he was. And that brand new shiny thing that you wanted so much just withered away and died. Well, I think that's the way Patrice feels about me. I can see the contempt in his eyes sometimes…but I think he can't bring himself to break it off with me because of old times' sake."

"How long has this been going on? Have I been harping on about how wonderful my life is, when all the time you've been miserable?" Dee was horrified. Bruce *must* be mistaken.

"Dee, I couldn't be happier for you! Things have been getting steadily worse with Patrice for a few months…you weren't to know. I've been trying to hide it."

"So, this isn't all in your head? You've discussed this with him?" Dee was finding this hard to accept. Patrice and Bruce had the relationship she had been aspiring to.

"As much as you can discuss something with someone when all you do is fight all the time."

"…Do you want me to talk to him?"

"Not really." Bruce shook his head dully.

"Ah, Bruce," she said sadly and put her arms around him because nothing she could say today, not even her very best pep-talk, was going to make this go away.

*

Felix decided that the coffee shop would be his first port of call because he simply couldn't stomach showing up at Dee's house uninvited. His obligation to Milo had already lapsed a week and he could not continue vetting all his calls. So today was the day to establish this once full of possibility, but now highly dubious, friendship with his cousin's wife.

Once inside the coffee shop, Felix feared his best efforts would be in vain since he could not see Dee anywhere.

"Infamous American alert," Evan said to Dee in a hushed voice as she was strolling out of the back office. She rocked Finn to and fro to send him off for his lunchtime nap after his feed. Evan was stacking a bookshelf with pre-loved popular women's fiction when Dee pulled up beside him.

"…What?" For a moment, her heart skipped as she imagined Milo had returned from his trip early to surprise her. She was soon slightly disappointed to see cousin Felix loitering around the second-hand literature section.

"Ooh, it's Felix Kellerman again," Bruce intoned excitedly, coming to join his boss and manager where they secreted themselves marginally out of sight at the back of the store. "Your cute, famous cousin-in-law. Do you think he might be gay?" he joked.

"Bruce, I've seen him with girls," she recalled blankly, not very often, but she definitely had.

"What do you think he wants?" Evan wondered.

"Hmm, I'll use my psychic powers, shall I? Jesus, I don't know! Oh...I hope nothing bad has happened," Dee suddenly thought better of her flippancy. "...I'd better go speak to him." Dee handed over her slightly grisly baby to Evan without asking permission.

"He's hardly going to stand there leafing through 'Anna Karenina' if there was some family crisis going on," Evan scoffed, cradling the child against his chest but Dee was already on her way over.

"Hi Felix, it's nice to see you," Dee began gingerly.

"Hi...yes, and you." He kissed her cheek with an awkward lunge then managed to quickly regroup. "...This is a really nice coffee-shop-come-second-hand-bookstore; I haven't been in before. I could see myself spending many a lonely lunchtime here," Felix commented politely.

"Oh, I really hope you'll reconsider, I don't think a little coffee shop like this could take the crush of all your adoring fans," Dee said, because an insolent comment was always her first line of defence when she was uneasy. He laughed knowingly and evidently relaxed with the presence of humour so she relaxed too; nobody had died and Felix understood her sarcasm.

"I see, so that's how it's to be." Felix rubbed his chin with a crooked smirk.

"Anyway, this is a long way to come to spend a lonely lunchtime. I'm sure there are some pretty good places to drink coffee and leaf through second-hand books in Chelsea."

"Are you this welcoming to all your customers? Anyway, I don't live in Chelsea anymore. My sister, Forrest and I moved into a rather nice place up on Richmond Hill yesterday." He leaned casually against a bookshelf, hoping it wouldn't topple over.

"So that really came off? Milo gives nice presents, doesn't he?" Dee arched a telling eyebrow. "Is it one of those really nice mansions up near Jerry and Elliott's?"

"Yep, it's a little ostentatious but we'll get used to it. You're welcome to come over and use our indoor or outdoor swimming pool, billiard room, home cinema or gymnasium anytime." There was a little flicker of mischief in his eyes and Dee sensed there was a game afoot. Dee could not resist a challenge as far as a decent game of put-downs was concerned.

She mock-yawned with a stretch of her arms. "...Yeah, if I'm passing. So, we're kind of neighbours now?"

"Kind of, accept my house is in a far better location and worth a shit-load more than yours." Felix grinned wickedly and Dee laughed out loud.

"Damn it – I'm the poor relation again. So what can I do for you while you're shirking your house-moving responsibilities and slumming it in my coffee shop?"

"Well, I never was very good at unpacking so I thought I'd leave it until later. And I was wondering whether I could take my cousin's wife out to lunch since she will know all the local haunts?"

"...Oh..." Dee was slightly thrown for a moment. "...Sure, that would be great. Will we be meeting Ginny and Forrest?"

"...Um, no. It's just me, I'm afraid. Or won't I do...? I can promise that my table manners are exemplary. I went to a really expensive school." Felix was starting to feel his control of the situation slipping from his grasp.

Dee laughed to conceal that she was annoyed with herself. A friendly gesture was made and she was automatically wary. "Oh Felix, don't be stupid, of course you'll do. We could go now if you like?" She rubbed her clammy palms together.

"Or we could take a rain-check...?" Felix gave her an escape route because she appeared to need one.

"No, no, I'd love to go to lunch," Dee insisted vehemently.

"But only if Ginny and Forrest accompany us? I pretty much gathered I was not your go-to cousin-in-law, but I'm new in town. I hoped you could show me the sights."

"Oh Jesus, Felix..." Dee groaned and rubbed the orbits of her eyes with her fingertips. This was excruciating for them both. "I didn't mean anything by that...when I asked if Ginny and Forrest were coming. It's just, I have this *jealous husband*..."

"No, really?" Felix gave her his best sarcastic gasp but she obviously didn't catch on.

"You saw him at the wedding! He can be really irrational sometimes. Did you know my only male friends he's actually happy about are gay?"

Felix almost guffawed. Oh yes, she *certainly* had a jealous husband. If only she knew. "I know that your husband is very protective over you, but he isn't jealous of *me*," Felix said blandly but he was, in actual fact, mortified. He had to think on his feet now. "...Look, to be honest, Milo and I are very close and he's called me a couple of times since he left. He would never admit it to you, but he's really worried about you and two small children being all alone in that big house night after night. So I thought I'd take the initiative and check everything was okay. I wanted to let you know that you're more than welcome to come and stay at ours if you feel a bit isolated..." Oh he was good; he was very good. Felix had to commend himself. A little bit of truth. A little bit of guff. If he could persuade her to stay at their house, his obligation would be laid to rest. Dee would be under the whole family's protection then.

"Oh Felix...that is so sweet of you." Dee gave his arm a friendly (possibly even patronising) rub, genuinely flattered. Felix watched her do this a bit uncertainly. "But you don't have to worry about me. I'm getting quite used to being on my own and I have a lot of nice friends really nearby if I was concerned about security. We live in a pretty nice part of London, y'know. And don't forget, we do have different gun laws to you yanks," she informed him with a jocular air.

"Yeah well, you know us Americans; always living in fear of some thieving intruder blowing our brains out. *Anyway*, now you know you have some *even nicer* friends nearby." He gave her arm a distinctly rigid pat in return and turned to leave. That could not have gone any worse if he had deliberately intended to screw it up.

"I really would like to go to lunch with you though...if you're still interested," Dee called after him and Felix turned to face her again with a wan smile. Ugh. It was painful.

*

The new acquaintances were seated outside Benito's coffee house under a brightly coloured patio umbrella on the café forecourt. Although it was barely mid-January; the sun was shining, their coats were warm and it was hellishly busy inside with no hope of housing two adults, a toddler and a baby in a pram. On their way, Dee had dropped by the nearby pre-school to collect Angel. Dee rocked the stroller containing the sleeping baby lazily with her foot on the large wheel. Angel was doing an odd little crab dance across the paving stones complete with pincer movements with her hands. The display wasn't even for her audience's benefit. Her face was set in determined concentration.

Felix watched the child thoughtfully. "...She's kind of-"

"I know." Dee scratched her nose.

"Does she get that from you? I don't remember Lance being particularly off-the-wall..."

Dee considered that momentarily. "Um...I guess..."

"So, any new murders I haven't been briefed about?" he asked blandly.

Dee gave a tight little smile that she simply couldn't pull off. "...That's a little insensitive, isn't it? A woman died in horribly brutal circumstances. It isn't really a laughing matter, Felix."

"Yeah but, she *was* a bit of a bitch and probably deserved it," he said with a clownish grimace and Dee gave him a withering (if a little forced) smirk.

Felix attempted to smooth things over as he was fully aware he had the propensity to come across as a little thoughtless and cocky. "So are Jerry and Elliott in the clear yet?"

"It looks that way. The investigations appear to have scaled down at the hotel because the police have virtually disappeared. I hope that doesn't mean they've just *decided* Lance did it. I'd like the real killer to come to justice." Dee bit at the patch of skin beside her right thumbnail.

Felix widened both eyes enough to see the whites, as though he thought she might be pulling his leg. "But surely any sensible person will come to the conclusion Lance arranged it. The woman was systematically destroying his life, so he must have snapped – you do *know* that, right…?"

Dee bristled then. "Whatever happened to innocent until proven guilty? You evidently think you knew my ex-husband but I can assure you I knew him better. He must have hated his secretary, sure, but it takes a certain kind of person to end somebody's life. And Lance wasn't that person. Whatever else he was, he wasn't a killer," she glowered.

"Alright." Felix gave a defeated shrug, there was just no telling some people. "I knew you didn't like me," he said blankly whilst crunching on a biscotti.

"What…?" Dee pulled a face, her black beret not quite obscuring her frowning eyebrows; still irritated. "I don't *dislike* you."

"But you don't *like* me either. If Ginny or Forrest had shown up at your store to take you to lunch, you wouldn't have thought twice about going."

"That doesn't mean I don't *like* you. That just means that Ginny is a woman and Forrest is a priest, but you're-" she stalled hesitantly. "You know what I'm trying to say, don't make me say it…" Dee groaned.

"I have literally no idea what you're trying to say…"

Dee sighed. "…Well, you're a funny and attractive guy. I just try to see things from Milo's point of view sometimes."

"You think I'm attractive…?" He sat back in his seat, giving her the most quizzical look she had ever experienced.

"Uhhhggg!" Dee grumbled, growing more and more exasperated with the awkwardness of this situation. "Look, *I* would feel a little weirded-out if Milo spent lots of time on his own with my cousin Cassie if I was abroad," she explained more expansively. "Anyway, I just try to steer clear of good-looking men if I can help it. He'd definitely rather the manager of my shop wasn't a man. He isn't even completely certain about Elliott and Jerry, and they're his half brothers. Although I did have a brief relationship with Jerry once – that might be why…" she added as an afterthought.

"You've got tickets on yourself, haven't you?" Felix smiled around the biscotti he was eating. "Do you think no straight guy could possibly resist you?" He began to laugh heartily which irritated her more so.

"What?" Dee smarted. "I *don't* have tickets on myself actually! I'm painfully aware that there is nothing special about me. Milo has dated some of the most beautiful women in the world. But for some insane reason, Milo happens to be the insecure one in our relationship and I'm just trying to spare his feelings," she concluded acidly.

"And *I'm* kidding," Felix replied softly with a glib little smirk.

"...Oh...well...that's not very funny." Dee flushed, noticeably.

"Look, I may be his cousin, but I don't know why you have such an insecure husband. Well, I *kind of* get it; he's got himself a new hot, young wife who he worships and he doesn't want to lose her."

"You think I'm hot...?" Dee gave him that same mock-quizzical look he'd given her.

"Oh dear God, let's never speak of this conversation again," Felix said with a weary sigh and they both burst into laughter, easing the tension somewhat. If only he could just *tell* her Milo had asked him to come! "Look, we're one big family now, so we should get along. Milo happens to trust me...because I'm the one who-"

"Yes, yes, the one who persuaded him to fight for me, that one has gone down in popular folklore..." Dee was relieved when Angel finally gave up on the crab-dance and sat down on a chair like a normal child. "Milo *asked* you to make sure that I was okay, didn't he...?" Dee asked in a softer voice and eyed him knowingly.

Felix watched Dee momentarily, well - he wasn't actually going to lie to her. Not entirely. "...No, maybe he wanted me to but he didn't say so - not in so many words, anyway. Like I say, I took the decision upon myself. Milo was just freaked out by that Cameron incident at the wedding-"

"I knew it..." Dee sighed, sipped at her coffee and decided to peruse the menu for a while. "Why can't Milo just accept that he won and Cameron lost - which is why Cam was upset? And now it turns out *you're* only here because he guilt-tripped you into it."

"I didn't say that!" Felix growled with a roll of his eyes. Man, she was perceptive! "I thought we decided at Christmas that we were going to be pals. You're fine with Forrest and Ginny, but even though we seem to have so much in common; music and films and books...and humour, *I'm* the one you're guarded with. I'm Milo's cousin!"

"Since when has that counted for anything in *this* family?!" she snapped.

Felix stared at her pensively. "I suppose you have a point...Milo said he would have taken you from Lance even if he *had* lived - and you hadn't left him…"

"I know…" Dee had begun to regret her outburst now. She still suffered with guilt issues over being married to one man and then his cousin (half brother) directly afterwards, but none of that had anything to do with Felix.

"All I'm saying is, although I'm a terribly funny and a deeply attractive guy; if you can resist me and you want to us to be friends…we can be…"

"I really hate you…" Dee let a begrudging smile creep across her lips.

"And I think you're ugly," he concluded.

"Thank you."

"You're welcome."

Dee sat thoughtfully for a moment. "You really make me laugh, Felix. I liked you when I met you at last year's Ball and I liked you even more after Andrew's funeral…and I always wanted to be friends. I guess I'm just a little skittish after the way Milo behaved over Cameron. I *really* love him and I've been through one failed marriage already so I just want to-"

"You'll grow old together," he assured her wisely. "And I like you too. It's nice to have a new friend I'm not related to, since I virtually know nobody else here." Felix watched as she fished out a box of raisins for her slightly odd little girl. "So, have you seen anything of Cameron since the wedding?" he *finally* managed to ask an hour and ten minutes after entering the coffee shop.

"No." Dee shook her head without any real interest in the subject. If Felix hadn't been strangely enjoying himself, he would have yelled with exasperation right there outside the café. "So, who are you seeing at the moment?" she asked bluntly.

"Are you always this insolent?" There was an incredulous smile on his face.

"Not always, but do you see how comfortable I am in your company? Do you see how we've bonded and struck up an instant rapport? So instant, I feel I can ask you the most probing and searching of questions?" Dee was barely stifling laughter and it was a good thing Felix was difficult to offend.

"You can go off people, you know," Felix reminded her. "Yes, I'm seeing someone. She's a singer - she sometimes sings at my club. She's fairly well known, actually."

"Well, if you mean well known in the sense that *you* are well known, I'm quite sure I've never heard of her." Once Dee had started in this vein, she found it hard to quit.

"That's because you are uncultured and clearly a half-wit." Felix chuckled. He was beginning to feel pleased he had run out on his unpacking duties. "Right, can we order some food now? I'm starving."

SUSPICIOUS MINDS

It was one of those rare occasions when Dee found herself entirely alone in the coffee shop. And she was terrified. Thankfully the lunchtime rush was over but what if a customer came in? What if they *wanted* something? Dee could just about manage a cake or a cold beverage but certainly nothing more! The bell over the shop door tinkled and Dee physically froze.

"Oh thank God it's you!" she exclaimed with relief on seeing Patrice.

"If only *all* my welcomes were so good. Where is everybody? Has there been another zombie apocalypse? I hate those..." he mused jovially and sauntered over to where she stood behind the counter. "Are you wearing an *apron*...?"

"Oh Patrice, can you stay and help me until Evan comes back? Otherwise, if a customer comes in, I'm totally screwed."

"Where are Evan and Bruce?"

"One of our food deliveries didn't turn up and Evan had no choice but to go to the cash-and-carry. He called me to ask if I could stand in - I couldn't go to the supermarket because he's very specific about what he wants. And Bruce is on a 'customer care' training day at the college. Didn't he tell you?"

Patrice glanced nervously at his feet, scuffing his toe on the lino floor. "No, I left early this morning...before breakfast..."

"Do you know how to use a coffee machine?" Dee whined unhappily.

"Of course I do, I'm a bar manager." Patrice stepped confidently around the counter and pulled a fresh apron out from one of the shelves beneath the till. As he tied it, he fished out a pair of glasses from his blazer pocket and squinted at the coffee machine. "Oh yes, we used to have this model in the bar..." Patrice advised her importantly. "Surely Evan shouldn't be calling on the *owner* to cover for him."

"It virtually never happens - and it's my fault for being so bloody inept. I'm not even entirely sure how the till works. Stupid baby-brain..." Not that the baby was any excuse. Dee had never taken the time to learn because Evan was so capable.

"Don't worry, I can teach you." Patrice pat her shoulder condescendingly.

"It feels like I haven't seen you for weeks," Dee said as he fiddled with the coffee machine settings.

"I know...it's been crazy-busy at the bar. We'll have to arrange a date to get together soon," Patrice replied with a polite smile.

Dee chewed on her lip. "Were you looking for Bruce - when you came in...?"

"Yeah, he forgot his house keys so I was dropping them in because I probably won't be home when he gets back..." Patrice was very definitely avoiding her eyes.

"Is everything okay between you? I get the impression-" Before Dee could make further inroads into this conversation, two customers came in. Patrice immediately set to work taking the couple's order. He made them a latte and a mochaccino and both wanted a piece of coffee and walnut cake. Patrice took his time serving them, making polite chit-chat, going as far as to talk to the pair about the weather. Dee wondered if he were stalling so that he didn't have to speak to her. Soon the customers couldn't be waylaid any longer and they took a seat near the travel books. "I should give you a job too - you'd be an asset."

Patrice smirked. "You couldn't afford me...and I don't think Bruce would be too pleased."

Dee shoved her hands in her pockets, watching Patrice make them both a coffee. She tried to commit the task to memory, but she just couldn't seem to...care. "Patrice...I know you're having problems. Bruce won't talk about it, but he's very upset. Is it just a rough patch or-?"

"It seems to be more serious than that. Will you take sides if we split up?" Patrice raised his head and fixed her with his eyes this time.

That caught her off-guard. "...No, I- you're both my best friends."

"But you love him more, right? Even though you knew me first..." He said it blankly, not accusingly. It was as though he just wanted to be sure.

"I won't take sides - I swear...but please tell me it isn't going to come to that. God, it would be like my *parents divorcing* if you two split up. You're the most devoted couple I know; there's no hope for any of us if you guys can't stay together." Dee could quite easily have cried. Because even though she refused to take sides, there would be a definite wedge, a barrier formed that wasn't there before. "...Do you still love each other?"

"I don't know." Patrice finished putting steaming foamy milk in both cups then set about tamping the loose coffee grounds into a tight puck into the portafilter. Then he slotted it skilfully into the machine. He would have made a great barista here.

"Is there somebody else involved...?" Dee held her breath.

"Yes and no..." Patrice pulled the lever to release the boiling water into each drink, then he just seemed to stop mid-flow during what he was doing. "There's someone...who likes me...somebody I work with. But other than telling Bruce about it, I haven't taken it any further. I just don't know what to do. Things aren't the same with Bruce and-"

"Please don't...please don't do anything unless you're one hundred percent sure." Dee wiped the beginnings of a tear forming in the corner of her eye. "Because once you've done it - you can't undo it..."

Patrice's eyes seemed to well up with tears too. "Oh Dee...I just don't know what I want anymore. Please don't get upset..." He rubbed her cheek.

"You guys are my family...and I feel like my family is breaking apart..."

"Honey, we can't stay together just because of you."

Dee pulled a tissue from her pocket and blew her nose. "I know...but are you going to try to work things out? Have you thought about counselling or-?"

"I'm going to see how it goes." Patrice eyed her momentarily, thinking something through. "But if it doesn't work out...I need you to promise me you won't cut me off."

It seemed that was incredibly important to him - as if that were the real reason he had come here today.

"I promise I won't. We'll *always* be friends." But it would be so much harder. Dee would have to divide up her time, worry about which friend to invite to what event; who could come for Christmas, birthday parties, drinks down the pub. "But you will try?"

Patrice put his arms around her. "I will try..."

*

The house was at its most immaculate since the Christmas guests had descended on her, but somehow Dee was determined to make an even better impression tonight. She had found the worsening saga of Bruce and Patrice was affecting her far more deeply than she could have imagined, so all Dee could do to take her mind off it was gather the people she loved around her. She had no control over those external things so needed to gain control closer to home.

"Great, you're here," Dee beamed as her uncle Gordon and her cousin Cassie arrived at the house early one evening about three weeks after Milo had left for the States. "Here, let me help you with your bags." She hurriedly took Gordon's large holdall from him. He wasn't long post-op cardiac surgery.

"Can't you just leave that to the butler?" Uncle Gordon joked in a teasing manner Dee was unfamiliar with.

Cassie rolled her eyes and Dee groaned. "Uncle, I'm not *that* rich," she complained. But she was. Well, *Milo* was. Dee just could not think of that money as anything to do with her. Milo had insisted on taking over the entire cost of keeping the house, of raising kids, the cars, the house in the country, any expenditure at all. Dee drew the line at the shop though. Milo was old-fashioned in that sense; believing it was the man's role to be the main provider for the family. Other than all things household, Dee tried to keep a distance between her and his money. "I have a nanny-come-housekeeper, but that's all."

"The disappointment is unbearable!" he chuckled, following her through to the lounge. For some reason, Dee felt more embarrassed about her recent second marriage into wealth whilst in Cassie and Gordon's company than in anyone else's. Even though she had not long met them, she was uncomfortable about the cash issue. They were her only living blood-family and it made her uneasy that they may think she had married for it, uneasy that it may cause a gulf between them.

"I'll show you to your rooms in a bit after we've had some drinks," Dee said, putting their bags down in the hall and loitering in the guest lounge doorway (the cubbyhole was for when they knew her better). "I'm afraid I couldn't keep the children up any longer. They were tired out so I put them to bed, but you can meet them in the morning, Gordon."

"Of course, I didn't expect them to be up at this time. This house is *amazing!*" Gordon continued with gusto, not picking up on the fact that Dee was still slightly on edge.

"Dad, it's a great house but you must stop going on about money all the time. Dee could be living in an enormous mansion but she doesn't because she's down to earth. She ought to be on honeymoon but she isn't because she won't leave her baby behind. Dee's normal, just like us," Cassie insisted, giving her father a withering look and sat gingerly on the sofa.

"I know that, what did I say? I'm only teasing the girl, Dee knows me," he argued with a roll of his eyes.

"But she doesn't know you, not yet."

"You're not offended, are you Dee?" Gordon protested, looking a bit anxious.

"Not at all," Dee smiled. Not offended, just worried about appearing to be somebody she wasn't.

"I know Dee, she's like my sister - but without the snobbishness. Dee is more street-smart and savvy than Rebecca ever was - having a tough childhood has ensured that. But she's her mother's daughter alright," he assured both the girls and Dee hoped he was telling the truth. She liked the look of her mother in the photos anyway; she had a kind face.

"Come on, Dee, I'll help you fix some drinks." Cassie rose to her feet even though she had only been sitting for thirty seconds and followed Dee out to the kitchen. "Sorry about my dad. He thinks you're best thing since sliced bread really. In fact, you're practically his sister reincarnated."

"Gordon does know I didn't marry for the money, doesn't he? I know I must look like a real piece of work on paper but I'm actually depressingly normal. The money is circumstantial. I married my first husband because I fell in love with him, and I only *met* my second husband because he was my first husband's cousin…and you *know* how much I love Milo. Once you mix in wealthy circles, well…those are the only people you meet and-"

"We know that. You don't have to explain yourself to us. Even though I've only known you since Christmas, I know you've a good heart. You're our family, one of us."

"Oh Cass," Dee sighed and gave her a hug. The doorbell sounded then and Dee wandered back out into the hall to open the door. "Jesus, you again?"

"I can see the money was well spent on your Swiss finishing school." Felix rolled his eyes and stepped through the door.

"Mm, I'm all about good breeding." Dee eyed him as he breezed past her. She had to be averaging a meeting with Felix once every other day and she had a feeling she knew why. Felix seemed to be finding settling into this new area slightly more difficult than he would like. The large mansion up on Richmond Hill had been segmented into three sections so that Forrest, Ginny and Felix had their own living areas and need never cross paths if they did not wish to. Ginny was spending a great deal of time with Jerry, who had become her boyfriend in all but name. Forrest was exceptionally busy with church business and was rarely home, so Felix was left to kick about the enormous house by himself. All his friends and haunts were back in Chelsea and Camden and even though he had been a fairly regular visitor to Richmond before his move here, he was feeling increasingly isolated. His very new friendship with his cousin's wife had, therefore, flourished. Their humour, although slightly juxtaposed due to cultural differences, was similar. Of course, Felix was better educated, more refined - but he found her crude and unconventional brand of common sense and wit rather refreshing. "My uncle and cousin have just arrived, actually. They've come to stay over for a couple of days so we can get to know each other properly."

"…Oh, I'm sorry…I should have called first." Felix ground to a halt as he reached the kitchen doorway and noticed Cassie perched on a stool at the breakfast bar.

"Hi, nice to see you again," she began pleasantly.

"Hey, it's the girl everybody's talking about…well, *Forrest* certainly is anyway," said Felix with a barely disguised smirk on his face. Cassie flushed an unattractive shade of crimson.

"Shut up, Felix, don't embarrass the girl." Dee whacked his arm fairly hard.

"Ouch!" he howled, clutching his injured arm. "If this is how you treat all your uninvited guests, I'll be off. I've been beaten and insulted so I'm getting out of this hell-hole. Shall I call in on you in the coffee shop tomorrow? We could have lunch."

"Felix, you don't have to leave on our account. My father is a big fan of your work, he would love to meet you," Cassie insisted. "You should stay for dinner…if that's alright, Dee?" she gulped, realising she had just invited some guy to somebody else's dinner party.

"Oh I don't mind. But Cassie, you don't have to flatter his ego, Felix is aware nobody has ever heard of him," Dee joked, ignoring the mock-evil eye he was giving her.

"You be quiet; I was talking to your more intelligent cousin. Are you sure, Cassie? Don't you guys want to catch up by yourselves? You've made plans-"

"If stuffing your face and getting pissed are classed as plans, then yes, go away," Dee muttered impudently.

"Well, I'd love to join you." Felix tactfully ignored Dee again. "I was *supposed* to be having a drink in town with Joanna, the singer I told you about?" Felix glanced briefly at Dee. "But she got a better offer - some gig or something. I don't know, I wasn't listening - anyway, she blew me off."

"You must bring Joanna over when Milo gets back. Or we could go out on a double-date. I'd like to double-date with Ginny and Jerry too but I think the cold war isn't yet over," Dee explained thoughtfully.

"…Hmm, maybe." Felix seemed to lose interest in the subject.

"Oh, I see." Dee gave him a coy little smile.

"*Oh, I see,* what?"

"Did you make her up?" Dee asked in that patronising voice one would use to speak to a small child.

"Dee! Stop being so mean!" Cassie frowned on Dee's pure insolence but she was not yet accustomed to the way Dee and the majority of her friends delighted in abusing each other.

"What? He's always talking about this *girlfriend*, Joanna Lake, but he keeps making excuses for not bringing her over."

"No, I'm just embarrassed to be friends with *you*," Felix gave Dee that pretend sneer. "Joanna's a very talented jazz singer and you're just some shop-girl." He pulled up a bar stool beside Cassie.

"Yeah-yeah. You made her up - she's probably inflatable..." Dee chewed blandly on her thumbnail.

"We're having a *wild* fling if you must know, Dee. You're just jealous because you're married and boring. Just the other weekend, we got caught by her mother doing it in the restroom on a visit to her parent's house." Felix said, almost as though he were bragging, yet completely nonchalantly. "*That's* how wild we are."

"Why do you Americans call it a restroom? You don't go in there for a *rest*," Dee asked blankly.

"Perhaps because we Americans are more genteel than you British, we don't feel the need to be so literal."

"You're so *genteel*, you weren't even in there for a rest *or* a bath..." Dee wrinkled up her nose sourly.

"That's true," he conceded with a wink. Cassie watched the pair in wonder. Dee and her relatively new acquaintance happily traded insults and discussed his sexual conquests as though they had grown up together, while Cassie just looked on. But Cassie did not possess that edgy, slightly spiteful drollness; her sense of humour was more gentle and forgiving.

"So, you met the parents, huh? Sounds serious," Dee observed dryly.

Felix shrugged blandly. "What can I say? I'm a catch."

"Okay, you guys go through to the dining room and prepare yourselves for some of my kick-ass, homemade curry," Dee said cockily.

"Homemade curry, huh? I didn't know you were a good cook, Dee." Felix climbed off the barstool and sauntered towards the door, looking half-way impressed.

"I didn't say *that*, I said I could make a kick-ass curry," Dee repeated but a little more slowly.

"Do you cook yourself, Cassie?" Felix wandered through the doorway with Cassie, glancing back as Dee produced a large (if slightly misshapen) tray of chocolate brownies from the oven and placed it on the work-surface for later.

"Only when she falls in the oven," Dee laughed at her own mirth but glanced at the vaguely perplexed expressions of Felix and Cassie who had stopped to stare at her from the kitchen doorway. The American and the Australian smiled vacantly. As another foreigner, Milo often gave her the same confused smile. "Les Dawson? No...? Catch up guys, English humour waits for no man."

"No, I got it - I just thought you could do better," Felix smirked, placed a hand in the small of Cassie's back and lead her to the dining room.

Dee called after him. "You won't be invited again, y'know. Not that you were invited *this* time!"

*

The dinner party had gone remarkably well for an evening that Dee had been anxious about and with the addition of an unexpected guest to cater for. Dee was glad Felix had shown up out of the blue, he had somehow taken the pressure off. Gordon and Felix seemed to instantly hit it off. They both had that same slightly cruel humour which ensured they got on like a house on fire. Dee watched the two men a little ruefully and could only hope that one day Gordon would take to Milo that way. Gordon's opinion was unusually important to her but she knew her husband was a far more acquired taste. Dinner and dessert soon turned to copious amounts of alcoholic beverages and at around eleven, Felix bid his tipsy goodbyes and climbed into a taxi.

"Now, that's the kind of man I could see *you* with, Cassie," Gordon informed her heartily.

"I don't think so," Cassie replied softly. They had adjourned back to the kitchen and Cassie was stacking the dishwasher even after Dee's protestations.

"No, I think she would be better suited to a certain American clergyman I know," Dee nudged her cousin from where she leaned against the counter and Cassie smiled with a sort of pleased bashfulness.

"Milo's brother? The one in the wheelchair?" Gordon piped up.

"Forrest has disabilities, but that doesn't define a man," Cassie said archly to her father. Dee was already beginning to glean they regularly rubbed each other up the wrong way.

"I didn't say it did," he argued.

"You'd really like him, Uncle," Dee advised (she did just *love* how the word 'uncle' sounded in her mouth. It was such a novelty. *Real*, blood-family - she couldn't get over it).

"I'm sure I would but I think Cassie would suit the witty jazz musician," he concluded in that roguish Scottish accent that Dee adored.

"I don't think so, Dad!"

"Oh well. Right, I think I'm off to bed." Gordon too said his goodnights and left the two girls to chat.

"...Sorry about him." Cassie rolled her eyes, embarrassed by him as she had been for much of the night.

"No, I think he's fab - I just wish he was *my* dad," Dee mused.

"You're welcome to him," she grumbled.

"Fathers are supposed to humiliate their daughters – it's the law," Dee advised her pragmatically. At least, she imagined they did, she didn't really know.

"...So, does Forrest ever mention me?" Cassie closed the dishwasher and turned to Dee coyly.

"Well, he does ask after your health more than is strictly necessary," Dee confirmed with a wry grin. "Why, do you like him?"

"I don't know, I've only really met him properly at the Ball that one time...but he did seem unbelievably nice," Cassie admitted diffidently.

"And he really is like that, all the time," Dee couldn't contain her excitement. How she would love for Forrest to get together with a girl as adorable as Cassie. He was so good-natured and she was terribly sweet - they were the perfect match. Forrest deserved someone as amazing as Cassie to love. "Well, I must accidentally-on-purpose invite you both over at the same time," Dee decided shrewdly. "What did you think of Felix? He's hilarious, isn't he? Did you like him?"

"Hmm, I think Felix likes himself enough for the both of us," Cassie glowered. "He's just one of those guys who will always be more intelligent, better-read, funnier, more talented and more articulate than you or I could ever be."

"Really?" Dee was a little taken aback; Cassie never seemed to have a bad word to say about anyone. "Maybe he's a little bit brash on first impressions, but he's actually really sweet once you get to know him properly. Your dad thought he was great."

"My dad has been wrong before." Cassie shrugged, appearing not to want to linger on the conversation.

Dee crossed her arms across her chest and frowned. "Well, what's wrong with him...?"

"What, *apart* from how he was flirting with you outrageously?"

Dee almost laughed. "*Me*? He was flirting with *you*, more like. Touching your back or your arm every five-and-a-half minutes."

Cassie cocked her head just slightly as though trying to comprehend something. "Did you really not see it...? He clearly fancies you."

"...*What*?"

"...Dee, I'd watch him if I were you," Cassie warned in a soft, serious voice.

"How do you mean?"

"I could be wrong but I don't think I am; I was watching Felix tonight. Every time I looked at him, he was staring at you. Every quip and every comment he made, he seemed to be looking for your approval. Every insult was just to get a rise or some reaction out of you. He bounces off you like there is some secret code between you…and I get a bad feeling about it."

Dee shook her head as if to clear it. "…No, I've got that kind of relationship with most of my friends - male friends anyway. It's just friendly banter, Cass."

"Felix is clearly not terribly interested in that woman he is seeing. From what you say, he seems to be showing up on your doorstep every day." Cassie stopped pretending to clear away the dinner things. "You're very recently, *very happily* married…and you've got to be careful of opportunistic men like him - they prey on good-natured women like you." Cousin Cassie, who was normally very gentle and soft in her demeanour, was wearing a hard expression.

"Cassie, he's Milo's *cousin*," Dee stressed emphatically.

"Adopted cousin, but yes - your point being?"

"My point being, there is just *no way* Felix fancies me. And reading between the lines, it sounds as though Milo hinted to Felix that he'd *like* him to check in on me - because Milo was worried about me being alone with two small kids." Dee couldn't help feeling annoyed and slightly insulted. Cassie had decided she was naïve too, hadn't she? Why did everybody come to that conclusion? "Felix has just moved to Richmond and his family are all otherwise occupied and he doesn't know anyone else here. What's more, it was Felix who persuaded Milo he should take a chance on me," Dee asserted, though she felt she had said and heard that sentence one too many times before.

"Well, I don't really know about that, but I do know something bugged me about him tonight."

"First impressions aren't always great to go on; I've learned that the hard way…" It was bad enough that Bruce and Patrice might be splitting up, Dee couldn't stomach her cousin taking against one of her new friends (not to mention Milo's *cousin*). "You should give Felix a chance. We're all family now and it would be nice if we could get along." Dee felt rather unsettled by Cassie's words. She did not see a problem but was troubled that Cassie did.

"Alright, I'm not one to judge a man unfairly. Everybody deserves a second chance." Cassie made up her mind not to rock the boat or write a man off for being too clever for his own good. Only, now she was watchful of him.

KEEP YOUR FRIENDS CLOSE

The next morning, the awkwardness of the night before seemed to be forgotten. Cassie and Gordon finally managed to meet the children properly. Gordon seemed to fall in love with them instantly, to the point where his eyes kept filling up with 'moved' tears. He assured Angel he was her new grandad and Angel (who hadn't really had a grandfather before, since Erwin Stark was dead and Austin Phillips had virtually nothing to do with their family) was rapturously pleased about this. She was even more pleased because Grandad Gordon had come bearing gifts for her. Whilst Gordon and Angel played a game of snap at the kitchen table after breakfast, Cassie and Dee loitered in the kitchen doorway sipping at mugs of tea. Cassie was cradling Finn in her free arm and Dee was keeping a beady eye on the workmen traipsing up and down the hall.

"So what room are they decorating?" Cassie asked brightly.

"Milo's study. Well, he's been using one of the spare reception rooms as a study anyway but I'm having it fitted out so he has a proper home-office here. It's going to look like this." Dee proceeded to show her the CGI mock-up of a large olive-coloured room with a huge mahogany desk at one end and a rustic sofa in the middle which sat by an equally rustic coffee table. "I mean, it was so good of Milo to move over here with me and I just want him to have a room that is entirely his; somewhere to escape - as well as being an office. Do you think it's going to be manly enough? I really want him to like it..."

Cassie wasn't really looking at the picture; she was watching Dee and smiled at her sheer excitement. "You love him to bits, don't you?"

Dee looked up cheerfully. "Well, yeah."

"You must really miss him."

"I can't wait for him to come home. I look forward to his calls every evening but it's not the same..." Dee gulped. She struggled with this long-distance relationship but tried to focus on the future; things would be perfect when he was home for good.

"Knock-knock," Felix intoned brightly as he appeared at the open front door. "I've just come to pick up my car." He gesticulated with his head at his racing-green Lotus out on the street.

"Morning Felix," Dee replied. She had completely forgotten about his car being left overnight. She glanced gingerly at Cassie who seemed to be wearing a fixed smile.

"So, today's lunch meet-up that we arranged last week, did we agree last night to reschedule or not? I can't remember – I was a bit drunk," he asked casually.

"Um..." Dee chewed on her lip. "If it's okay with you, I think I'll raincheck. I'm not going to bother going into the shop today either - I thought I'd spend a day with my family," she gulped. Dee had this overwhelming need to be polite and ask Felix to join them but with another quick glance at Cassie, she decided against it.

"Oh, okay...no problem," Felix said urbanely.

"Is that Felix?" Gordon called from the kitchen. "Come on in for a coffee!"

"Hey Gordon!" Felix called back. "...Listen, um - I've got an idea. Why don't you two girls spend the day doing those girly things girls do, and I'll take your uncle to my club in Camden. He said he really wanted to see the place and I was going to swing by this morning anyway."

"Oh, well - that's very kind of you," Cassie began, "but he's been looking forward to spending some quality time with his grandkids and-"

"Nonsense." Gordon had arrived at the kitchen doorway with Angel clasping his leg and tagging a ride on his foot. "I can catch up with you girls and the kids later this afternoon. And we're spending another night here too. I wouldn't want to pass up on an opportunity to visit 'The Black Keys'." He took a big sip of his mug of tea.

"Hello Unca Flix." Angel disentangled herself from Gordon's leg and climbed up onto Felix's hip like a monkey instead.

Felix smirked at the child, looked to Dee for a reaction then said, "I don't want to mess up your plans..."

"Don't be silly," Dee piped up because she really felt she had to. "My uncle is going to be spending loads of time with me and the children - it would be nice for him to see your club."

"Okay, great...are you ready to go now, Gordon?" Felix shoved his hands awkwardly in his pockets. He couldn't shake the feeling that something was afoot here. He smiled weakly at Dee again whose returning smile was equally weak.

"Yep, yep - I'm all yours. Let me just get my jacket." Gordon smiled jovially and hurried upstairs.

"Well, thank you, Felix. My dad will be in his element, I'm sure." Cassie forced a grin, she probably wasn't giving Felix a fair crack of the whip. Maybe Felix, with all his wit and cleverness, just made her feel jealous if she was honest - a bit inadequate. And possibly she didn't want to share her new cousin with this new, brash American man just yet. But officially he had been here first, and maybe she was just going to have to.

*

As January gave way to February, a couple of evenings after Gordon and Cassie had returned home, Felix sat in Dee's TV cubbyhole. He distractedly fingered the remote control. The Hitchcock movie was on pause while Dee went up to check on her crying son. This was the second evening in a row that Felix had dropped by. He saw so little of his sister and his cousin Forrest of late but he felt he had neglected to investigate the Cameron issue. The problem was, it was very easy to forget what he was primarily here for because Dee was so easy to be around. *So* easy that the friendship appeared completely authentic. No, it *was* authentic; Dee and Felix were incredibly alike - it was just Milo's request had turned it into something deceitful. Still, in all the time he had spent with her, he had seen nothing of Cameron so Milo probably had nothing to worry about anyway.

Dee returned with a weary sigh and sat beside him on the sofa.

"Did Finn go off to sleep again?" he asked brightly.

"Yeah, eventually. Some evenings he doesn't want to be left but he's slowly learning that nothing bad will happen when I'm gone." She felt Finley was doing rather well for a baby who would only turn five months old at the end of this month. Dee concluded motherhood had proven easier the second time around, even if the father wasn't around as much as she would like.

"He's growing up so fast." Felix felt privileged to have been allowed to spend so much time watching the baby progress and change, and witness the joy her little girl was becoming. If only he didn't have to feel so guilty about his underhand secret agenda, perhaps they could even be *proper* friends like they had initially planned to be. "So, have you seen Cameron around?"

"No, he seems to have dropped off the face of the earth, I think the wedding brought it all home to him. Anyway, how come you keep asking after Cameron? Are you in love with him or something?" She rolled her eyes with a disinterested sigh.

"I'm just being a concerned friend and making sure he isn't bothering you. Cameron struck me as relatively unbalanced. You would tell me if he were making a nuisance of himself, wouldn't you? You can rely on me while Milo is away if there *is* a problem."

"Oh don't be so melodramatic, Cameron isn't a threat to *anybody*. I feel sorry for him if you must know. Anyway, like I say, I think he finally understands that Milo is here for the duration. I wish Cameron well; I hope he meets a nice girl," Dee said absently. "Listen, if you're drinking, you can stay tonight - save getting a taxi back." She noticed he was already halfway through his second Budweiser.

"Oh...okay, thanks." Felix had stayed once before at Christmas and found the spare room to his liking. "Dee...am I imagining things, or have I done something to upset Cassie?"

Dee exhaled slowly, it was too late in the evening and she was too weary to make up an excuse. "...Well, not exactly," she began tentatively. Cassie thought Felix was *into* her, and not only did Dee find that notion ludicrous, she found it hugely embarrassing. "I know it's stupid but it's just that...she thinks you might be harbouring some kind of-" The pair pricked up their ears to hear the sound of the key in the lock and Dee glanced at Felix, slightly confused. Then she smiled. "Did you know about this...?" Dee elbowed him in the ribs.

"Know about what?" Felix gormlessly watched Dee rise with barely concealed excitement to her feet and hurry out into the hall.

She was quick to fall into the arms of her husband as she caught sight of him in the half-light of the passageway.

"I wasn't expecting you for another couple of weeks! You have to stop surprising me..." But she was cut off by his eager lips meeting hers.

Milo murmured between kisses, "I've been longing for you for hours..." He kissed her so hard and so passionately, she almost forgot Felix was in the other room until she realised he was pressing her against the wall and attempting to undo the buttons of her denim shirt.

"Felix is here..." she whispered and Milo disappointedly rest his head upon her shoulder.

"...Shit," he sighed.

"It's okay...we'll have time later," Dee grinned whilst leading him into the cubbyhole.

"Hi Milo, I didn't know you were due back tonight..." Felix stammered uneasily. "Listen, you guys must have a lot to catch up on so I'll take off."

"No, don't be silly. You've been drinking, stay the night," Dee insisted adamantly.

"Of course you must stay," Milo agreed, perching on the arm of the sofa.

Dee briefly ran her fingers through Milo's hair. "D'you want a cup of tea or anything, honey?"

"Um, no- actually, yes please..."

"Okay." She happily kissed the top of his head and strode off to the kitchen.

"So," Milo began once he was sure she was out of earshot. "I haven't heard much from you, super-sleuth."

Felix shrugged dispassionately. "There was nothing to tell you. Cameron appears to have left the building. I think he's finally given up on her after the wedding saga," Felix informed him.

"Great, that's great." Milo smiled to himself contentedly. Cameron was a constant source of worry for him.

"So, now my job is done, I think I'm going to hang up my spying hat and slink back into relative obscurity," Felix said with a hint of regret. He hoped he could remain Dee's friend, but he would miss the regularity of his visits.

"What for? I'm only home for a few days. It's only been a few weeks since the wedding and maybe Cameron is just licking his wounds before he starts pestering her again. Besides, you're family. You're Dee's friend, and you've every right to be here."

"I think she's starting to get suspicious as to why I'm coming over so often. I'd like to think we'll still be friends, but I need to cut back on how often I'm taking her to lunch or showing up here," Felix explained logically. "You know, when I first looked in on her in the coffee shop, Dee was really anxious about it because she was afraid you'd be jealous of *me*. She thinks you've got some kind of jealousy problem." Felix threw up his hands in mock-disbelief. "Weird, right?"

Milo laughed self-deprecatingly. "Well, I suppose I have. But women like my wife don't come around very often, so I try not to be complacent."

"Look Milo, I've grown very fond of your wife and if she ever found out we'd made this *arrangement*, she would never forgive me...or you."

"Well, she's never going to find out so it doesn't matter. Anyway, why don't you want to be here? You either like my wife or you don't. Isn't she witty or smart or well-bred enough to be a close friend of the famous Felix Kellerman?" Milo narrowed his eyes, pressing what he thought were the right buttons.

"Don't try to play me, Milo. You heard what I just said; I think she's great and you know it. I just don't want to be here under false pretences."

"Then don't be, I just want you to be around. She trusts you now and I know she would confide in you if she were in trouble. Felix, this is the first time I've been away and felt confident that Dee and the kids were safe. Other than Forrest, you're the only man I trust...I just didn't expect the moral indignation from you."

"...Look, I'll drop in from time to time, but only when it's convenient."

Felix finished off his beer in one action.

"That's alright, and when I go back-"

"*I'm* going away too in a couple of weeks. I'll see her as and when - on my own terms. And I'm only here as her friend. I'm not doing this for the sake of reporting back to you anymore, okay?" Felix put his foot down, this deceitful business had to stop.

"Okay, fine..." Milo held up his hands in surrender. "We don't even need to talk about this again...not unless something happens." Milo patted his cousin's arm.

Although Felix was horribly uncomfortable with all this subterfuge, he was also reluctant to walk away entirely. "Anyway, I'm beat. I think I'll go to bed." Felix rose to his feet.

"...Okay - sleep well..."

"Say goodnight to Dee for me. I'll see you in the morning." Felix gave a bit of a fake stretch and wandered out into the hall and up the stairs.

Eventually Dee returned from the kitchen with a big mug of tea. "...Did Felix go to bed?"

"Yeah."

"Huh, he didn't even say goodnight. *Rude*," Dee said with mock-affront and put Milo's tea on the coffee table. "Oh yes, I need to show you something," she remembered, grabbed his hand and pulled him to his feet. Milo followed her willingly to the study. Dee snapped on the light and stood aside proudly.

"Oh wow..." Milo regarded the newly painted and furnished room with surprise.

"I thought I'd renovate your home-office so you'd enjoy working here when you come home. I spoke to your secretary and everything and she gave me some idea of what you'd like...so I hope you do like it..." Dee suddenly sounded a little unsure of herself.

"You did this for me...?" Milo turned to face her, astonished.

"Well yes...I thought there should be a place in this house that was just for you. I kind of hoped it would make you want to stay home more often," Dee admitted diffidently.

"I don't stay away because I *want* to." Milo kicked the door shut and gave a sly smile. "Anyway, do you want to christen it?"

Dee laughed. "Man, you've got an obsession about christening rooms."

"It's just my ingenious ploy to get you to have sex with me as much as possible." Milo was already kissing her throat.

"It's not that ingenious, I saw right through it..." Dee let him guide her over to the huge sofa in the middle of the room. "...Milo, Felix is here..."

"No, he went to bed."

"What if he comes back?" she mumbled between kisses but he was already pushing her down amongst the plush cushions.

"He won't..." Milo assured her, ripping open the popper-buttons of her denim shirt and pushing it off her shoulders. As he straddled her hips, he surveyed his wife just momentarily. "...God, you're beautiful..."

"...I'm not sure we should have sex on this sofa, it's worth a stupid amount of money," Dee said doubtfully, but she was already undoing his belt and unfastening him. She wanted him as much as he wanted her.

*

When it was over, Dee lay completely naked with her husband resting on top of her; his head buried in the crook of her shoulder. Dee reflected that she had never felt this intimately close with another human being in her entire life. Milo was part of her now, just as much a part of her as either of the children. To lose him would be akin to losing a limb.

"Are you warm enough?" he murmured, eyes closed, weary enough to fall asleep right here inside of her.

"Yes, I've got my human duvet." Dee coiled his hair around her fingers.

He chuckled sleepily. "I *am* your human duvet," Milo agreed.

"I miss you..." Dee confided softly. He was so quiet, she wondered if he had fallen asleep.

Milo kept his eyes closed; his breathing was deep and heavy. "I'm miserable without you..." he replied finally. Milo lifted his head, resting his chin on his hand, his eyelids droopy yet his eyes were sharp, fixed on hers. "Whenever I leave, I'm okay for a couple of days...and then the isolation starts to get me down. I find it hard to work, longing for you like I do. Then my mind starts to wander - and I dwell on Andrew...because I haven't got you there to make it alright."

Dee was surprised at this sudden, post-coital candour. He virtually never brought up the subject of his son unprompted. "...Milo, do you think it's healthy that I'm your only support system? I mean, I'm happy to be, but if something ever happened to me-"

"If anything ever happened to you, I would kill myself," he said abruptly and rest his head beside hers again.

"No you would *not* kill yourself; you'd have two children to take care of," Dee asserted firmly.

"You can't leave me with those monsters," he retorted and they both burst into laughter. Dee watched the gentle shake of his shoulders as she continued to stroke his hair. She glanced at her wedding and engagement ring, entwined with strands of his beautiful salt-and-pepper-coloured curls.

"I know you've said 'no' in the past, but would you consider getting counselling? Would you do it for me?"

"You've lost two parents and a husband and you've never had a day of counselling..."

"I had child-therapy when my parents died, for your information. I didn't have any choice - they made me," Dee told him bluntly. "It's just...I don't think you've grieved; I think you bury it. And one of these days, I worry that you're just going to explode..."

"I don't need to speak to anyone. I'm fine...as long as I've got you," Milo insisted brusquely. But Dee knew after all these months that she alone couldn't completely fix him. Of course it was flattering to be needed, but his total reliance upon her was rather daunting sometimes. She knew she would have to persuade him over time, but tonight wasn't the night. Milo didn't want to hear about therapists or bereavement or depression.

"...We should go to bed."

"Can't we stay here...?" he mumbled, virtually drifting off to sleep again.

"No, Mrs Dawson is coming early and Felix is in the house and I don't want to be caught naked down here. Come on." Dee physically heaved his dead-weight off her body.

*

The occupants at the breakfast table the next morning included Milo, Felix and Angel. Working quietly at the kitchen surface, Mrs Dawson prepared one of her famous continental breakfasts. Milo assisted the toddler with her meal and chatted happily to her as though he had never been happier talking to another human being. Angel giggled at all his silly, fatherly jokes and Felix watched him rather glumly. He was tired, he hadn't slept well.

Dee arrived in the kitchen with her son in her arms, freshly changed and fed and joined the men and her daughter at the kitchen table. She greeted everyone in the room, carefully placed Finley in his high chair and from behind, proceeded to drape her arms around her husband to give him a loving kiss on his cheek as though they were alone. Milo would have purred contentedly if he were a cat.

"Mrs Dawson, Felix, I'm sorry you had to witness that, but I am married to the most adorable man in the world and I can't help it," Dee mused happily as she sat down and set to work slicing open a croissant.

"It's only natural, you are still newlyweds after all," Mrs Dawson piped up.

"I'd have thought you'd have had enough of each other after last night," Felix grumbled, rubbing his bloodshot eyes.

Milo laughed in surprise. "I'm sorry, Felix. Did we keep you awake?"

Felix hadn't thought through his comment before uttering the words and he instantly regretted it. Glancing at Dee, he noticed her breezy air of just a few moments ago seemed to have disappeared. In fact, she appeared distinctly embarrassed. She flushed a very vague shade of red, lowered her eyes and pretended to be fascinated with her breakfast.

Milo continued obliviously, "you have to understand, Felix, I've been away for weeks and my wife is really hot," he chuckled.

"...Milo," Dee groaned.

"What? You're gorgeous and I can't keep my hands off you." Milo kissed her neck and Dee felt her face growing hotter and redder still. Mrs Dawson rolled her eyes good-naturedly and went off to dust the lounge.

"Listen, I'm going to take off." Felix stood up just then.

"Aren't you staying for breakfast...?" Dee asked weakly.

"No, I'm really just a black coffee man in the mornings. So how long are you around for, Milo?"

"I don't know for sure, a few days, maybe a little longer. I've chosen my predecessor but I need to work closely with him before I can really base myself in England for good."

"But I thought..." Dee began to complain.

"I won't be away so long the next time, okay? Soon we'll be together practically all the time, I promise," he assured her in a placating voice. "Anyway, you can always come with me if you can't bear to be parted from your amazingly virile husband." Milo laughed out loud, winking at Felix.

"Alright guys, I'd better make like a tree." Felix grimaced. "You have to come and see the house, Milo. You'll be so jealous," he smirked but he was not his typical, flamboyant self as he grabbed his things from the hall and left the house.

"Milo, can we not talk about our sex life in front of Felix or Mrs Dawson? I'm really not that much of an extrovert. I was actually very embarrassed," Dee said in a hushed voice.

"What? *I* didn't bring it up. Anyway, Felix was only kidding. He's a man of the world, he understands," Milo shrugged indifferently.

"You know, Felix has been around an awful lot...and I was wondering if everything was alright. Do you think he's okay? I'm a little worried that he's struggling with this move to Richmond. That new house is so huge; it's divided into *wings*," she said as though that was a ghastly arrangement. "Even if it wasn't, Ginny is always with Jerry, and Forrest is never around. I think Felix is lonely," Dee confided.

"Well then, it's lucky he has a friend like you..." Milo stalled for a moment while he thought about how to throw Dee off the scent.

"I just didn't want you to get the wrong idea, I know what you're like and I wouldn't want you to feel uncomfortable with our friendship. You know I would never even look at another man now," Dee insisted adamantly.

"I know that, crazy woman - I'm not jealous of my *own cousin*. There is only one guy that bothers me and that's Cameron. Felix is family and I trust you both implicitly. You know, I'm glad he's been around because I worry about you so much when I'm away."

Dee narrowed her eyes shrewdly. "…Did you ask him to keep an eye on me?"

"…No, I may have mentioned how anxious I was - perhaps he took it upon himself…" Milo chewed the inside of his mouth.

"Well, just as long as you're okay with it…but, to be honest, it has been really nice to have Felix around. I do get lonely without you. I haven't seen much of Bruce and Patrice socially because they are having relationship problems, so it's been good for me," Dee confided. "But I am concerned about Felix. Maybe you shouldn't have pressured him to move here. All his friends and haunts are in Chelsea."

Milo wrinkled his nose derisively. "I didn't pressure him. They *all* wanted to move to Richmond. And Felix doesn't have a wealth of friends or haunts in Chelsea. He spends half his life abroad, living out of a suitcase because of his work. Felix is a bit of a loner - hanging out with you has probably done *him* some good."

Dee sniffed, unconvinced. "Well, maybe you should spend some time with him while you're back. Perhaps he needs a guy's company - to help him settle in," she added.

"Sure," Milo agreed readily. She did not seem to suspect anything, not really, not the actual truth anyway.

TROUBLE AND STRIFE

The hotel bar was predictably quiet at mid-morning. Though Patrice noticed there was that self-same middle-aged gentleman who appeared to be staying for the duration as a long-term hotel guest. He sat thoughtfully in his usual booth drinking a glass of G&T even though it was only 10:00am. Patrice pondered what path would lead a man to stay in a hotel for months on end, drinking from the early hours right through until lunch, then return at teatime and drink until closing. He must have been wealthy to afford to stay here endlessly, but surely completely alone in the world to feel the need to do it. Patrice reminded himself it wasn't his business and decided to simply use this as a lesson never to end up that way.

"Who's this smartly-attired and debonair young man I see before me?" Dee said, sidling up to the bar to surprise him.

"Hey, you." Patrice stopped what he was doing (going over the stock list) and leaned across the bar to give his friend a hug. "What are you doing here? I haven't seen you in the hotel since...well, the wedding."

"Gosh, has it been that long?" In truth, Dee was finding excuses to run into Patrice or she feared she would never see him at all. It was easy to catch up with Bruce, he toiled (well, drank a lot of coffee) in her shop every day. But she could lose touch with Patrice if she wasn't careful. Dee was always careful where friends were concerned.

"You okay?" he asked sagaciously.

"Yeah, awesome. Milo came home last night," Dee replied, keeping a bright disposition - she didn't want these visits to appear forced.

Patrice arched his eyebrow with a wicked grin. "Oh, so you haven't had much sleep then?"

"God, I didn't realise my sex-life was such a hot topic for debate these days." Dee scratched her nose, trying to quell that new nagging doubt that had come into being this morning.

"It isn't. I just know what you newlyweds are like." Patrice loosened the knot in his tie and seemed to relax in demeanour as he did so. "It's nice to know you've still got time for your less-amusing other best friend."

"I've always got time for you Patrice," Dee chided, "particularly with your hotel staff discount. So, are you free to come for morning coffee and very possibly a huge slice of cake? We can stay in the hotel if you haven't much time - and you'd like to use that aforementioned staff discount on me..."

"Says the richest woman in Richmond." Patrice pushed his glasses up on his head. "Um...I can be free in about half an hour. I've just sent my staff off for their break."

"That's fine, I suppose I can loiter with intent for half an hour, I'm good at that," Dee mused.

"Hi Dee..." came a diffident male voice beside her. Cameron stood with a buttoned-up thick wool coat and a preppy university scarf about his neck. "Patrice..." he then acknowledged Dee's friend as a secondary matter. Both Dee and Patrice stared at Cameron in silence for a moment.

"...Oh...hi..." Dee glanced at Patrice warily. "What are you doing here, Cam?"

"I'm um...meeting a friend for coffee. I was waiting in the lobby for her when I saw you come in. I thought I'd say 'hello'..."

"Aren't you barred from this hotel?" Dee asked, not meaning to be rude, but she couldn't help but feel it was an odd place for Cameron to choose to meet anyone.

"Not that I'm aware of. I got thrown out on the night of your wedding - but nobody ever said I couldn't come back..." He awkwardly shoved his hands in his pockets. "I've wanted to come and see you about that...have you got five minutes to chat...?"

Dee looked to Patrice again for reassurance - he only shrugged. "...Well, I really do only have five minutes. I'm here to see Patrice for coffee."

Cameron cleared his throat. "Honestly, just for five minutes. I'm meeting somebody too." He led her over to one of the sofas, Dee looking back at Patrice one last time and they gingerly sat down. Dee looked across to the seating area beside the fireplace where she and Milo had finally decided to be together nearly a year ago. Well, more correctly - the decision had been finalised in the car park. "Look, I wanted to say I'm sorry for causing a scene that night. I hadn't intended it to play out that way." Cameron fiddled anxiously with a coaster. "I had been toying with the idea of coming earlier in the afternoon - to try to stop the wedding during the vows. But I just sat in a bar and got drunk instead."

Dee narrowed her eyes. "This isn't sounding a great deal like an apology..."

"Just let me say my piece. You're married now, so I know it's over."

Cameron was staring distractedly into the middle distance. "And I'm moving on too. I'm meeting a girl today..." He gesticulated toward the lobby with his thumb.

"I know, you said."

Cameron chewed on his lip. "I was just hoping that maybe when things have settled down, someday you might want to consider being friends again."

Dee shook her head decisively. "No, I don't think that's going to be possible. Too much has happened and my husband detests you."

"But if you made him understand that I've changed. I just want to salvage what's left of our friendship – I know we could never be completely the same as we were, but I'd hate to throw what we had away. I'd like to be in Angel's life in some small way."

"I'm sorry, I'm not trying to be mean but Angel and I can't have you in our lives anymore. You and I were never really *just friends* so we can't try to recreate something that didn't really exist. Milo is adopting Angel - that should be finalised any day now, and I don't want to confuse the child any further. She *has* a father. You just don't have a place in her world anymore." Dee was struggling to remain polite and trying not to be cruel, but she wasn't about to give him false hope either.

"Do you really think Milo is going to be good for her? He's so much like Lance - they're cut from the same cloth. And it turns out Lance was evidently a dangerous person. Your late husband very probably *killed* that woman..."

"Why do you keep bringing that secretary up? It's got nothing to do with Milo. And I don't believe it had anything to do with Lance either. And it's certainly got nothing to do with *you*," Dee assured him acidly. "It sounds as though the police are going to close that case so we'll probably never know what happened. I for one would like to put that episode behind me. You can't keep dredging up that awful incident to compare my two husband; they're two different people. And that's how I know you aren't capable of changing."

"But I *am* changing," he insisted bitterly. "I can accept you're married to Milo if that's what you really want. I just want to be your friend."

"And I don't. I don't need you, I don't even miss you," Dee told him bluntly. *Cruel to be kind, cruel to be kind, cruel to be kind,* she kept telling herself. "I wish you well. I hope this woman you're meeting today is *the one* - I hope she's the perfect girl for you. I want you to be as happy as I am. But I want you to live your life at a distance from mine, okay?" Yes, firm but fair. This was the only way he'd ever understand.

Cameron searched her eyes for a moment and slowly nod his head. "...Okay...but if you ever change your mind-"

"I won't," Dee asserted and rose to her feet. Cameron stood too.

"Alright...good luck with everything," he offered sadly. Dee gave a curt little nod in recognition of this and turned to walk back to the bar. When she chanced to look back, Cameron was already on his way back out to the lobby. Patrice was frowning as he stacked glasses from the dishwasher onto the shelf when she returned.

"Can you keep a secret?" Dee asked.

"Yes...?" Patrice replied hopefully. She was his confidante again - Bruce didn't own the rights to that.

"Can you keep *that* secret?" Dee rolled her eyes over to the place where she had been sitting. Patrice tried not to appear too disappointed that he wasn't going to be let in on something he didn't already know about.

"Why?"

"Because Milo has some pretty big jealousy issues - and *this one* isn't exactly unfounded. I just don't want to upset him. You saw how Milo reacted at the wedding..."

"I suppose," Patrice agreed.

"Anyway, Cameron finally seemed to understand it's over now that I'm married. I think this problem, at least, seems to be resolved." Dee rubbed her face to clear her head, just relieved to see the back of it.

*

Felix had worked up enough appetite to eat a brunch of sorts with Forrest in the dining room that same morning up at the new house. It was a rare thing lately that the two men were ever around at the same time long enough to do any more than say 'hello'.

"So was Dee pleased to see Milo again last night?" Forrest, however, wasn't eating. He merely refilled his cup with black coffee after black coffee.

"What do *you* think?" Felix didn't raise his eyes from a couple of slices of Marmite toast - that was a habit he had picked up whilst living here. "Next time I stay over, remind me not to sleep in a spare room anywhere near theirs. No, in fact, remind me not to stay over at all. My God, they were at it like knives."

"Too much information!" Forrest gulped, waving his coffee spoon at Felix discouragingly.

"I didn't get a wink of sleep; every time I was just about to nod off, they started up again...was it two, three times? I lost count - seriously. Oh, and they're not afraid to express themselves - no, no, no. You needn't worry your pretty little head about that. There's no danger of them being sexually repressed. At one point, I thought he was-"

"Alright, alright! I really don't need to hear any more details," Forrest warned him sourly. "They're a married couple who haven't seen each other in weeks - a *newly-married* couple, I might add. It's great that they haven't gone off sexual activity after having a child so recently."

"Oh, trust me, that's not a problem."

"They're in a healthy relationship that even God Himself wouldn't frown upon. It takes sex to procreate, don't forget. Where did you think Finley came from, did you think the stork brought him? Did you think they never *did it*?"

"Perhaps it was a virgin birth," he replied brusquely. "Actually, I like to imagine that Finn was just the product of a one-off drunken fumble one cold Christmas night-" Felix mused without monitoring what he was saying. Then he checked himself and began again. "It's just, now that I know her - she seems so innocent and childlike. I don't like to think of her like that, just like I don't like to think of *Ginny* as a sexual being either...Dee's kind of like my surrogate little sister."

"Hmm, that's sweet, but she's not," Forrest frowned. "Look, nobody likes to think of their loved-ones in a *physical* sense. I think you're in a bad mood because your girlfriend is away and you'd like to be-"

"Please don't finish that sentence," Felix begged.

"When is Joanna back from Europe anyway? You should bring her over for dinner here when she gets home. I know Ginny isn't hugely fond of her, but I actually think you make a great pair; both in the arts industry, both exceptionally talented," Forrest pointed out philosophically. "I know you're fickle, but the fact that you have so much in common with her makes me think that she could possibly be the one-"

"Must you do this matchmaking thing every time? Isn't one wedding in the family enough to satisfy you?" Felix rolled his eyes condescendingly. "Anyway, Cupid - you ought to stop meddling in *my* love-life and go sort out your own. There's an Australian girl I know who's just sitting there frustrated, waiting for some procrastinating clergyman to ask her out on a date."

"Oh shut up," Forrest glowered. "As I've told you a million times, that isn't going to happen."

Felix smirked. "Why? You're not a *Catholic* priest."

"You're unbearable when you're like this. Maybe you should go back to bed and catch up on your sleep. Perhaps you'll be in a better mood when you wake up," Forrest muttered waspishly.

Felix thought about that for a minute. "Maybe you're right." That would explain his morose mood. "But I might go back and crash at the Chelsea apartment instead." The flat that he owned with Ginny was still on the market but it was kept looking like a show-home whilst it was on sale - so it still had a bed. "Then afterwards I can pop in on my friend Alistair who owns the seafood restaurant on the Fulham Road. Did I ever introduce you to Alistair?"

"No." Forrest didn't know any of Felix's Chelsea friends other than to look at. They all seemed to be incorrigible womanisers with more money than sense and barely-disguised alcohol problems. In fact, he wondered how somebody as affable and charismatic as Felix *had* such horrible friends.

"Yeah, he's having some issues and I've been promising to go back and see him since I left Chelsea," he continued. "Forrest, seeing that you're a man of the cloth and you're well versed in giving good counsel - I need to ask you for some advice on his behalf."

"And what advice would that be?" Forrest continued to stare absently at his coffee. He wasn't wildly interested in helping *Alistair*.

"Well, he's not sure but he thinks he might be developing a very minor crush on a very married woman...she's a friend and he doesn't know what he should do about it. I'm really awful at giving advice so I thought I'd ask someone who has a decent moral compass...since I don't have one..."

"I thought Alistair was married..."

Felix chewed on his lip, "...I thought you said you didn't know him?"

"I said you hadn't introduced us. I know *of* him."

"Well yes, he's married, *unhappily* married...what advice shall I give him...?"

Forrest sighed; he still did not meet Felix's eyes. "What does this married woman feel about *him*?"

"Her? Well, I think it's safe to say that she's not interested in him in that way," Felix asserted sagely.

"Then what advice did you expect a man of God like me to give? They're both married. Alistair knows exactly what he has to do." Forrest finally looked up. "He has to back off and leave her alone for a while...until those feelings pass...because they always do."

"...Back off...right," Felix answered gingerly. "...But what if it's circumstantially impossible to do that?"

"Nothing is impossible."

Felix pursed his lips pensively. "...Okay, you've hit the nail on the head, of course. I knew that was the answer, he just seemed so genuine about it - not his normal woman-chasing self. I'll be sure to pass on what you said."

He rose to his feet cautiously. "...I think I'm so tired I might just crash here and swing by Alistair's restaurant this afternoon. Thanks Forrest, I'm going to get some shut-eye." He walked briskly to the door of the dining room.

"Felix, is there something you want to talk about...?" Forrest asked evenly and Felix turned to face him.

"...Me? No, why...?"

Forrest eyed him with a melancholic, level gaze. "You just seem so...distracted by something lately..."

"No, no, I'm cool. Nothing new to report - nothing you don't already know. I'll catch you later, Forrest." Felix quickly turned and left the room. Forrest sat very quietly for a while after that, until church matters called.

THE GREEN-EYED MONSTER

The coffee shop was remarkably busy some days later. The lunch rush had been and gone but even the aftermath of that was hectic. All were glad business was booming but it didn't help to lessen the anxiety and stress that success brought. It was overwhelming sometimes.

"Bruce, do you ever feel your conscience is pricked by how little work you do?" Evan remarked coolly as he made another sweep past the table where Dee and Bruce sat drinking coffee in the window of the store. Bruce was watching Ginny and Felix waving and bidding their goodbyes as they left the shop.

"I do as much work as Dee," Bruce stated blandly, still otherwise preoccupied.

"Dee owns the shop!"

"Sorry Evan, I was just waiting for Ginny and Felix to leave." Dee jerked to attention. "I'll come and help you now. Just tell me what needs doing." She brushed her choppy blonde hair from her eyes which was now long enough to sit about her shoulders.

"I'm not asking you, Dee. I'm talking to your layabout, freeloading friend over there," Evan muttered darkly. He had grown very fond of Bruce in truth, but he was fully aware the man would never pull his weight. "What do you actually pay him to do?"

Bruce stared from the window. "I don't get paid anywhere near as much as you."

"There's no reason you should, you don't do anything!" Evan retorted.

"I'm still on my break!" Bruce barked.

Evan was brimming with barely suppressed annoyance. "Your break finished ten minutes ago!"

"Evan, he's not having a good day, I'll come and help," Dee insisted. "You go for your break and I'll serve for a while." Dee detested serving, but stocking-up or cleaning the kitchen didn't seem like a viable option when Evan was rushing about on the shop floor like this.

"I don't want *you* to do anything, Dee." Evan just didn't seem to want to ask anything of her. It was like she was the boss and he needed to prove to her that, he as the manager, could cope adequately.

"Evan, don't be ridiculous." Dee got to her feet. Angel instantly appeared from the play corner and started skipping about her feet.

"I'll serve if you could just clear some tables. And tell Bruce to give me a hand when he's finished staring into the street!" Evan wandered off to the counter, muttering to himself. Dee grabbed an empty tray from her own table and began placing the used coffee things on it. She observed Bruce, still watching Felix and Ginny window shopping a little way down the lane.

Dee narrowed her eyes. "What's up with you today? You hardly said a word to Ginny and Felix. Have you quarrelled with Patrice again?"

"Yes...but it's not that. And while we're on the subject of Felix, why is he always hanging around?" Bruce obviously thought better of his apathy and began to help her, but with no trace of his usual good humour or sarcasm. "I come over to your house, and there he is. We're in the middle of a juicy conversation here at the shop, and he rocks up to whisk you off to lunch."

"What are you talking about? This is the first I've seen of him since Milo came home." Dee pulled a face. "Anyway, I thought you liked Felix."

"No, I've gone off him. So, am I being replaced as best friend?" Bruce asked quite seriously.

Dee sighed. "Oh Bruce, is that what all this is about? You *know* that other than Milo, you are my best friend in the whole world. I do like Felix a lot, he's really sweet but you're my closest friend and you always will be." She just couldn't ever say that whilst Patrice was in earshot. "God, you never made this much fuss about Milo when he first showed up."

"That's different; I knew you and Milo were meant to be the minute I set eyes on him. I was happy to step aside for true love. Felix is just some annoying hanger-on who thinks too much of himself and quite clearly has a thing for *you*."

Dee stared at him, aghast. "...Why does everyone keep-?"

"So I'm not the first person to notice...?" Bruce observed shrewdly. "Who else-?"

"Oh you're being ridiculous! He barely even spoke to me today!" Dee huffed, stacking used cake plates and tea cups from another table noisily, Angel pulling at her sleeve but she was too cross to acknowledge her. Why *hadn't* Felix spoken to her today? He barely made eye-contact. Bruce stopped the pretence of trying to help clear up and simply followed her.

"Didn't you see how he was *watching* at you every time he thought you weren't looking?"

"What are you talking about? Why are you being like this? What you ought to be doing, instead of needlessly making enemies with my friends who've done nothing to hurt you, is try to work out your differences with Patrice. You're in a serious relationship, you *live* with the man - and have you been to couples-therapy like I've been begging you to? *No!*" Dee glowered hotly.

"What's the point if he's shagging some other guy?"

Dee immediately stopped what she was doing. "...What?"

Bruce sat down at the empty table and picked at his nails sulkily. Dee sunk down beside him and helped her daughter up onto her lap. Angel put her arms around her mother's neck for a cuddle. "His name is Trey or something...he's the new finance guy at the hotel."

Dee pursed her lips. "You can't *know* something physical has happened. Patrice promised me he wouldn't ever-"

"I didn't think you'd seen anything of Patrice?" Bruce looked up, breaking his previous teenager-pose.

Dee cleared her throat. "I've seen him a few times, *he's* my friend too...and I know for fact he wouldn't lie to me."

"Patrice didn't come home last night. He texted to say he wouldn't be back but didn't say why," Bruce explained softly.

"No, maybe he offered to do somebody else's nightshift at the hotel." Dee shook her head adamantly. "Patrice isn't that kind of man. He wouldn't go behind your back. At the very worst he would come to you and tell you it was over, but he wouldn't-"

"Can we not talk about this anymore? I wanted to work things out with Patrice but he doesn't want to work things out with me. We're over in all but name - and it's just going to be a case of sorting out our living situation next. I know this isn't what you want to hear - I know you've seen us as your substitute family for years but we can't stay together just for you." Bruce reached across the table and pushed his hand into hers. He knew she was swallowing back tears as he spoke. "We both love you Dee, but you can't fix us. What I really need right now is to know my best friend is *still* my best friend..."

"Of course I am...Felix could never replace you."

"Look...I admit that I'm jealous of him. The way he thinks he's so clever and funny grates on my nerves-"

"But he *is* quite clever and funny...that's not a reflection on you. You're the funniest person I know."

"It's more than that. There's just something about Felix that makes me uncomfortable. And it isn't just sour grapes..."

"Felix is just a little lonely since he moved to town and I expect he'll get bored of me once he's settled down." Dee gripped Bruce's hand tighter. "I know; why don't we spend an entire day together this week? That means no children and no partners and no coffee shop - just you and me. We can do whatever you want."

"Will Milo mind? He hasn't got much time left with you before he goes back again," Bruce mumbled, but he was coming around and she knew it.

"Milo will understand," she insisted and was glad when he finally graced her with a reluctant smile. Still, she was aware that Bruce was the second person in her social group who had quite suddenly taken against Felix for no obvious reason. Well, their reason was the same impossible one. But Felix had no designs on her, Dee would swear an oath on that. He was Milo's loyal cousin and her new faithful friend. Yes, Felix was a strange one, maybe - perhaps he was an acquired taste. A taste *she* had acquired and her friends just needed to catch up.

"And yet again, he's sitting down doing nothing!" Evan growled from across the room. Both Bruce and Dee stood up with a start and a guilty smile.

"You'd better do some work or I'm afraid Evan will fire you and I won't be able to stop him." Dee gave Bruce a huge bear-hug just to prove she was there for him. She would *always* be there for him.

*

Ginny linked her arm through Felix's as they strolled from The Lanes into George Street on leaving Dee's coffee shop. Ginny gazed unseeingly into shop windows with no real intention of buying anything. He was silent too, lost in thought.

As if she had read his mind, Ginny began, "you didn't have much to say for yourself today? You and Dee are normally competing for the wise-cracking crown but your head evidently wasn't in the game."

"...Oh, I've got work stuff on my mind. I've got to go away again soon." He strolled along with his twin sister, no idea of where they were heading.

"Oh but you enjoy your work and being away, I know you do. I've never met a man who likes hotel rooms more than his own home the way you do," she said. "Dee seems so much happier now Milo is back, doesn't she?" Ginny remarked absently, completely dismissing his worries about leaving.

"I suppose."

"I hope he's back more or less for good soon. She does miss him terribly while he's away and they're so perfect together," she said distantly, thinking how she would miss Jerry if he was constantly abroad on business.

Felix rubbed at his eyes with one hand; they felt gritty like they often did when he hadn't been sleeping. "...I just wish Milo didn't talk about her the way he does since the wedding. Have you noticed he only ever refers to her as his *wife* now? Even when Dee is sitting right there. It's like she doesn't need a name anymore now they're married - like he owns her. He's all, '*my wife*' this and '*my wife*' that. I mean, I think the poor girl deserves a name," Felix muttered belligerently.

"Good grief, Felix, I thought you were the founding member of the 'Dee and Milo fan club'."

"Oh I wish people would shut up about that. As if anything *I* said would make him decide to marry her, as if Milo ever did anything because another person told him to!"

Ginny arched an eyebrow. "If I didn't know better, I might even think you were jealous," she laughed lightly.

"Don't be stupid," he growled.

"...Is this about Joanna? Are you seeing what Dee and Milo have and missing your girlfriend?" Ginny asked. "Look, call her and ask her to come home. She would if you asked her to. I know I've taken a while to warm to her, but if she's the one for you - I can get past that-"

"It's nothing to do with Joanna! All I'm trying to say is, I know Dee better now and I think she's a really special person," he attempted to explain - this was his twin sister, surely she could understand what his problem was better than anyone (maybe even better than he did). "I care for Milo, of course - but I don't always trust him. I think we all thought he was this new man when he met her but he's still *Milo*, he's still devious and manipulative. That sort of trait doesn't just go away overnight." Felix knew that best of all.

Ginny shook her head. "God, you're sounding more and more like Forrest every day. In fact, Forrest doesn't even talk like that anymore."

Felix ignored her. "Milo never was very good at treating women like human beings but even though he very obviously worships Dee and doesn't womanise anymore, he treats her like a *possession*. And now they're married, ownership is complete."

"So? The only person who should rightfully have a problem with that is Dee. She clearly loves the attention he lavishes on her. She's spent the majority of her life without any family, remember; Milo being slightly overbearing is probably a complete novelty for her," Ginny reasoned. "And it's not like Dee's some submissive female or that he dominates her. Milo is always saying that *she's* the boss in their house - which he secretly revels in, by the way."

"Lance was pretty obsessed with Dee too, if I remember the stories correctly. And he probably killed another woman just to make certain he didn't lose her-"

Ginny stopped and turned to him, stunned. "What on earth is all this about, Felix? Milo isn't like *Lance*. They're a really lovely couple - I thought we all agreed on that. Milo isn't perfect but he loves Dee more than anything - and he loves those kids. Maybe you shouldn't spend so much time around there if it bothers you so much."

"What is that supposed to mean?"

"It means you spend an awful lot of time with Dee lately and I don't understand what's going on with you. Maybe you should keep your distance because it's making you act really strangely..." Ginny hadn't started walking again.

This made Felix finally think and check himself. "It's not really about Dee...I'm happy for her and Milo, I really am. It's about me. I'm just tired of being on the road all the time when I want to settle-in here. Maybe it's just because I'm getting older, maybe I just need to make myself a real home – a proper base," he tried to explain. "I'm just so tired and I'm not sleeping..."

"Can't you turn down this next job? I've never seen you this low - perhaps you really do need to relax at home for a while." Ginny rubbed his arm worriedly. He was deathly pale, now she came to think of it, and this just wasn't the Felix she knew and loved. "It's not like you need the money."

"I can't, I'm committed now and you're only as good as your last body of work. But maybe I'll pass on the next one." Felix wandered ahead and Ginny watched him go with a nameless, but nevertheless real, unease. He had disquieted her mind and she just couldn't shake this new anxiety instilled in her.

*

Just spending an afternoon with her husband was something Dee relished; it did not matter what they actually did. Just kicking around at home, walking in the park with the kids, shopping - *anything* was good if it was with him. Today was no exception as Milo drove Dee back from a restaurant in town where they had enjoyed a wonderful lunch together. He had held her hand across the table practically the whole time (apart from when he was eating – and even then a little) and Dee just couldn't tire of this quality time with Milo.

Dee jabbered on in her usual way and Milo sat and listened with half a smile on his face.

"And Felix thinks my intellect is inferior to his because I like Jackie Chan and martial art movies, but he doesn't understand the complexities of filming that particular genre or mixing martial arts with comedy. Some of the films even have subtitles, so if that doesn't make me intellectual, I don't know what does," Dee reasoned.

Milo pulled up in a long queue of traffic on George Street and turned to face her. "You know, it's lucky I still really fancy you because half the time, I haven't a clue what you're talking about," he said with a well-meaning sincerity and gave her lips a soft kiss.

"*Fancy* me? My God, what's happening to you? You're already picking up the lingo. You've been here too long," she teased and he turned away to look back at the traffic again with a good-natured shake of his head. Soon the trail of cars began to move and Milo took an unexpected turn-off.

"I've just remembered; I want to show you something." He pulled up outside a smart-looking office block and looked to Dee for a reaction.

"Yes, stunning brickwork - typical of Richmond architecture." Dee rolled her eyes. "What about it?"

Milo sighed and smiled all at once. "It's the new Richmond branch of 'M. Phillips Property Holdings Plc'."

Dee broke into a childish smile. "...Really? You're going to be working around the corner from the coffee shop? That's great!" She threw her arms around him and he seemed pleasantly surprised to receive a hug for his efforts. "At last, you're going to be home for good and we can have lunch together every day and I can just call you whenever I want to and-"

"So you won't mind that I'll be heading back to New York again tomorrow just to sort out some final preparations?"

The smile fell from her lips and Dee stared out somewhere into the middle distance. "How long for this time?" she said in a monotone voice.

"Two weeks max. Once this trip is over, I promise I'll only ever need to go back every now and then...four times a year at the most."

"Hmm, you've barely been back a week this time and Finley turns five months old the day after tomorrow. You'd think you would want to stick around for that at least..."

"...Dee...Dee, look at me..." Milo physically had to move her jawbone to turn her face to meet his. "You knew it was going to be like this when you agreed to marry me," he reminded her gently. "But I'm moving heaven and earth to be with you and the kids - you can see that."

"It's weird because we're married and we've had a child together, but I feel like I barely know what it's like to live with you. When you come home, it's as though you're an honoured guest. I haven't cohabited with you long enough to learn what your annoying habits or pet-hates are. When you go back to America, I'm so cut off from you...your life is a complete mystery to me." Dee scratched the back of her neck. "You're the one man I want, Milo, but you're also the one man I can't completely have."

"What...?" He pulled a face, bemused.

"Honey, I trust you one hundred per cent. I *know* you'll always be faithful. But do you ever see Amber when you're in the States? I know she's a friend of the family and I wondered if she ever drops by..." Dee asked diffidently.

"...No, I haven't seen her since the Ball when I split up with her after kissing *you* at midnight..."

Dee bit her lip. "But you'd tell me if you did see her sometimes, right? I'd just rather we didn't keep things from one another..."

Milo watched her with a faintly amused smile. "My God, you've got it bad...nearly as bad as me."

"What's so funny?" Dee frowned, thrusting her bent knee up beneath her chin, preoccupying herself with her skate-shoelace.

"I've just realised something; you love me as much as I love you."

"Yeah, so?"

"But you trust me one hundred percent...and I don't think I do you the courtesy of trusting you as much as that..."

"...Oh-" Dee's face took on that crestfallen appearance.

"No, hear me out...if I just gave you more credit and had as much faith in you as you have in me, we wouldn't have this problem," Milo decided - it all seemed so obvious now.

Dee shifted in her seat uncomfortably. "...You think we have a problem?"

"When I go back to the States, every five minutes I'm wondering what you're doing. I wonder if some guy in the coffee shop is looking at you in the wrong way. Sometimes I imagine that you're thinking you've made a terrible mistake tying yourself to me when it's a big world out there with lots of younger and nicer men in it."

"You don't still think that?" Dee almost laughed.

"Deep down, I've always believed that I was more in love than you were. I've always thought I was lucky that you settled for me...and every day I'm secretly jealous of any man under the age of fifty who may or may not be staring at my wife." Then he chuckled to himself at his own insecurities. "And for the first time, I realise that you're just as insecure as I am."

"Well, I don't deny that. I trust you not to do anything about it, but I still worry about all those women you used to date throwing themselves at you, turning up on your doorstep totally naked but for a raincoat..."

"That has literally never happened to me - or *anyone*," Milo laughed. "...I just never thought you were actually serious. I thought you must be humouring me. But now I know that you worry just as much as I do - I think I feel better…" Milo suddenly felt terribly silly about all this cloak and dagger nonsense he had been putting poor Felix through. Cameron was history and had never been a figure Milo needed to fret about. Dee would always be faithful, in fact, she was as pointlessly jealous as he was. "I know I have trust issues, but I want to work on that…so I don't mess up what we have…"

"I'm sure you wouldn't find it so hard - but we're not together enough for you to develop any real faith in me."

"Well that is all going to change." Milo placed his hands on either side of her face. "Just so you know - I am totally incapable of cheating on you, Dee. I love you so much that sometimes I worry I'll scare you off. I pretend to play it cool now and then so that you don't get irritated by the way I constantly stare at you like a love-sick idiot. I guess I just haven't been with you long enough to get used to you." Milo smiled and was glad when she kissed him.

"But soon you will and I'll just be your boring old wife…once you see me day in, day out." She placed her arms around his neck. "And I can't wait for the time when we're always together; knowing the other inside out, irritating the hell out of each other."

"It's going to be great. And now the adoption has finally gone through, I can be a *real* father to Angel as well as Finley. Everything will work out, you'll see." Milo laced his fingers with hers. "Two weeks max," he repeated sagely.

"Yeah, yeah - it better be. Shall we see this new office of yours?" Dee let him go and pushed open the car door.

"Yep, and we should totally christen it."

Dee gave him a withering look. "…Again with the christening thing? Seriously…?"

*

It was a chilly February morning that Felix found himself sloping back into Dee's coffee shop after a short absence. His former daily routine had begun to follow a vaguely familiar pattern; breakfast, composing on the piano, seeking out his new play-friend for lunch, nightclub, calling in at Dee's for TV and more chat before retiring to his house. However, things had been different since Milo had been home for his week-long stay. It seemed inappropriate for the super-sleuth to call in on Dee when the alpha male was in residence. Now the alpha male had flown back to America again, it was with some relief but a little reluctance that Felix made a visit to the shop again.

"Hey," Felix greeted Bruce behind the till in a virtually empty shop. "If this place is always *this* busy, you might need to look for another job - I can't sustain the business alone by being your only customer. There's only so many lattes one man can buy," he smirked. "Is the boss around?"

Bruce looked up with a deliberate casualness. "If you're talking about Dee, I would have thought *you* were the authority on her whereabouts," he stated evenly and Felix was quiet for a moment whilst he digested that comment.

"...Um, nope. So, does that mean you don't know...?" Felix tried not to rise to the bait - Bruce was being unnaturally cool with him, right? He wasn't misreading this?

"That means I don't know," Bruce confirmed icily and busied himself by placing some huge frosted cupcakes behind the glass from a plate with a pair of tongs.

"...Bruce, have I done something to offend you?" Felix leaned up against the counter and gingerly fingered the *'The Little Book of This'* and *'The Little Book of That'* (or something) which sat by the till in a little stack to be purchased.

"You may have everybody else fooled, but I know what you're up to, Felix," Bruce assured him coldly and Felix stood stock-still.

Wearing his most casual exterior, Felix said, "...oh, and what is that?"

"I see the way you look at her. You're here all the time and if you're not here, you're at her house. Dee is a happily married woman; happily married to *your cousin*, I might add. Do you think I'm stupid? Did you think nobody would notice? Dee may be gullible about men but I'm certainly not." Bruce's face became flushed but his voice was like acid, calm but seething with a malevolent anger underneath. "I do recognise when a man looks at a woman that way."

"Oh. My. God, I'm so bored of this! First Cassie and now you - what the hell is wrong with you people?" Felix complained.

"Cassie, huh? She's a sharp one..." Bruce mused.

"No, she's got too much time on her hands - much like you!" Felix could have laughed until he perceived that Bruce's suspicions were a far worse evil than any knowledge of his recent subterfuge (coerced by Milo). "I've only ever tried to be a friend to Dee, but you pit bulls who *call* yourself her buddies, are just so consumed with jealousy-"

"Jealousy?" Bruce rolled his eyes.

"Are you sure you aren't getting your panties in a bunch because, actually, you're afraid you've lost your monopoly over your best friend?"

Bruce did not blink his glassy blue eyes. "No, no. I will *always* be Dee's best friend - long after you've gone and been forgotten. But she is *my* best friend, believe that. And I've been here through some of the worst times of her life. That girl has suffered and struggled more than you'll ever know and finally I get the opportunity to see her the happiest I've ever seen her...and I'm not going to sit by and let you ruin it."

"How am I going to ruin it, you ridiculous little man?" Felix could feel himself growing wild with anger. What had he done to deserve this malice? What had he ever done but try to help ease Milo's jealous mind? And what did he have to show for it? Dee's so-called friends turning on him out of envy, cloaked in some pretence about protecting her. "I'm Milo's cousin! I have no designs on her! You've got completely the wrong end of the stick!"

"No, I'm never wrong about these things." Bruce shook his head blandly. It was that nonchalance that pushed Felix over the edge.

"Well, you're wrong about this!" Felix was so sick and tired at all this spite directed at him that he decided to sell his cousin down the river. What else was he supposed to do? "There is only one reason I've spent so much time with Dee, and that's because Milo *asked* me to!"

"...What do you mean?" Bruce suddenly seemed to lose a little of his confidence, a little of his edge over Felix.

"When Cameron gate-crashed the wedding and caused that fight, Milo started to believe he was unhinged or something. He thought Cameron may be danger to Dee and the kids. Milo asked me if I would befriend Dee while he was away and tell him if Cameron ever showed up to hassle her. That's the one and only reason I'm here..."

Bruce stared, not quite comprehending what he was hearing. "Cameron is a simpering loser, but he was never a big concern to Dee or the children. Nobody has even seen him since the wedding. Are you telling me the truth? Because if you are, it sounds to me like Milo has conned you into spying on his wife because he- he doesn't trust her..."

"...Perhaps," he shrugged with faked disinterest. Screw Milo! Felix didn't care anymore. "I've told Milo repeatedly that Cameron simply isn't on the scene, but I made him a promise, and he doesn't seem understand that my presence isn't necessary."

Bruce narrowed his eyes suspiciously but he clearly doubted himself now. "So you don't have a thing for Dee, then...?"

"I swear to you, I am not harbouring any kind of inappropriate feelings towards Dee," Felix stressed emphatically.

"So you never wanted to be friends with her in the first place?"

"I didn't say *that*..." Felix replied, irritably shoving his hands in his pockets. "Don't say anything to her, okay? Think how upset Dee would be if she thought her husband didn't trust her." He watched Bruce's face contort in a suppressed kind of annoyance. "I don't even think it's about lack of trust. He just worries about her...and sometimes he deals with things inappropriately. But Milo is a good man and he'd be devastated if Dee thought badly of him..." He now began to regret his disloyalty.

"...I can't keep that from my best friend." Bruce did not meet Felix's eyes but his conviction seemed to be dying.

"...Well alright, tell her then. Do whatever you want, St Bruce of Richmond. But just ask yourself, are you doing this out of concern for her - or out of spite because you're jealous of me?" Felix eyed him knowingly. "All I know is, I'm done with this whole thing. I try to help someone and all I get is accusations." After playing the hard-done-by card, Felix turned and strode to the shop door.

Before Felix could flounce out, Bruce said, "...I won't say anything...but stop coming around here. Dee says you're going abroad for work, so just go - and don't renew your friendship when you come back."

Felix sneered. "You'd just love that, wouldn't you? As long as you get to be top-dog, it's fine to put the kibosh on any friendship she had with me."

"If you don't have feelings for her, then that shouldn't matter to you."

Felix turned as if leaving, and then his indignation caused him to look back. "You know how highly she values her friends...she'd be hurt if I just disappeared without an explanation."

"I'm sure she'll get over it." Bruce refused to meet his eyes again. As far as he was concerned, the conversation was over. And so it was. The conversation, this whole episode; it had to be over.

*

When Ginny cooked, it was never a run-of-the-mill meal. She had to source the finest and most unusual ingredients. It also had to look just as good as it tasted. So she found herself thoroughly enjoying herself pottering around the kitchen one evening. Her twin daughters sat at the table with their heads together playing some secret game that nobody other than them could ever decipher. Forrest sat across from them checking his emails on his laptop.

"What happened to Mrs Thingimyjig? Did she die?" Felix said as he rakishly flounced in wearing his smart overcoat.

"If you mean Mrs Right - she always has Thursdays off. So you have the pleasure of my cooking today. It's my amazing risotto," Ginny said brightly.

"Oh I can't - I'm off to the club," he replied.

"...Oh, but I thought Tony was playing tonight?" She was a little put out, she'd included him in the numbers.

"No, he isn't feeling very well so I offered to step in."

"But you've got other pianists to do that. I thought you were going to take it easy for a while?" Ginny planted her fists firmly on her hips.

"It's fine - I don't mind."

"When are you leaving for your next composing job...?" Forrest looked up slowly.

"In about ten days." Felix shrugged and grabbed an apple from the fruit bowl, ruffled the twins' dark curly hair, bit into the apple, said a brief, "bye," and left.

Ginny sighed and waited for Forrest to turn to her, she had been sure he would. And he did. "Forrest...are you worried about Felix...?"

Forrest closed his laptop. "Worried in what way?"

Ginny shifted uncomfortably from one foot to the other. "He just doesn't seem himself." She gave Forrest a searching look to try to glean if he knew anything but he remained blank-faced. "...But if you haven't noticed anything." She cunningly turned her attention back to the hob.

"...I may have noticed something..." Forrest began again and Ginny gave a secretly satisfied sigh, she knew how to make him cave.

"...Does it involve Dee...?" she said quietly but didn't turn around to face him yet.

"Why, what do you know about Dee?"

"Forrest!" Ginny spun around, frustrated.

"Alright, yes...it might involve Dee." Forrest scratched his head.

Ginny came to sit down beside him, wiping her hands down her apron. "Are you thinking what I'm thinking...?" she asked gingerly.

Forrest brushed a hand over the closed laptop. "It depends what you're thinking-"

"I swear to God - I'm going to make you wear this meal if you don't stop it!"

Forrest sighed. "Look, he hasn't confessed anything to me so I don't think I'm betraying a confidence..." he gulped and seemed to lose his nerve, but then continued, "but I'm concerned about the way he talks about Dee, yes - if that's what you're alluding to."

"...And when you say, *'the way he talks about Dee'*, what do you mean?"

"Ginny! You know exactly what I mean! I think he's developed feelings for her, okay? Are you satisfied that we're on the same page now?"

Ginny didn't know whether to be relieved that he agreed or horrified that he confirmed her fears. "Then what are we going to do about it? Should we-? Are you thinking about an intervention?"

"No I'm not thinking about an intervention! Do you even *know* Felix? If we box him into a corner, he will only deny it and then he won't trust us!"

Forrest shook his head. "He'd be mortified if he thought *we* thought-"

"But if he knew *we* knew...he would have to rethink his feelings on the matter, we could be sure he wouldn't act on it."

"Don't you think we should give Felix a little more credit? He does know right from wrong," he insisted vehemently. "Look, have a little faith in your brother. It's not a crime to be tempted. It's not a sin to *think* about sin..."

"Oh good grief, do we always have to make it about religion?" Ginny huffed.

"Yes actually! I'm a clergyman if you'd forgotten!" Forrest lowered his voice as the children had cottoned-on to the fact there was a disagreement ensuing. "...Felix is going abroad in ten days or so and he'll have a long period of time to reflect on this...indiscretion. I know my cousin - *your* brother - and he has a good heart. One day we'll laugh about this, I promise you. Secretly, of course - but we'll laugh about it..."

PREVENTING THE UNPREVENTABLE

It was not easy to extinguish an enjoyable habit, even if it was a habit that had been only a few weeks in duration. Felix sat in a racing green Lotus outside Dee's house and thought about the best way to engineer the end of a very agreeable friendship. Perhaps he should creep back into obscurity without a word so as to avoid suspicion, but that would appear *awfully suspicious* to Dee. Or perhaps he should manipulate an explosive argument with her so that she could never forgive him. But how was he supposed to pick a fight with her? They'd never quarrelled about anything before now.

Felix slowly pressed a button to wind up the electric window. As he climbed from the car, he turned up the collar of his overcoat to keep the cold air away from his neck. He trudged through her gate, along the path of her short-ish front garden and up the steps to her house like a man walking to the gallows. Felix berated himself for ever getting into this. He could just be enjoying a *normal* friendship with her right now if he'd only said 'no' to Milo in the first place. But now there were secrets and deceit between them that couldn't be overcome; not with Bruce and Cassie whispering malicious things about him in her ear. If he could only have come up with a decent plan before embarking on this today...

"Hi Felix, come in," Dee said with a cheerful smile on answering the door. Felix couldn't even remember having rang the doorbell. "I'm afraid it'll have to be a quick one because Mrs D is just about to take the kids and Bruce is coming over in a bit - we're spending the day together." Dee made that clear from the outset, there was no way Bruce was about to brook the presence of Felix for any length of time, the mood he was in lately. Dee was even wearing her grey padded and hooded body warmer and a cream cable-knit beret, so she was obviously expecting to be gone soon.

Felix gnawed on the inside of his cheek. Not only was he having to wing this exit from her life, he was going to have to do it quickly. "...Oh, that's okay - I was just passing so I thought I'd say 'hi' since I haven't seen much of you lately..."

"Yeah, I know - why is that? I've hardly seen you in days." Dee closed the door behind him once he had sauntered through into the hall. And when she had seen him, he was in the presence of Ginny or Forrest and he barely said a word. In fact, ever since that night Milo had come home and Felix had stayed over, things had been distinctly odd between them - frosty even.

"Oh, y'know - Milo was home, I thought you could use the time alone together."

"Oh that's alright then...I was beginning to think I'd done something to upset you. Coffee?" Dee asked out of sheer politeness, loitering at the kitchen doorway. She didn't have time for coffee really.

Felix opened his mouth to form a reply but the ringing of his mobile phone inside his overcoat breast pocket caused him to close his mouth again. He slid out the phone, evidently recognised the caller and frowned. "I'm sorry, do you mind if I take this? It's kind of important..."

"Of course..." Dee watched him turn away and head towards the guest lounge, answering the phone as he went.

"Hi...where are you...? In the car...?" Felix said into the cell phone as he entered the lounge and pushed the door to behind him. Dee twisted her mouth. No, things were still weird and she couldn't fathom why. Before Dee could begin to dwell on it, there was a familiar wrap at the door and she answered the door for the second time - on this occasion to Bruce.

"That's a first, you're ready to go." Bruce rolled his eyes.

"Not exactly, Val hasn't left yet and Felix has just shown up. But he knows we're going out in a minute," Dee explained.

"Felix...?" Bruce pushed the front door shut behind him. "Where is he?"

"Oh, in the guest lounge on some important business call I think." Dee scratched her head watching Mrs Dawson bustle downstairs with Finn in her arms and Angel trailing behind. Dee proceeded to fuss over her children, piling on coats and hats and scarves before they went out into the cold. Bruce paced from Dee's hall into the cubbyhole impatiently. He folded his arms and tapped his foot whenever he stopped.

"Dee, I'm going to put the children straight into my car. They will roast in all these jumpers and coats," Mrs Dawson sighed. Sometimes her employer was overly neurotic and it was something she just had to live with.

"Yes Val, but your car is maybe fifty meters from the house. It's freezing out there," Dee insisted, buttoning Angel stiffly into her overcoat.

"Mummy!" the little girl groaned.

"Dee, we are supposed to be catching a film in town, remember?" Bruce grumbled. Dee ignored him and proceeded to wrap a blanket around the already overdressed Finley. "We need to go now. Val can let Felix out, can't you Val?"

"No Bruce. Val has to be at toddler group and I need to say goodbye to Felix. Now he knows you've arrived, he won't expect to stay for coffee," Dee assured him. "Do you have everything you need, Val?"

"Dee, even if I didn't, I have everything the children could want at my house once I get back from toddler group. And I'll be bringing them back here before dinner so we'll be fine. I am an experienced nanny; just relax."

Dee smarted. "I am relaxed. I trust you implicitly, Val, but it's a sad world if a mother can't fuss over her own kids anymore," she protested.

Mrs Dawson rolled her eyes good-naturedly. "I'll see you at five, enjoy your day out." She left the house with her hand in Angel's and the bundle formerly known as Finley in her other arm.

Dee turned to Bruce. "You know what the older generation are like. They just don't worry enough about anything. They'll leave your kids out in the boiling hot sun without sunscreen or freezing in a tee-shirt out in the snow and tell you it's natural and that you're an obsessive mother for questioning their judgement..." she muttered.

"Yeah, yeah, now just tell Felix he needs to leave because we have to go," Bruce told her forthrightly.

"I can't do that - he's just on a call. He'll be finished in a minute." Dee scurried off to find her car keys. Bruce wandered back into the cubbyhole again and stared frustrated from the window. He had agreed not to mention Milo's overly-controlling habits of late if Felix agreed to keep his distance from Dee. But here the annoying American cousin was *again* in the other room. Bruce's annoyance began to get the better of him.

"...Dee, can you come here a minute?"

Dee flounced into the room with car keys in her hand like a truculent teenager. "Do you want me to get ready or not?"

*

After a few well-chosen words and Dee staring at him as though he'd gone completely off his trolley, Bruce witnessed that same look of bemusement change to a piteously disconsolate expression. She put a great deal of faith in her friends; before the arrival of Cassie and Gordon, they were the only family she had. "...Bruce, I'm really sorry but I need to sort this out. Can we take a rain-check on the cinema...maybe tomorrow...?" she murmured with her downcast eyes on the floor.

"Dee, maybe I should stay with you..." Bruce stuttered, "he might deny it and-"

"...I know you'd never lie to me Bruce, so if you say it's so - then I believe you. But you'd better go so I can deal with this or I won't be able to think straight. I'm sorry about our plans...we'll definitely go tomorrow." Dee rubbed his arm affectionately as if to reassure him when perhaps she was the one who required reassurance.

"...Okay, but you will call me as soon as you can, won't you?" Bruce scratched his head uncertainly, beginning to fear that maybe he shouldn't have started this; not with Dee being the way she was about friendships. He sensed something ominous was about to happen and if it did, it could only be his fault.

"...Of course I will. I'll call you later, Bruce."

Bruce opened his mouth as if to say something further but closed it again. What was done was done and he needed to be somewhere else while events unfolded. He touched her back gently and wandered grimly out of the house, down the Vineyard and out towards town.

Felix was still standing in the middle of the lounge, he pulled a box of cigarettes from his inside coat pocket and was about to light one until he remembered Dee wouldn't like it. He was still having trouble getting a word in edgeways past Milo's infernal rebuttals and denials. "Milo, did you even listen to anything I just told you? I'm trying to make you understand I don't want to do this anymore..."

"I know, you just said, and I said that was fine," Milo retorted innocuously down the telephone line.

"Yes, but what does that mean? Today it will be fine and tomorrow you'll play on my heart strings and guilt-trip me into doing something else underhanded that I don't want to do? I mean what I say; I've had enough of pretending to be Dee's friend just to keep you in the loop about Cameron."

"And *I said,* that's fine - about three times," Milo said with a deliberate slowness, spelling it out for him again. "Look, when I left last week, I didn't get to speak to you. I wanted to tell you that Dee and I had a long chat and I realised I've nothing to worry about. She loves me as much as I love her and Cameron could never come between us. So I don't want you to do anything you're becoming uncomfortable with."

Milo's sheer casualness infuriated Felix. "*Becoming* uncomfortable? You knew from the start that I was unhappy to deceive her and manufacture a friendship just so you could stay informed. You've conned me into spying on an innocent, if gullible, woman and I feel absolutely despicable! Cameron was never a concern to Dee or the children. He was never unhinged or dangerous at all. I've not seen him grace her presence even once since the wedding!" Felix knew he was becoming more and more irate. Milo had got him into this, Milo was the despicable one.

"Okay! Okay! I was out of line and I shouldn't have asked you...but I thought you liked being friends with Dee, I had no idea it was such an awful ordeal for you."

"...It's not that. Bruce knows..."

"...Bruce knows *what*...?" At last Milo voice sounded 'concerned' too.

"About our arrangement. I was dropping in on Dee so often; he thought I was trying to steal her from you...so I had to tell him the truth." Felix cringed as he awaited his cousin's reply.

Milo's voice was as cold as ice when he retorted, "why would you tell him that? You could have invented any excuse in the world but you told him *that*?"

"The whole thing was going to come out anyway so I thought I'd head him off at the pass...but Bruce is always going to be Dee's loyal henchman. He said he wouldn't tell her but you know he will. Those two are as thick as thieves..."

"So the truth of it is, you aren't pricked by your own conscience at all, you've just been found out and you're deserting the sinking ship!" Milo growled maliciously.

"What ship? This is *your* ship; your marriage and I should never have had anything to do with it! I was just some distant cousin Dee barely knew and now I've been sucked into this devious little plan to make her think I was her buddy, when I was only there because you coerced me to be!" Then Felix had the strangest sensation. There was a prickling at the back of his neck and he had the funniest feeling that he was not alone in the room. Felix turned his head and found Dee's face staring at him from the open door to the hallway. "Ah..." Felix stood motionless *and* speechless for a moment; surveying her face to see the exact level of trouble he was in. Dee's formally surprised expression turned to one of dejected resignation. She had been betrayed. She had heard everything.

Dee turned on her heel, stalking back out into the hall and into the kitchen.

"Felix? Why have you gone quiet? What's happened?" Milo's voice sounded at last.

"Nothing, I have to go," Felix blurted, hung up the phone, and hurried to catch her up.

Dee was already unzipping her gilet and throwing it and the beret angrily on the breakfast bar when Felix found her. He closed the kitchen door behind him as if trying to dampen the impending explosion. "I have nothing to say to you, Felix!" she snapped as he drifted closer, before he could even open his mouth. Dee thought she would want to fix this - but actually she wanted nothing more than for him to go.

"Dee...listen to me. You need to listen to me-" Felix tried to grasp her wrist but she slipped free with a jerk of her arm.

"Do I? I heard everything! There's nothing you can say to wheedle your way out of it. You admitted it to Bruce and now I've heard it for myself!" Dee replied waspishly. "Well, you are released from your obligation to Milo, so now you're free to go! Go on, sod off! You don't have to *pretend* anymore!"

"...You aren't being fair, Dee. You have to hear my side of it. I never wanted to lie to you but Milo is so good at cajoling people into doing things he wants them to do," he insisted. "Look, he persuaded me to look in on you, that's all. Come on, you virtually *guessed* that he had."

"You said you'd 'taken it upon yourself'. But now I know he *made* you," she said with a quivering lip.

"It wasn't like that!" He took her arm again but before he'd constructed a defence, tears were spilling down her face. Most people would have been hurt, sure, but Dee was actually traumatised. And he understood why. Friends and family were one and the same in her neat and ordered little world. She hadn't had any blood-relatives other than the children until the arrival of Gordon and Cassie. Dee had hand-picked her own little family over the years - and accepted Felix into the troop. She had trusted him; taken him into her confidences and invited him into her world. To Dee, that was tantamount to being family and Felix had totally abused that trust. He couldn't be more disgusted with himself.

"I'm just sorry the ordeal was so beneath you!"

"*Beneath* me...?" Felix shook his head.

Dee wiped her face with her free forearm. "How awful it must have been for you, befriending a dense woman like me..."

"Don't be ridiculous! You know me better than that! Milo asked for my help - sure, but I'd *always* liked you. Remember? At Christmas? We agreed to be friends," Felix reasoned. "The only thing I was unhappy about was the deceit, I wanted to know you *long* before Milo asked."

"Do you think I'm deaf *as well* as gullible? I just heard you on the phone!" Dee emphasised with a flash of her eyes. "You just told Milo you were sick of pretending and you wanted out!"

"Surely you know that's not what I meant!" Felix asserted. "I *always* wanted to be noticed by you...to be friends with you...but on my terms, not Milo's..." He noticed she was watching him uncomprehendingly but he ploughed on. "I won't have you think badly of me. It isn't fair!"

Dee began again, but this time more softly. "...You've totally taken advantage of me, Felix – you're a horrible person. I thought we had a bond...but none of it was real. You were only here because my husband doesn't trust me."

"You're not listening! All of it was real! I love hanging out with you! Don't you get it yet?"

"Only two minutes ago you were telling Milo you wanted to get out of this *manufactured* friendship!" Dee shouted at him, exasperated with all the lies and twisting of the truth.

"That? I was just saying that for Milo's benefit; so he wouldn't get the wrong idea – because of what people are saying about us. But not because I didn't think you were good enough!" Felix finally let go of her arm because she seemed to have calmed a little. "...People *are* talking, Dee; Cassie and Bruce are accusing me of-"

"...Which is laughable now that we know the complete opposite is true," she retorted bitterly.

Felix blinked. "...You know?" He stalled just for a moment. "...Well, what would you say if they had been right...?"

"What do you mean? What the fuck are you even on about?" Dee whined, nearly hopping up and down with frustration.

"Bruce didn't just *happen* to guess Milo had asked me to keep tabs on you. Bruce thought my interest in you was far unhealthier – that I had feelings for you..."

"I *know* that, he told me! What a fucking joke!" Dee was virtually laughing over the stupidity of the notion.

Felix sighed. Which was worse, Dee thinking him a treacherous liar or Dee knowing the truth? Honesty was always the best policy, right? Felix made his decision. "...You and I were on course to be close friends anyway... but it happened sooner than I planned," he began uncertainly. "The one and only reason you've just overheard that bullshit about me trying to get out of this friendship is because - I can't believe I'm saying this out loud – I haven't even admitted it to myself before," he muttered almost feverishly, rubbing his mouth. "I've developed this horribly inappropriate crush on you, Dee...." Felix confessed. The words in his ears shocked him as much as they did her. It wasn't as though he didn't *know*, but to finally declare it- "I didn't want to mess up your marriage. So I thought if I just got some distance...if I could just not see you for a while until this stupid infatuation passed..."

Dee was momentarily quiet whilst she digested this. "...Are you fucking mental? How on earth do you think making up shit like that will help you?"

Felix smarted in disbelief. "...You don't believe me?" His behaviour had been obvious enough for Cassie, Bruce and possibly even Ginny and Forrest to become suspicious, yet she saw nothing. Nothing at all. "Here I am, laying my cards on the table, admitting to just about the worst thing I've ever done and she doesn't even believe me," he said to himself rather theatrically. "You think I'm a horrible person and you're probably right - but for all the wrong reasons. I care for my cousin, but if I thought you were interested in me...I would probably go for it even though it would ruin my life! Oh, and a word to the not-so-wise? *That's* how fucking mental I am!" Felix was livid now. How dare she disbelieve him after an admission like that? And why could he only think about how pretty she looked, glaring at him balefully with those oddly pale blue eyes?

  Dee stared at him, astonished. "...What a load of crap!"

  Felix shook his head, stunned. "...How naïve *are* you?"

"If one more person calls me nai-!"

  But her protestations were cut off as he took her face in his hands and kissed her hard on the mouth. Dee stumbled in confusion but Felix caught her in the small of her back to steady her. Everything seemed to go into slow-motion then. During the effort of jerking away, the kitchen door opened and the two broke apart to find Milo there in the doorway watching them.

IN THE AFTERMATH

All three were silent and Dee had a strange feeling of dizziness as she tried to make sense of what had just happened. What *had* happened? Had Felix Kellerman, Milo's cousin and her new friend, really just...*kissed* her?

"...What's going on?" Milo asked in a surprisingly small voice.

Dee herself couldn't answer because she didn't honestly know and couldn't honestly speak. The back of her hand had strayed to her lips, as if trying to wipe away any trace of his kiss. Her eyes were staring wildly at Felix; accusingly, like daggers.

"...Milo, how can you be here?" Felix replied stupidly. "...I called you on your cell phone. You said you were in the car – in New York..." Felix seemed unable to get a grasp on the horrid reality unfolding before him.

"...I was in the car...but I didn't say I was in New York..." He was still watching them with a painfully confused expression. "...I was coming back from the airport," Milo said blankly.

"But you only left a few days ago..." Felix realised he wasn't making this situation any better but he was finding Milo's presence difficult to make sense of.

"...It's the anniversary of Andrew's death today...and I wanted to spend it with Dee and the kids so I came home early...I wanted to surprise them," Milo continued in a toneless voice. Dee's pounding heart nearly stopped. The first anniversary of Andrew's death. She had forgotten. "Why are you kissing my wife?" he asked, crushing any deluded hope that he hadn't walked in on them in time to witness it.

"...I don't know, it just happened," Felix sputtered.

"Are you having an affair with my cousin, Dee?" Milo asked quietly, closing the door and coming further into the kitchen, a steely flicker flashing across his brown eyes. Dee had seen that glint only once or twice before, and she had never cared for it.

"No I'm not! Jesus, Milo..." Dee was genuinely appalled. "I didn't even know Felix was going to kiss me, honestly!" she appealed to him, more than ready to desert Felix in his darkest hour.

"...But you didn't push him away. You let him kiss you. I was standing right there..."

"Milo, I just froze! It must have looked awful, you walking in on that but-" Dee began with a painful awkwardness. She was cringing as she spoke, knowing she was innocent but feeling so guilty. And every stammering word she said sounded like lies in her own ears - so how must it sound to Milo? "...I swear, I didn't-"

Felix stepped in at last. "Milo, Dee's telling the truth...none of this is her fault. We were having an argument about the arrangement I had with you. She overheard me on the phone just now, and she was upset - so I kissed her."

"...Why would you do that?"

"I- it was a moment of madness...I don't even know why. I'm so sorry..." Felix professed shamefacedly.

"People don't go around just kissing random people..." Milo shook his head, his eyes wide with disbelief. "Do you love her?"

"No, no – this is the first time I ever kissed Dee and I don't *love* her...maybe I have a bit of a thing for-"

Dee knew it was coming before it actually did. She saw the rage well up in her husband before it erupted like molten lava. "What have you done?! You're sleeping with Felix, aren't you?"

"Milo, no!" Felix exclaimed fearfully. "She didn't do anything wrong!" But before he knew it, Milo's fury was transferred to him. Milo unexpectedly struck out his fist and hit Felix hard in the mouth. Felix fell back heavily. He awkwardly hit a breakfast bar-stool and slumped to the floor.

"No!" Dee screamed without even meaning to. She crouched down by her friend, helping him to sit. "...Why did you have to hit him?" And why did she recall having said something like that so recently? Dee realised tears were streaming down her face again. What on earth was going on? Did Felix really just kiss her? Did Milo really just catch him doing it? This whole thing was slightly blurred; like an out-of-focus, bizarre dream. No, a nightmare. "Nothing happened, I swear nothing happened..." she sobbed.

Milo was at full throttle now. He hauled Felix to his feet, manhandling him up against the breakfast bar. Felix was visibly shaken from his battering. He had not actually been physically assaulted in a very long time, and to be struck by his own cousin was particularly upsetting.

"How could you do this to me? I trusted you! You were the best man at my wedding!" Milo shook him so hard, Felix feared there was more violence to come.

"Felix, just get out of here!" Dee skilfully separated the two before Milo could continue to use him as a punching-bag.

"I'm not leaving you alone with him!" Felix seemed horribly serious.

"Just go!! Don't you think you've done enough? Please, just go!" Dee cried so harrowingly that Felix gestured with a discreet nod of his head in agreement.

Shaking, Felix left the kitchen and slipped from the house. His hands trembled as he unlocked his car and climbed in. Felix sat there, too numb and dizzy to drive - but he had no intention of leaving. He wound down the window and listened out for any strange thuds or screams. Not that he was certain he would hear anything from here. Nevertheless, he sat and waited it out.

*

Milo was crying. This was always a very rare occurrence. If it did happen, it was about Andrew. Perhaps if he hadn't seen what he'd seen today, it *would* have been about Andrew. But not now. Now their perfect marriage was falling apart at the seams. Dee tried to hold his hands where he stood but he shook her off.

"What did I do to deserve this?" he wept brokenly.

"Nothing happened!" she professed. "You've got it all wrong! There is no affair, nothing is going on!"

"Then why was he kissing you?!"

"I don't know!" Dee screamed at him, but then attempted to calm herself. "...We were quarrelling about you...you know that. You were on the phone to Felix just ten minutes ago so you know what we were quarrelling about. You had no faith in me, Milo! You didn't trust me to be faithful and you coerced your cousin into pretending to be my friend to spy on me!" Dee was shaking. This was insane. Milo loved her, and surely she could make him understand, right?

"Well, evidently I was right not to trust you!" Milo almost laughed, but it certainly wasn't a pleasant laugh. "I was always afraid you still might carry a torch for Cameron...but I was worried about the wrong guy, wasn't I? I sent Felix in here to help me but in the end, I drove him into your bed instead!"

"I'm not having an affair with Felix!" Dee cried. "...I think he came here today because he was actually trying to *stop* this from happening. Felix said he wanted to get away because he had developed a stupid crush on me...but I wouldn't believe him..." Dee spoke quickly because she had no idea how long he would listen before he stormed from the house. "...I was upset that you didn't trust me. And I was upset that someone who I thought was a friend had lied to me. I guess Felix, in his wisdom, thought he had to prove he was telling to truth...by kissing me."

"No, you *wanted* him to kiss you! I saw it. He kissed you, and you didn't recoil - you closed your eyes. You didn't even try to push him away!" he glared, his eyes blazing like a madman's. Dee feared that *her* Milo may not even be in there now.

"I just froze, Milo! I pushed him away as you walked in! I didn't even see it coming, I swear!" she wailed, actually sinking to her knees right there on the kitchen floor in emotional exhaustion. How could she make him understand when she didn't understand? Why *had* she frozen like that? If only she'd jerked away an instant more quickly. Milo crouched down with her, just to keep eye contact.

"You're lying!" he hissed, lips virtually hidden they were so tight with anger. "This has been going on for weeks! You've been fucking my cousin behind my back because I wasn't around!"

"It's all in your mind," Dee groaned, worn down to nothing. "...I love you more than I've ever loved anyone. Why would I cheat on you when we had to fight so hard to be together?"

"Because I wasn't here! Because you've cheated on every man you've ever been with!" Milo yelled in her face and Dee winced again. "...People were forever telling me to be good to you. I was warned on a daily basis to treat you right. But I knew. I knew if anybody was going to cheat in this relationship, it wouldn't be me. I loved you too much to even think about straying, but you're so fucked-up in the head, you don't know a good thing when you've got it! In your deranged little world, I bet it seemed like a good idea to sleep with Felix so you could keep him in your life. I bet you've been doing it since you were a girl - offering yourself to men because it's the only way to make them stay! You think sex will make men care for you but that doesn't make them your friends, you little fool!" he growled like an injured animal.

"I'm not like that! You know me better than that!" Dee protested, horribly, horribly hurt.

Milo shook his head vehemently. "...I don't know you. We had a life together, we had children together; we were a family...but you threw it all away," he cried bitterly.

Dee was at a complete loss. "...Have you gone completely mad? I didn't do anything wrong, Milo. Maybe I misjudged a man's affections for me...but I didn't do *this*. I'm so sorry I forgot today was Andrew's anniversary but you're not in your right mind – you've made a huge mistake," she said sorrowfully.

"He was kissing you!!" Milo bawled again, grasping her shoulders now so that she had to look at him. But she was too horrified at this car crash of an event to even think of looking away. "Just tell me why. I know I wasn't here enough, but I've worked so hard to be at home with you and the children. I asked Felix to keep an eye on you but I didn't really believe you had intentions towards another man. I just wanted to make sure Cameron didn't come sniffing around. I just wanted to know you were safe. Now I'm finally home for good and you've gone and done this..." Milo lowered his eyes sadly, the rage finally seeming to subside - replaced only by misery. Was he relenting at last? Did he realise that the red mist which descended over him so rapidly had made him see things that simply weren't there? "...I trusted you, Dee. I've never trusted anyone before. You restored my faith in people, in love, in everything...and now you've broken my heart."

Dee touched his face gently – and he let her. Could she finally talk him down? If anybody was capable of calming him, she was. "...Why can't you just be *normal*? Why do you have to be so controlling? If you hadn't engineered it so that Felix was forced to spend so much time with me and left fate to run its natural course, he wouldn't have got the wrong idea about me. None of this would have happened..." She wiped the tears from his eyes with the pads of her thumbs.

"If I didn't engineer my fate, you and I would never have happened in the first place," Milo informed her flatly, his eyes hardening again. "Remember? The only accidental meeting in our relationship was when I first met you at Lance's funeral. Everything else was staged." The blandness of his voice made his meaning sound even more sinister.

"...I know that...but that doesn't matter – because we love each other. But you and I were meant to be, we would have found a way to be together if you hadn't felt the need to be so underhanded..."

Milo laughed at her bitterly. "But I *am* underhanded, Dee – always have been. I don't believe in fate so I control my own. And I do it because I can. I'm used to getting what I want, but I couldn't have you and you were the one thing I really wanted."

"...But you didn't *need* to meddle in anything, I was falling in love with you anyway!"

"No, you're here because I arranged it. I arranged our whole future together because I'm conniving and controlling. That's what I am and that's the man you married. I'm master of my own destiny."

"But you're not master of *mine* and I fell in love with you without any help! Okay, so you put yourself in the right place at the right time but you didn't fake your whole personality. I grew to love you, Milo, the real you.

You didn't engineer *that*!"

"...Maybe not...but what use is all that now? Everything is ruined." Milo stood up brusquely and brushed himself off as though he were through with the conversation.

"You forced that friendship with Felix down my throat...but that's all he was - a friend," Dee reasoned. "You have to believe me, there is no affair going on." Dee stood too and caught his hands again while trying to catch his eye.

Milo surveyed her quietly for a short time. He seemed far less certain, was he wavering? Just fractionally? "...I don't know, Dee. But he *did* kiss you and you did respond. Even if this was the first time...if I hadn't come home when I did-"

"If you hadn't come home when you did, I would have pushed him away! A millisecond later, I would have fought him off or punched him! The idea of it is revolting to me! I don't want Felix, I want you!" Dee held his hands tighter, desperately. She had to keep him talking, she had to keep him here...if he would only see reason.

He shook his head despairingly. "...No, it's over...my whole world revolved around you but now I can't even think of you in the same way." Milo gently but physically removed her person from his path to the kitchen door. Only momentarily did he glance back as he left the kitchen, and then almost seemed to stagger out into the hall like a physically wounded man.

"It can't be over, we just got married! We've just had a baby together! Please, don't do this to me and the children," she pleaded, tears spilling down her face all over again.

"I'm not doing this to the kids. They're innocent in all this. You know I will always love them and provide for them...I just can't be with you anymore." Milo wiped his eyes with the heel of his hand, then placed that hand on the door handle. Dee could not afford to let him leave; she could convince him surely if she only had more time. Milo loved her, deep down he must know she was not capable of this.

"No, please Milo!" Dee begged, grabbing his arm but he shook her off.

"I can't do this! You're never going to tell me the entire truth but I think you're having an affair - or *something* is going on with you and my cousin. At the very least, he kissed you and you wanted him to...and I'll never be able to get it out of my head!"

"Milo, please don't leave like this! I'll move to America with you - we never have to set eyes on Felix again. Just tell me what to do and I'll do it!" she whimpered but he was already leaving through the front door.

"No, I can never trust you again. We're finished, Dee," he said in such a small and fractured voice that Dee strained to hear him. Then he turned, stalked through the little garden, out through the gate and onto the street. He jumped into his Aston Martin and sped off in the direction of town.

*

The moment the Aston Martin had torn off down the street like a streak of lightning, Felix Kellerman leapt from his car and hurried up to Dee's house to find her sitting outside on the stone steps. She was wearing a rather vague, distant kind of expression as he slumped down beside her.

"...Did he hurt you?" he gulped.

"...No..." Dee replied blankly, using both her hands to wipe her tearstained face. A trickle of blood was drying on Felix's mouth but Dee did not care sufficiently to bring it up. They were quiet for a time.

"...Dee, I don't know why I-"

"Why you ruined my life? No, I don't know why you did either," she said flatly. "He's left me, Felix, because of what you did," Dee began again. "I don't know what I did to make you think it was okay to kiss me...but I *loved* Milo...and now he's gone."

Felix gulped emotionally. "He'll be back. Milo just needs to cool off. Andrew's anniversary must have tipped him over the edge – because he clearly wasn't in his right mind just now. But he loves you, so he'll come back."

Dee looked up with a desperate kind of hope in her eyes. "...You think so?"

"...Sure, I- at least...I think he-" he stammered uncertainly. "...Dee, when you came along, you set a precedent. Milo never loved anyone before you, so I don't know what he'll do if he thinks he's being cheated on..."

"I didn't cheat on anyone!" she barked. "You kissed *me*! I didn't even see it coming!"

"I know! I don't know what came over me. You were just so upset when you thought I'd lied to you and didn't care about you. I just wanted to show you that...I did."

"By kissing me?" Dee shook her head, incredulous of his stupidity.

"It was an idiotic thing to do, I see that now...and I don't know what possessed me-"

"No-no-no, you said and did a *lot* more than kiss me!" Dee narrowed her eyes shrewdly. "I covered for you in there; I told Milo you had a crush and you were trying to distance yourself from it. I told him you just kissed me in the heat of the moment. But *you* said if you thought I was interested, you would have gone for it - even though Milo was your cousin!"

Felix kept his eyes on the step beneath his feet and licked his top lip with the tip of his tongue. "...Then you know what I said was irrelevant, because I knew perfectly well you weren't interested..."

"But if I *had* been...? Is that true what you said? Is that the kind of man you are? You'd screw your own cousin over for a woman?" Dee glared hard at the side of his head but he still wouldn't make eye contact.

"...Look, I didn't know how today was going to play out when I came over. All I knew was that I had to find a way to distance myself from you. Cassie and Bruce were already onto me...but worse than that...I was afraid of what I was capable of doing if I didn't get away. Even though you were my cousin's wife, I didn't trust myself," he admitted disgustedly. "I thought about staging some kind of fight with you - but I knew you wouldn't fall for that. I'm going abroad for work soon so I could have just exited from your life in that way. But I knew you would wonder what had gone wrong between us when I got back and stopped coming around. Of course, Bruce already knew about Milo so I had to come here to try to smooth *that* out. Then I thought I'd just tell you the truth so you'd accept that I couldn't be around you anymore...but you wouldn't believe me. You were *so* upset that I just wanted to show you that-"

"You've wrecked my marriage, that's what you've done," Dee assured him rancorously, then was quiet a moment. "...Tell me what I did wrong. I'm clearly terribly gullible or stupid or whatever when it comes to men," she continued. "Most straight guys only seem to want me for one thing - and it isn't friendship. I know I'm not particularly pretty or sexy, so it can't be that. Bruce says there is something naïve and childish about me - which is a pretty creepy thing to find attractive in a woman. I've given men the wrong idea before and I want to know why..." she muttered. "Tell me what I did wrong so I never do it again..."

"You've done *nothing* wrong. I *did* want to be your friend...but I spent too much time with you and I - I got confused."

"If you give a damn about me, if you care for me and my children at all, you'll go and speak to Milo. You have to tell him that you did an insane thing and that I had no part in it. Please, you have to straighten this out. I don't want to live my life without him," she beseeched Felix rather desperately.

"...But I don't know where he's gone...and he'll only hit me again..."

"Felix, you caused this and now you have to fix it!"

"Okay, okay!" He rose to his feet. "I'll try to find him and tell him it's my fault. I'll do my best...I'm sorry, Dee. I'm sorry I screwed everything up..." He waited a moment for her to look up at him and perhaps share some of this blame but she did not. Felix turned away, walked back through the garden and out onto the Vineyard to where his car had been parked for the longest time.

WHAT TO DO, WHAT TO DO

When Dee reached Forrest and Ginny's house up on Richmond Hill, she found Ginny had only arrived shortly before her. Ginny had opened the door to her looking rather flushed and out of breath and lead her silently through to the lounge. Dee took Ginny's quiet demeanour as a realisation of what she had feared; that Ginny would blame her. Well of course Milo and Felix's family would think it her fault - they were bound to stick together. Sometimes non-blood-family didn't mean a great deal when push came to shove.

"...I guess you've heard what's happened then?" Dee followed her sullenly, that same sickly feeling growing worse again in the pit of her stomach.

"Yes, I've just met Felix in town, he's very upset," Ginny replied as she stopped in the middle of their extravagantly lavish sitting room.

"I guess you must think this is all my fault and I don't blame you. Even though you and I are friends, Felix is your brother and your loyalties must be with him. But I don't think I really did anything wrong..." Dee stupidly began to cry again and Ginny turned back to face her with a far gentler expression.

"Oh no, honey, I know you didn't have anything to do with this. Felix told me exactly what happened." She suddenly clasped Dee's hands in that dramatic way she had. "I happened to be in town and Felix called me as soon as he'd left you. We met up and he's admitted everything. Then he dashed off to try to find Milo to make things right. So I then called Forrest, who I didn't realise was here with Milo. It seems Milo left not too long before I arrived...and that was ten minutes before you did."

"...Where did Milo go?" Dee asked rather desperately.

"To some mystery hotel, he's sworn Forrest to secrecy. Forrest won't tell me and he certainly won't tell Felix. Come on, let's sit down and have a nice cup of tea. We'll all calm down and think logically about how we are going to fix this," Ginny then seemed to have a change of mind about where she wanted to be and took Dee through to the dining room. Forrest sat at the head of the table and was staring blankly at a tray of tea things.

Forrest glanced up just then. "...Oh Dee, I was hoping you would come," he smiled sadly and Dee came to sit beside him. He gave his sister-in-law a comforting hug since she appeared so thoroughly upset and began to pour the tea into bone china cups. "Before you say anything, you don't need to explain yourself to me. I know you didn't have anything to do with this. Felix made a pass at you, he admitted it to Ginny and to be honest, we've both been expecting something like this to happen."

"You have?" Dee scratched her head.

"Well yes, he's been talking about a married woman he had a bit of a thing for - well actually, he pretended it was a *friend* who had a crush on a married woman. And I feared that it he may be talking about you. Honestly, the way he goes on and on about you, it was obvious to both Ginny and I. But we truly didn't think anything would come of it."

"Well *I* did...and I said we should intervene, Forrest - but you refused," Ginny asserted pointedly. "You see, we're to blame too, Dee..."

"We couldn't possibly know Felix would act on his attraction to Dee! I felt sure he was a better man than that." Forrest couldn't help but feel terribly betrayed too.

Dee sighed. "...Why didn't I see this coming? It was obvious to everyone but me." She rubbed her aching head. "And I didn't even remember today was the anniversary of Andrew's death...I knew the date was coming up, but if only I'd not forgotten and called him earlier, maybe this would never have happened..."

"It's not your fault, Dee. This date is ingrained in Milo's mind but nobody expects it to be so for you," Ginny insisted.

"But I'm his wife! It's my job to know! Poor Milo, going through the loss of his son all over again and then seeing me with Felix like that and thinking-" she cringed. "No wonder he flipped out. Forrest, you have to tell me where Milo is staying so I can try to talk to him," Dee said firmly.

"No Dee, I made a promise and I won't break it - not yet anyway." Forrest shook his head. "Look, Milo is in a terrible state and I really think he needs to calm down before he talks to either you or Felix. He's not himself and I'm worried he may do or say something he'd regret. All you need to know is that he's staying at a hotel in London for a few days until he's had a chance to think."

"But he *has* to come home. This is all a mistake and if he'd just listen to me-" she gulped. "What am I supposed to tell Angel when she comes home tonight? That her new father has left her just like her last one?" Dee wiped her eyes at the very thought of her children.

"Don't tell Angel anything. She wasn't expecting her father back so soon so she needn't be told anything just yet. Once Milo has come to his senses-" Ginny began.

"Ginny, don't get Dee's hopes up. We really don't know which way this is going to go. You didn't see Milo so you don't know how badly he has taken this. You see, I've never seen him like this, Dee, not since Andrew died. He *really* loves you and he feels so terribly let down. I think you were the most important person in his life; he trusted you to love him, warts and all."

"Which I did," Dee stressed adamantly. "...Well, I have to admit, I didn't honestly take on board quite how calculating he was. You're not going to believe this, but other than Lance's funeral, all the times we coincidentally bumped into each other at the beginning...well, he'd actually *arranged* it. He knew where I would be and accidentally-on-purpose decided to be there too..."

"Oh yes, we guessed *that*." Forrest twisted his face and glanced despairingly at Ginny. "London is a big place. How likely was it that he should *accidentally* come across you quite so often?"

"You knew?"

Forrest shrugged. "Yes, we always found it highly unlikely and I told him so...so he admitted it. I thought you must have guessed the same."

"I thought fate was playing a hand in our relationship...and I didn't know until he told me when we finally got together," Dee mumbled, embarrassed.

"That's how we know you would never have betrayed Milo. You're so adorably innocent," Ginny said with a fond smile. Adorably stupid more like.

"...Yes, so people keep saying. Look, I can't sort this out with Milo if I don't know where he is. You must tell me, Forrest...I've got to speak to him."

"Really Dee, I can't. Call him on his cell phone if you want to; if he's ready to talk to you, he'll pick up."

"...What am I going to say to make him believe me? He's adamant that I have feelings for Felix. He says that because I *closed my eyes* when Felix kissed me, I must want him. But honestly, I was so shocked that I just froze. Milo thinks that if he hadn't turned up, I would have slept with Felix. Then, at the same time, he's accusing me of having this affair for weeks. Do you see what kind of irrationality I'm dealing with?"

"Yes, well he *is* the most jealous man in the world." Ginny rest her chin on her hand glumly.

"Do you think Milo will go back to America for good? If he does, I have no chance of ever convincing him." That worst case scenario came into Dee's head and she suddenly felt quite nauseous again.

"I don't know what he'll do. But Ginny and I will do our utmost to persuade him that you're innocent." Forrest grasped Dee's hand but she felt no better. Getting Milo back seemed more unlikely than ever.

*

Bruce Yates felt an utter heal the next day at the coffee shop and there was nothing Dee could say to alleviate that. Even Evan, who never missed an opportunity to tell Bruce how his behaviour was childish and destructive, must have taken pity on Bruce - because he just patted his arm, placating him now and then.

"If I'd just kept my big mouth shut, none of this would have happened!"

"I keep telling you, the fact that you told me about your conversation with Felix is irrelevant. Felix had come over to discuss it with me anyway. The outcome would have been the same even if I hadn't had prior warning…" Dee insisted. She didn't believe that at all, but had no desire to make Bruce feel worse. Bruce had made her angry; angry enough not to hear Felix out – and Felix then felt he needed to prove something. The three coffee shop staff sat glumly at the shabby-chic table in the window and stared dejectedly out into the street.

"But did I really do it for you or did I tell you because I was jealous? I was upset about all the time you were spending with Felix and not with me," Bruce sniffed and was actually on the verge of tears.

"The only person to blame is Felix," Evan pronounced, "and Milo for acting like a lunatic and not trusting Dee in the first place." It was a rare thing for Evan to defend Bruce but the poor man was so miserable, he did not have the heart to rub it in.

"I can't understand why Milo is behaving like this. I thought he was a sound guy," Bruce mumbled, shaking his head.

Milo's mobile phone had been switched off since yesterday and Dee had drawn a total blank on the business of contacting him. She had rung around most of the top hotels in West London. Nearly all took confidentiality seriously enough to be unable to tell her if a Mr Phillips was staying and others had never heard of him. Milo could theoretically be in *any* hotel in London or staying under a pseudonym. It was hopeless unless he wished to make contact with her.

"He's got to talk to me sometime, hasn't he?" Dee asked hopefully. "Milo is going to want to make arrangements to see the children at the very least, so he has to get in touch."

"Of course," Evan agreed.

"…I didn't sleep a wink last night and I'm so tired. I kept running it over in my head and I was thinking of all the things I could have done differently. If I'd just taken notice of the doubts that Cassie had about Felix or looked into why Bruce had taken against him, maybe I could have prevented all this," Dee said quietly. "Milo was perfect for me and I should have made sure that he didn't have any reason to mistrust me. If I was just a little better at forming friendships with women, this wouldn't have happened. But I always choose to believe I have more in common with men and I must give off some signal that makes them think I'm available. I'm so bloody stupid..." Dee snivelled and wiped away another bout of tears. She had gone to bed incredibly late because she had spent all of the evening texting or trying to call him, or pointlessly calling hotels. Dee even emailed him a letter. But still, there was no response to any of her efforts from Milo.

"Now that's enough of that. I'm a man and you've never given me any reason to believe that you're out for a fling or anything else. What's more, I don't find you in the least bit attractive," Evan said with an almost straight face. "All you ever did was go on about how amazingly wonderful Milo was, so Felix must just have seen what he wanted to see," he told her firmly. "You mustn't blame yourself."

"...Guys - I only came in to let you know what was going on, but I think I'd better go home." Dee packed her things together before she began to sob uncontrollably again. "I need to be there in case he shows up..."

"And what are you going to do about Felix? You can bet he'll be back on your doorstep to try to salvage any remains of a friendship with you," Bruce piped up.

"Well, I can't have anything to do with him. I can't give Milo any reason to believe there is anything between us. Besides; I don't think I can forgive Felix. What if Milo never comes back? What if my kids have to grow up without a father because of this?" That was the most heart-breaking thing about this situation. Those poor, innocent children could miss out on everything; no dad around to play football in the park or roughhouse games, or to check their maths homework or make them laugh with his silly jokes at the breakfast table. Just as Dee had no father figure, neither may her two children - not in any day-to-day sense anyway.

"Please stay. You need some company right now and Milo will know where to find you if he wants you," Evan said worriedly.

"No, I can't. I'll see you later." Her voice broke and Dee was out of the shop in seconds and both men didn't feel like talking anymore.

*

It was pretty galling to think that she had only been married for eight weeks and already Dee's second and most promising marriage had already gone wrong. At the beginning of March and three days after the awful 'kiss' catastrophe, Milo finally came to call. Unfortunately, the malevolent expression her smartly dressed husband wore ensured that Dee was painfully aware this was no time for reconciliation.

The two sat formally at the table in the kitchen after Milo had refused drinks or food or any kind of hospitality, he immediately began to discuss terms.

"Wait a minute, Milo. Aren't we even going to talk things over before you draw up some kind of a deal?" Dee interrupted Milo before he could open his briefcase (Dee thought it ominous that he had brought one).

Milo twisted his face incredulously. "I want a divorce, Dee - but I'm not here to discuss that today. I'm only here to talk about access to the children for now."

"You want to divorce me…?" Dee gawped at him, open-mouthed. The world really had gone insane. "Can't we have counselling before you make that kind of decision? I still really love you and I think this marriage is worth saving…" Dee did her best not to cry but was almost ready to start begging again – the miserable creature she was. "…We only got married in January, Milo, surely we can-"

"If I could get an annulment, I would, but my lawyer says we're not entitled to one. And we can't get divorced until we've been married for a year. So I'll apply for the decree nisi as soon as I'm able and then the decree absolute six weeks after that," Milo said as if reciting the facts parrot-fashion from his legal team. "So it's too early to discuss the divorce in any detail. Although I will say I was short-sighted enough to think we didn't need to sign a pre-nup before we married, but we'll talk about money and what you want at a later date." Milo still seemed to be ferreting in his briefcase but never actually produced any documents.

Dee stared at him blankly. "…I don't want your money, I never wanted your money," she shook her head in disgust. "And I don't want a divorce either! Felix kisses me against my wishes and suddenly we have to separate?"

"No! We are *not* separating; we are not taking some time out or having a break - we are through! I caught you in the throes of passion with my cousin and I've heard all the excuses I need to from you! I have grounds for divorce. Now I want to talk about my kids!" he barked.

She lowered her eyes, simply shell-shocked. Yes, the world and everybody in it had gone crazy. "…I will never keep your son from you," Dee murmured weakly.

"Don't even start! Angel is my little girl too; she's my blood and I adopted her because I love her, I didn't do it for you! I want fair access to both my kids!" Milo shouted vindictively but finally managed to calm himself. "...I want to see them for two consecutive days a week - *both* of them."

"...Well alright...I just wasn't sure how you'd feel about being Angel's father since you don't seem to want *me* anymore..."

"Angel didn't cheat, Angel didn't lie!"

"And I didn't either!" Dee rubbed her eyes, if she could just clear her head and wake up - this might just be a horrible dream, right? "This is crazy - I just don't understand what's going on..."

He seemed to be ignoring her angst entirely. "Right, so we're agreed on the kids. Here's my new address and phone number. I'm moving in at the weekend." Milo finally produced a card from the briefcase. "When they stay with me, they'll have their own rooms so they can sleep over. You were going to stop breast-feeding this month so I think I can cope with Finn by myself now."

"...You have a new address? Already?" Dee was wondering if she had entered some kind of alternate universe. Milo had left her three days ago and already had a new home with room for his children but not for her.

"That's right." He watched her staring vacantly at the address of his new flat in a luxury apartment building on Richmond Green. "It wasn't difficult. I'm in Real Estate."

"This is fucking insane! You've left me, you want a divorce, you've bought a new house and you want to take my kids away for two days a week! I don't feel very much like being cooperative today - you can go now." Dee stood up angrily.

"They're *our* children and we need to talk about this," he said, for the first time unnerved.

"You don't want to talk about repairing our relationship and I don't want to talk about sharing custody of the children. Isn't life a bitch?" Dee was about to lose it. She had spent days crying over him, longing for him to come home and when he finally showed up, *this* was all she got. Her tempestuous nature was brought to the fore and Milo would rather have avoided her rage. "Here I am, begging you to come home and you expect me to comply to your terms for sharing the children? Fuck you, Milo! If you hate me so much, why don't you go back to the States? Why get an apartment here in Richmond? You're just being pathetic! Right, since this isn't your home anymore, you can leave." She crossed her arms and glared at him and Milo felt this really was a good time to go.

"...Okay, I'm going." Milo rose to his feet. "But for your information, I'm staying in England for my children, not for you...for now anyway. I'll be in touch." He stalked coldly from the kitchen and out of the house. But Dee followed him, she simply couldn't help herself.

"Why are you doing this? This isn't fair! I've done nothing wrong!" she screamed at his back.

"There's something going on with you and my cousin!" he yelled, spinning around on the doorstep.

"Felix kissed *me* and I had nothing to do with it! There's nothing going on...I haven't even seen him since it happened! We aren't even friends anymore! Why can't you just be rational and talk to me instead of ranting about divorce and access?" Dee grabbed his arm and, crying, she said, "...I love you. I'm always going to love you..."

Milo watched her momentarily; his steely eyes seemed to soften for a second, welling with tears. "I just can't get it out of my head...I see you with him every time I close my eyes and I-" his voice cracked. "How can I forgive you...?" There was a definite chink in his armour, his resolve was crumbling and he was much less certain – Dee was so sure, the feeling was tangible.

"I haven't done what you think I've done. I belong to *you*...we belong to each other, remember?" She clutched both his hands now. Dee wasn't too proud to beg and plead with him again, if she could just make him understand that he was mistaken. And now was indisputably the time because he was definitely wavering. Dee had to stop this inexorable train before it came off the tracks. "We could get away from here - live anywhere you want. You, me and the children...we never have to see Felix or Cameron or anyone else you don't want to see again..."

Milo gulped back the pain that was so evident now yet so well hidden when he arrived. His watery eyes searched hers desperately and he began, "...I just want-"

"...Is everything alright?" Felix asked as he crept quietly up the steps from the path.

Milo stiffened, the window of opportunity slammed shut with a bang, and he cast Dee a hateful look. "Ah, your boyfriend's back," he snarled, barged past Felix and stormed out through the garden to his car.

Dee glowered at Felix reproachfully, scrubbing at her eyes with the back of her sleeve. "...Your timing is fucking impeccable."

I WISH I MAY, I WISH I MIGHT

Felix's lips were moving but Dee heard nothing but the tone of his voice. She was thinking about the look on Milo's face as he stood at the door. Although his words showed no real sign of backing down, the obvious sorrow in his eyes suggested he loved her so badly; he would simply die if they could not be together. That was before this idiot showed up and ruined all the hard work it had taken to break through Milo's icy resolve. If she could only see him on his own for a decent amount of time and talk about their relationship - where things had gone wrong. One kiss could surely not have caused all this; there must be a fundamental lack of trust which made this event inevitable. Andrew's anniversary must have unhinged him too. If he was simply prepared to entertain counselling and not hurry down the road of separation, perhaps this awful rift could be fixed.

"Dee, are you listening?" Felix asked softly. He was sitting where Milo had sat at the kitchen table, drinking a mug of tea Dee had begrudgingly made for him.

"No, not really," she admitted bluntly. "I was thinking about my husband. I really think I was making some headway in getting through to him until you showed up. I was just telling him I hadn't seen you since it happened and then there you were to spoil everything."

Felix blanched. "...Well, I didn't know he was going to be here and we haven't seen each other since it happened. I'm sorry I interrupted you, but I came because you and I have some things to resolve too."

"Do we? I don't think there's anything left to say," Dee shrugged dismissively.

"Look, this whole thing has been blown out of proportion. Milo should have trusted you enough not to need me to keep tabs on you and I should have been man enough to refuse him. But what happened has happened, and yet we *have* become friends in spite of everything. You're a really special person and I feel privileged to know you; I just wish I hadn't confused my feelings for you." He scratched the back of his neck nervously. "...I admit I still have a bit of a crush on you which was why I-"

"Why you destroyed everything!" Dee glared. "If you knew it was just an inappropriate crush, you should have ignored it and waited for it to go away. You knew I loved Milo and you knew I would never leave the father of my children, so why take a stupid infatuation to the next level and kiss me? I don't understand how your mind works!"

"If you'd never found out about my arrangement with Milo, if you hadn't got so upset about me deceiving you, I swear I would never have laid a finger on you. I would have gone abroad for a while and waited for this stupid crush to go away - which it would have. It was just seeing you cry made me want to console you..." Felix touched her hand but Dee pulled away coldly.

"I'm a thirty-one-year-old married mother of two and I can console myself perfectly well without needing to be kissed by you!" Dee growled.

"...I know that. But your friendship meant a lot to me. I've made a mistake and I'm sorrier than you'll ever know, and it will never be repeated. Do you think we could get past this and be friends again one day...?" he asked hopefully.

"Are you the most self-centred man in the world or what? My husband has just left me because of your *mistake*. He says he wants a divorce, he's moved into a new apartment on Richmond Green, he wants to take the children for two days a week and have nothing more to do with me because of your *mistake*," Dee explained with exaggerated patience. "So you see, your friendship is pretty low down on my list of priorities. I want Milo back, Felix, and your presence here makes that prospect even more unlikely. I'm going to do everything in my power to make Milo love me again and if that means cutting you out of my life, then that's what I'm going to do. I asked you to talk to him but it appears you haven't even bothered."

"I tried to find him but only Forrest knew where he was. Do you really have to cut me out of your life? Is that what he wants?"

"I don't know what he wants! He won't talk to me!" Dee rubbed her face, she really couldn't take much more of this nightmarish episode of her life; her mental health seemed to be deteriorating before her very eyes. "I can't see you anymore. If you're not around then maybe one day he'll realise there was nothing going on with you," Dee decided.

"It shouldn't be like this. You didn't do anything wrong - *I* messed up. If he trusted you, he should have believed you straight away. He has the right be angry with me, of course, but even I deserve the right to be forgiven some time." Felix shook his head fretfully. "I did the wrong thing, but can't you ever forgive me...?" he asked dispiritedly.

Dee rose to her feet, itching to have him out of here in case Milo should decide to come back. Felix must never be here in this house or in her presence again – his being here could only ever give Milo the wrong impression. "No I can't, your friendship has cost me my marriage. We part ways here and now." Dee continued to stand and glare so that he got the message that it was time to leave. "You ought to be more concerned about fixing your relationship with your cousin, it's him you should be fighting to keep in your life."

"I want that more than anything...but that doesn't make you less important to me," he tried to explain.

"You need to go now, Felix. And I don't want you to call me or to show up here or at the coffee shop anymore," Dee said determinedly.

"...If that's what you really want," he muttered, unable to believe he had been shut out by both his cousin and his new friend. How had things come to this?

"That's what I want." Dee showed him to the door. Felix gave her an imploring glance before realising that she was unmovable. Then he left.

*

Bottle feeding Finley full-time was not proving to be the easiest transition. The little boy had been fed from a bottle plenty of times before but it never was what he *really* wanted. Dee was finding the change a somewhat tricky adjustment too; she was having to let her milk dry up before she was truly ready. It was painful physically and mentally. Still, it was very nearly time to start him on solid foods - so it was going to get easier, Dee had to keep reminding herself of that. She stared sightlessly at Angel's discarded colouring book and crayons; the child had utilised every colour she possessed in her arsenal. But this masterpiece had been abandoned as soon as her gymnastics lesson had begun. Dee was left to loiter in the gym café-viewing area with Finn where she sipped on an overly-weak cup of tea and chewed on an uninteresting digestive biscuit. Milo had departed two weeks ago and Dee was still trying to contemplate life without him. Every day that went by, his loss seemed more real, more permanent.

"Hi Dee, I was hoping I would bump into you today," Ginny pronounced, sitting down at the table. Dee glanced down through the glass wall into the gym below where Paddy and Melody had belated joined their gym class which ran alongside Angel's. "I've been trying to call you."

"...Hi Ginny, sorry I forgot to charge my mobile and I've just been out and about with the kids all day," Dee explained. A few days ago, that would have been unthinkable - Milo might call at any time. But recently Dee had realised he was in no rush to talk to her. This amazing turn-around she had been hoping for might never happen at all.

"Well I'm glad you're still managing to get out and about," Ginny smiled and Dee nodded dully. "I didn't know you were bottle feeding Finley now," she remarked.

"Yeah, well he's nearly six months and I was probably going to stop breastfeeding then anyway. But now Milo has moved out, I thought I'd better start bottle feeding him all the time. His father has to be able to look after him without me. I'm starting him on solids this week too...so Milo really should be as capable as I am," Dee sighed. She would be sending the children over to Milo's this weekend for the first time – without her.

"Hmm, I'd love to see him cope with the broken nights of sleep and when the children are sick or having tantrums," Ginny scowled.

"You do think Milo will cope, don't you?" Dee put down a green crayon she had been fiddling with.

"Of course he will - he has no choice but to cope. But there's no substitute for a child's mother, I don't care what anyone says," Ginny spat fiercely. As a single mother herself, she had no real faith in the 'new man'.

"But you think the children will be safe?" Dee enquired worriedly. What if one of them *should* be unwell? Could Milo really cope alone with that?

"Milo would never put Angel or Finley in danger, Dee. I would like to murder my cousin sometimes, but he does love the children. If he's out of his depth, he will call you or failing that, Mrs Dawson or even me." Ginny stared at the menu but took none of it in and then gesticulated down at Angel on the gym floor. "Does she know what's going on?"

"...Sort of. She knows her daddy and mummy have quarrelled and are taking some time out to think things over. Milo is taking them to his new apartment on Saturday morning for the weekend, so she had to know the truth." That had been the hardest conversation in the world. Angel had cried a little but took the news better than expected. Dee had explained how it was similar to when Angel fell out with friends at nursery (which it wasn't).

"This whole thing is ridiculous." Ginny shook her head. "Why does he have to find himself a new apartment so soon? Why can't he stop and think about it before being so final about everything?"

"...I can understand why he's upset. If I caught him in a clinch with another woman, I would be furious too." That was fairly new. Dee was *trying* to see things from Milo's perspective. "But I'd like to think that once I'd gone away and thought about it for a few days, I would have come to my senses and calmed down. It was just a kiss, for God's sake - not an affair. It wasn't even a kiss I had consented to!" Dee still felt so hard done by. She knew she had been pretty dim not to suspect Felix was forming feelings for her when he was constantly turning up on her doorstep, but she just hadn't imagined he would do such a thing when he had been such a supporter of Milo's and her relationship. "I expect Felix has told you that I don't want to be friends anymore..."

"Yes," Ginny admitted.

"Ginny, I think it's really big of you to want to be my friend. I know you must have the greatest allegiance to Felix because he's your twin brother. I just want to say that I'm really grateful you haven't turned on me because that would have made my life so much worse. Other than my cousin Cassie, you're the only female friend I have," Dee confessed. "But I do understand if you feel Felix has become a bit of a scapegoat. I've been thinking about it a lot. He really did screw up, but I honestly believe he hadn't set out to make a pass at me that day. I'd like to forgive him but if I did, there's just no chance Milo will ever come back."

"I do love my brother, but if I were you, I wouldn't waste too much of your pity on Felix. This isn't the first time he's done something like this - which is one of the reasons I was so quick to believe you were innocent," Ginny confided.

Dee raised an eyebrow. "...How do you mean?"

"I think Felix has some issues with boundaries when it comes to women he can't have. He did the same thing with one of Milo's other girlfriends – well, his *wife*, actually."

"Renee?" Dee gasped but Ginny was staring distractedly over her shoulder.

"...Um Dee, I'm sorry but I forgot to tell you Jerry was with me. He's just been on a business call in the car," she grimaced.

"You brought Jerry to the girls' *gym class*?" Dee suddenly looked about her as if in a panic. "Oh Ginny, I don't want to see Jerry! He'll only sit there and gloat." She hurriedly tried to scoop Finn and the kids' things together, not really knowing where she was supposed to hide whilst Angel was in a class. But she knew it was too late when Jerry appeared at the viewing-room door and caught sight of her at the table.

"Dee, how are you?" Jerry said as he sat down at the table with a rather pitying look on his face. "How are you feeling? I thought you might come and see me. I know you probably thought I was going to say 'I told you so' but I really wouldn't have."

"No, of course you wouldn't," Dee replied grimly. Her mind was still reeling over the revelation about Felix and Renee. She would love to ask more but was not about to do that in the presence of Jerry Stark.

"But I *was* right about Milo, wasn't I? I said he was no good…" Jerry eyed her pointedly, ruffling Finn's hair.

Dee gulped down a lump of rage threatening to well up and burst forth. "Jerry, this isn't entirely Milo's fault. It was the anniversary of Andrew's death and he must already have been upset. He overreacted to something he *thought* he saw – but didn't. You must understand why he'd feel so hurt. Yes, he has some jealousy issues, but he's not a naturally cruel person." Even now, Dee would defend him to the end. Especially in front of Jerry. "This is totally out of character for him…"

Jerry twisted his mouth, bemused. "Out of character? No Dee, the only out of character thing Milo ever did was *marry you*," Jerry said with a stoic yet underlying patronising tone. "The Milo I know would want a fling with you, sure, but nothing more. Then his son died and you got pregnant. Probably in a rash moment he thought he could make a life with you, but the real Milo was going to surface eventually. Him *leaving* you, now that's in character."

"Jerry, what an awful thing to say! That's my cousin you're talking about!" Ginny argued, totally incensed.

"Yes, and *my* half brother, and evidently I know him better than both of you."

Dee shook her head adamantly. "I knew you would never give Milo the benefit of the doubt, but what you're saying doesn't add up. He loved me, I know he did - he wanted to get married more than anything. Milo was the one who desperately wanted to bring the wedding forward. Why would a man go to all that trouble if he wasn't fully committed?" Her husband's past passionate adoration was all Dee had been clinging on to. His former kindness was all she had left to give her any hope. And Milo had been incredibly kind and considerate and loving - there was no way that was an act.

"I'm not actually saying he didn't *love* you. I have a feeling he probably did in his own twisted way. But you two barely knew each other. Maybe he just realised too late he couldn't live that kind of run-of-the-mill life. Maybe Felix was the opening he needed for a way out."

Completely against her wishes, Dee found herself crying again; big tears rolling down her cheeks. It was so unexpected and sudden that she couldn't control it. She shamefacedly covered her eyes with her hands - why was she doing this in front of Jerry?

"Jerry! How could you?" Ginny gaped, repulsed by her boyfriend's harshness.

"I'm just offering an unbiased opinion because none of the Kellermans or

Phillipses see him for what he really is," Jerry said defensively.

"It's not true! Milo loves me! He's just trying to punish me, that's all...I know he'll come back!" She desperately mopped the unwelcome tears from her face and Ginny tried to comfort her.

"Well, I doubt that very much, and I think you'd be happier in the long run if he didn't. Don't think this is me giving you permission to start seeing that flake Felix..."

"You say one more word about my brother-!" Ginny threatened him menacingly.

"What? I mean, I know he's your twin so you have to defend him but he's not exactly suitable for Dee, is he? He's like a big child flitting from one affair to another, never settling down - and he's hardly dependable," Jerry continued arrogantly, absolutely refusing to see he was on rocky ground.

"I don't have to listen to this," Dee seethed, scooping up Finley unceremoniously, knocking over a chrome chair in the process.

"I'm on your side, Dee! I'm just being honest with you – you'll only ever get honesty from me..." Jerry explained, still managing to sound aloof. "You can't still be defending him after what he's done?"

"Milo got the wrong end of the stick, but he's not a bad person! He's going to snap out of this and come to his senses because he loves me and he loves his children!" Dee glared, just about to stalk out in anger but too late remembering the half-completed gym lesson. She supposed she could sit in the car and wait...

"...Dee, don't worry," Ginny said, jumping to her rescue. "I'll um...I'll drop Angel off at your house when they've finished up here."

"Thank you, Ginny," Dee said gratefully. "But don't bring *him*." She glowered again at Jerry and bustled angrily from the room.

Ginny turned her attention back to Jerry in stunned disgust. "...What is wrong with you?"

PERSONA NON GRATA

Dee knew April would be an unpleasant month before it even arrived. She was standing listlessly in a cash machine queue on George Street thinking about how she had been pregnant this time last year and life was just about to take an upward turn. A year later, all those dreams had turned to mush. Dee would have been better off if she had turned Milo's marriage proposal down back then. At least the heartache would have lessened by now.

Milo had left her nearly a month ago and Dee had suffered a couple of two-day stints without the children. The anguish she had experienced spending those few nights away from her six-month-old baby and her little girl had been excruciating but she felt she was unable to deny Milo this right however much she wanted to.

"I knew it was you from a hundred yards down the street," said a friendly American voice. "Nobody else dresses like that around here."

Dee turned to face Felix and was too intrigued to maintain a cold front. "...Like what?"

"Like a thirty-two-year-old female, mother-of-two gangster," he smirked, shoving his hands in his trouser pockets and surveyed his ex-friend. She wore a black woollen beanie rammed down on her head and was cocooned inside a large khaki parka.

"I'm not thirty-two until October, thank you," Dee replied with a good-natured frown. She was so busy wondering if she really did dress inappropriately for her age and character, she forgot to be frosty with Felix.

"Aren't you a bit warm in that? Spring has sprung and all," Felix remarked.

"How long have you lived in England? Spring happens when it bloody well feels like it, not because it just happens to be April," Dee assured him forthrightly. This April did not want seem to be able to outrun the winter no matter how much one wished it would. "Anyway, I feel the cold more than most..."

"...Yes, I remember," Felix said with a fond smile. "So, the big guy turns forty-four next week, huh?"

Dee sighed. "...Yes. What *do* you buy for the man who has everything but hates your guts?"

He laughed. "I don't know - does Hallmark do a card for that? Y'know, for separated-wives and despised-adopted-cousins?" Felix let his eyes fall to the ground more sombrely. "...Well, if they do - I couldn't find one. So I'm just sending a regular birthday card...with a short note to say I'm sorry. If I send anything more, it seems like I'm trying to buy his forgiveness and if I don't send anything at all, it looks like I didn't care enough to remember," Felix figured.

"...I don't think there's any more we can do than that," Dee agreed sadly. "So have you managed to see him yet - to apologise...?"

"Sure, if you class me turning up at his new apartment a few times but never getting past the door as an apology."

"...Mm, he only lets *me* in to drop off the children..." She stared out into the busy High Street absently. "It seems like I haven't seen you in weeks..."

"Well, yeah...because you asked me not to come over anymore." Felix kind of grimaced awkwardly.

"...Oh yes..." Dee laughed more out of embarrassment than anything and he laughed with her. She had been so thoroughly depressed about Milo, she had forgotten how much she missed Felix, how much she missed his sense of humour.

He stared at his feet again momentarily. "...Are you taking the kids to his party?"

"...What party?" Dee murmured with a gulp.

"You know - the party he's throwing at his house on Saturday. Aren't you invited...?"

Dee exhaled again, even more miserably. "I shouldn't think so, I'm just hearing about it for the first time from you, aren't I? Are you going...?" she ventured diffidently.

"Oh sure! I'm guest of honour!" Felix chuckled a little bitterly. "No, I certainly won't be there. Which is why I was thinking maybe us outcasts should really be sticking together..."

Dee felt her stomach tighten and close in on itself. Then she looked around worriedly. "...I'd better get going, Felix."

"You haven't even withdrawn any money from the bank yet." Felix gestured with a jerk of his head towards the ATM queue which had long left her behind.

"...It doesn't matter. I'll only spend it. Well, I'll see you around-" Dee stammered a little nervously.

"Are you afraid to even be *seen* with me?" Felix asked with obvious disappointment on his face.

"Well, yes..." Dee admitted. "If he keeps seeing me with you, he'll never come back," she declared with a rather desperate tone and an expression that told him she knew this was pathetic; *she* was pathetic.

"I have a horrible feeling that he's never going to come back whatever you do..." Felix advised with a sullen sigh.

Dee looked out at the street again glumly. "...Well, I have to hope." But every day her hope diminished just a little more. Nearly a month had passed her by and he hadn't come home, he'd barely even spoken to her.

"...Okay...I understand. Anyway, I'm glad I bumped into you because I just wanted to say goodbye," Felix added fairly brightly just as she was turning to go.

"...Goodbye?" Dee stood stock-still.

"...Well, not forever - I think. I'm just going to New York for a couple of months to oversee the opening of a play on Broadway - I composed the music," Felix explained.

"Oh, I'd forgotten about that..." Dee was quiet as she digested this for a second.

"I was supposed to have left a couple of weeks ago but I stuck around because I'd hoped to try to fix things here with Milo and your good self before I left. But I haven't been able to do that..." he confessed guiltily.

"...Felix, I hope you're not going because you feel you *have* to. You can't be forced out of the town in which you live. You were in England long before Milo, don't forget that." Dee just felt incredibly sad about the whole thing. She had hated Felix for a few days; blamed him for everything, but she just didn't have the stomach to keep that up. Poor Felix had lost everything too, even the respect of his family.

"No, I have to go for work...honestly. Anyway, I'll be back by summer I think."

"Well, as long as you're just going for work purposes and not because people have driven you out," Dee replied doubtfully. "I know you made a dumb mistake but I do feel guilty that you've had to shoulder all of this on your own. Even your own family have been more compassionate towards me than they have been to you. I don't think I really blame you anymore and if I could be friends again, I would. But I'm afraid I can't..."

"...Do you want to go for one last coffee before I never darken your doors again?" he offered hopefully.

"No Felix..."

"What if we grabbed a takeaway Styrofoam cup of that hot, muddy water they sell at the mobile burger van in the park? That hardly counts as coffee at all." Felix had always been a bit of a chancer. "Nobody will see us there. C'mon, if we're never allowed to speak to one another again, I'd just like to be able to explain myself properly – maybe have one last banal conversation...like we used to."

Dee watched him uncertainly for a second. "...Well...alright..." she reluctantly agreed and wandered off in the direction of Richmond Park with her ex-friend.

*

Dee watched disconcertedly as Felix paid for two white cardboard cups of what she would soon discover was the nastiest tasting coffee she had ever experienced. Then he handed one to her. She gingerly added a level spoonful of sugar because there was no sweetener, stirred whilst trying not to look at him, and they continued to stroll on.

"...So, you said you wanted to explain yourself properly?" Dee began after quite a long and stilted silence.

"...Did I say that? Well, perhaps I didn't mean 'explain' exactly because I've already told you *why* I kissed you. I'm still really embarrassed about it so I'd quite like it if we swept it under the carpet for the rest of our lives!" Felix smiled pleasantly but then his face took on a more serious pose. "But I've had more time to think about what I did...and I'd like for you to appreciate how deeply I regret it. I don't claim to be quite as miserable as you...but rest assured, I feel like shit."

"I do appreciate that you've suffered, Felix – it's obvious that you wish it had never happened," Dee conceded. "And if were up to me, I'd sweep it under the carpet for the rest of our lives too - but Milo will never let us forget it so I guess we can't." She kept her eyes on the pathway ahead of them, further along they would pass by a play park if they got that far. "Do you want to tell me about you and Renee...?"

Felix stopped in his tracks and stared at her, fairly stumped by that question. "...You know about me and Renee?" But he supposed there was no point in feigning ignorance now. "I suppose a little bird named Ginny told you? Because nobody else knows."

"She meant well." Dee had wanted to keep Ginny's name out of it if she could - and had failed miserably. "Is that why you kissed me? Is there something about Milo having something you don't that makes you do crazy things?" she asked bluntly. Dee noticed she was standing by a park bench so thought she may as well sit down on it.

Felix followed suit and sat beside her. "...Renee was completely different," he grumbled under his breath, seemingly a touch disgruntled that Dee knew about her.

"Okay...then tell me about it," she said pragmatically.

Felix shook his head as though he'd really rather not recount this to her. "...During the last six months of their marriage, there was just something between us. We weren't friends like I am with you. There was just some kind of sexual chemistry going on. She looked at me in a certain way and I looked at her the same manner, I suppose." He rubbed his eyes, distinctly uncomfortable now. "Anyway, they split up like we all knew they would. They had both been seeing various other people during the marriage and once it was over...well, she came to call on me one day."

"And you had a relationship with her?" Dee enquired as reasonably as she could.

"I wouldn't call it that," Felix answered blankly. "We slept together a few times about a month after they decided to part ways..." He was quiet for a little while. "Renee was unbelievably beautiful...and I guess I just wanted to know what it would be like to sleep with such an amazing-looking woman. But that was all it was for me...so once we'd done the deed a couple of times, the fascination was gone. I don't know what it was she saw in me, but she didn't pursue me again either." The embarrassment etched on Felix's face was evident. "Now before your little mind runs away with itself, that isn't how it was with you. I developed a really strong friendship with you...and I just began to want more."

Dee had found herself staring at him during the course of his admission. She had barely given him eye contact before now. "...When did this *crush-thing* start, Felix?"

Felix pursed his lips and mulled that over. "...Probably this Christmas."

"Christmas? But we weren't even friends by Christmas, not properly anyway." Dee was startled by his reply. It went back as far as that?

"No, but that was when the *attraction* started I'd say. I mean, I didn't stop and think, *'I really fancy Dee'*, I just remember having this *feeling* about you. I remember hoping that I would meet somebody like you someday. And once we got to know each other better - well that subliminal attraction just got...less subliminal."

As much as Dee truly didn't want to get into this, now this discourse had started, she desperately *needed* to talk about it. "Felix, I need to ask you a question and I want you to be completely honest with me, don't just tell me what I want to hear..."

Felix seemed disconcerted by that request. "Alright..."

"The one thing Milo keeps saying when he will design to talk to me, is that when he walked in on you kissing me-" Dee stalled for a moment and seemed to need to regroup before she could recommence, "...he says that it looked like I *wanted* you to kiss me. He's got into my head - and there's nobody else I can ask. I'm even beginning to doubt myself now..." Strangely enough, Dee felt the overwhelming urge to burst into tears - but she steeled herself against it.

"No." Felix was already shaking his head adamantly. "If you're asking me to tell you if I think you responded? If you're asking me to tell you if I think you wanted to be kissed? Then no, I don't think that at all." He continued to shake his head. "It was exactly how you first explained it - you completely 'froze' in my arms. Honestly, I'm not just corroborating your story - that was exactly how it felt. And it was a split second thing - there was no time to think or feel or...want anything...."

Dee could have hugged him. Almost. Milo had made her feel so thoroughly rotten about herself, made her question her every action on that fateful day. Why had she closed her eyes? Why? Was it because that was just something you did when somebody kissed you - even if you didn't consent to it? Even if you were repelled by it?

"...Good...that's good then." She sipped at her hot coffee and made a face. It really wasn't pleasant. Dee put the cup down on the ground beside her feet. She rubbed her arms briskly, perhaps she had been sitting still in the cold for too long.

"You're right, it is pretty cold for April," Felix pulled his navy blazer closer to his body. "I should climb in that huge coat with you," he smiled wolfishly. Dee grimaced at him. "...What?"

"When you say stupid things like that, I just-"

"Oh come on, stop overthinking everything." Felix rolled his eyes.

"Maybe that's my problem - I don't over-think things enough. Everybody knew about your attraction to me...but me," she divulged, ashamed of that childish propensity to believe the best of everyone. "Acid test - would you make that kind of remark to a male friend?" Dee frowned reprovingly.

"I-" Felix scratched his head. "God, I don't know. You've got me analysing every little thing I say now. I bet most men who have a female friend flirt a little and don't mean anything by it, that's normal. I bet most men have thought about sleeping with that female friend too..."

Dee rubbed her temples anxiously. "You are *so* not making this any better..."

"If I hadn't kissed you, you wouldn't think twice about-"

"Yes, but you did!"

Felix huffed. "This whole thing has been blown *way* out of proportion! I was delighted Milo found someone like you. You made him happy, you were good for him and he was a far nicer person for having met you. I was proud that he asked me to be best man and I meant every word I said at the wedding. I just spent too much time with you and got confused about my feelings..." he explained to her again, vehemently this time. "So I did a knee-jerk thing...and it has cost me dearly. Half my family are barely talking to me - *you* don't want to talk to me." Felix angrily kicked a stone with the toe of his shoe, watching it skitter away. "If I could turn back the clock; if Milo could respect me again, if I could have you back as my friend...I think I'd do anything. But I can't."

"I just want him to forgive me...I want him to forgive us both."

He sighed mournfully. "You did nothing wrong, don't forget that. Dee, I think there is a very slim chance Milo may come back home to you...but there isn't a hope in hell that he'll forgive me." Felix stared at the sky before he looked at her again. "I know what you must be thinking. If you tell Milo about me and Renee, he might think that there is a pattern in my behaviour and he'd realise you were innocent. You *are* thinking that, aren't you?"

"It hadn't even occurred to me, Felix. And I don't happen to think it would do either of us any good," Dee shrugged.

"Well, if you want to tell him, you can. I'm deeply sorry I caused this...that's all I can say." Felix rose to his feet and smiled down at her warmly where she was still sitting wrapped up like an Eskimo on the park bench. Dee knew he was making to leave.

"...Felix, what did I do that made you feel that way about me? Was I giving off some kind of signal? Is this my fault?" Dee asked a question that was constantly whispering away in her head, day and night. She had to ask him now because she had this unpleasant feeling she may never see him again and America would claim him back because of this.

"...No, Dee. You were just being yourself, and Dee being Dee is a really attractive quality. All I would say is, just be wary of guys in the future. Some men get feelings of friendship and attraction mixed up. Men are really dumb...well, *I* am anyway," he qualified. "So, I guess we've been chatting out in the open for far too long and I don't want to cause you any more trouble." Felix seemed a little distant for a minute and when he spoke again he sounded rather hoarse and emotional. "I wish you all the best. I hope that you'll find happiness soon, whether he comes back or not. You're a fantastic person and you deserve only great things...and I'll never forget you," he said rather weakly and it was then she felt certain she would never see him again. Felix quickly turned and walked away. No 'goodbye' or anything.

Dee desperately yearned to call him back as he briskly stomped off to the exit of Richmond Park but she had to let him go. If she hung on to this friendship, she may as well kiss her marriage goodbye. Standing partially obscured by the burger van, Milo Phillips morosely observed his wife and cousin Felix part company.

SWEET REVENGE

The Saturday afternoon of Milo's birthday brought with it real spring weather and the first actual warmth of the year. April *finally* shook off its winter coat and wild flowers bloomed in every patch of earth or any crack between the paving stones. This should be a magical time of the year; a time for new beginnings. But Dee did not want a new beginning, she wanted to recapture the happiness of the past.

"It's a lovely building," Cassie commented as the elevator doors opened on the third and uppermost floor of the apartment building. It was an old converted stately home divided into three huge living spaces. Dee happened to know that Milo owned the entire pristine building on Richmond Green but lived in the top-floor flat himself. And although the building was undeniably breath-taking, there was something rather clinical and cheerless about it that suggested to Dee that this place may not be a permanent fixture in Milo's life.

The two women gingerly crept along the hallway with Dee's two children, glancing at the classical paintings in burnished gold frames on the wall. The ceiling towered above their heads and the lush red carpet was soft beneath their feet. Their eyes were drawn to the magnificent staircase they had chosen not to climb leading back down to the opulent foyer. Yes, it was beautiful, but neither felt comfortable here. "So, the plan is, we drop the kids off then we're out the door. We'll head straight down the pub to meet the others to watch the rugby game, alright? Remember, we're in and we're out," Cassie confirmed, sensing Dee was becoming increasingly overwhelmed with this occasion. Milo was turning forty-four and she was not even invited to the gathering. One year ago, Dee had been the guest of honour at Milo's birthday dinner at a swanky restaurant in the West End. Her whole night had been spent explaining to excited family members and future-friends how she and Milo had finally put their differences behind them and got it together. And her future husband had stared at her adoringly all night, absently playing with the back of her hair.

"...Alright," Dee agreed, trying to shut off those recollections.

"And Mrs Dawson is going to be here?"

"Yes - at some point, she's taking the children to stay at her house tonight when the party really kicks off." Dee had been over this before but somehow the planning of their arrival and exit from this building had turned into a military procedure. "...Cass, I don't think I can do this...we should have just let Mrs D bring the kids..." Dee ground to a jarring halt outside the door to Milo's apartment. They could hear music and chattering coming from the other side. "...Can *you* do it? I might go and sit in the car."

"No, Dee. You have to be strong. We're going to go in there looking really cool and carefree and drop the children off - and breeze right back out again. He's going to see you looking so pretty and indifferent and realise he's made a huge mistake." Cassie had it all mapped out in her mind's eye.

"...B-but..." Before Dee could make some more excuses, the door opened without their having to knock and Forrest welcomed them in.

"Hey Dee, kids...hello Cassie – I thought I heard voices. Well, you two ladies are looking rather stunning," he said with most of the comment directed at Cassie.

"Yeah, we're off down 'The Dorchester' to watch the rugby with Bruce, Patrice and Evan," Cassie stated quickly before Forrest got the wrong idea and thought they were gate-crashing the get-together. Everyone knew The Dorchester. It was a popular and lively pub that Dee and her friends often frequented before Finley was born. Cassie had insisted on 'going out make-up' and new outfits so she and her cousin could look their absolute best.

"...Oh, well surely you could stay for a drink or two?" Forrest seemed rather disappointed that the women would be leaving so soon.

"We just wanted to drop off Angel and Finn and go," Dee replied warily as she passed Forrest to step over the threshold into the apartment hallway. She couldn't quite believe how on edge she was; like a wild animal fenced in, looking desperately for an escape route if one was needed. Dee soon found herself in the lounge of this sparse open-plan home Milo had created for himself without a place in it for her. Dee was greeted with a large gathering of people, most of whom she did not know. Milo was nowhere to be seen so Dee instantly felt better. Perhaps they could make a quick exit without even being spotted by him.

"Dee, I was wondering when you would get here," Ginny greeted Dee. The two women hugged and Ginny gave Dee a strange kind of grimace which Dee didn't really know the significance of.

"Did you bring Jerry?" Dee asked as Ginny's two daughters scurried over to hug Auntie Dee and then proceed to play with Angel.

"Of course not, he refused to come. But Elliott is supposed to be showing his face later tonight."

"...Oh," Dee gulped, unable to help feeling rather put out by that. Surely Elliott was her friend first and foremost. But then, Milo *was* his brother. And she was the one who had seen to that. "...Hey, Ginny, watch this." Dee placed her son down on the polished wooden floor and the little boy proceeded to crawl off into the party.

"Oh my God, he's crawling!" Ginny clapped her hands and Forrest smiled warmly.

Just then, Dee raised her eyes and saw Milo standing a few feet away in a pale blue cashmere sweater with a white t-shirt just visible underneath and a pair of well-fitting blue Levi's. He was his usual smartly casual self and as handsome as the day they had met. Their eyes fixed on each other's once he had witnessed his baby son crawling for the first time. His expression was unusually...friendly, and there seemed to be an unspoken bond solidifying between them; a silent but obvious exchange that said, 'look at our beautiful, clever son. *We* made him.'. The six-and-a-half-month-old baby crawled readily to its father and Milo scooped Finn up in his arms. Milo stared at Dee again and came a few steps closer, almost appearing glad to see her.

"...Thank you for bringing the children...can I get you a drink?"

Dee thought about accepting that drink but Cassie glared at her warningly. No deviation from 'the plan'. "...No thanks, we're going to the pub for the England-Australia rugby game. These are for you. Happy Birthday," Dee said, carefully giving her husband three cards and two presents. The two extra cards and two presents were from the children.

"...Thanks. Well...don't drink too much. You know what you're like when you have too many," he replied remarkably genially. "Mrs Dawson isn't here yet but she'll take them home before their bedtime."

"...Okay. Well, have a nice birthday party..." she replied awkwardly because he was still watching her so intently. Perhaps it was because Cassie had made her wear her hair down and styled it differently so that it framed her pretty, doll-like face. Perhaps it was her new short black skirt and heeled black ankle boots. But he was definitely staring, yet saying nothing. Dee knew she should do the tough thing and leave now - but she longed to talk to him, and just maybe he needed to talk to her.

"Oh hello, Dee. It is Dee, isn't it...?" said a stunningly pretty woman with honey-blonde shoulder-length hair. She draped herself around Milo's shoulder and Dee suddenly realised she knew this overly-familiar woman. It was Amber Williams, his American ex-girlfriend who she had not seen since the New Year Ball before last. Milo's good-natured expression was gone and his replacement expression appeared rather pained and even nervous...no, embarrassed.

"Jesus Christ," Cassie exclaimed under her breath standing beside Dee. Dee just watched without comprehending what she was seeing. Amber was here. *Amber was here?* What was she doing all over Dee's husband? And although he seemed distinctly uncomfortable in this elongated and toe-curling silence, Milo wasn't exactly shrugging this woman off either. Why wasn't he...? Then Dee belatedly understood.

"...Right..." Dee murmured with an agonising realisation of the truth, that awful woman still smirking at her like a Cheshire cat. "...Hello Amber, how is your village coping without you?"

"...Village?" Amber cocked her head to one side, baffled by Dee's unusual question.

"Well, every village needs its idiot."

"Dee, shall we get going?" Cassie asked, agitatedly clearing her throat. Amber was glaring acidly at Milo's wife.

"...Um, yeah," Dee agreed and shot Milo a reproachful glance. Forrest sighed sadly as sat in earshot, watching Cassie take Dee's arm, rapidly steering her back out into the hall before Dee could even say goodbye to her children. Ginny followed closely after and caught Dee before she reached the front door.

"...I'm so sorry, Dee-" Ginny declared with actual tears forming in her eyes.

"You knew about this? Why didn't you tell me?" Dee was already crying before she had time to consider curbing it until later.

"...No, I only found out when I got here...and I didn't know how to-"

"What is Amber doing in England? Is he seeing her?" Dee felt herself beginning to panic.

"As far as I know she showed up in London a few days ago and must have heard on the grapevine that you and Milo had split up. Forrest has discovered she's been on his case ever since he got together with you, calling him up whilst he was in the States to try to entice him back but he didn't want anything to do with her then. I think Amber's been staying with him for a couple of days," Ginny tried to explain in a hushed voice but she herself did not know the facts for certain.

"...Is he sleeping with her?" Dee was forced to ask, but in truth, she did not really want to hear the answer.

"...I don't know; I honestly don't know. I tried to get him alone to discuss it but he told me to mind my own business."

Dee could hardly breathe. "...It's just like Jerry said. Maybe Milo has been seeing Amber all along in America and was looking for a way out of our relationship," Dee sobbed, beginning to lose it now.

"...No, Dee...that just doesn't add up. Why would he be so desperate to marry you as soon as possible if all along he wanted to be with another woman?" Ginny shook her head.

"You can never understand the workings of a man's mind." Cassie scratched her head.

"I've got to get out of here." If Dee didn't get some fresh air very soon, she would begin to hyperventilate.

"Come on, Dee." Cassie opened the apartment door and took Dee out before Ginny could say anything else. Dee was in a daze as she was hurried down the impressive staircase out to Cassie's car but before she could get in, Dee doubled over and began to dry-retch.

"...I think I'm going to be sick," she heaved. But even as she said it, the feeling was passing. Dee was only glad she hadn't eaten anything.

"Okay, take deep breaths...shall I take you home?"

Eventually Dee stood up straight and said, "...no, I need a stiff drink. Lots of them..."

*

The atmosphere in the pub was decidedly melancholy and none of the group had given much attention to England's rugby match with Australia which was now long over. Cassie hadn't even had the heart to crow about how her beloved Australian team had whipped England (like they all knew they would). The group had done their best to support their respective countries but, after what had just happened, the outcome of a sporting event had been put horribly into perspective. Bruce, Patrice and Evan had met Cassie and Dee at The Dorchester as planned and all five sat glumly around a table contemplating the mounting empty drinks glasses before them. Dee had almost got her hopes up that Patrice and Bruce had patched things up (she hadn't seen them out together in the same place for months) but they sat as far away from the other as possible, never gave the other eye contact and never once responded to any comment the other would make. Evidently they were both only here for Dee - and Patrice wasn't giving up his friendship with her just for Bruce. Sometimes Dee felt she was almost involved in a custardy battle; her being the child.

Late afternoon had worn into evening and all would have been nicely merry if today's events had not cast such a big shadow over their night out. Instead they were inebriated with an unpleasantly depressed feeling attached to it. Her friends couldn't help but watch how Dee stared into the middle distance with an expression of dismay etched across her face...no, it was more like despair. Her entire world was collapsing around her for no good reason.

"...Is it me, or is this whole thing just insane?" Evan piped up again after a time of uncomfortable silence.

"Evan, I don't want to talk about it anymore," Dee groaned. Milo's new romantic liaison had been discussed to death and was running around her head, infecting all her other thought processes until she could barely stomach contemplating it anymore.

"But how can one little kiss that you played no part in cause all this? How can Milo accuse you of cheating and then start sleeping with someone else almost immediately?" Evan truly couldn't get his head around this fiasco, nobody could.

"He's trying to punish Dee, we've established that," Cassie sighed. "At least Dee got out of there with as much decorum as possible. She even managed to wise-crack on her exit. I mean, you've got to applaud her for that if nothing else." She rubbed Dee's arm.

Patrice burst into laughter and somehow that eased a bit of tension. "*Village idiot* - you're my hero, Campbell..." he grinned fondly across the table at her. Dee tried to smile back but not even a sassy zinger as an exit-line was enough to lift her mood.

"Y'know, we don't actually *know* anything has happened between Milo and Amber yet," Patrice reasoned stoically. "Amber may just be crashing at Milo's for a couple of days because he's a friend she happens to know in London. You guys were only in that apartment for five minutes, so you don't know what's gone on."

Cassie shook her head regretfully. "You weren't there, Patrice. That woman was all over Milo like a rash."

"...But Amber *isn't* Milo's friend. He's never mentioned her whilst we've been together. Why should she be crashing with *him*?" Dee repeated something she had said countless times this evening.

"Yeah, but Ginny told you Amber's been contacting him every time he went back to America. So it sounds like they were still friendly but you just didn't know about it," Bruce reminded her. There was more to this Amber business than met the eye. Milo had definitely been hiding something all these months.

"...Guys, I'm gonna' go..." Dee scraped a hand through her hair. She was still reeling over the news that Milo and Amber *had* been in contact in the States. Surely Milo would have mentioned if Amber were hassling him? Yet it was Dee he felt needed to be spied upon... "I shouldn't have come here tonight, I've just ruined everybody's evening and you were all looking forward to the game..."

"Dee, if you stay here - we worry about you, if you go home - we worry about you," Evan began logically. "At least if you're sitting here in front of us, we know you haven't slit your wrists." He finished his fourth pint of beer and Dee laughed (it was more of a sniff, but close enough).

"No, please don't slit your wrists!" Bruce threw himself across her lap theatrically.

Dee really did laugh this time. "I won't - *I can't*, I've got two kids to take care of!" Dee patted his back affectionately and noticed how Patrice watched the interaction. She knew he was trying to curb a smile. Maybe she could put her own problems on a back-burner for a while and try to help patch up *their* differences. Bruce seemed horribly resigned to the fact that his relationship was on its way out; Patrice was sleeping in the spare room and nobody was prepared to divulge whether he was seeing another man or not. But Dee just wasn't prepared to believe that these two adorable men who were both so kind, loving and thoughtful, had changed so much that they detested each other. There must be some misunderstanding that hadn't been thoroughly discussed. There must be some soul-searching conversation that hadn't been had that could reunite them. Before Dee could formulate a strategy in her devious little mind, the door of the pub burst open and a large group of people crowded in. The faces coming through began to look rather familiar and Dee had the feeling she had seen some of these people before until she spotted Ginny, Forrest, Milo...and Amber.

"Oh for God's sakes, can't he give you a moment's peace...?" Cassie gasped, incredulous of what was happening before her very eyes.

"What are that lot doing here? Did Milo know you were going to be in this pub?" Evan gawped in surprise. This unpleasant situation had gone much too far for his liking.

"...No," Dee said in a very small voice. "We told him we were going to the pub but we didn't say which one..."

"Forrest knew where we were going to be!" Cassie argued pointedly. Her face had turned bright red; she was absolutely livid.

"But why have they come *here*?" Dee exclaimed plaintively. "...I thought they were having his birthday party at the apartment..." Just when the dust began to settle, her crazy world began to spin again like an out-of-control rotunda ride.

"...Well, it's a popular pub, I suppose," Evan said in the most patient voice he could manage. "Shall we go somewhere else?"

"No, why should we? We were here first!" Cassie snapped defiantly. "If

Milo has any decency, he will leave when he spots us. Not that it will be of any surprise to him because he knew Dee was going to be here!" This dissolution of Dee's marriage had brought out a different side of Cassie's character that none of them had witnessed before. She was fiercely loyal to her cousin, to the point of being a bit of a dragon. Dee remembered Felix had once described her as a 'pit-bull' for this very reason.

Dee was quiet. She didn't know if she could stomach sitting here with Milo *and* Amber in eyeshot. Even thinking about them together was crucifying her, let alone *seeing* them. She did not know if her bruised little heart could take it. But all too soon Forrest and Ginny were on their way over once Dee's little group had been spotted.

"...Hi Dee, we're so sorry about this," Forrest began immediately as he joined them. Ginny loitered awkwardly beside him while Evan and Patrice gingerly shifted aside to encompass Forrest's wheelchair and Ginny's stool that she had dragged over from a nearby table.

"...Err, Bruce, would you help me get the drinks in?" Evan asked with a secret head-gesture directed at Bruce. He felt Dee deserved a little privacy if she was to hear that her husband truly was having an affair.

"No, I don't want one..." Bruce was too wrapped up with what was going on at the table to even think of leaving. And Patrice, who was normally the most sensitive of the pair, completely ignored Evan - clearly he was not shifting if Bruce wasn't. Was this a battle of who was the better friend?

Evan was already standing so he could hardly sit down again. "...Right...so same again for everyone else? Forrest, Ginny, can I get you some drinks...?"

"...Oh, um, just a couple of beers, please. Whatever you're having," Forrest said with his mind on something else completely. And of course Cassie refused to take the hint too. She had taken on the job of Dee's protector and defender today and Evan had no choice but to leave Dee and her henchmen to it (and procure the large round of drinks by himself).

"...Honestly Dee, we didn't mean to barge in on your evening out with your friends. Milo insisted on coming here even though I tried to talk him out of it," Forrest babbled worriedly.

"But he knew full well *I* was going to be here...or at least *you* did." Dee rubbed her clammy palms on the seat of her chair, glancing frantically over at the bar. Milo momentarily caught her eye as he bought a round of drinks for his numerous friends. The expression he wore was difficult to read from this distance but Dee felt sure she saw pure, abject misery in his big brown eyes. He was soon forced to break his gaze when Amber re-joined him where he stood propped against the bar, gushing over him and pressing her body alarmingly close to his.

"Well, yes...I did happen to mention where you'd gone. But I was as surprised as you are when he and some of his friends decided they wanted to go out...for a change of scene," Forrest gulped nervously. "He rounded up the guests and booked a bunch of taxis to take us here. I told him this was a bad idea but he insisted you'd be gone by now because the rugby was over." Forrest glanced around at the unconvinced and barely disguised angry faces at the table. "...I don't imagine we'll be here for long, no more than a couple of drinks...not now that he knows you're still here. There was talk of a nightclub anyway." Forrest seemed horribly ashamed about the whole situation. Dee arched an eyebrow; Milo? In a nightclub?

"But why choose The Dorchester? It's hardly Milo's local!" Cassie narrowed her eyes and Forrest turned to her wordlessly for a moment.

"...It's a popular bar and good for a large gathering, I suppose," he mumbled.

"Bollocks!" Cassie was turning out to be a very fiery and determined woman when she wanted to be. "Milo is trying to hurt Dee and flaunt that bitch in her face and you know it!" Everyone at the table watched her; some with a new-found respect, some simply stunned into silence. They had never seen Dee's cousin so vexed about anything.

"...I did try to-" Forrest stuttered. But Dee was watching Milo again and her heart nearly stopped when Amber placed a lingering kiss on his mouth.

"...Oh my God," Dee said aloud without meaning to. She covered her mouth in disbelief. "...Amber just kissed my husband..."

"That fucking dickhead!" Bruce growled, ignoring Patrice's lightly restraining hand on his arm.

"Is he...*sleeping* with her...?" Dee asked in a terribly strangulated voice. Forrest and Ginny gave each other a momentary look. "Please, I have to know..."

Ginny sighed unhappily. "...Sweetheart, we don't know. We really don't. He refuses to discuss it but something is clearly going on..." she spoke for the first time since arriving at their table with a sincere look of regret on her face. "I'm so sorry..."

"Of course he's sleeping with that cow, the cheating little shit!" Cassie glowered furiously. "I'm going to go over there and slap him!"

Bruce picked up his own untouched glass of gin and tonic and placed it in Cassie's hand. "Cassie, if you do that – and then slap Amber - I am going to literally buy your rounds for the rest of your life," he assured her.

Patrice grinned. "And I'll go halvesies with you," he chipped in. Bruce and Patrice smirked at one another. Dee was in emotional agony and they were not in any way making light of it, but their shared gallows humour was their only means of dissolving this tension. It was like a powder-keg at this table right now.

"...I can't believe this is happening." Dee placed her face in her hands. "...We split up a month ago and he's already found someone else..." She was crying. Again. Dee was beginning to grow accustomed to this regular occurrence.

"...Oh honey, don't let Milo see you cry." Cassie placed a comforting arm around her cousin. "Guys - block his view!" Cassie forcibly shoved Bruce's chair right beside Patrice's with a kick of her foot so Dee was obscured from Milo's line of vision where he stood at the bar. Dee was glad her new cousin was so on the ball. Bruce and Patrice glanced at each other again, reminded of another night in a restaurant in Covent Garden when it was *their* job to ensure Milo didn't see Dee cry whilst in the company of yet another girl.

"...Looks like our work here is done," Patrice remarked glumly to his partner.

"Evidently so..." Bruce agreed. It was kind of sad really, for years they had taken the place of the much-needed girl-friend in Dee's life. But now that much-needed girl-friend was here in the flesh.

"...You said Amber's been contacting him every time he went to the States?" Dee dabbed at her eyes with her sleeve, unable to shake the image of another woman kissing her husband (and her husband not pushing said woman away).

Forrest reached across to pat her hand with well-meant but ineffectual sympathy. "It turns out my mother has been letting Amber know whenever Milo went back to America. I suppose it's because my mother...doesn't like you. As I understand it, he refused to see Amber when she tried to make contact. But my mother must have slipped the information to Amber that you and Milo had split up. It can't be a coincidence that Amber has come over here on business the moment he left you..."

"Does he have real feelings for her? Surely this has got to be out of spite...?" No matter how she tried to calm herself, Dee was becoming distraught. "...Ginny, do you know if Felix is contactable in New York? I really need to speak to him," Dee snivelled.

"Dee, I don't think that's a good idea," Ginny whined with obvious reluctance.

"Why not? I need to tell Felix what's going on. He's been ostracized by everyone; forced out of the country because of what he did when it turns out Milo may never have had his heart in this marriage anyway! Felix has been the bloody scapegoat throughout this whole mess! He needs to know that he's been treated unfairly, we both have!"

Ginny gave a chary shake of her head. "Dee, if you call my brother, you'll be all upset and he'll rush home and decide he needs to comfort you…and then something you'll both regret might happen," she hinted heedfully.

"I don't want to have *an affair* with him!" Dee snapped waspishly, completely appalled at the suggestion. "Felix is my friend and he's going through the same hell as I am!"

"I assure you he *isn't*," Cassie scoffed. "Felix *caused* this nightmare in the first place, remember?" she said in no uncertain terms. Ginny eyed her sharply although she was actually inclined to agree.

Dee could barely speak she was crying so hard. "…What did I do to deserve this? What did I *do*…?"

"Don't cry, sweetie," Ginny said. "Milo is *here*, isn't he? He's clearly playing games – and that must mean he wants you back," she spouted impetuously. Forrest shot her a look. No raising Dee's hopes, Ginny had been warned.

"Come on, Dee. Let's go to the loo to sort your face out," Cassie insisted, glaring acidly at the usurpers at the table.

THE NIGHT OF NIGHTMARES

Dee dabbed at her eyes with scrunched-up toilet paper before any more tears could escape down her face. Cassie had done such a sterling job of touching up her makeup, Dee was determined not to spoil it. She was beginning to feel the effects of all the alcohol they had consumed finally catching up with her now that she was in a standing position. Dee could safely say, judging by the spinning of the bathroom they stood in, she was pretty bombed.

"Lucky you wore waterproof mascara," Cassie said, surveying her cousin in the mirror of the ladies' toilets.

"God, this is bad, Cass," Dee declared with a shake of her head. "I can't believe he's doing this to me…"

"You know it's all to get a reaction, right? That's why he left his own birthday party to parade Amber in front of you. And that's not the behaviour of a man who doesn't love his wife anymore," Cassie reasoned.

"What good is that to me if he's *sleeping* with her?" Dee couldn't seem to come to terms with the fact that Milo was even capable of this kind of cruelty; the man *she* knew wasn't the man out there.

"…None of this makes sense to me. He went to such great lengths to find my dad and me just to make you happy." Cassie chewed on her upper lip. "Milo worships you, I know he does…and eventually he's going to snap out of this period of insanity. If it isn't too late by then…" But was it too late already? Now Milo was having some form of dalliance with somebody else?

Dee eyed her thoughtfully. "Cassie, I know we've had a few to drink but I have to tell you something." She took a steadying gulp. "…I know we've only known each other for a few months but I feel like I've known you all my life. You're more like a sister to me than a cousin and I want you to know that I really love you," Dee sniffed and was a little surprised to realise she had made Cassie cry.

"I love you like a sister too," Cassie howled and threw her arms around Dee. "I wish we'd grown up together."

"Even if it's over with Milo, at least I have you because of it…" Now they were both crying, partly due to the drink, partly due to the emotional circumstances of the day but mostly because they really meant it. "You've been so brilliant through all of this and I don't think I could have handled it without you," Dee confessed.

"Okay, stop mucking up your makeup - I've only just fixed it. Let's get out to the bar and drown our sorrows and I'll try to accidentally-on-purpose spill my pint over Amber," Cassie joked (but she would happily do it).

"You'll have to stand in line." Dee linked arms with Cassie and they wandered out from the ladies' toilets back into the noisy bar but were met by the anxious figure of Milo standing there. It was as though he had been waiting for them. Dee made to walk by but he stopped her just by manoeuvring his body in front of hers to block her path.

"...Cassie, can I talk to my wife alone please?" he asked softly; a strange, desolate expression on his face.

"Stop calling me your wife, I'm not *your* anything!" Suddenly, as if by a snap of the fingers, the belligerent Dee he had first met was back. And all the walls, all those barriers and barbs, were firmly up again.

"How could you do this, Milo? I could strangle you for doing this to my cousin!" Cassie began angrily.

"If it weren't for me, you wouldn't know *your cousin* at all." Milo eyed her coldly.

"Cassie would have found me with or without you," Dee assured him with a hateful sneer. "Now fuck off back to your girlfriend and leave me alone! I have nothing to say to you!" Dee furiously barged past him and hurried at a near-run through the bar.

*

Dee had to get out, to get some air, to escape this nightmare. She had just made it out through the side doors and found herself at the bottom of a short flight of stone steps that led up to the street when Milo burst out through the doors behind her and caught her arm.

"You have to listen to me!" he insisted, seemingly rather agitated, and panicked even.

"I don't have to do anything! Why did you come here? Did you feel some need to rub your affair in my face?"

"It's not an affair and I didn't think you'd still be here. This is just a coincidence..." he groaned, seemingly on the verge of exasperation.

"There are no such thing as coincidences when you're involved, Milo, remember? You engineer everything to suit your plans! You told me that yourself!" she snapped.

"Why would I pick another fight with you? What good would that do me?"

"You could have gone to any pub in Richmond, but no - you show up *here* with rent-a-crowd the minute the rugby finishes!" Dee huffed.

"Rent-a-what?"

"You and all those *fake friends*. Who are all those people? I've never seen them in my life - they're not your friends! You don't *have* any friends!" Dee glowered. "The only friend you had in England was me and you don't even have that anymore!"

Milo was glaring at her as though he didn't know whether he wanted to kiss her or kill her - no it was definitely more like 'kill her'. "...Most of them flew in from the Sta-"

"I. DON'T. CARE!" Dee shouted before he could finish.

"And what about you? Do you always go to watch the rugby dressed like *that*?" He looked her over with barely disguised malice; her short skirt and heeled ankle boots.

"Like what?" Dee gave herself an exaggerated check-over then. "Like a girl? Like a girl going out on the town? Did you really think I'd dressed like this for *your* benefit?" Dee almost laughed in his face (actually she *had* dressed like this for his benefit, on Cassie's instructions, but he didn't need to know that). "Well go on then, you have my attention, what do you want?"

Milo was quiet for just a millisecond, searching her eyes. "...I wanted you to know that I didn't come here to hurt you..."

"Oh really? How did you think I'd feel seeing another woman kissing you?"

"Well now you know how it felt for me catching you with Felix," Milo muttered resentfully.

"So, you *are* doing this out of spite then?" Dee retorted.

"No," Milo sighed. His demeanour suggested he was as exhausted and miserable as she was.

"Why is that bitch staying at your apartment?"

He answered reluctantly. "...Amber came over to England on business. She works for an American agency that recruits models and she's over here looking for new talent. I'm just about the only person she knows in London, so she contacted me needing a place to crash for a few days."

"Can't she afford a hotel then?" Dee sneered. "Forrest says she's been calling you whenever you went back to the States on business. I bet something has been going on with her all along, hasn't it? Jerry was right about you, he says you were looking for a way out of our marriage and I haplessly gave it to you. Perhaps I should have sent *my* cousin Cassie out to America to befriend and spy on *you*!"

"You don't get to be morally outraged! You don't get to absolve yourself of any guilt!" Milo shouted back at her. "All of this is happening because of what *you* did! I never saw Amber on my trips to America. Yes, she did call me now and then but I made it clear I was in love with *you*. I never told you about it because I didn't want you getting the wrong idea."

"...Have you slept with her...?" Dee's belligerence fell away. She was so tired and she just had to know. But Milo hesitated to reply just a little too long.

"...Once..." he said with a tone of voice that said this was like crucifixion for him. "...There was no point in pining for you or hoping for some kind of reconciliation when there isn't going to be one..."

"What have you done?!" Dee screamed in his face. "Why are you doing this to me? I love you so much and you're torturing me for something I didn't even do!" She hammered her fists on his chest and was crying so brokenly he felt compelled to try to comfort her.

"...You're the mother of my children and I'm always going to care about you, but what you did-" There were tears running down his face too. He reached out and touched her agonised face, then motioned to put his arms around her.

"Don't touch me! You don't ever get to touch me again!" she hollered rather wildly.

Milo recoiled, spurned. "What did you expect me to do? You either had or are having a fling with my cousin, and I'm expected to stay faithful to a woman who has betrayed me?"

"I never did anything to you! There was never any me and Felix! It was all in your head!" she wept bitterly. "You're the only cheater in this marriage, you're the one who destroyed us! So you send me those divorce papers the minute you can and I'll sign them; I'll sign anything you want as long as it means you're out of my life!"

"...We need to talk about the children..." Milo wiped his eyes shamefacedly.

"I've bent over backwards to make sure I didn't exclude you from those children's lives! I let you keep my six-month-old baby overnight when you knew I wasn't ready to do it – just so you didn't feel shut out!" Dee shook her head. "I've begged you, I've pleaded with you; I wrote you emails, texted, called...*everything* to get you to come home. I'd have prostrated myself on the floor if you'd just agreed to give me a chance," she glowered. "We've only been apart one month and already you're fucking someone else?! Well, I'll tell you something for nothing; you'd better dine out on the memory of me begging - because needy, pathetic Dee has gone. I will

NEVER ask you back again! We're finished!"

Something in the maliciousness of her final words seemed to disturb him more than any of the screaming or the tirade of anger that preceded them. "...You started this..."

"You fucking childish little prick! I'm done with you - and I will 'talk children' when I am good and ready!" Dee stormed up the stairway onto the street.

"You can't take my children away from me! I'm a good dad and I don't deserve that!" he called up after her, following her up onto the street into the fresh night air.

Dee spun around. "You're not a *good* anything! If there were no kids involved, you would never set eyes on me again...but there are, and I'm not going to punish them for your mistake. So you'll get to see them but you *will* be sorry, I can promise you that," she told him coldly. "One of these days you're going to realise you've made a monumental mistake...you drove away the only woman who ever *really* loved you, the only woman who ever could. But by the time you realise that, I will have moved on. So you just go and pick up where you left off with your sad little life; sleep with hundreds of women, catch an STD, smoke like a chimney, get lung cancer and die a sad and lonely man! I wish you *were* dead!" And with that final stinging insult ringing in his ears, she made off down the street in the direction of the taxi rank.

Milo watched her go and dried his face with the heel of his hand. His head and his heart were a tornado of confusingly mixed emotions; love, hate, revenge, sorrow - and he was too screwed up now to think clearly enough to stop his world spinning out of control.

KEEPING A DISTANCE

A couple of miserable weeks had passed since that hauntingly memorable night at The Dorchester and Dee had heard nothing more from Milo. He did not even request to see the children, but Dee sent them over regardless in the charge of Mrs Dawson on his weekly designated periods with them. She would keep up her end of the bargain but nothing more. Never again would Milo be allowed to make her feel how he had that night; worthless, hopeless. Forrest assured Dee that Milo had not been in touch because he was very upset about the 'incident' and was still licking his wounds - but Dee refused to believe he cared enough to be capable of *being* upset. So as April was coming to a close, Dee was surprised when her doorbell sounded, only to find an old friend on her doorstep.

"Felix, you're back..." Dee said, a little taken aback. But she had to admit she was terribly pleased to see him.

"Dee, I'm so sorry. Ginny only called me a couple of days ago to tell me what happened. I got a flight as soon as I could get away." Felix stepped through the door and closed it behind him. He observed her quietly for a minute, trying to assess how the land lay now he was back, now everything had changed. "...Can I give you a hug?" he asked hopefully.

"Of course," Dee replied with a weak and broken smile. Her voice cracked and her eyes immediately misted over and he placed his warm arms around her. Both felt the instant sense of comfort that only an embrace like this could give. "This just goes from bad to worse. I'm so sorry for what's happened to you..." Felix pulled back and stared at her momentarily. Dee had this funny feeling he was going to kiss her again, but was nevertheless surprised when he softly placed his mouth on hers.

Felix hadn't planned on doing this, and was fully expecting Dee to rebuff him again - but oddly enough she responded and kissed him back. Dee had felt so utterly lonely and unloved for so long and there was something extremely consoling about being kissed again. The pair stumbled a few steps against the open kitchen doorframe. Felix kissed her harder. He was definitely becoming more amorous; his hands in her hair, trying to prise her lips apart with his tongue. Just like last time, this felt like an out-of-body event to Dee, she felt as though distanced from it; on the outside looking in. But she felt no urgency to recoil from Felix either. Milo didn't love her anymore. Milo was with someone else - he was *sleeping* with someone else. But this was *Felix*...and Dee didn't love Felix.

"...*No!*" Dee pulled away and scraped back her hair, exasperated with herself - far more than she was with him. "I don't want this."

"I'm really sorry...I honestly didn't set out to do that-" Felix appeared as shocked by the event as she was.

"The one thing that has kept me sane is the knowledge that I'm innocent - I'm in the right," Dee explained warily. "This must never happen again. If we do this, then we're guilty of everything Milo says we are."

"I know - I know..." He rubbed his eyes. "...But you *have* to stop crying in front of me because it makes me do stupid and totally inappropriate things like that," Felix laughed nervously, he just had to break the tension.

Dee chewed on her lip and said, "I promise not another tear will be shed in your presence. I'm sick of crying anyway – I feel like I have a permanent headache from blubbing all the bloody time..." At last she smiled weakly and led him through to the kitchen, because somehow that felt safer than the guest lounge or cubbyhole which housed soft furniture that one could lie down on... "So, is the musical going well...?" Dee scratched her head, trying to regroup.

Felix followed her uncertainly. "...Yeah, ticket sales are good. I think it will be pretty successful. I stuck around as long as I needed to and now I think I'm surplus to requirement," he said. "So, does this mean we can be friends now?"

Dee shrugged. "...Well, I suppose so. Milo clearly isn't coming back and I wouldn't take him if he did."

"...That's it then? Your marriage is really over?" Felix sat down at the breakfast bar while Dee filled a kettle.

Dee kept her back to him and said in a soft voice, "...yes. Milo is sleeping with somebody else..."

"But *Amber*? Ginny told what he'd said to you at the pub – it's just...*Amber*?" he repeated dubiously. "I *know* Amber of old and I know for a fact Milo detested her." Felix shook his head, baffled. "So for him to hook up with a woman he despises means he *really* believes you were sleeping with me. Did Milo say it was a one-off? Or do you think he's having a full-blown affair?"

"...When I saw him at the pub, he said he'd slept with her once...and that was two weeks ago. So I expect they're planning their engagement party by now - because they certainly don't seem to let the grass grow beneath their feet." Dee added milk to the tea, stirred and placed a mug before Felix on the breakfast bar. She realised she hadn't even asked Felix what kind of beverage he wanted, but she remembered he once said he'd grown fond of tea since living in the U.K. "I guess he doesn't despise her anymore…"

Felix gingerly sipped the tea. "…I'm surprised you're even talking to me."

"Why?" She pulled up a stool and sat beside him.

"I'm to blame for everything that's happened."

"Maybe you are, maybe you aren't. Jerry reckons his relationship with Amber goes further back than this. I've since found out she used to contact him whenever he went back to New York. What I don't understand is, if he wanted to be with Amber, why did he even bother with this pretence with me?" Dee sighed. "What if Milo only took up with me because he was recently bereaved and I was having his baby?"

"That doesn't make sense at all," Felix said dismissively. "If he was with you just for the baby, he wouldn't have been so obsessed with you. I actually thought his adoration was a little unhealthy because it was bordering on…well, *needy*."

Dee stared into the middle distance. "…No, none of it makes sense, does it? Milo loved me – he *did*. Sometimes his reliance on me was a bit overwhelming. He used to say if anything ever happened to me, he'd kill himself…and every time he went to the States, he begged me to come. If Milo never really wanted to be with me, why say things like that?"

"Because he *did* want to be with you, Dee," Felix assured her. "When Andrew died, you were the only one he wanted there to comfort him; he never once asked for *Amber*. This whole thing is about revenge. Everything he's doing now, it's just to hurt you."

She frowned. "…Well, that may be so – but the damage is done. It doesn't matter if he slept with her once or a hundred times, nothing will ever be the same," Dee said mournfully.

"You mean that? If Milo walked through the door right now and begged your forgiveness, you'd turn him away…?" Felix arched an eyebrow, unconvinced.

"…I-" Dee stalled. She wanted to be strong and say she would never show Milo any forgiveness, but in her heart she longed for his return. "No, some things can't be forgiven…" But she was ashamed of her hesitance.

"I can't believe one stupid kiss has caused all this. Sometimes I feel so bad about it I just have to go to bed so I don't have to think about it anymore. Then I wake up in the morning and all the problems I created are still there," Felix confided rather emotionally.

"You mustn't berate yourself like this anymore, Felix," Dee insisted kindly, touching his hand. "Milo had the right to be mad...but he didn't have the right to *go* mad..."

Felix looked away regretfully, unable to accept her forgiveness. "I know your life is wretched, and I know two children have lost their father – because of me. If I'd not acted on an impulse, if I'd not let myself get carried away and allowed myself one moment of madness...none of this would be happening." However, that 'one moment of madness' was now 'two'. Two kisses – the second far more passionate than the first. But Dee was tired of hating him, so she swept it under the carpet. She was good at that.

*

It wasn't often that Evan actually called Dee into the coffee shop to discuss business. In fact, whenever Dee did show up for work, he always gave her a bit of a faintly surprised expression. She was actually fretting about it on the drive over - was 'Bookish' in trouble? People often joked that the store appeared as though it was part of a set from a, *'life after total world nuclear warfare'* movie. But Dee always thought that there were just busy periods and lulls. She couldn't afford for the shop to go under now - not with a possibly messy divorce to contend with at the end of the year. Plus, she needed this place, needed the distraction from the rest of her troubled life. Dee carried her infant son against her chest as she followed Evan into the back-office which they shared (whenever she cared to grace the place). He placed two cups of coffee on his desk and sat in his swivel chair with a rather nervous look on his face.

"...Should I be worried?" Dee grimaced, pulling over her office-chair to join him.

"...Worried? No - I don't think so anyway..." Evan scratched his head.

"The shop isn't in trouble then...?"

"Oh no, the accounts are looking healthier than they've ever looked in the history of this store!" he laughed awkwardly. "I asked you to come in because I have a proposal for you..."

"...Oh?" Dee looked down at Finn who was whining a little. She fished a packet of rice-cakes from her bag and proceeded to give him one to gnaw on.

"...I want you to hear me out before you say anything. Now I've been putting some money aside since you bought the store from me and put me in charge as manager...and I've been speaking to my bank who've agreed to give me a loan..." he said rather anxiously, noticing she was watching him with squinted eyes, her head slightly cocked and her mouth open a little (that gormless look she sometimes wore but he chose not to tell her about). "What I'm trying to say is...I wondered whether you'd consider letting me buy back half the shop...?"

Dee closed her mouth again and stared at him, nonplussed for a moment. "...You want to buy me out completely, don't you? You want your shop back..." she said in a small little voice. Was she about to be *entirely* purposeless now?

"No, no not at all - I want to be partners," Evan stressed vehemently. "I love working with you - when you came along, you took the pressure off. It's great having somebody like you around to bounce off too...but I'd just like to part-own the place again. I thought you might appreciate the extra money...now that your marriage is coming to an end. And once we're fully established and we've made a decent profit, I thought we could buy some more shops together - make a 'Bookish' a chain, even." Evan still didn't know how to take her silence. "But of course you can say 'no' if you want to, it's *your* store..."

Dee gulped and sort of smiled. "...I *could* use the extra money...and it would be a weight off my shoulders knowing that you co-owned the shop with me. I do worry about the financial implications of running my own business..."

Evan suddenly appeared extremely relieved and even a little excited. "Are you sure? You won't regret it - we're going to make great partners!"

"Oh, I'm positive." Dee was relieved too. "As long as you're sure you can really afford it."

"I'm certain, I've gone over my figures," he asserted. "Dee...things *are* financially okay with you, aren't they?" He seemed concerned then.

"Oh yes, I'm fine. I just want to be a bit more careful now I'm on my own," Dee assured him stoically.

"I know you are intent on being independent from Milo, but your husband is a very rich man. And he was the one who walked out on your marriage - not you. You have two kids...he *owes* you," Evan reminded her.

"He may be a very wealthy man but that wealth has nothing to do with me. I didn't earn any of it."

"Now don't you go agreeing to anything stupid just because you're being all self-reliant. You're entitled to some of his money after what he's put you though," Evan insisted rather hotly. "It's not like he'd miss the cash!"

"I know and don't worry - he will provide for his child. I'm not stupid or pig-headed enough to let my kids suffer." Dee cringed as Finley dribbled some of the rice cake onto her hand. "I've got to say, you buying into the shop has come at a great time though, Evan. I can use the money to buy

Bruce's new house."

"...You're buying Bruce a house?" Evan stared at her, aghast.

"Well he and Patrice really need some space or they're going to implode. I'm still hopeful that they can patch things up but I think the best way to do that is for Bruce to move out - give them both some room and time alone to think," Dee said sagely.

"Is this a good time to be doing something like that? You said you needed to be careful with money..."

Dee rolled her eyes. "Oh Evan, stop being such an old woman. I'm not *that* financially insecure! I've been married to two rich men on the bounce!" she laughed, even though she was a little bit ashamed of it. "Look, property is always an investment. And if Bruce and Patrice get back together, we can rent it out. It's a win-win for everybody."

"And Bruce is just going to let you do this, is he? He's going to let you buy him a house?"

"Oh, Bruce is being just like you about it - irrational! But I'm going to do it anyway, Bruce is family. And I'd do the same for you too," Dee said archly. "If there's one thing this break-up has taught me, I now realise who my real friends are...*you* guys are my family and I'm going to look after you."

Evan continued to stare at her as though she were quite mad for a while but Dee simply chose to ignore him.

*

Milo hadn't much to say to his lawyer as they sat outside Benito's coffee house. The two men sipped on their lattes and Milo proceeded to light a cigarette, nervous about the impending meeting. April had sluggishly become May and he hadn't seen his wife in three weeks – not since his birthday. For some reason he felt incredibly anxious about setting eyes on Dee again. Always true to her word, Dee's texts and emails stopped dead - it seemed she had been serious when she had vowed never to ask him to come home again. Milo just knew how she was going to behave today; she would be the Dee of old, the one he met after Lance's funeral, the Dee that made him irrationally crazy. Eventually Dee came sauntering along, flounced into the confines of the café courtyard and slumped down at the table. She had that sulky air of a teenage boy about her - she was even wearing that annoying sulky-teenage-boy baseball cap. Dee *always* wore that when she was in a bad mood - she used it as some kind of emotional crutch; as though it had the power to conceal her true feelings. And Milo was dreading the prospect of this meeting even more now.

"...Can I get you a coffee, Dee?" Milo asked urbanely. He decided that his being affable would put her on the back-foot.

"Nope, I'm not planning on being here long enough to drink a coffee," Dee advised him coolly. Milo exhaled slowly, there was absolutely no chance of this going smoothly. Dee had received a call from Milo's lawyer asking for the couple to meet here to discuss terms. She was particularly incensed that her gutless husband did not feel he could ring her himself to arrange the get-together. "So, get on with it."

"Mrs Phillips, I expressly I asked you to bring a legal representative," Mr Mahon, Milo's lawyer said rather brusquely.

"Well, Milo may feel he needs to fly you in from America - though why he can't just use an English lawyer, I'll never know - more money than sense, probably. I, on the other hand, don't *need* legal representation. I don't want anything. Now, what do *you* want?" she asked in that same frosty, flippant manner.

Mr Mahon cleared his throat uncertainly. "Mr Phillips is happy with the arrangements for two days' access to the children a week...but he went against my advice initially and did not set up a prenuptial agreement before the marriage. So we're here to discuss a settlement that would be agreeable to both of you. We'd like to keep this out of court. So the question is, how much do you feel would be a fair amount?"

"I've already told you, I don't want anything. I don't need his money." Dee was staring out into the street serenely and this was beginning to irritate Milo (just like she knew it would).

"Well that clearly isn't the case," Milo began waspishly. "When I first met you, you weren't terribly financially stable *then*. The little you *did* have, you spent on a coffee shop which appears to be empty of customers half the time. And now I understand you're having to sell half of the place back to the previous owner!" he glowered.

Dee bit her nails with that same neutral look on her face. "Who told you that?" She was actually extremely cross that Milo should know this information already but hid her anger under a mask of disinterest. "And, by the way, my monetary situation is no longer any of your business."

"It *is* my business when my children are living with you! Look...I want to contribute to raising our kids, even you can see that's the very least Angel and Finley deserve." Milo finally managed to calm himself, thinking if he kept on appearing reasonable, then maybe she would be forced to reciprocate.

Dee had actually been tunelessly whistling during the course of his patronising speech. *Whistling*. Milo could feel a blood vessel throbbing in his temple. Dee shrugged her shoulders. "Okay, that's fair, I guess. Just the standard rate of child-support for Finley...and set up a trust fund for him which he can have when he turns eighteen or something."

"Angel is legally my child too, I've adopted her and I wish you would stop pretending otherwise! I have already set up a trust fund and child-support for *both* children!" Milo had not fully expected to be attempting to force money on her but knowing Dee, this should have been no surprise to him. Dee had been slandered as a 'gold-digger' for the majority of her adult life; this was her big chance to prove she was nothing of the sort. Of course she was going to take it.

Dee gave an overly-theatrical, impatient sigh. "Milo, what I want is to live my life as if you'd never existed. Now I can't precisely do that because I had your baby. But as it is, I own a house, I still have some of the money Lance left me and the coffee shop is *not* empty - it's doing really well. So just pay the child-support, for both kids if you must, set up the trust funds and we'll leave it at that."

He narrowed his eyes. "That is not how this is going to work. I am going to continue to fund the running of the house and provide a monthly income made payable to you - to contribute to the day-to-day costs of raising children. I want to pay for their food, their clothes, their schooling – everything." Milo was insistent on this, he was really rather old-fashioned at heart and believed a father should be the sole provider for his kids.

"*No.*" Dee exaggerated the word as though he were stupid. "You're not doing this out of the kindness of your heart. You just want to control me - but I mean to be free of you. So I want you to stop paying all those bills and costs of running the house, and I want everything to be put back into my name," she said tonelessly, wrapping her fingers on the table. "I won't be beholden to *you*."

Milo's mouth was a thin, hard line, his brow knitted in vexation. "I WILL contribute to our children's lives and you WILL accept this money from me. I am their father and I want to be involved in their upbringing!" He scowled malevolently. She had barely made eye contact with him once and that made him furious.

"Mr Phillips!" Mr Mahon warned him. "Mrs Phillips has every right to-"

"Why don't you think of this as a lucky escape and save your money for your *next* divorce? Because unlike me, she will certainly only have married you for your money and you are going to need all your cash to pay *her* off..."

"Whereas you are holier than thou, aren't you? You *certainly* wouldn't marry for money. Yet oddly enough, you seem to have married two wealthy men one after the other! Go figure!" Milo barked.

"I've got a good idea, why don't you take your money and shove it up your arse?" Dee replied with the same banality but her eyes glinted like steel. Keeping up the placid exterior was too tough. "I invested everything I had into this marriage! Oh, and I'm talking emotionally, not financially. Can you reimburse me for *that*?" She had promised herself she wouldn't lose her cool, but he brought out the very worst in her.

"*You* invested everything? I had my heart ripped out - I would have died for you!" But luckily for her, Milo was losing it big-time.

"Well, be a sport and go kill yourself now - do us all a favour!"

"My kids are going to be brought up in the manner they have become accustomed to!"

"They aren't exactly destitute now, you stuck-up wanker!" she snapped finally, then instantly dialled down her anger a notch since her indifferent attitude seemed to score far more heavily. "Fine, buy your kids off with your guilt-money so you can make yourself feel better about being an adulterer. But *I* don't have to accept another penny from you. Can I go now?" Dee scraped her chair from the table and stood up. "As I see it, we don't need to speak again in person until the end of the year. The minute you can rustle them up, send me *any* documents to do with the divorce and I'll sign it. The sooner we can end this farce of a marriage, the better. I will send Mrs Dawson over with the children on Saturday morning." She turned to walk away.

"I hear Felix is back," he piped up bitterly before she could leave.

"Yeah, what of it?"

"I guess that means you can carry on where you left off? I take it you're still screwing him...?"

"Unlike you, I've not screwed anybody else. But since your opinion doesn't matter to me anymore, yes I'm friends with Felix again. Hey, I can be friends with anyone I like now - maybe I should look Cameron up," Dee considered mockingly and sauntered off back onto the street and disappeared from view.

"Well, that went better than we could have expected," Mr Mahon smiled. "I must say, you've really dodged a bullet there. She wasn't at all what I expected - I almost liked her." He turned to Milo who was now seething with barely contained anger. "But why on earth she turned down a big settlement, I'll never know. She clearly needs the money."

The fury Milo had been ramping up to suddenly dispersed. "Why does she *clearly* need the money...?" he said sharply.

"Well, apart from selling half her store back to the former owner, she's put her summer house up for sale - so I'm guessing she's tightening her belt."

"Summer house...?"

"Yes, the house in Wiltshire," Mr Mahon explained.

"...But-" Milo began. The house where they first fell in love. The house where they spent that idyllic Christmas as a family with Andrew shortly before his death. How could she? "Buy the house."

"...What? Why?" Mr Mahon sputtered.

"Just do it – buy it under one of our subsidiary companies and put the house back in her name. But keep my name out of it."

"But she's going to know *you* bought it for her..." he shook his head incredulously.

Milo shook his head. "She has other rich relatives - it could have been purchased by anyone," he smouldered. Yes, anyone; Jerry, Elliott...Felix.

"Mr Phillips, your wife wants nothing from you. We're going to need to move quickly and make her sign a legal document stating that - before one of her friends gets to her and convinces her to take you for all you are worth. I've seen it happen before," Mr Mahon warned him quite seriously.

"Never mind that - you need to find a way to ensure she has no choice but to accept *this* much money from me on a monthly basis." Milo scribbled down a figure on a scrap of paper and shoved it unceremoniously at Mr Mahon.

"...Mr Phillips, are you sure you realise what you're asking me to do? You employ me to make sure that you and your assets are protected," he blustered.

"I employ you to do what I say," Milo snarled, got up and charged off down the High Street with no destination in mind.

*

Milo wasn't the only one brimming over with fury. Dee ground her teeth as she jumped into her car after her meeting with Milo. All that repressed rage she had concealed at the café overflowed now. How dare Milo persist in talking about money? She had never been interested in his wealth, yet his lawyer was petrified she would rinse him for every penny he had. Dee decided to take herself on a little jaunt out of town to calm her frustrations. She switched on an album of favourite music as she slipped onto the dual carriageway and forced herself to sing along. Singing usually calmed her down. But all too soon Dee realised the first track was about lost love and she found her eyes beginning to tear up again. So it was with an outer-body kind of calmness she first spotted a white van pulling out prematurely from a slip road. Of course Dee instinctively slammed on the anchors but she certainly didn't seem to be stopping. And Dee remembered thinking, wouldn't it be odd to die in exactly the same way as her parents?

CRASH AND BURN

Later that afternoon, Forrest had visited Milo's apartment and the two men steadily made inroads through a bottle of red wine. Amber breezed into the room with her matching luggage and dumped it by the door. She stood behind Milo where he sat on the sofa and leaned over his shoulder to kiss his cheek.

"I'm all set. I'll only be gone for a couple of days. Will you miss me?" She nuzzled his neck but Milo barely responded. He stared fixedly at his wineglass, aware Forrest was watching him.

"You'd better get going, you don't want to miss your flight..." he murmured.

"No, that's true. Well...b-bye Milo, bye Forrest," Amber beamed across at her new beau's brother and bustled out of the apartment.

Forrest continued to stare at his motionless brother for a while. "Why didn't you help with her bags...or drive her to the airport?" he said, studying Milo as he deftly knocked back half a glass of wine.

"I'm tired. And she has a rental car," Milo said with an absent shrug.

"...If you let her stay with you for much longer, you will never get Dee back," Forrest promised him sourly.

"What makes you think I want Dee back?" Milo snapped suddenly.

"Well, you clearly don't want *Amber*. You can hardly bare to look at her."

Milo morosely glared into his empty glass. "...I saw Dee this morning with my lawyer, I tried to talk terms...y'know, money. Mahon was spitting feathers because I hadn't drawn up a pre-nup. So I offered her a deal that was more than fair...but she said she didn't want it. Dee wants nothing from me at all..." he said distantly.

"Well you'd better make sure those children are provided for, I don't care what brave-face Dee is putting on. You have an obligation to-"

"Of course I'm providing for the children! What kind of man do you think I am?" he rumbled but then became vacant again. "She just looked at me like I was dirt. To be honest, she didn't really look at me at all..."

"What did you expect? Your behaviour on your birthday was despicable!"

Forrest ranted as he had a dozen times before. "And what's more, you turned Ginny and I into accomplices! Dee and her friends blamed us for allowing you to come to the bar - as if we could have stopped you! She's barely spoken to us since!" he complained. "Dee was devastated - I've never seen her cry like that before, it was awful. You're sleeping with another woman out of pure spite when Dee didn't actually do anything wrong!"

"When is anybody in this family going to take my side? You weren't there! You didn't see what I saw!" Tears appeared in his eyes again and he shielded them from his brother by scraping a hand through his hair. Forrest recalled how he had seen this very reaction from Milo when he had initially caught Dee and Felix together. Milo had arrived at the house absolutely distraught. He must have cried for twenty minutes, inconsolable by Forrest who could not remember ever seeing Milo so upset other than that awful February when Andrew had died. Forrest wished he could tell Dee how horribly broken Milo was over all this but Milo had sworn him to secrecy. And as a man of the cloth, he took that seriously.

"...I'm sorry Milo, I am always here for you...but I just don't believe anything was going on between them. If they were having an affair, why would Felix take the entire blame and swear he was the one who had made a pass at her? The poor man has been completely alienated from the family - and if they had been sleeping together, surely you would expect him to want her to share some of the responsibility? Felix really isn't that noble," Forrest reasoned. "Both Ginny and I had a worrying feeling that Felix was developing some inappropriate feelings for Dee. He used to talk about her constantly - once he asked my advice about a crush he had on a married woman who had no feelings for him. Dee was oblivious to the whole thing!"

"But I saw her, Forrest. He was holding her and kissing her and her eyes were closed and she was making no attempt to break away..."

Forrest sighed. "Look, what you thought you saw does not warrant you taking up with an old flame and having a fling with her in some twisted fit of revenge. My loyalties will always be with you, Milo, but I won't just say what you want to hear. One of these days you are going to realise you've made a dreadful mistake. If you leave it any longer, Dee will have become too cold and remote to reach. Please, I just want you to consider what I'm saying whilst Amber is away, because very soon she will be back - and you are clearly miserable with her hanging around."

Milo removed the moisture from his eyes with his forefinger. "I don't think I can forgive Dee, Forrest. I hate my life and I miss my kids and my home - and I miss *her*..." he admitted out loud for the very first time. Yes, he missed his wife; those funny little things she said and did - half of which he didn't understand but he loved them anyway. He missed the way the small curve of her body snuggled in against him at night, the feel of her tiny hand in his. Everything. "...But I can't forgive her." Before he could embarrass himself any further, the telephone began to ring. Milo was glad of the distraction as he picked up the handset. "...Yes...that's right, I am. She did what...?"

*

When Dee finally came around that evening, she found herself in an unfamiliar bed in a clinical-looking white room. There were various medical items dotted around which gave her a clue as to where she was before she remembered what had happened. Felix was fast asleep in a chair beside her, his head cradled in his arms on her bed. It took her a while to be fully focused enough to speak; her head ached, her body ached and her mouth was bone dry.

"...I just love my life..."

Felix's head came up with a snap. "...Dee..." Before he could say anything else, he put his face in his hands and started to cry. She had seen him tear-up once or twice in the time she had known him, but never actually *cry* before.

"...Am I dying?" she asked blankly.

"No..."

"...Then what are you crying for?"

Felix gave a confused laugh. "...I guess I don't know," he smiled. "You were in a car crash."

"Yeah, that's kind of coming back to me. Is the other driver okay?" Dee asked apprehensively.

"Yes, he got away with nothing more than bruises," Felix advised her. "The police are about, actually. They were waiting for you to come round to ask you some questions."

"It's wasn't *my* fault!" Dee protested rather too vehemently.

"Dee, we know that. There are witness accounts to say he pulled out on you, the police just want your statement, that's all," he assured her with a comforting hand on hers. "...I was so worried about you."

"...I feel kind of terrible, what did I do to myself?" Her head pounded and inhaling was somewhat painful but other than that, she was not sure why she had been hospitalised.

"You hit your head on the windscreen and you've bruised your brain which was why you lost consciousness. That sounds worse than it really is, but they'd like to keep you in for a couple of days to keep an eye on you. Oh and you broke your wrist and a couple of ribs. Other than that, you're at the peak of your physical fitness," Felix finally joked with her. She *must* be okay.

She surveyed the plaster of Paris cast on her left wrist which was neatly wrapped in brightly-coloured purple tape. "Thank God the kids weren't with me. Oh my God, did I kill the car...?" Dee groaned and covered her face with her good hand.

"Oh yeah, it's totalled." Felix noticed her expression of pure disgust with herself. "Now be reasonable, Dee. A car is just a car and can be replaced-"

"I'm getting divorced at the end of the year and I'm going to be a single mother, I can't afford to go around crashing cars willy-nilly!" she whined.

"You have insurance, don't you? You're the injured party so you've nothing to worry about. Jesus, I'll buy you ten cars if that is all that's upsetting you..." he began but noticed the steely look she shot him. Dee hated having money thrown at her – which was why she was refusing almost all financial aid that Milo was arrogantly trying to thrust in her direction. Felix, although extremely rich like the rest of the family, had never dared to insult her like that before. "...All I'm saying is...you're alive and that's what's important."

"...Has Milo been in?" Dee suddenly asked with barely disguised hopefulness.

"...No, not yet..." Felix looked away with some embarrassment. "But everyone else has - your uncle, Cassie, Jerry, Ginny, Elliott, Bruce, Patrice, Evan and Forrest. In fact, I think a lot of them are still milling around the hospital. Forrest was with Milo when he first found out. The hospital called Milo as your next of kin. Mrs Dawson is taking the children to stay with their father because it was thought best that they didn't see you until you were awake."

"...So, he'll bring them in this evening before visiting ends - or tomorrow...?"

"...Well, either that or Mrs Dawson will..."

"...I see," Dee mouthed quietly. So, now she discovered that her husband didn't care whether she lived or died. No, he would probably prefer that she'd died. What a fabulous day.

"...Look, I don't know exactly what Milo is thinking right now, but I do know it's him who should have been sitting by your bedside for hours. And if he can't sort his priorities out enough to do that, then I think you're better off without him," Felix insisted and Dee was rather taken aback by that.

"...Didn't he even say anything?"

"Forrest told me Milo was obviously very upset when he found out – but I guess he couldn't make the leap to forgiveness. Forrest offered to take him to the hospital but he said he needed some time alone to think," Felix sighed resentfully. "Even if *you* haven't given up on Milo, after today, I certainly have. When Forrest rang me to say what had happened to you, I just ran to my car to get here. I couldn't believe it. I just felt sick to my stomach..."

"...It's okay, Felix, no real harm done. Maybe this head injury will be a blessing in disguise; I might stop marrying complete dicks," Dee smirked, and squeezed his hand that was still in hers.

Felix grinned and ran his fingers across her palm. "...Can you see yourself ever feeling that way? Y'know, stop falling for megalomaniacs and choose somebody a bit more down-to-earth next time? Somebody more like you...?"

Dee observed him warily. "...I don't know; I'm not sure even brain damage can cure my terrible taste in men..." She casually took her hand away, ignoring that searching look in his eyes. Dee had got away lightly after this car accident, but the emotional harm done was irreparable.

*

With a mildly warm plastic cup in her hand, Cassie Grant stepped out of the elevator and promptly bumped into Forrest, nearly spilling the coffee cup contents over his lap.

"...Oh, sorry..." Cassie stuttered.

"It's fine, you didn't catch me." Forrest smiled up at her from his wheelchair.

"...Any news?" Cassie asked tentatively.

"The nurse has just told me Dee is awake. Felix is with her now, explaining what's happened..."

"Oh, thank God!" Tears sprang into her eyes, for a while there Cassie thought she was going to lose her brand new cousin no sooner than she'd found her. "...Have you told Milo? Is he here yet?"

"...I called him but I don't think he's bringing the children tonight," Forrest grimaced.

"Priceless!" Cassie huffed and stormed on by but Forrest caught her wrist.

"Hey! Don't take it out on me! I'm his brother, not his conscience!" Forrest snapped, rather disappointed that Cassie had cooled towards him since Milo had left Dee.

"You should be doing more to talk him round! He's clearly making a complete fool of himself and everyone seems to be treading on eggshells around him instead of giving him the good slap he deserves! Well, I'll tell you what, if I see him anytime soon, he'll wish he'd never hired a detective to find me!"

"I've talked until I'm blue in the face, Cassie! Milo has never listened to me in his life! He didn't listen when I asked him to stop driving his car so fast and consequently wrapped it around a tree, and he won't listen now!" he barked and Cassie turned very pale. Everyone knew the disability story by now.

She sighed, chagrined. "...I'm sorry. I know it's not your fault but I just needed to vent some anger, I guess. I apologise," she said mournfully as she turned away but he was still hanging on to her wrist.

"...Cassie, I thought...I actually really like you but since all this happened, whenever I see you, you won't even make eye contact with me anymore." Forrest tugged at his dog collar. "I was thinking about calling you up one day and asking you out to dinner or the movies or something...but I guess that's a bad idea, right?"

"No, that's a good idea-" Cassie said rather doubtfully. "But do you think that would be a little disloyal to Dee? Oh, are we talking date-date or platonic-date by the way?" She was really rather blunt when one got to know her, a quality she shared with her cousin. Although the 'Antipodean' in her made her bluntness slightly more pronounced.

"Date-date," Forrest confirmed. "And I certainly don't think you would be disloyal to Dee if you accepted because I'm still very good friends with her...or at least I hope I am. She will always be my sister-in-law as far as I'm concerned. In fact, I would go as far as to say Dee would be pleased if we went out on a date-date." The corners of his mouth turned upwards into a small smile.

Cassie grinned back coyly. "...Yeah, I think she would...but we won't mention it tonight. Shall we go in to see her?"

*

The next morning, Milo busily dressed his son while giving Angel as much help as he could to pull on her denim jacket and baseball cap. She was beginning to look (and dress) just like her mother, and he couldn't help but like that.

"Honey, come on, we have to go see Mommy in the hospital," Milo explained for the umpteenth time. This was actually his second attempt to visit Dee in her sick-bed. When Mrs Dawson had dropped the children over early yesterday evening, he had finally pulled himself together and asked the nanny if she could stay with the kids at his apartment for a couple of hours. Before visiting hours ended, Milo needed to see with his own eyes that his wife was okay like Forrest's texts suggested. But something had stopped him in the hospital car park. It was probably the sight of Jerry milling around with Elliott at the main entrance. Jerry chatted and Elliott puffed on a cigarette. Milo had waited a long while for the pair to leave but they *didn't* and he just couldn't face getting into another argument with Jerry. And he wasn't sure if there was another entrance. So, in frustration, he had turned the key in the ignition of his Aston and driven back home.

"What's wrong with Mummy?" Angel repeated the same question she had asked all morning (and yesterday evening).

"Mommy had a little accident in her car but she's just fine now," Milo insisted as he pulled on Finley's soft shoes. "Alright, I think we're all set. Let's go." He grasped Finley in one arm and picked up a beautiful bunch of red roses in the other while ushering Angel out the door.

"...Hey, where are you off to?" Amber was standing out in the hall with a suspicious look on her face and her luggage in her hands.

"...Amber...you're back so soon...?" he gulped. "...Dee's been in a car accident and I'm taking the kids to the hospital to see their mother..." Milo said edgily because he was anxious to go. He couldn't even make room in his brain to ponder why Amber had returned only the morning after she had left.

"Yes, I heard. Milo...you know how I feel about you seeing Dee." Amber came in and closed the door behind her.

"Amber, Dee needs to see her children," Milo sighed.

"Then get the babysitter-woman to take them. Have you forgotten what your ex did to you? So she was careless driving her car, does that mean you forgive her everything?"

"I didn't say I forgave her, but I do need to see if she's okay..."

"Then ring your brother or call the hospital to find out. You don't need to see her in person. As soon as I arrived at my apartment in New York, your mother called to tell me what had happened, so I knew I just had to catch the next flight back to London to be with you."

"My mother? How did she know about Dee?"

"I don't know, perhaps your brother or one of your cousins called her. Anyway, you know your mother and I are very close and she thought I should know," Amber shrugged, her honey blonde hair bouncing around her shoulders. It was becoming clear to Milo that perhaps his mother was spoon-feeding Amber to ensure Dee would never be allowed to be a factor in his life again. Although that bothered him, it made no real difference. His marriage was over before anyone else had chosen to interfere.

"Look, you don't have to worry. I have no plans to get back with my wife but I do need to see for myself that she's safe. Whatever she has done, I don't want to see her hurt. She's the mother of my children and she's a good mother too…I will always care for her."

Amber frowned. "…So why the red roses? Red roses don't imply you care, red roses mean 'love', don't they?" she inquired and Milo realised that he may not get to the hospital on this particular occasion either.

"Amber, I really don't want to have this conversation in front of Angel, okay? I'll drop the kids off at Mrs Dawson's and she can take them to visit their mother…"

"No, no, I'll call Mrs Dawson and she can pick them up from here. That way we can spend the morning together." Amber kissed him sweetly and brushed by to reach for the phone.

*

The nurse was talking but Dee was having trouble listening because all the time she was hoping to interject with a question. She had slept very little during her first night in hospital and was looking forward to getting home and being with her children. The nurse shone a pen-torch in Dee's eyes, watching for pupil dilation, and tested the equality of strength in her arms and legs for the zillionth time. Bruce watched avidly as he loitered on the window sill. He was a keen fan of hospital dramas.

"So, if everything seems to be okay, can I go home today?" Dee asked with a childlike little grin on her face.

"No, because you've had a head injury and you lost consciousness, the doctor would like to keep an eye on you for another twenty-four hours and then you can go home in the morning."

Her hopeful face dissolved with the disappointing news. "But I'm fine, you said so yourself. I promise I'll just go back to my house and lie on the sofa. If I feel a little dizzy or strange, Bruce will bring me straight back."

"We'd just like to keep tabs on you to be on the safe side. It's only one more night." The nurse touched her arm and left Dee and her friend alone to chat. Dee came to sit beside Bruce.

"Bollocks," she sighed.

"Cheer up, the nurse said Mrs Dawson is on her way with the children," Bruce reminded her.

"Yeah, that's true…I guess Milo still doesn't care enough about my health to bother…" She stared distractedly from the window.

"Well, it's become clear to me that Milo is a fucking cock and he didn't deserve you. He had us all fooled," Bruce said rather sternly. "But I can promise you, he will come to regret his actions one day."

"…I've had to put on a brave face for everybody else. They all want me to do the 'tough Dee' thing so I do it because I don't want to keep sobbing on people's shoulders who can't deal with any more of my bellyaching. But I can't lie to you, Bruce. This thing with Milo has just ripped my heart out," Dee admitted, tears standing in her eyes. "I know it's over, but I feel so horribly sad about it. Other than you, he was my best friend in the world - my soul mate. But now I'm not even allowed to speak to him anymore." Her lip quivered and she wiped her eyes. "I know I'm more or less okay after the car accident, but he doesn't even care enough to come and visit me in the hospital. The man I love, the man I can't get out of my head, hates me so much he probably wishes I've not survived," she sniffed.

Bruce sighed. "...I *know* Milo loved you...and that can't have changed overnight. Every horrible little thing he's doing to you is his way getting revenge. That's the only way I can make sense of this." He held her hand gently.

"...That doesn't make me feel much better if it still means he's never coming back."

"You can't honestly want him back after everything he's done?"

She stared absently at her cast. "...I wouldn't *take* Milo back...but I *want* him back. I can't really imagine my life long-term without him; I certainly can't see myself meeting anyone new. I know I'll never love anyone as much as I loved him," Dee confessed painfully.

"...You thought that about Lance," Bruce reminded her.

"I did love Lance, I really did...but the way I felt about Milo, it was like falling in love for the very first time..." Dee shifted uncomfortably on the window sill. Her ribs were awfully painful, probably the most aggravating of her injuries. "But he's slept with another woman, he's admitted it. So even if he came to his senses and asked to come home, I'd have to turn him away...I'd *have* to," Dee said, almost exasperated with herself. She dreamed of him coming back just so she could humiliate him the way he had humiliated her - but was she brave enough to do it?

"But *would* you, Dee?"

"I'm in hospital and he isn't here, so I think we can safely say he's never coming back. And I'm never going to have to find out what I'd do..." Dee was glad when Bruce put his arms around her. She let herself cry because she knew it was okay to do that with him. Bruce didn't need to see feigned bravery or a stiff upper lip. Dee's current situation was terrible and there was no point in pretending otherwise.

*

The next morning, Dee was struggling to pack her holdall so Felix proceeded to take over the job for her. Dee held a squirming Finley in her good arm while she sat on her hospital bed. She distantly watched her daughter skipping about the room, wondering when this permanent low-level sickness in the pit of her stomach would ever wear off. Dee had felt this relentless nausea ever since Milo had left. The only relief from it was when she finally managed to fall asleep at night.

"Come on, cheer up. You've been harping on about going home for the last two days and now we're finally out of here," Felix chirped as he zipped up her bag and scooped up as many bunches of flowers as he could be bothered to carry in his free arm.

"...Yeah, I know. Let's go..." Dee smiled wearily, rose to her feet and followed him out of the room with her baby in her arms and Angel in tow.

Perhaps fifteen minutes after they had left, Milo arrived at the door of Dee's old room with a fresh bunch of red roses in his clutches. He stared at the empty bed and began to panic.

"Nurse," he said, grabbing the nearest passing uniformed woman he could find. He didn't really know *what* her job was, "...what happened to my wife?"

"Oh, you must be Mr Phillips. Mrs Phillips has been discharged – actually she hasn't long gone." The pretty black nurse smiled pleasantly.

"But the woman at reception said I could come in and see her," Milo sighed, relieved Dee wasn't dead but still extremely disappointed he hadn't caught her before she left. Now Dee would never know he had cared enough to come visit her.

"I'm sorry. I guess it hasn't filtered back to the ward-clerk that Mrs Phillips has actually been discharged. She left with her children. Oh, and a chap with a nice tan; he had wavy black hair...with a five o'clock shadow...if that helps?"

But it didn't help. Milo's heart sank. "...Oh, okay...thanks..." He didn't actually see the nurse depart because he was too wrapped up in his own thoughts and personal miseries.

NEED YOU LIKE A HOLE IN THE HEAD

Why did sickness always strike at some ungodly hour of the night? It was almost exactly three o'clock in the morning when Dee found herself kneeling on the bathroom floor with Angel's head in her lap. Dee had only been released from hospital a couple of days previously, she was supposed to be recuperating, not spending half the night holding her little girl's hair out of her face as she vomited down the toilet. But the job of a mother could never be put on hold, it was never suspended. The children needed her and Dee must attend to those needs.

Her skin prickled as she heard a rattle at the front door, a key turning in the lock downstairs. Well, burglars didn't have keys. So who was it at this time of night? Mrs Dawson surely didn't know Angel was ill - she wasn't psychic. Whilst Dee was wondering who else she had haplessly doled out keys to, the footsteps coming up the stairs finally arrived at the open bathroom door. It was Milo, of all people.

Dee was almost too stunned to speak for a moment before her anger made its way back to the surface (where it pretty much lived these days). "...Why have you still got a key?" she said, affronted - forgetting her hair was all over the place and she wore only a vest and PJ bottoms.

"...I thought I'd keep it for emergencies," he said awkwardly, standing there in jeans and a crumpled sweatshirt. For a man who was always pristine, his hair was almost as tousled as hers; he could easily have just scrambled out of bed, thrown on the first thing and jumped in his car.

"It's three in the morning, what are you doing here...?" She screwed up her face, confused.

Milo finally knelt down beside her in the doorway. "Bruce called me...he said the kids were sick..." Bruce had actually said an awful lot more than that. He had been staying with Dee for a few days to help out the invalid - but Dee had sent him home that evening when she had noticed Angel going downhill. There was no point in spreading this bug to friends. Bruce had actually called Milo 'a waste of space' on his rant down the phone; he said Milo was a 'disgrace' and ought to be 'pulling his weight' while Dee was recovering from her injuries - and that his family needed him. That and a few choice swear words.

Dee looked down in her lap. "...It's just Angel..."

"...You've just got out of hospital...when did you last sleep?" Milo reached out to push Dee's hair from her eyes but she automatically flinched from him. Her face was hard and Dee kept her eyes averted and said nothing. Milo slowly withdrew his hand, spurned.

Angel suddenly raised her head, peered at her father and said, "Daddy, I sick..."

"I know baby-girl," Milo replied sadly - he raised his hand again to comfort the child but Dee shook her head.

"It's not worth all of us going down with it," she scolded. Angel placed her exhausted head back in her mother's lap and promptly fell asleep again. Dee used to love it when Milo called Angel his 'baby-girl'. Funny, now she loathed it.

"Go back to bed, Dee...I'll stay up with her," Milo said softly, glancing at the plaster cast on her arm. Surely Dee couldn't cope with this in her present state of health?

"No, she needs her mummy when she's sick - that's what she's used to," Dee insisted sharply then thought slightly better of it. "...Take Finn back to yours...please. I don't want him catching this bug too..."

Milo nodded his head, wishing he'd thought of that. "Okay..." He climbed to his feet then disappeared along the hall. Dee wondered if she were dreaming, she had sat in that hospital room for two days and hoped and prayed Milo would come to see her. But he never did. Had this selfish pig of a husband actually come to help her now? Well, only because Bruce had called and berated him down the phone, she bet. She would bloody kill Bruce!

Finally, Milo returned with his half-asleep son wrapped up in a grow-bag. He held a small bag of Finn's things and a blanket in the other hand.

"...When will you bring him back?" Dee kept her eyes on the floor. A tear was tracking down her cheek and she didn't want Milo to see. She had never felt more alone in her life, and this was the way it was always going to be - Dee realised that now. If she had raised her eyes, she would have noticed Milo's eyes had pooled with tears too. He used to be a part of this household, they were a team once - dealing with these little blips in family life together. Now he didn't belong here; he didn't really belong anywhere.

Milo tried to hide the hoarseness in his voice. "...Just call me when Angel is forty-eight hours clear...and I'll send him home..." He stood there for a moment more - he with one child, her with the other, wondering if maybe she might look at him. But Dee never did. So he turned and slowly descended the stairs with his son in his arms. Dee heard the front door open and close again.

She would try to make the best of this. At least Finn was one less dependent to worry about, maybe she and Angel could sleep late tomorrow and catch up on some much needed shut-eye. Dee contemplated how she would sit still on this cold bathroom floor for another hour or two until she was sure Angel had stopped throwing up, then she would take the child back to bed with her - it would be just like the old days, when Dee and Angel were all the other had.

*

Halfway through May and a couple of weeks after the events in the middle of the night at her house, Dee strolled along George Street with Bruce during their lunch hour. The weather was warming up and Dee wore no more than a lightweight black leather biker jacket which was unusual for her, being that she was such a cold-blooded person. Without discussing it, they turned into the alfresco area of Benito's and were about to take a seat when Dee eyed Milo sitting at a table with Amber roughly ten yards away. Milo was staring distractedly into the distance while Amber chatted to him and ran a finger over the back of his hand which rested on the table. They looked like the perfect couple; tall, attractive, immaculate. Dee just bet she had looked incredibly incongruous when she had been with him - the odd couple; no wonder it hadn't worked. Then Milo caught sight of her and Dee recognised that expression of sheer distress she had noticed before on his birthday at his apartment.

"...Shall we go somewhere else?" Bruce asked warily.

"No, he's seen us now," Dee said quietly and sat down. "We're going to be bumping into him fairly regularly so we'd just better get used to it." But Dee found having the sight of him constantly rubbed in her face when she couldn't have him very hard to take sometimes. Milo was *sleeping* with that woman, *her* Milo - or at least he was once. Just then an elderly couple ambled out from inside the coffee shop, holding hands. Both Dee and Milo noticed them, strolling out onto the street happily. That should have *them* one day; Dee honestly thought they'd grow old together. Milo caught her eye again, sorrowfully, as if in agreement. But Dee looked away. She nonchalantly flopped open the work-diary she had been carrying and proceeded to make a business call without giving her husband a second glance. 'Tough Dee' was in order today. Bruce wondered how she managed to put on such an amazing act when he knew how badly bruised she was over her husband.

Milo watched her carefully from the corner of his eye. This was the first time he had seen her since that night at the house when Angel was poorly. Dee had since dutifully sent the children over with Mrs Dawson every week and after two days, Mrs Dawson brought them home again. Dee and Milo need never set eyes on each other, or at least that would have been her plan if only they did not live in the same town. Her right wrist was still cocooned in the white plaster cast, covered in purple fibreglass tape. Her favourite colour. Dee's movements were awkward which he presumed was still due to her broken ribs. Milo wondered how she was coping. He hoped she wasn't in too much pain. He thought about how inappropriate it may or may not be to go over there and wish her a speedy recovery, but Dee had been injured *so* many days ago that it was now too little too late.

"I'll pay the bill," Milo sighed as he rose to his feet and wandered dejectedly into the restaurant, keeping an eye on Dee as he went. Not once did she return his gaze.

Bruce grinned as Dee finished her call. "Did you see Milo staring at you? He was feeling very sorry for himself, just longing to catch your eye. Well, let him look at what he can never have, the prick."

"I wasn't looking," Dee shrugged with a fake indifference. But now she noticed that Amber was eyeing them with a measured stare and proceeded to rise from the table and totter over in incredibly high black heels and a slinky black shift dress. Dee glanced ruefully over her own outfit of jeans and shell-toe Adidas - she just wasn't in the same league.

"...What the fuck does she want?" Bruce muttered under his breath before Amber reached them. The intruder pulled up a chair and was now wearing the sickliest, most pitying and patronising expression ever witnessed in modern society.

"Hello Dee." Amber committed the most foolish and unthinkable act by actually *sitting* on that chair and joining them. She ignored the disgusted looks she was greeted with. "I was wondering how you were after that horrible accident?" Amber persevered when she received no answer. "...Look, you know there was no ill-feeling on my part when Milo left you for me. You must remember that he was my boyfriend first when he decided to take up with you after that Ball. I really think if Andrew hadn't died, Milo wouldn't have taken leave of his senses the way he did...because your marriage was really very badly-matched. I suppose even you see that now. Anyway, I just want you to know that when we see you around town, we don't wish you any animosity."

And that was too much for Dee, that woman speaking for Milo as though they were a proper couple. But Dee had to broach this the right way because too much emotion was never a good image to portray. Dee turned theatrically to Bruce. "Why is Gash-Mouth talking to me?" she asked with mock-disbelief. Bruce went on to impersonate the action of wielding a knife, making sharp stabbing motions while humming the high strings section of the 'Psycho' theme tune to underline his point. Then Dee joined in with the low strings cello section and the pair burst into hysterics, got up and left her there at the table. They wandered off and Amber could hear them laughing long after they disappeared from view.

When Milo returned, he found Amber sitting red-faced at the table Dee and Bruce had been occupying. He slowly journeyed to join her. "...What are you doing over here?"

"I just came over to wish her well after the accident – I just wanted to be pleasant and grown-up about it. But they started singing the 'Psycho' theme tune and laughed at me like a couple of children!" she said furiously.

Milo could not stifle the snigger that burst from his mouth. He rubbed his lips to disguise his amusement. "...Oh, you just have to ignore Dee when she's with Bruce. They're incorrigible when they get together."

"She called me Gash-Mouth!" Amber protested and Milo steeled himself not to laugh again. Amber did have rather a large mouth when he stopped to think about it. Milo put his hands in his pockets and sighed. He missed Dee's silly, schoolgirl humour. In fact, he missed every little quirky, neurotic thing about her.

*

It was only a day or two later that Dee received the first of her obnoxious phone calls. She was actually not at home when it arrived but she was none-the-less shocked when she pressed the button to hear the messages on her answering machine one day.

"...You're going to be very sorry for making fun of me at the coffee shop. The gloves are now off, bitch!" the malicious female voice threatened. "I tried to be civil with you for Milo's sake and because I pitied you, but nobody laughs at me and gets away with it! He's mine now. You stole him from me but the tables have turned. You only got your claws into him because Andrew died and you took advantage of that! It's me he really wants. Did you know he wants to marry me? Did he tell you that?" Amber ranted. "The minute he can divorce you, we'll be getting hitched. And you know what else? You're not even plain like he says you are; you're just ugly." The message ended there and Dee could not help but feel rather unsettled by it. She cautiously decided not to delete the message, or any other messages, that may follow in case it was ever required in court one day.

But the calls kept on coming - usually one a day. One morning when Dee was alone in the house, the phone rang again. People who knew her normally just rang her mobile so Dee was instantly filled with rage as she grabbed the telephone receiver. "Hello?" She was greeted with quiet little sniff. A woman's sniff. "If that's you Amber, you can say whatever you have to say to me right now! I'm here in the house so you don't have to leave one of your cowardly little messages! Or better yet, meet me in town and say it to my face!" Dee seethed, almost shaking with anger. How dare that woman repeatedly belittle her?

"...What...? Dee, it's me...Cass," the fragile voice sounded and sniffed again.

"Oh Cassie, sorry. I thought you were...somebody else," Dee stammered, not wanting to get into the 'Amber' thing. She was actually too embarrassed to tell her friends about it. "...Are you alright?" She gnawed on her lip, there was something about that small little voice; it was tentative and...broken...

"...Dee, it's my dad...he had another heart attack...they've just taken him away," she said before her voice dissolved into wracking sobs, barely able to get the rest of the words out. "He- he didn't make it this time..."

LOVE YOU TO DEATH

Forrest anxiously wheeled himself along a gravel path to get to the roadway in a Wimbledon cemetery. He couldn't seem to propel himself fast enough, so intent was he to be hidden from visibility by the crop of trees from the congregation gathered by the hole in the ground. His tailored black suit seemed to be restricting his ease of movement.

"Milo, I'm really not sure it was a good idea that you came," Forrest announced upon reaching his brother who stood (evidently unsuccessfully) out of site by the trees. Milo shifted his weight from foot to foot, loosening his tie.

"I'm not planning to stay long – I just wanted to pay my respects..." he said, craning his neck to try to catch a glimpse of his wife by the graveside. "I can't believe Gordon's really dead. He seemed in good health when I last saw him."

"We knew he had heart problems, unfortunately his heart gave out for good this time. Cassie said it was instantaneous, so I imagine he didn't suffer," Forrest explained. Gordon had literally dropped dead whilst pottering in the garden of their Wimbledon home. "Look, I know it was me who called to let you know, but I didn't really mean for you to come here. Dee will just get mad and you aren't Cassie's favourite person either. Let me pass on your condolences for you," he said pragmatically.

"Is Dee alright?" Milo asked with a kind of quiet desperation, still trying to catch site of her in the group of people all dressed exactly the same in black. "She barely has any family as it is, and for Gordon to be taken from her at a time like this-" he stalled. At a time like what? *This* terrible time that he had brought about?

"...I don't really know. She's trying to be strong for Cassie," Forrest advised gravely.

Milo suddenly looked back into Forrest's troubled eyes. "Yes, of course...poor Cassie. She must be taking this very badly...how is she?" he asked almost as an afterthought.

"Not good, obviously..." But Forrest was interrupted by a small

243

commotion just a few yards behind him on the path. An irate Dee and an equally disgruntled Bruce were marching over to greet the two men.

"What the fuck are *you* doing here?" Bruce snapped before Dee could open her mouth, which had become merely a screwed up opening in her face.

Milo ignored Bruce entirely and met Dee's eyes with a sincerely tormented expression in his own. "Dee, I'm so very sorry for your loss...I only came to pay my respects, I didn't mean to intrude-"

"Well you are intruding! Nobody invited you so I'd like you to leave before Cassie catches sight of you. She's in bits as it is!" Dee glowered, but the anger belied the pure misery written all over her face. Red, blotchy patches circled her eyes and her face was clearly tearstained. Another bereavement, one of too many.

"I- I can imagine she's distraught. Please tell her how sorry I am. But I just wanted to see if *you* were alright, you'd only just found Gordon and now..."

Bruce stepped in front of Dee as if to shield her from him. "Dee doesn't need your concern or your sympathies anymore. *We* are her friends, not you. You don't belong here. The only thing you need to do is be a father to your children, if you think you can manage that." His hands were balled into little fists as though he could happily strike Milo.

Milo was quite taken aback by all this spite, he hadn't expected a warm welcome exactly, but this? And Bruce had been such a loyal supporter of his when he first arrived in Dee's life. "I only wanted..." Milo's eyes strayed to the congregation again. "...Is that Felix over there? What is *he* doing here?" he asked confusedly.

"Unlike *you*, Felix had befriended my uncle. He took him to his club lots of times, they were friends – he took the time to get to know him!" Dee glared, rubbing the cast on her wrist distractedly. "Felix was invited to this funeral, you weren't!"

"...But why Felix and not me? I was the one who found Gordon and Cassie..." he stuttered; wounded and under attack. He had only come to offer some kind of comfort, but Dee evidently despised him now.

"Oh I wondered how long it would take him to crowbar *that* in!" Bruce spat.

Dee narrowed her eyes disdainfully. "You're not still expecting kudos for that, are you? You paid a man a lot of money to find them and you've had your thanks. So go away and let us grieve in peace!" She watched Milo menacingly, her eyes angrily roving over his suit and tie in the darkest of charcoal greys. Dee just bet it was chosen with the greatest precision; dark enough to be similar to black for a funeral if he were welcomed, but *not* exactly black in case he was turned away.

"Dee," Forrest intervened at last, "Milo is only here out of concern for you, he means no harm..."

Dee suddenly turned on Forrest then. "Get your brother out of here before Cassie sees him, okay? She can't cope with anymore drama today!" she ordered, briefly flashed another frosty glare at Milo and spun on her heel, marching back in the direction of the graveside. Bruce had put an arm around her shoulder and escorted her away. Milo stared after them wordlessly.

*

Relations were so incredibly poor between the married couple these days, that it was at the beginning of June that Milo paid his first visit to the house in weeks. Dee wasn't exactly welcoming. She knew he had been licking his wounds after Gordon's funeral, but she didn't care how hurt *he* felt. So she was instantly on her guard, because there had to be something he wanted or his liaisons would have been made through Mr Mahon or Mrs Dawson. If it hadn't been for the night he had come to the house when Angel had been unwell or the funeral debacle, Dee may have been forgiven for believing they may never actually need to speak in person again.

"What is it now?" Dee asked harshly as he stepped through the door.

"Ah, the old Dee I used to know and love," Milo was (perhaps inappropriately) attempting to be light-hearted but it fell on deaf ears. Still, the irony wasn't lost of either of them. It was the same kind of hostile Dee that he had first met almost two years ago and it was hard enough to break the ice the first time. Now it seemed impossible. He took on a sorrowful expression. "...Look, if you thought that my showing up at Gordon's funeral was in poor taste, then I'm sorry. But I just wanted you to know I cared. If I'd have sent a text or flowers or a card...or just said nothing, you'd have thought that was in poor taste too. So I couldn't really win whatever I did," he tried to explain softly.

"Always the injured party, aren't you?" Dee scornfully raised an eyebrow, turned her back on him and went through to the kitchen.

"...Really though, Dee – how are you? Losing your uncle so soon after finding him must have been-"

"I wish people would stop asking me that with those hang-dog eyes. It's Cassie everyone should be worried about. She's lost her *father*." In truth, Dee just didn't know how to feel about her late uncle's death. She was heartbroken, of course. Newly introduced into her life after years of never knowing of the other's existence, and then he was gone. But Dee felt guilty over her grief. Yes, it was yet another bereavement, but she hadn't really known him as well as she would have liked. The new relationship was still being forged just as it had been severed. "And it's our kids you should pity; coming from a broken home, just getting to know the closest they were ever going to get to a decent grandparent - unlike those evil bastards you call *your* parents - and now Gordon has gone..." For one moment, it appeared Dee was about to burst into tears. But she seemed to shake herself and the hurt etched across her face was instantly buried. Dee had hardened her heart so much after Milo, she was still too numb to let this new grief in.

"...I know...I thought of that. And it must be awful for Cassie being an Australian bereaved here in the U.K. Thank God she has you," he said, and then, more tentatively, "...how are your injuries?" Milo mainly wanted to change the subject. But in all honesty, he just wanted to know how Dee was coping and had never got the chance to ask.

Dee rubbed her cast as she stood in the middle of kitchen and thought about it. "...Well let me see, I had double vision and headaches for a bit. My wrist feels okay now but it still aches, the cast comes off soon. It's my ribs that have been the worst problem because I can't turn over in bed. But since in reality, you're not really bothered, why don't you get on with what you actually came to talk about?" Dee stiffened again, he hadn't been concerned enough to visit her in the hospital so it was too bloody late for his concern now! She skulked off to stand at the breakfast bar, her back to him again.

Milo gritted his teeth. "Hey, I am bothered! I came to the-" he began to insist, coming further into the kitchen but soon decided it was futile to try to defend himself. Dee was now climbing up on a stool at the breakfast bar, pondering over a magazine and tapping a biro between her teeth. Milo gathered this was the occupation his arrival had interrupted. "...Are you always going to treat me like this?" he said ruefully. "You can't just pretend I didn't happen. I mean, *you* should have called me for help when Angel was sick, not Bruce. You had a broken wrist and you needed me. I'm still a part of this family - I have responsibilities to you guys. I ought to have been invited to the funeral too. At the very least, can't we agree to be civil for the sake of the children?" Milo asked plaintively. He was so very tired of the constant hostility - it was wearing him down.

"If the children were here I would be, but they're not."

Milo signed resignedly. "...So, where *are* the kids?" There was no breaking down her walls this time. Even though she was doing the 'impassive thing', Dee was always inclined to be hot-headed and there was just no point in railing against her when she was like this.

"Angel is at nursery and Finley is with Mrs Dawson," Dee replied. "Now anytime you feel like getting to the point, you just let me know," she said without looking up, an imperturbable tranquillity about her. Milo could not pretend her coldness did not sting because once they had been each other's closest friend. Now she was the insolent Dee of old who was so belligerent and spikey, he could not even attempt to get close to her.

"...I just wanted to know if I could take the children on Thursday and Friday because I'm flying to New York at the weekend." Milo rubbed his eyes. A stress-headache was beginning to brew.

"You came here to ask me that? Why didn't you send a text or a message through Mrs Dawson or, failing that, send your man-servant?" Dee twisted her face.

"I don't have a man-servant," Milo groaned wearily.

"Yes, I suppose that will be okay," Dee shrugged, barely even gracing him with her attention. She was jotting something in her magazine and Milo guessed it was one of those annoyingly easy crosswords or a romantic quiz. He knew it was a ruse to display her best unfeeling act, but it still hurt.

Milo frowned. "...Dee, did you really need to be quite so mean to Amber the other week? I know it was inappropriate, but in her misguided wisdom, she was only trying to be friendly."

"Was she? *Was she though*?" Dee said in a mocking voice, still greeting him with only the sight of her back.

"Amber was really upset you'd nicknamed her '*Gash-Mouth*'. Maybe she does have a fairly large mouth...but you and Bruce needn't always be so childish," he mildly rebuked her, merely wanting to keep the conversation going if he was honest. He even sat down at the kitchen table, hoping to chat a while, hoping she'd offer him tea so that he could stay longer. But it didn't appear likely, the way she sat facing away from him.

"You should hear what we call you," Dee drawled, smiling to herself.

"...I have a nickname now? What is it?" Milo was almost amused.

"Well I'll give you a clue; if you've ever read 'Paradise Lost', that might give you a hint..."

Milo bristled because he had. And he knew all too well it was about the various different devils that had formerly been angels but were thrown out of heaven to occupy hell. "...You call Amber and I whatever you like if it makes you feel better."

"Feel better? Now that would imply that I give a shit," Dee retorted while scratching her head calmly with the end of the pen, then she twisted around on her stool and gave him a neutral stare, mulling something over. "Talking of Amber, when you come back from New York, there is something we need to chat about..." she said, seemingly anxious about something.

"No, let's talk about it now." He narrowed his eyes, this sounded ominous.

"...Okay, well at first I ignored it but the more I think about it, I'm beginning to feel concerned..." She twisted her mouth uncertainly.

"...About what?"

"Your girlfriend has started nuisance calling. If I actually answer the phone, she hangs up but if the machine picks up, she's leaving unpleasant messages." Dee chewed her lip. For some reason, she was nervous about telling him. She would have thought she would have enjoyed rubbishing Amber but she felt somewhat like a tell-tale, snitching on his girlfriend to score points.

"...What, Amber? Don't be silly," he scoffed, but somewhat half-heartedly - anxiously even.

"How did I know you wouldn't believe me?" Dee sighed, picked up the phone and dialled her voicemail and put it on speakerphone. "I'm many things Milo, but I'm not a liar." She waited patiently for the incriminating messages, she had saved every one.

The pair listened to the recording of the malevolent woman cursing and hurling insults at Dee's expense. Milo's shoulders were already beginning to sag and his face turned an awfully pale, waxy shade. Amber continued, "did you know we're already talking about the wedding? We'll be getting married in America and I've persuaded him to move back there with me. I'm going to start a family straight away and once I've given birth to the *true* Phillips heir, your two little brats will barely exist in his eyes. Not that Angel ever mattered to him. Milo only adopted her to keep you sweet. You and Milo were a mistake - everybody said you looked ridiculous together; even he admits that now. He's *mine*. As if a plain and inconsequential girl like you would have a chance against someone like me-"

Dee switched off the machine and stared at her ashen-faced and silent husband. "...And so on and so on. I've got quite a few messages just like that – if you want to hear them. The thing is Milo, Angel could have been with me and overheard some of the vicious things that woman has been saying and it's just not on." Dee folded her arms.

"...I never said I was going to marry her...I never said I was going back to live in America either! And *nobody* said you and I looked ridiculous together - least of all me!" Milo gaped. "And I'm certainly not starting a family with her! You know I love Angel like my own and Finley-" He shook his head, totally aghast.

"Did you hear what she called your children? Brats, she called them brats. I'm sorry, Milo, I want you to see your kids as much as possible but I don't think I can allow them to stay with you if I know she's there. I'm not being vindictive but I am the only advocate Angel and Finley have and I've got to think of their safety," Dee explained. "It's becoming clear that Amber bears a grudge against them so how can I knowingly entrust them to her when they're in your care? How do I know you won't leave them with her for a few minutes? How do I know she won't give them a quick slap to teach them a lesson when you aren't around?" Dee watched him in utter turmoil, sitting there at the table. "I don't care what you do or who you sleep with anymore, but if you marry her, well then I'm going to have to rethink how we go about you having access to the children. You're going to have to buy her an apartment or something and she's going to have to stay *there* when you have the kids over - not at yours," Dee said. "You're lucky I'm not calling the police..."

"I am *not* going to marry her!" Milo declared again, throwing up his arms, exasperated. "This is insane! I haven't even-" His head was in his hands, and he was muttering something under his breath about, 'madness' and 'gone too far' and 'out of control'.

Dee didn't think she had ever seen him quite so agitated. Milo was clearly suffering and it suddenly dawned on her that when she had prophesized at The Dorchester that he would regret the day he had ever started this - and how he would be sorry, well *today* was that day. It was funny how Dee wasn't as exultant as she had expected to be. She almost felt a bit sorry for him. "...Of course I trust you, I don't like you very much but I trust you implicitly with the children. You're a good dad...but Amber? There's just no way I'm letting her anywhere near them again when it's quite clear she detests them," Dee proclaimed. "What sort of mother would if I be if I sent them to your house when I now know her to be unhinged? I mean, I know Bruce and I joked about her being a 'psycho', but I didn't know it was going to turn out to be true." She took a breath and assessed the damage again, he was staring absently at the grain in the wood on the table-top. Dee leaned back against the breakfast bar. Could she really kick a man when he was down like this? Yes, yes she could. "...I can see this has upset you...but I'm afraid when it comes to me, you get back out what you put in. And you've knocked every last bit of compassion out of me. You've made me what I am," she continued putting the boot in. "You brought this on yourself, Milo...and if Amber is still the woman you want to spend the rest of your life with, then good luck to you, mate - because you're going to need it."

"Of course I don't-!" But he was too deflated to continue. "...I'm so sorry. I had no idea, I swear. I had no idea," Milo said very quietly. "This will never happen again. I promise she will never bother you again." Finally, he stood up. He looked at her as though he were about to say something rather meaningful. "...I'm truly saddened about Gordon, but I'm glad to see you're feeling better after the accident. I was really worried, you know. Goodbye, Dee..." Milo walked gravely from the kitchen and left the house.

*

The next answering machine message Dee received was from Milo. He had called the following day to say he would not be taking the children this week after all because he was flying to America early and staying out there until the end of the month. Amber's calls stopped abruptly.

GONE

Forrest and Ginny sat bickering at one of the tables in Dee's coffee shop on a lovely June day; the first time since the incident at 'The Dorchester' that they had visited. They sat on one of the sofas with Bruce and Evan and argued the toss about Milo's sudden disappearance. Cassie hadn't been out much of late, unsurprisingly. She was still suffering greatly over the loss of her father and Dee tried to spend as much time with her as she could, but also tried to balance that with giving Cassie space to grieve too. Dee thought her four friends were currently squabbling rather well without her opinion about Milo, so she stayed silent and sauntered in her flip-flops over to the till to serve two customers. Just lately, she had started enjoying working in the shop - even serving. Dee loved being a mother, but she liked having a purpose outside the home too. And since Milo had left, she needed to keep her mind as occupied as possible. She had actually found she was oddly good with the general public too; she laughed at their jokes about the weather and joined in with their small-talk.

"Oh my God...my little bird has flown the nest." Evan pretended to cry whilst watching Dee. The others smiled. "So Bruce, I hear you're moving into your new house next week?"

Bruce looked up warily. "...Um...yeah..."

"Oh yes, Dee bought you a house, that's so *nice*." Ginny pat Bruce's knee somewhat patronisingly.

Forrest wrinkled his nose. "...Can Dee afford to be doing that right now?"

"She didn't exactly *buy* me a house," Bruce complained. "I said 'no' about a million times but she was insistent. So I tried to get her just to pay the deposit but she wouldn't have that either. Anyway, Dee's bought the house and I've convinced her to let me pay her the mortgage...mates-rates, of course."

"You don't have to justify anything to us, Bruce," Ginny assured him. "Property is always an investment."

"That's what Dee keeps saying," he shrugged awkwardly.

"So you are splitting up with Patrice then?" Ginny said.

Bruce sighed. "...Well, maybe. We've actually been getting on a lot better but we've agreed my moving out will be for the best to give us some space..." There was the small matter of the other guy on the scene but Patrice insisted nothing physical had come of that and never would until he had decided where his relationship with Bruce stood.

"Did you see that?" Dee came bounding back over. "I actually made a mochaccino and a skinny decaf latte without anybody's help! Boom!" She sunk down on the sofa beside Evan who grinned at her with a roll of his eyes.

"So Dee, Milo didn't say if he was actually flying out *with* Amber?" Forrest began pretty much where he had left off.

"Oh God, you're not still going on about that? I actually went over there to serve *customers* to get away from this," Dee grumbled, picked up a horribly bland financial report Evan had prepared for her and proceeded to pretend to read it.

"Come on Dee, you must think it's all a bit strange," Ginny pressed.

"Milo has been acting strangely since he left me and I've never pretended to understand it." Dee did not meet their penetrating stares, flicking through the report instead.

"But you must have a theory about it? This all started with Amber making malicious phone calls to you," Forrest said. "I saw him just before he left and he wouldn't tell me anything but there were deep scratches on his face. Do you think they fought?"

Dee feigned indifference, although the 'scratches' were new on her. "I don't know. Maybe he strangled her, chopped her up into little pieces and buried her in Richmond Park," she grinned blandly. Ginny and Forrest stared at her with horrified expressions on their faces and then glanced worriedly at each other. Laughing, Evan placed his mug of hot chocolate on the coffee table. And since Dee had an appreciative audience, she continued, "and if he hasn't, I will."

"Can I help?" Evan chuckled.

"You can do the chopping," Dee assured him. It was a bit of a sick joke really, especially since it had become known what had befallen Lance's secretary. And Lance's name had never been, or probably ever would be cleared.

"Guys, don't joke about these things...perhaps something *has* happened to her..." Ginny's hand strayed nervously to her mouth.

"Don't you guys know Milo at all? He's an arrogant, manipulative little shit, but he wouldn't hurt Amber. She and Milo have probably had a big fight and gone to America to patch it up properly. And what's more, I don't even care anymore so can we stop banging on about it?" Dee rolled her eyes.

"Here-here," Evan agreed, sipping his drink.

"You know, you don't do yourself any favours with your 'I don't give a crap' routine," Forrest said rather sternly.

"I've never heard you say 'crap' before. Say some other swear words and I'll record them on my phone," Dee said indolently, actually pulling her mobile out. "I've been looking for a new ringtone..."

Forrest ignored her. "Milo says you're so aloof around him lately that you're just impossible. You need to learn to be friends for the children, at least. I told him this hard-nosed act you do is a coping mechanism. I told him deep down you are still very upset about losing him, but I really think you should try to be a little nicer if you do actually want him to come back."

"Who are you to tell Milo that? I never said you could speak for me! It isn't for you to tell him how I feel! I don't know what planet you're living on, but everyone else knows that Milo and I are never getting back together. Even if he did see the error of his ways, which I sincerely doubt, I wouldn't take him back because he's shagging another woman. You religious-types do understand that adultery is *wrong*, don't you?" Today Dee was not to be trifled with, not since she had become her old irascible self was she someone to be trifled with. Forrest was lost for words for a moment.

Forrest gave her a withering look. "I realise he has hurt you but surely you still have the capacity for forgiveness? And should you really have befriended Felix again? That just puts an even bigger wedge between you and Milo."

"Are you listening to yourself? A wedge between me and Milo? The wedge between us is the woman he's fuc-"

Ginny intervened then. "...Forrest just wants you back in our family, Dee," she said softly. "We all do. I know when you've been hurt, sometimes it's easier to wear a hard shell, I've done it myself. But I know you're terribly unhappy, I know how much you loved Milo."

"So what? He left her? What do you expect her to do?" Evan began antagonistically. "Milo was the one who walked out. He was the one who had an affair with another woman. Do you think Dee should still be calling him daily to beg for a reconciliation? Dee did all that at the beginning, but there comes a time when a person needs to focus on their self-esteem; because sometimes that's all you have."

Ginny eyed him suspiciously. "Everything I have ever said and done has been in defence of Dee. I want her to be happy just as much as you do," she protested.

"Yeah, and what about your boyfriend? It seems you're quite happy to let him browbeat Dee about how 'stupid' she was to ignore his advice about marrying Milo. You allow Jerry to constantly berate her and tell Dee 'he told her so'."

"Jerry is a person in his own right. I don't happen to agree with his opinions but I can't change them."

"The very fact that you continue seeing someone who is obviously an obnoxious oaf is tantamount to condoning his behaviour. It's abundantly clear to everybody else but you that Jerry is a bitter and unpleasant little man. Dee may be alone now but it's better that than being with a person who makes you feel small. Why don't you sort out your own messed up life before you start telling Dee how to run hers?" Evan argued hotly.

Ginny's mouth fell open. "…What has Jerry's and my relationship got to do with anything? What has it got to do with *you*?"

"Well, since Dee's private life is up for discussion, why not yours? Why not mine? I just happen to think you're an intelligent woman and you could do a lot better."

"Well, let's talk about your private life, shall we? Who are you? How come you're so perfect and self-actualised?"

"Nobody said I had it sussed. My wife died and now I raise an eleven-year-old daughter by myself because I haven't found the right woman for me. I'm single and I'm not terribly happy about it but I'd rather that than be with someone who's evidently wrong for me and detrimental to my happiness."

"Who says Jerry is wrong for me?" Ginny was beginning to become irate. "And since when were you appointed Dee's personal guard-dog?"

"Whoa! Time-out, guys!" Dee interrupted, subconsciously using some of her husband's lingo. "Evan, I'm truly flattered that you should defend me but it really isn't necessary. And Forrest, Ginny, I'm honoured that you care about me but your well-meaning advice isn't going to change anything. Milo and I will be getting divorced whether you like it or not. But Forrest, you'll always be my wonderful brother-in-law and Ginny, you will always be my great friend – whatever happens," Dee promised. "Do we always have to argue about my mixed up personal life? I know I make it a very easy topic to fall back on but sometimes I'd like to talk about something more mundane. Although, the subject of *Ginny's* relationship and Evan's *lack* of relationships was a nice distraction, cheers for that. But there's enough animosity between myself and Milo and I'd really like it if my friends could get along."

"You're right, Dee. I'm sure nobody meant to be overly opinionated," Forrest smiled and patted Ginny's hand to calm her. She and Evan were still glaring at each other.

"So Evan, would you help me at the counter for a moment?" Dee forcibly grabbed Evan's hand and dragged him to his feet and over to the coffee machines, pretending to fiddle with some buttons. "What was all that about, Evan?" she whispered. "Why were you picking on Ginny?"

"...I wasn't picking on her...but if you're willing to tell people how to run their lives, you have to be prepared to have people inflict their opinions on you," he huffed.

"You know Ginny only wants to help. She has never taken sides between me and Milo and she really could have. She could have blamed me for the whole thing and said I led Felix on – but she didn't."

"How noble of her." Briefly, Evan was required to use the espresso machine for real as a customer came up to the counter for a macchiato and a millionaire shortbread.

Once the customer had gone, Dee said, "I know you and Bruce aren't keen on Felix and I understand why you feel like that...but don't you like Ginny either?"

"Well, of course I do!"

Dee watched him with a measured gaze. "...You don't *like* her, do you?" She finally worked it out.

Evan turned to her and pursed his lips. "What if I do? What difference does it make? She's dating your late husband's idiotic brother!"

"I didn't know you were interested in Ginny...how long have you felt like this?" Dee gaped.

"...Since Christmas, but she barely gives me the time of day. But then I'm not a rich hotel-chain-heir from an important family with a big house on Richmond Green. I'm just the manager of a stupid, inconsequential coffee shop!"

"*Part-owner* of a stupid, inconsequential coffee shop, actually," Dee reminded him sullenly. The store was really doing rather well and was making a name for itself in the town. "...I'm sorry you felt like that and I didn't even notice...but I think Ginny and Jerry are pretty happy together. And Jerry really isn't so bad. He treats Ginny really well and the things he says about me are only because he cares. I've known him for a very long time and he's always been very good to me. You're a great guy and someday you're going to meet someone really special. It's hard to get over the loss of a loved one and I admire you for waiting so long – I didn't and perhaps I should have. But I *did* fall in love again after Lance so it shows it's possible."

"I think I'll pass if it only ends up the way your current marriage has." He caught the spurned look in her eyes and immediately regretted his outburst. "I'm sorry, I didn't mean that. I know you really loved Milo and you were right to take a chance on love again. It's just a shame you seem to have such terrible luck with men." Evan gently rubbed her arm.

"Guess what?!" Ginny was suddenly hopping about excitedly on the other side of the counter. The two turned to look at her. "I've just found out Forrest had a date with your cousin Cassie last night!"

"What? That dark horse, he took his time!" Dee enthused, now she too was jiggling about like she needed the toilet and hurried over to question Forrest. Ginny glanced up at Evan who was now ruefully turning a new batch of cakes with tongs so their more presentable side faced the customers.

He gave her a baleful half-smile. "I'm sorry if you thought I was picking on you before. Will a free cup of coffee make up for it? I'll throw in a muffin if that would swing it."

"It will have to be chocolate chip. I won't negotiate on that," Ginny grinned sheepishly as she watched him serve up the freebees.

"...I had no right to say those things about your boyfriend. I'm just having a bad day."

"You really don't like Jerry much, do you?"

"It doesn't matter what I think."

"And you are super defensive over Dee..." Ginny lowered her eyes with a twist of her mouth. "You're not thinking of becoming the next Mr Campbell, are you...?"

Evan raised his eyebrows. "Me? *God*, no!" he exclaimed but thought better of his outburst. "Don't get me wrong - I think the world of Dee and I'd do anything for her. But sometimes I think she has the emotional maturity of...well...my daughter," Evan laughed. Of course he meant no offense; he adored Dee like a sister - a *much younger* sister.

"That's a bit harsh." But Ginny couldn't help but feel brighter after that reassurance. "...Dee says your wife died of breast cancer. What was her name?" she enquired.

Evan was surprised she knew even a little about him or had bothered to commit it to memory. "Her name was Sarah..."

"Your daughter Mia is really pretty. Does she look like her mother?"

"She looks more and more like her every day."

"My little girls and your daughter got along really well at Christmas and at the wedding, didn't they? I know there's a bit of an age difference but kids love kids, don't they? You should bring Mia over to my house some time. My girls would love it." Ginny took her free coffee and muffin back to the table where Forrest and Dee were chatting animatedly. In all honesty, Dee was doing most of the talking. Evan watched Ginny walk away in that refined and elegant way she had.

*

It was another warm morning at the end of June and no different to any other summer morning accept that it was special to Dee on two counts. Angel sat at the garden table eating a bowl of cereal on a wooden garden chair on the patio. Nine month old Finley sat contentedly in a high chair beside her smearing porridge over his face and hair; watching the birds hop about the lawn. It was the best time of the day, warm enough to sit outside but cool enough to enjoy it. Dee pottered about in crumpled shorts and a vest by the large wooden swing-set with a monkey wrench in hand, haphazardly tightening some bolts under the seat.

"Whose flowers, Mummy?" Angel asked, staring at the bunch of lilies and chrysanthemums on the garden table. She had forgotten again. She had turned three just this week and Dee had thrown a little tea-party with all her friends and family. Milo had called home with profuse apologies but said he honestly could not make it back because he was too ill to fly. Instead he sent a truck-load of presents and promised to have a second birthday celebration on his return. Dee was enraged over that, and saw it as a symptom of the disease that was Amber. Dee imagined they were having a romantic vacation and Amber probably would not allow him home just for his 'daughter'. Dee wondered if he would have returned for Finley's birthday; a child who was really his.

It was the final nail in the coffin of their marriage - another final nail. Milo continued to give her reasons never to forgive him; his affair with Amber, his absence after her car accident and now his nonappearance on Angel's birthday. Dee hadn't even needed additional reasons, and yet they kept on coming.

"Uncle Jerry and Uncle Elliott sent them to me," Dee finally replied.

"What for?"

"...Um...because they wanted to be nice." Dee stared at the lilies and chrysanthemums in commemoration of the second anniversary of Lance's funeral. They sent flowers on the day of his death and the day of his funeral - the Stark boys had done this for the last two years, commemorating his funeral like another landmark. Dee sighed, just wanting to enjoy this beautiful morning (she was able to wear shorts in *England* for goodness' sake!) but circumstantially, she just couldn't. Dee had been secretly hoping to receive a *different* kind of flower this morning – like a bunch of red roses. Today was also the second anniversary of the day she and Milo had first met. Perhaps this anniversary didn't need to be marked anymore since she had now married him, or more importantly, now that they were on the verge of divorce. But it meant something to her. So many reasons to hate him yet Dee had to admit that, stupidly, she still loved him.

"Who died?" Felix asked as he breezed into the garden, having strolled around the side of the house when Dee hadn't answered the door, jovially patting the children's heads as he passed. He stopped beside Dee labouring at the swings in her cut-off denim shorts.

"...Lance - two years ago," she said. "Well, it's the anniversary of the funeral actually."

"...Sorry..." Felix cringed. "Damn, what idiot says '*who died?*' when there's a bunch of lilies on the table? And not long after what happened to...poor Gordon." He actually slapped his own forehead in mortification.

Yes, it was a *bit* tactless. Dee lowered her eyes. "...Don't worry, it's not for you to remember the second anniversary of my late first husband's *funeral*. You didn't even know him that well," she tried to remark pleasantly. "It's just Jerry and Elliott's way. They send me flowers on the anniversary of our wedding, his birthday, the anniversary of his death and now the anniversary of his funeral. Just in case I should forget."

"...Bit weird." He watched her smile and shrug all at once. "But doesn't that mean that today is also the second anniversary of the day you met Milo?"

"You're on fire today." Dee pointed genially in his direction with her monkey wrench.

"Well, the visual clues and the faux-pas helped," he admitted jocularly. "...Did he forget?" He took her derisive snort as confirmation that Milo had. "I'm surprised you expect anything from that man after he didn't show up for-" Felix trailed off. He did not want to mention Milo's lack of presence at Angel's birthday while she was nearby. "And I don't believe for a second that he was ill," he said very quietly.

"I'm inclined to agree with you. Yes, I don't know why I continue to feel let down by him either...but I do." Dee pushed her hair away from her face. "And I doubt he forgot – he's not the type to forget something like that. But he does seem to enjoy being spiteful." Yet another nail.

"...Yes, 'Vindictive' should have been his middle name," Felix said absently, then met her eyes again. "So, are you going to fight this divorce when he petitions in December? Because theoretically you could make him wait...if you felt like being vindictive too."

"Why would I want to do that? Why fight to stay married to a man who doesn't want to be married to me?"

"Do you think he's with Amber in the States right now - even after what she did?"

"Why should I imagine anything else?" Dee gazed at Angel who was searching the cereal box for its hidden toy. She sometimes wished she could end this marriage sooner, because being in limbo really sucked.

"You know you're worth ten of him." Felix eyed her thoughtfully.

Dee swallowed her low mood, shrugging it off like a coat that was too heavy for the weather. She looked up at Felix where he stood three feet away, not a great deal taller than she was. Dee found herself perusing him with an appraising eye - she didn't really know what made her do that because she never had before. He was dressed unusually casually for him; he wore a green t-shirt with the picture of a saxophone emblazoned in the centre and long corduroy shorts with his swarthy, thin, brown legs sticking out the end, finished off with a pair of green Converse. "You look nice today, really cute-" she remarked, then noticed the arch of his eyebrow so hurriedly thought she ought to qualify that. "I mean, *cute*...you know, like a little boy..." she stammered.

"...Oh good, because that's the look I was going for...*a little boy*..." He gave an incredulous shake of his head and Dee burst into laughter.

"...I didn't mean it like that." She wiped her streaming eyes with the knuckles of her spanner-hand. "I just wanted to pay you a compliment, and as you can see, I'm unusually gifted at flattery..."

"And what the hell are you doing with *that* thing anyway?" Felix grinned good-naturedly, gesticulating towards the monkey wrench.

"Oh, tightening this swing-seat up, it's getting loose..." Dee surveyed her work casually. "You know me, I'm a tight-ass - never pay a maintenance man when you can muck it up yourself."

Felix was quiet for a time, watching her approvingly, shading his narrowed eyes from the glaring sun. He took the monkey wrench from her hand and gently tapped her on the arm with it. "...I never met a girl who was a dab-hand with a monkey wrench before..." Felix stated in a soft voice and Dee felt slightly odd. Something unspoken and a little bit awkward and a little bit embarrassing and a little bit...*exciting* passed between them during that measured gaze he gave her. She squirmed beneath that gaze and just had to break the silence.

Dee laughed uneasily. "...Well, you still haven't. Health and Safety will be cordoning that thing off with red and white tape any minute now." They both laughed about that.

"...And I never met a girl who could make me laugh the way you do."

"You need to get out more..." Dee joked gingerly.

"...I've been out enough," he assured her. "I remember a time when we always used to laugh like this and nobody ever questioned our motives..." Felix seemed melancholy for a moment and Dee just didn't know what to say. But then he suddenly appeared to think of something that cheered him. "Well, this is a pretty horrible day for you on many levels, isn't it? But I have a plan; why don't I take you to my club tonight? We're having one of our special 'big band' nights – we only do a couple of those a year as they're so expensive to put on. It's Friday night, you need a night out and you've always said you'd come see me play one day. Today should be that day."

"Oh, that's sweet of you but Bruce, Patrice, Evan and Cassie had the same idea. They thought I would need cheering up so they're taking me out tonight...although I think it's Cass who *really* needs cheering up."

"Well...unless they've got definite plans, why don't they come to the club too? My treat. It's going to be an *amazing* night. Yours truly is doing a set with the full orchestra and then we have three amazing singers, dancers-" Felix stalled when he saw her uneasy expression. "I know Bruce doesn't like me...and Evan, Cassie and Patrice are pretty suspicious too, but I'm your friend just as much as they are. I think it's time we all made an effort to get along. Milo is a lost cause now, so your friends and I may as well patch up our differences."

She pursed her lips for a moment. "...Well...alright...I'll call them and see if they're up for it." Dee glanced across at her son. He was growing a crop of curly blonde hair and watched her adoringly with his piercing blue eyes. The eyes and hair (apart from the curls) were hers, but every other aspect of him belonged to Milo. If only the beautiful boy wasn't the spit of his father and didn't serve as a constant reminder of everything she had lost.

HAPPY ANNIVERSARY

That evening, much to Bruce's consternation, he reluctantly found he had indeed been enticed to Felix's club. He, Patrice, Evan, Cassie and Dee had crammed themselves into his car and shared the journey into Camden. They met Felix at the club, he always arrived early to prepare. Bruce had elected to drive so the others were at liberty to get completely trashed while he maintained control of when they left.

"This place is *amazing*," Dee said again, sitting at their table for six. She looked around at the large and impressive club like an awestruck child. 'The Black Keys' was loosely based on 1930s and 40s American ballrooms Dee had seen in all her favourite old movies. She felt as though she was in America – in another era. The band up on the stage played 'big-band-style' swing music, complete with a Frank Sinatra impersonator and dancing girls in amazing costumes. "If I owned a club, this is exactly how I would want it to be," she enthused brightly. This elegant ballroom - its enormous glitter ball high up on the ceiling, the numerous round tables with white linin tablecloths, well-dressed diners in dinner jackets and cocktail dresses, waiters darting about with magnums of champagne in ice buckets and the wonderfully infectious music - it was like a fairy-tale to Dee. Of course, not every night was as extravagant as this, but what better night to see her dear friend Felix play? "Felix, why didn't you tell me you owned a club like this? I'd have come ages ago," Dee insisted. She couldn't help feeling Felix was jolly clever.

"You've only known me for two years and you've been promising you would visit since then," Felix said, feeling rather satisfied. He noticed that Dee kept giving him sidelong, admiring glances to. She didn't give out compliments readily (apart from the one this morning in the garden about him looking *cute* - and even that hadn't come out right) so it meant even more.

"Well, I always thought it would be dark and seedy," she admitted.

"Do I look dark and seedy to you?" he replied and Bruce was physically restrained from answering that with a sharp kick from Patrice. Oblivious to this, Felix continued, "I mean, obviously every night isn't like *this*."

"Well thanks so much for inviting us - it's fantastic," Patrice agreed heartily, ignoring Bruce rubbing his shin.

"And the tickets cost a bomb tonight too – so I'm glad we're your guests, Felix!" Evan added with a wry smile. He, Bruce and Patrice were beginning to feel more relaxed in their tuxedos now that they were in the right establishment. They had felt pretty silly dressed up in this attire during the car journey from Richmond in a Ford Focus. But Felix had insisted on the smart dress code. Dee and Cassie wore designer evening dresses; Dee was pretty in white and Cassie elegantly wore black.

"All we need now is a mob shooting and police raid and we'll be set," Bruce remarked and Felix laughed despite himself.

"Now don't spoil the finale," he said.

The evening was going rather well and the six had already made their way through two courses and were about to start dessert before the dancing began later. The wonderful evening was flying by all too quickly for Dee. For once, she had actually spent large chunks of time not thinking about Milo at all. Everyone except Bruce were becoming nicely drunk on copious amounts of champagne (anything they wanted - on the house) and most were rather enjoying being the pampered guests of the genial host and club owner.

"So, I noticed Ginny was chatting to you at the coffee shop again yesterday. I take it your fall-out is long forgotten then?" Dee turned to ask Evan quite innocently.

"...Well," Evan began, shifting uncomfortably in his seat, fully aware Ginny's twin brother was sitting right beside him, "I apologised for my outburst, so-"

"You fell out with my sister?" Felix piped up.

"...Well there was a heated discussion about Dee and Milo's relationship going on at the store – which is quite a common occurrence these days," Evan explained apprehensively. "I was just a little irritated by some of Forrest and Ginny's comments about what Dee should and shouldn't be doing to get Milo back – and so I said a few unpleasant things about Jerry."

"Well, I'm right behind you there, buddy," the American agreed, finishing the contents of his champagne glass. "I never could stand the overbearing idiot."

"Really?" Evan suddenly brightened in mood.

"Oh yeah, whenever Jerry stays over, I feel I have to get out of the house."

"Oh come on, that house is so enormous, it's like three houses in one," Dee protested.

"When Jerry Stark is sharing your living space, there isn't a house big enough," Felix assured her and Evan laughed out loud.

Dee frowned. "None of you give Jerry a chance. He can be overly-opinionated and a little crotchety, sure, but he's only been that way since Lance died," she insisted condescendingly.

"That just isn't true, Dee. I've known Jerry off-and-on since I was a little boy and he's *always* been like that," Felix stated. "I don't even know why Ginny took up with him. He's not even her type. He's not anyone's type really. Do you know what I think? She'd be better off with a guy a bit more like you, Evan. But then, my sister has never taken any notice of what I think." After that, he and Evan seemed to get on famously, which evidently irritated Bruce. Both were very intelligent and well-read men and discovered that they actually had a lot in common. Dee felt rather pleased about this.

"Hey Cass," Felix leaned across and placed a hand on hers. "I wish Gordon was here with us tonight. I know I said this at the funeral, but I miss that fella. He was such a character, your dad."

"I know," Cassie dabbed discreetly at her eyes with a cream serviette. "He would have loved this...he thought *you* were the bee's knees. When Milo left Dee, he used to say, *'why couldn't Felix have been the American cousin who introduced himself at Lance's funeral?'*" she smiled. Dee and Felix glanced at each other uneasily, only to instantly break eye contact.

He cleared his throat. "...It's going to take time – but you're going to get through this," Felix continued kindly.

Cassie flashed a tearful little smile. "Thank you, Felix."

Dee gave Felix a watery smile of her own, putting an arm around Cassie. "...So, Mrs Secretive, how are things with you and Forrest?" She decided to draw Cassie into the conversation more so since she had been rather quiet before Felix had spoken to her.

"...Oh...he's awesome...I've seen him every day since we started dating." Cassie rubbed her palms on the seat of her chair, now she was the one feeling apprehensive. "And he's been so supportive over my dad..."

"I've been meaning to ask about you and Forrest – he won't tell me anything!" Felix grinned at Cassie, pleased to have found a way to pry into his cousin's private life without badgering Forrest himself. "Is love in the air? Can we expect another union of our families?"

"...Oh, it's early days Felix - we're just dating. But we get on really well. He's such a sweet guy, a real gentleman. Still, I have a feeling it's only going to be a platonic relationship," she confided awkwardly, "which is fine, if that's all he wants..."

"Oh, I doubt that. The way he looks at you does not say platonic to me," Felix insisted.

"Have you *done* anything yet?" Bruce's interest in the conversation was now fuelled, and he was never one to be backward in coming forward.

"Bruce!" Patrice rolled his eyes. "Maybe Cass doesn't want to divulge her private life to all of us."

But Cassie seemed eager to respond, if only to receive advice, or maybe just to talk since she hadn't been amongst them much since her father's death. Even a table-full of people didn't put her off. "...He gave me a goodnight kiss a couple of times. Could his hesitance be anything to do with his job?"

"I should imagine so – Christians are not supposed to practise...sex before marriage," Felix said diffidently.

"Does that mean he's *never*-?" Bruce began.

But again he was interrupted by Patrice. "You can't ask *that*, Bruce - he's Felix's cousin and-"

"It's okay, I'm just not really sure." Felix was beginning to look a little 'put on the spot'. "Forrest just isn't the sort of guy you can discuss that kind of thing with. He did get into the clergy pretty young though – so I wouldn't have thought-"

"*Can* he have sex...?" Rather tipsily, Dee asked the question nearly everybody else was thinking.

"...Um...look, if you don't mind, I'm a bit uncomfortable discussing that in his absence – he's my best friend and all," Felix squirmed.

"...Oh, I'm sorry," Dee gulped and lowered her eyes, embarrassed that she had asked such a stupid and inappropriate question. It had really just been a thought in her mind which had haplessly found itself being said out loud. How had she expected Forrest's cousin-stroke-best-friend to react to a personal question like that?

"No, it's cool. I just don't feel I should discuss his private life too freely..." Felix began regretfully, trying to catch her eye.

But she was deep in concentration, pouring herself a drink. "No, it's fine. You're right."

"Well actually, I don't know anything about Forrest's situation, but it's a common misconception that all paraplegics can't have sex," Patrice turned to Dee advisedly. "It depends whether the severing of the spinal cord is partial or complete."

"Forrest's is only partial," Felix confided, still directing himself to Dee. "And I'm sure he wouldn't mind if you asked him..."

"I can safely say that is *never* going to happen," Dee intoned mainly to herself, still refusing to look at him.

"I hope he can, I haven't had sex in two years!" Cassie laughed heartily and the others joined her, so relieved to see her being more like old self. She was mostly mild mannered but had that blunt characteristic at times which shocked some but that Dee loved about her.

"Seriously though Cass, do you think you'd be okay to wait with the possibility of never-?" Bruce grimaced without finishing his sentence. "At best, you'd have to marry him first, and at worst..."

"It isn't the most important thing in the world, Bruce. I just really like Forrest, I like being around him; he's so bright and interesting and he's so passionate about helping others. If friends is all we are destined for, then so be it. Who's to say he even likes me like that?"

"Cassie, he couldn't fail to like you *like that*," Felix assured her. "If you're interested in Forrest and are happy to wait – then just go with the flow for now."

"Yes, I think I will. Thanks Felix." Even Cassie was beginning to warm to Felix tonight. Dee gave him an appreciative smile at last and he smiled back, she was so pleased he was making such an effort to fit in with her friends and family.

After a while, Dee turned to Cassie and repeated, "have you *really* not had sex in two years?" The two women burst into laughter. Felix noticed with some amusement that Dee was really quite drunk – and he was glad, she needed to have some fun for once.

"You must have grown a skin over it by now," Bruce interjected, beginning to enjoy the evening too. Dee covered her face to muffle her chortling.

"Bruce, just when I think the tone of the conversation can go no lower, you're always there to prove me wrong," Patrice sighed witheringly, but even he was smiling at his estranged boyfriend. Dee noticed how their interaction with each other had warmed during the evening, she hoped tonight could be a turning point for them.

"Well Cassie, I think a good man is worth the wait," Dee insisted, then laughed. "Look at me giving you my shitty advice, I haven't had sex in nearly five months and I'm already frustrated!" she mused without keeping her honesty in check. "But it's not so much the sex you miss, is it? It's the affection, just knowing you can have a hug whenever you want one...or someone to cuddle up to at night..."

"Yeah, that is the worst part," Cassie agreed. "I miss holding hands down the street or having someone to call up just to hear a friendly male voice."

"Well I have a friendly male voice - does that help? What the hell are you women talking about? You can't beat a good, thorough shafting." Bruce rolled his eyes, ignoring that Patrice's whole face was now in his hands. "Dee, I don't know why you don't just find some random guy tonight and get this shag you so badly need out of the way. Milo's fucked off for good now, so you're a free agent."

Dee gave him a good-natured yet 'shut up' glare. "I may be frustrated and alone Bruce, but I'm not desperate yet," she told him with an impudent and sassy smirk. She then noticed Felix was watching her with a quizzical expression while he ate his dessert. So Dee decided to curb this inebriated candour because coming across as a drunken slut was never a good look.

"Are you still dating that singer, Felix?" Cassie asked politely.

"...Joanna Lake? Yeah, sort of. She's singing on my set tonight actually," he stated blankly. Dee studied him with a frown. She didn't know he was still seeing the jazz singer. He never told her anything and yet her life was an open book. Her friends were all very bad at sharing their secrets so Dee determined to play her cards a little closer to her chest in future.

"Great! Let's talk about Felix and Joanna!" Dee clapped her hands together with a wicked grin.

"No, let's not." He eyed her with a good-natured yet 'shut up' glare of his own.

"What time is your set?" Evan said looking at his watch.

"As soon as I finish this glass of champagne," Felix smirked and drained the glass. He rose to his feet, asked the party of friends to wish him luck, gave Dee a friendly brush on the shoulder as he passed and wandered up to the stage.

"Flash bastard," Bruce muttered.

"Bruce, give him a break. He's okay once you get to know him and he's been really generous to all of us tonight. I haven't enjoyed myself this much in ages," Evan said, being his sensible and diplomatic self. As Felix mounted the stage, the audience seemed to instantly recognise him and broke into rapturous applause.

"You're just saying that because you have a thing for his sister, you turncoat," Bruce grumbled. "He's a cock and I'm the only one with the guts to say it," he mumbled but nobody was listening.

"Yes Bruce, he's been so kind to us tonight. We haven't paid for a thing and he's been nothing but pleasant!" Cassie rebuked him.

"Sucking up you mean..." he grumbled. Cassie turned away as she knew how difficult Bruce could be when in this kind of mood.

"I didn't realise he was quite so famous," Patrice gaped at Dee, sounding rather impressed.

"Well sure, only in his own club," Bruce sneered.

Just then, Felix was joined on the stage by a beautiful woman in a silver dress which plunged at the neck and back to reveal her beautiful figure. Her long chestnut hair fell about her shoulders and was set in the style of an old black-and-white movie star.

"Is that her?" Cassie clutched Dee's arm as though the Queen had just sauntered onto the stage.

"...I guess. Gosh, she's *really* pretty," Dee admitted. She couldn't understand why Felix didn't rave about her more.

"Yeah, and he's so ordinary," Bruce observed. But Dee didn't think there was anything ordinary about Felix. The talented American jazz pianist began playing 'Feeling Good' while the powerful voice of Joanna Lake accompanied him. The hairs actually stood up on the back of Dee's neck. But Bruce was still ranting, "in fact, I would go as far as to say he was a bit weedy and swarthy-looking."

Dee considered this. Felix wasn't a great deal taller than her - maybe five-feet-seven or eight? And he was slight in frame, but he had a sweet face and the most exotic dark brown eyes. His very short hair was so dark it was almost black and his five o'clock shadow complimented his olive-skinned face. Felix was probably the best musician Dee had ever heard live, not that she was an authority on that kind of thing. But she did have tonnes of Frank Sinatra, Ella Fitzgerald and Billie Holiday's music and loved the works of Gershwin and Porter - so she knew he was good. And there was just *something* about talented men.

Evan watched many of the diners take to the dancefloor. "Shall we join them?" he suggested, standing up and taking Dee's hand.

"Yeah, come on – I could do with a dance," Cassie agreed, determined to enjoy yourself, dragging Bruce onto the dancefloor after them. Patrice rolled his eyes with a smile, happy to sit this one out. The two couples whirled around and Dee was reminded of better times; namely the New Year Ball – the day of her wedding, not the one before.

"Felix is really talented, I never realised," Evan began.

Dee glanced back up at the stage where her friend was performing and she felt rather proud of him. "Mm, he is pretty clever but we won't tell him that or he'll only become even more conceited."

"He's quite a nice chap actually."

"Yeah alright, why do you keep banging on about Felix? Do you fancy him or something?" Dee joked.

"...No, do you?" Evan arched an eyebrow. "Dee, I've been thinking..."

"I wondered what that burning smell was."

"Right now, Milo is probably in New York with Amber...and there has been talk that he may never come back," Evan continued.

"So?" she frowned. "...Anyway, that's just speculation. Nobody has spoken to him since Angel's birthday and I can't believe he would want to live in a different country from his children – well from his son, at least," Dee explained weakly, not really believing it herself. "...Not after what happened to Andrew..."

"Maybe, maybe not, but what I'm saying is; you'll be divorced by next year and after you've had a period of grieving for the loss of your marriage...you might want to start thinking about moving on," he said softly.

"I can't believe I'm hearing this from you of all people. Your wife passed away years ago and you haven't dated a single woman. Milo only left me a few months ago." A lump grew in her throat. Talking about the future and moving on was just too much on a day like today – the anniversary of their meeting. All Dee wanted tonight was to be drunk and to forget.

"I know and I'm not saying you should rush into anything but you wouldn't be doing anything immoral if you started dating again after...I don't know - a year say – whenever you feel ready."

Dee sighed as he attempted to (badly) ballroom dance with her. "...I don't think I could, Evan. I know I was talking about missing intimacy before...but in all honesty, I don't think I can see myself ever dating anyone. I can't put my kids through all that again – finding a new father-figure only for him to fuck off and leave. I should have been more careful after Lance died – like you were, but I honestly thought Milo was the real thing."

"We all did. But you're so young and you have a lot of love to give. Yes, you do have kids so you have to be careful, but you don't deserve to live out the rest of your life alone," he reasoned.

"I've had two husbands already and that's enough for anybody," Dee argued.

"I'm not suggesting you should look for a third husband, but I don't want you to rule out the possibility of someone new. Milo has moved on and soon it will be time for you to do the same."

"How exactly do I move on?" Dee gulped, tears welling up in her eyes.

"Well, I don't know exactly because I haven't managed to move on myself yet-"

"No, exactly! Why is it alright for you to be by yourself and not me?"

"I don't *want* to be single! People weren't meant to be alone, and being single for a while is okay but deep down, nobody really wants to be by themselves for the rest of their lives," Evan explained with a frustrated tone. He watched her lower her eyes with that teenage sulk she often wore these days. "...It's just - after tonight I can't help thinking you could do a lot worse than Felix..."

"Felix?" If Dee had been drinking her champagne, she may have choked on it. "God, for a worrying minute there, I was thinking you were going to suggest *you and I* should make a pact to hook up in a year if we didn't meet anybody else!" she teased.

"Good Lord, no! I think the stress and the drama of being with you would knock twenty years off my life! You're such hard work!" he laughed out loud and Dee smiled tightly, trying not to appear offended.

"But, Felix...? You didn't even like him until five seconds ago." She shook her head at his fickleness. "How can you even *think* that would be a good idea? He's Milo's cousin..."

"And Milo has gone now. I've really come to care for you like a little sister and I don't want to see you settle for just *anyone* - because your happiness is important to me. But maybe Felix could be really good for you in the future. The more I see him around you, the more you guys make sense. Milo will always be the children's dad, but your kids already know Felix and like him. You could keep it a secret from them until you're confident that things could work out between you," Evan said as though it would be the easiest transition in the world. "You must have noticed it too, the way he's been looking at you tonight; always seeking your approval, always trying to catch your eye and looking for an opportunity to touch you. If he makes a joke – you're the first face he looks at to make sure you're amused. I clearly know guys better than you do and I'm telling you-"

"No, it isn't like that with us! I don't *want* it to be over with Milo!" she blurted, gulping back the tears. "I know I act like I don't care about him anymore, but I do..."

"I know, I know – and I'm sorry this happened to you. But it *is* over...you're going to have to come to terms with that. You're going to need some time, maybe you're going to need a *lot* of time, months or years even," he cajoled. "But once you feel ready to move on, maybe you shouldn't rule Felix out. He's intelligent, he's funny, he's good-looking, he's talented – and not that it matters to *you*, but he's also loaded. And he obviously likes you an awful lot. But you can't afford to make Felix wait *too* long because he might find somebody serious and I know you would kick yourself because you're just so alike. I always respected Milo before he did what he did - but you and Felix are more akin than you and Milo ever were." Evan took a look up on stage at the man in question again. "You can't honestly tell me that the relationship you have with Felix is the same as the one you have with Bruce or Patrice or me?"

"Oh for goodness' sake," Dee grumbled.

"Dee…Bruce, Patrice and I think you're just adorable…but Felix can't keep his eyes off you; he hangs on your every word. Whilst we've been having this conversation, he's been glancing down at you from the stage in the vain hope that he's impressed you. Honestly, you could do a *lot* worse than a guy who clearly idolises you."

Dee stopped dancing and looked up at the stage once more at a man she truly respected and admired. Felix had kissed her once - *twice*. The first time was just a huge shock, but the second time…she had wanted him to. It felt…nice; warm and comforting. And tonight she was just so proud of him; proud to be in his entourage, proud to be his friend. But could she really see herself as anything other than his friend in the distant future? Joanna Lake was draped across the grand piano whilst singing, 'How About You?' and staring lovingly into Felix's eyes. Dee suddenly felt very angry with herself then for even considering it. Angry with Evan for turning it into an option. "What is this sudden fascination with Felix? And look up there, do you need any more evidence to prove that it's never going to happen? He *has* met someone serious – there's his drop-dead-gorgeous girlfriend up on stage mooning at him. I'm not even divorced yet, okay? And I'm certainly not getting involved with another man from *that* family!"

"Okay, okay." Evan held up his hands as a gesture of surrender. "But FYI, every time Joanna moons at him, Felix is cringing and looking across at you in case he's made you jealous. Oh, and he would drop that Joanna in an instant if you said the word…"

Dee sighed. "Can we not talk about this anymore?"

"Alright - I only brought it up because it just occurred to me tonight how good you look together," Evan said with a meek smile.

"…Well, thank you for worrying about my future happiness but I'm going to give singledom a go - I've hardly given it a chance in my entire adult life," Dee reminded him. "Oh, and don't mention this conversation to Bruce either because he'd bloody kill you if he heard you suggesting such a thing."

"Of course, I may have no idea about relationships but I'm not entirely stupid. I know how much Bruce hates Fe-"

"Do you mind if I cut in?" Felix suddenly asked with his hand on the small of her back and Dee very nearly jumped out of her skin.

DANCING IN THE DARK

Dee found herself on the middle of the dancefloor now in the company of two men. Felix was standing right beside her and she could barely look him in the eye for some odd reason. He'd only been up on stage a minute ago. God, she hoped he hadn't heard the tail-end of that conversation. Evan more than readily let her go with a big grin on his face.

"Bloody hell, did you *run* down here?" Dee gulped and Felix laughed.

"Hi Felix, of course you can cut in." Evan passed Dee's hand over to the other gentleman's. "Your set was amazing." If short. "I hope you're playing again?"

"Yeah, I'll do another couple of songs a little later." Felix gripped Dee's hand with a wink.

"Great, now we're an even number again, we can *all* dance. I'll see if I can get Patrice to dance with Bruce - maybe we can entice those crazy kids back together!" Evan hurried off through the crowds.

"Enjoying the show?" Felix asked, taking Dee in his arms for a slow dance - 'The Man I Love', to be exact. The same song the band had been playing at her wedding whilst she danced with her new husband just a few short months ago.

"...Oh y-yeah, it's amazing. So if you're here, who's minding the piano...?" Dee peered up at the stage where Felix's stand-in was happily banging away at the piano keys. Joanna had also disappeared.

"That's the perks of being the owner, I don't have to play all night," he confided with a smile, swinging her around in a semicircle so that she was facing in the other direction. Dee couldn't help but notice there were people in the crowd giving them discreet little glances and smiles. Felix sure did seem to be a big deal in this place, and here he was dancing in amongst the crowds with a small blonde girl in a white evening gown.

"You only did two numbers." Dee didn't mean to sound critical but somehow it came out that way.

"...I had no idea you loved to hear me play so much," he smirked. "Don't worry, I'll play a couple more just for you later on."

"Nice work if you can get it," Dee muttered before she realised the pun.
"Hmm, I was thinking of playing that too."
Dee was about to suggest a couple of songs she would like to hear but suddenly noticed a familiar face in the crowd. It was Cameron dancing with a young lady with short dark hair and a red dress. He spotted Dee and gave her an unassuming, if ginger, little wave and he and his partner slipped away into the throngs. That was odd.
"...Was that your ex Cameron?" Felix followed her line of vision and frowned.
"...Yeah, weird that he should be here tonight...I didn't know he was a fan of *yours*." She furrowed her eyebrows. "But he looked happy enough dancing with his new girlfriend, didn't he? So that's nice, I guess," Dee mused thoughtfully.
"Huh, there's me hanging around your house for weeks waiting for Cameron to show his face, just so Milo could discover his feelings for you. And now he shows up here at my club, completely disinterested in you with another woman! If I'd known he was a fan, I've have sent him goddamn tickets to one of my shows months ago and asked him his intensions outright myself – saved us all some time and heartache!" Felix said a little bitterly.
Dee wrinkled her nose. "In all fairness, he's unlikely to be a fan. He probably came to the wrong club by mistake..."
Felix grinned at her wolfishly. "...So, are you alright? You looked kind of...flustered before," he noted perceptively. "I saw you on the dancefloor with Evan – did you have some kind of altercation...?"
"No, no – we're fine. The Milo issue reared its ugly head again but I'm alright...if a little drunk." Dee wished her palms weren't quite so clammy; one of her hands was still in his as they danced. Suddenly, after speaking to Evan, she felt incredibly klutzy around Felix.
"...Aha," he said, eyeing her with that unreadable look. "Hey um, I didn't mean to sound rude at the table...about Forrest and the paraplegia thing..."
"No don't be silly. I shouldn't be so nosey...but you know me, I never stop to think before I speak..." Why did she feel so utterly tongue-tied? He was one of her best friends!
"You weren't being nosey...and I'd be happy to discuss anything with you - just not in front of a table-full of your friends," he explained in a logical tone of voice.
"Honestly, it was none of my business...and like I say, I'm *really* drunk," she said artlessly.
"I know...I like it when you're drunk..."

"...So, your set was utterly brilliant," Dee began again, taking another gulp of air. Why was this conversation so weird and stilted? "I don't think I actually realised how bloody good you were until tonight..."

"I played at your wedding," he said with a blank stare.

"Yeah, but I wasn't listening," she joked. "I know you did, Felix but there was so much going on that I didn't get the chance to stop and really appreciate it. And I was pretty drunk *that* night too."

"I remember. We should be drunk together more often."

Dee bit on her upper lip. Was he being oddly intense tonight or what? "...Anyway, I'm just saying - watching you tonight, well I take it all back. If you really are famous like you keep insisting...then I can see why. You're very talented and all these people here are clearly big fans. Now savour that compliment because the next time I see you, it will just be business as usual." Insults were so much easier.

Felix laughed. "I know how hard that must have been for you...so thank you," he said magnanimously but there was something brewing. Dee could just feel it. He was far more fervent than usual and certainly not as jocular.

So Dee thought the best course of action was to keep on yammering. "And Joanna Lake is SO beautiful, why didn't you tell me that? What an amazing voice! I think you make a really cute couple – you must introduce me to her," she insisted, trying to think of more filler for his brooding silences. God, why did Evan say those things? Perhaps Felix was being completely normal but now Evan had put this notion in her head, maybe she was looking for signs that weren't really there.

"...I'd rather not."

"...Oh?"

Felix pulled her body closer to his as they danced, his arm around her waist. "...I like her well enough...but I don't think she's going to be the one."

"Maybe love doesn't always have to hit you like that, maybe it can grow from something else - like friendship."

Felix was giving her that very flat gaze that made her squirm. "...Mm, I certainly agree with *that*, about love being slow-growing and maybe developing from a really nice friendship...but I think everybody wants to experience 'the one' whether it works out or not. I think I'd know by now if Joanna was going to be the one for me..."

"...Well maybe," Dee shrugged. "I still don't see why you wouldn't want to introduce me to her though..."

"Because Dee, I'm plainly screwing around...and maybe I don't want you to think of me like that."

Even Dee and her infallible smart-tongue couldn't think of an answer for that. Felix was watching her, perhaps for some kind of reaction and Dee had this horrible feeling that this was it. Evan's words were screaming around her brain, interrupting her thought processes to the degree that she just could not imagine how she was expected to respond.

"...How do you want me to think of you...?" Worst. Retort. Ever.

Felix replied evenly, "do you really want me to answer that...?"

Dee licked her lower lip. "...I could never feel disappointed in you merely because of your choice of girlfriend if that's what you're worried about..." she stammered but he was still staring pensively, as if waiting. There was a look in his eyes that she couldn't even put a name to. If only he would stop watching her like that!

"Hey Dee, you've *got* to see who I've found!" Bruce had scurried over with an excited bounce in his step. He grabbed Dee's hand and dragged her away from Felix.

Dee looked back at Felix anxiously and called through the crowd, "you coming, Kellerman? Let's get another drink!"

Felix frowned, put his hands in his tuxedo-trouser pockets and followed at a slow amble.

*

When Dee arrived at the table, there was a mystery man standing by their empty places with a half-full champagne glass in his hand.

"It's Oliver! Isn't this a coincidence?" Bruce said over the noise of the music, pointing directly at the poor fellow.

Dee, even though thankful for a get-out of that weirdly earnest conversation with Felix, looked gormlessly at the fairly handsome man in his late thirties or early forties. Oliver (whoever Oliver was) was now wearing a vaguely embarrassed expression, being put under her scrutiny. He was rather tall but not pulling himself up to his full height, perhaps because he felt on display, but had an affable face and floppy brown hair with a slight wave.

"...Um...I don't mean to be rude but I- wait, I do recognise you from somewhere but I can't quite place your face. I'm so sorry," Dee babbled on, readily helping herself to a glass of this crazily expensive fizzy stuff before she even sat down. Felix had arrived at her side rather surreptitiously but she couldn't bring herself to look at him.

"Oh that's quite alright," he said with a smile as all four seated themselves at the table. "You don't really know me as such. I'm just a regular customer at your coffee shop actually." He held out his hand. "I'm Oliver Brooke."

"Oh, I thought I recognised your face. Sorry, I'm Dee Phil- well, I'm going to be Dee Campbell from now on actually. It's nice to meet you." She took the hand he had offered and shook it.

"Yes, I'm ever so sorry to hear about your divorce. I've seen your husband only once or twice but I often see your children with you in the shop. They are lovely, aren't they?" He was terribly, terribly posh and Dee was usually intimidated by upper-class accents but Oliver was such a friendly chap, Dee found she was quite at ease chatting to him.

"Oh, thank you. Yes, they're great. I'm sorry I haven't spoken to you before but I have seen you about the store from time to time. I wasn't being rude. I just tend to flit in and out of the shop in all honesty. You're a friend of Evan's, aren't you?"

"Yes, I suppose I am. I'd been visiting his bookshop for years and years. I always loved popping in when I was on my break, but I must say I absolutely adore what you've done with the place. It's so much brighter and more inviting and it's wonderful that you can actually grab a bite to eat there now. A coffee shop really was the sensible way to go," Oliver enthused. "I actually quite liked the dark and dingy place it was but time moves on and there's no money in bookshops these days. Evan was never going to survive in today's competitive market."

"I guess, but he seems happy enough managing the place, and hopefully having part-ownership and more control makes it feel like it's still his baby..." Dee sometimes felt very uneasy that Evan had no choice but to sell his shop to her. And that was only due to the fact his wife had died and he couldn't really afford to raise his daughter as a single parent and shop keeper.

"Absolutely, I think even Evan would have to admit you're the best thing that ever happened to the place," he replied and Dee was surprised he knew so much about her and the business, but if he were a friend of Evan's, that would explain a lot. "I've been divorced myself actually. It's a pretty bloody awful business."

"Oh I'm sorry to hear that. Yes, it wasn't my decision," Dee found herself admitting.

"Well, I can identify with that. My wife left me two years ago, but it does get easier."

"Did you have children?"

"Thankfully, no. That would have made the whole situation so much harder. How is your little girl coping?" he asked and Dee found, for a posh person, he was really very easy-going. Not that there was anything wrong with posh people, Dee just didn't know many. She supposed the Starks may be considered 'posh' by some, but they were better described as 'wealthy'; new money. This chap was clearly a class *way* above that. She noticed after a little period of chatting amiably to this relative stranger that Felix was watching her through narrowed eyes.

"...Well, she misses her father Um...I'm sorry, I haven't introduced you to my friend, Felix Kellerman. He's my husband's cousin," Dee finally said and wondered if that were the crime Felix seemed to feel she had committed. She was very bad at introducing people. They always gave a feeble 'hello' and looked uncomfortable so she didn't enjoy doing it. Dee certainly did have the feeling Felix was unhappy with her about something.

"I'm a big fan of yours, Mr Kellerman. I'm quite a regular at your club too. I trust you will be playing again tonight?" Oliver beamed.

"...Uh, probably..." Felix shook his hand tentatively, noticing Bruce was smirking at him in a way he didn't like.

"You're a fan of Big Band music too, Oliver? Dee loves that kind of crap!" Bruce gasped theatrically and clapped his hands together. "You've got so much in common! I just bet you like the same kind of films; anything with Doris Day or Frank Sinatra or Jimmy Stewart? She's also crazy about martial arts films and period dramas – you don't happen to be into any of that shit, do you?" Bruce interrogated but before the baffled Oliver could answer, Bruce continued, "It's so weird seeing you here. You'll have to come and have coffee with us at the shop since we're all friends now."

"...Yes, that would be very nice," Dee agreed, knowing Felix was still staring at her with daggers. As much as she tried to ignore it, this was making her terribly anxious.

"Well, it was such a pleasure to meet you at last, Dee - you too, Mr Kellerman. Anyway, I must go and have a chat with Evan. It was nice speaking to you all." Oliver Brooke rose to his feet and they all bid their goodbyes. Bruce cruelly winked at Felix and left the table too, disappearing into the crowd.

Felix was positively staring murderously at her now. "Who the hell was *that*...?"

"Felix, you were sitting right next to me - you know as much as I know." Dee shook her head, taking another slug of champagne. What was going on with him tonight? "...I can recap if you want. He's called Oliver Brooke and he's a customer who comes into the shop...and he seems nice – if a bit posh," she shrugged, watching how he narrowed his eyes even more – they were virtually just little slits in his face. No, it was definitely not all in her mind. Something was positively 'up'.

"He's not your type at all. He's way too upper-class for you for a start," he scowled.

"Who said he had to be my type? What are we talking about?" Dee scratched her head, flummoxed. "Wait, you think I'm common...? I could have *him*," she chuckled to herself, (because she very probably couldn't) but was unaware quite how badly she was winding Felix up.

"I see, and is he going to be the *random guy*?"

"...The what?" Dee blinked without an ounce of a clue what Felix was insinuating or what he seemed to be so irate about.

"You know, the 'random guy', the 'random shag' Bruce said you needed to get over Milo," Felix continued as though he were really put out about something.

Dee stared at him in surprise. "...I wasn't planning on it, no." She gave a nervous smile. "Are you alright, Felix? You're being really weird tonight..."

"If the 'random guy' should be anyone, surely it should be me."

"Huh..." Dee gave another stupid, shaky laugh but then registered the seriousness of his face, not to mention the seriousness of his comment. It actually knocked the breath out of her. "...What...?" she gulped, turning to him but he didn't say anything. "I think you've had a little too much to drink, Kellerman," Dee attempted to make a joke of it, but even she knew that wouldn't wash.

Felix shook his head to brush her comment off. "Don't you sometimes think that you and I may as well be guilty of what everybody already thinks we're guilty of?"

"...What...? No!" Dee complained. "Only *Milo* thinks we're guilty of that. And he's going to divorce me to make me pay for a thing that we didn't even do. If you keep saying things like this, you'll never fix your relationship with him either," Dee assured him vehemently.

"I don't want Milo in my life anymore. After everything he's done to you...I can't forgive him," he said. "And I don't want to be innocent anymore either. *I'll* be your random guy...if you want to get over Milo, you should be doing that with somebody you trust - like *me*," Felix stated as though it was the most natural solution in the world.

"But you're not exactly *random*, are you? You're his cousin; the one who ended our marriage in the first place!" Dee looked away irritably.

"Even more reason why it should be me," he asserted, softening towards her now. "...I've wanted you so badly for so long that I can't even remember exactly when it started. I knew you didn't feel the same initially so I've tried to leave it alone. But this morning in your garden, I just got this feeling that maybe you felt something too," Felix admitted and Dee realised the garden incident wasn't just another figment of her imagination either. "You're so kind and funny and pretty. And you and I have so much more in common than you and that Oliver guy – apart from the period dramas and the martial arts, I'll never understand what you see in that..." he smiled, pushing her pale hair from her eyes. "...If you could just be a little braver, you'd realise we can finally do this now, Dee. You're free, I'm free." When did he get so close? His breath was hot on her cheek.

Dee closed her eyes. The champagne was hitting her brain cells just at the wrong time - but drunk or sober, she had to accept that she was so very lonely. And there was something about the prospect of being wanted that was dangerously appealing.

"...We aren't free. You have a girlfriend and I'm not even divorced..."

"You know I'm not interested in Joanna; I would leave her in a heartbeat for you. Milo has left you and your children for another woman. He didn't care if you lived or died after your car accident - the person sitting by your bedside for hours praying you'd be okay was *me*. How much more does he need to do to you before you'll give up on him?" he whispered sensuously.

Dee was at a loss for what to do or say. So this was the cause of all that intensity? Felix was making a play for her again? Her heart was hammering in her ears. Was she actually excited at the prospect of this? "...Felix...I don't think I'm ready for this..."

"...Maybe not before now. But tonight...I think you are." Felix gave her one of his most endearing smiles. It was easier now his anger had subsided. "...Unless you find me utterly repugnant that is, because you need to fancy me...that's the bare minimum..." he grinned roguishly.

"I do," Dee blurted out before she had time to decide if it was right to admit that to herself, let alone to him.

"*Finally,*" Felix said softly, entwining his fingers with hers under the table. "I've been waiting for you to catch up..."

"...But I didn't before, it's important you know that," Dee stressed, not wanting to withdraw her hand from his. "...When you kissed me initially, I'd never even thought of you in that way. But a lot has happened since then..."

Felix watched her thoughtfully. "...I have a small apartment above the club. I stay there sometimes when I finish a late show. I can take you there after my set and we can *be* together. I know underneath all that bravado how broken you are...but I can make you feel good about yourself again..."

Dee turned to him and was unsurprised when he kissed her mouth. And she responded. She let herself be kissed, let his tongue between her teeth and into her mouth. She needed an escape from the ceaseless pain tearing around inside her. Dee felt his fingers in her hair, his other hand on her waist, the taste of his lips on her mouth. It was so...different. Dee broke away suddenly and looked about her skittishly, unable to see any of her friends.

"Are you nuts, Felix? Your girlfriend is here, and all my friends are here!" Dee rubbed her face in distress and tried to clear her foggy head. "...I can't do this, I just can't..."

Felix still hadn't let her go but his face was awash with confusion. "Why?"

"...It's who you *are*. You're his cousin...not some random guy. A random guy is just somebody who doesn't mean anything, and you do..."

"You've made mistakes in the past with men. Your next experience should be with somebody you trust. That's me, by the way," he said, still smiling amiably at her. "And you shouldn't be wasting that experience on somebody undeserving of it..."

Dee shook her head adamantly. "...That somebody *cannot* be you."

"...I don't suppose I will ever be good enough for you, will I?" Just like that, all his good-humour had disappeared again. "Maybe I'm just not enough like Lance or Milo - not enough of a bastard. I couldn't possibly treat you as badly as you clearly like to be treated. It's okay, I get it now." Felix nodded resignedly.

"No Felix, that's not it at all!" Dee complained.

Felix rose to his feet. "...I um...I need to go and play these last couple of numbers..." He turned and stalked away in the direction of the stage.

"Felix!" she called after him but he evidently wasn't coming back.

TO DO OR NOT TO DO

Dee sat alone for a while, catching her breath and taking stock. What on earth was she doing? Kissing Felix Kellerman in the middle of a crowded club in which he was well-known and where, in any corner, one of her friends or his girlfriend could be lurking? He was a *friend* and she was allowing the friendship to be destroyed. Or was Dee being unnecessarily cruel to Felix? He quite genuinely cared for her; he was the one who had sat by her bedside when she was unconscious in hospital. He was the one who had come over virtually every day once she was discharged to help out because he was so concerned she couldn't cope with a broken wrist. He was the one who had shown up at Angel's birthday party with armfuls of gifts and chased her and all the other screaming kids around the house in some crazy game of birthday-tag. Milo had done none of those things; for months he hadn't been present in her life at all.

Dee rose sorrowfully to her feet and went in search of the others. Soon she found Cassie, Evan, Patrice and Bruce all dancing merrily together. Patrice even had his arm around Bruce's waist in a drunken display of camaraderie. Dee was so pleased to see this she almost broke into a smile. Almost. Felix was hammering out a tune up on stage, his eyes solely on the keys; not on Joanna slinking around with a microphone, inappropriately singing 'Too Marvellous for Words', not on Dee in the crowds. Just on his fingers on the keys. Dee knew he was uncharacteristically angry - all because of her.

"...Hi guys. I um...I think I'm going to get out of here," Dee said, forcing on the bravest face she could find in her arsenal.

"Are you okay? Where's Felix?" Cassie asked worriedly, noticing instantly Dee wasn't okay.

"...Up on stage again." Dee gestured with her head. "We had a bit of a falling out. Don't worry - it'll blow over...but I want to go home now. Apart from being here with you lot, it's been a rough day for me..." And a fairly rough evening too.

"Oh, well...we'll all go together," Bruce insisted.

"No, no, you guys carry on and enjoy your evening. You know, the night is still young and I don't want to bring everyone down. I'll get a cab back home. I just need to be by myself for a while..." Dee said as brightly as she could. Milo was back in the States and possibly never coming back. Felix had set his cap at her again only to be turned down - and now he clearly didn't want to be friends either.

"Oh honey, it won't be any fun without you..." Patrice groaned.

But Dee couldn't help but feel that they seemed to be having a great deal of fun, and she simply wasn't. "Of course it will. I um..." she cleared her throat, "...I want you all to know that you're my best friends in the world - you're my family..." Dee didn't know why she had to discuss this right now, but for some reason it was imperative that she did. "And I need you to realise how grateful I am for that," she declared. Maybe it was the recent near-death experience, or Gordon passing away so soon after his arrival in her life, but Dee wanted the people she loved to know *they* were loved.

"Oh Dee, we all think the world of you too." Cassie placed her arms about her and glanced at Bruce because now she was concerned.

"I don't think I would have got through any of the catastrophes in the last few months if you lot hadn't been there with me..." Dee tried not to cry, but she *really* wanted to cry. She had no right to be acting this way when Cassie had recently lost her father, but Dee was miserable and desperate to be out of here.

Bruce chewed on the inside of his mouth. "Yeah, I know; I'm awesome, Cassie is awesome, Patrice is awesome, Evan is awesome...but what's going on?" This out-of-character display of affection had put him on edge.

"Oh nothing, I'm drunk and if you can't tell people how awesome they are when you're drunk, when can you?" Dee advised with a weak laugh.

"Dee, I really think we ought to come with you..." Evan said more insistently.

"No-no, I won't allow it. I really need to go now. I'll see you guys tomorrow." Dee hugged all four of them one by one and quickly departed before they could change her mind.

"Oh crap..." Bruce cursed. "I should never have flaunted Oliver Brooke in front of Felix like that – that's what has caused this falling out between them. I was practically trying to set them up on a date and Felix had a face like thunder."

"Bruce, why would you do that?" Patrice said reprovingly. "Felix has been so nice to us tonight and you *know* he still likes Dee..."

"*Everybody* knows Felix still likes Dee," Evan sighed. "He makes it so obvious, well it's obvious to everyone but her. And Dee's been so reliant on him lately. I hope they can patch it up – she looked so upset just now."

"I worry so much about her...do you think she'll be okay?" Cassie asked with a feeling of gloom about her newly appointed cousin that she simply could not explain.

"I've known Dee for quite a few years and I can safely say she's rarely ever okay..." Bruce replied mournfully.

*

Dee grabbed her clutch bag from the table and made up her mind to leave. She headed in the direction of the exit, fishing around for the ticket for the coat-check girl. Once she had obtained her jacket from the foyer, she popped her head back in the club one last time. It would have been an amazing night if it hadn't been for her ruining everything. Then she spotted Felix at the bar, nursing a glass of scotch in a tumbler and absently staring into the middle distance. He couldn't have played any more than two or three songs because he had made it back to the bar for a drink pretty damn quickly. Dee stood and thought about her options for a minute. Poor Felix, all he ever did was care for her – perhaps a little too much.

"...Hi," she began gingerly. Dee needed to bid farewell to her host too - maybe even part friends tonight if she were lucky. Perched on the barstool, Felix eyed her darkly before continuing to sip his drink. "...I didn't mean to-"

"No more explanations are required, thanks." Felix held up a hand to block out further excuses she may come up with. "I think we've done this to death."

Dee sighed sadly. "You have no idea how much I care about you...and you are more than good enough for me. Please don't think that all I want in a man is a *bastard*, because I don't. You're lovely and *normal* – in a good way - and I'd choose you in a heartbeat if I could. But maybe I'm just not good enough for *you*..."

"Wow, I haven't heard that one in ages," Felix sniffed but the joke wasn't shared with Dee, he didn't even design to look at her.

"That's not what I'm trying to say. If you'll just listen to me-"

"I've listened and I've been patient and I've waited. But I'm tired of pretending and I'm not waiting anymore for somebody who never really wanted me as anything more than a distraction from her problems," Felix told her, still not gracing her with eye contact. "You've just rejected me, and even though you have every right to do that, I'm not a machine and it still hurts. And I have a right to want you not to be here while I get my head around it," he said. "So if you'll forgive me, I'd really like to end this right now. Is that okay with you? Because perish the thought that you should have *your* feelings hurt..."

"...Are we not friends now?" she asked meekly. She felt that sudden urge to cry again.

"You have plenty of other friends. I'm not even the best of them. I pretty much don't have a place in your life," he explained flatly.

"...Felix, that isn't true-"

"Weren't you leaving?"

"Not without you," Dee said, deciding just at that very moment what she really wanted. She leaned in to kiss him.

Felix seemed rather stunned at first but then his coolness slowly melted and put his hands around her waist. Reluctantly, he broke away. "Wait...did I just guilt-trip you into this...? Because that's not what I want at all..."

Dee was still nestled between his firm thighs, it felt nice to be this close to him. "I'm allowed to change my mind, aren't I? Look, I want to move on, and I want that to be tonight...and I want that to be with you..." Dee slipped her hand into his. "...Shall we go then?"

"Go...?" he said rather stupidly.

"...To this flat upstairs you were talking about. You were going to show me," Dee said as firmly as she could, although she was absolutely petrified and her heart was pounding in her chest.

Felix was still searching her eyes. "...Do you *honestly* want to do this...with me...?"

"...Yes, I do. Come on," Dee said more decisively and Felix held her hand as he led her out of the club through a different exit.

*

Dee found herself at the bottom of a dark stairwell. She was so afraid of what she was about to do with one of her best friends, she feared she may actually be trembling - she feared Felix may even notice. Still holding her hand, he led her up the stairway. "...Up the wooden hill to Bedfordshire, huh?" Dee said the first thing that came into her head just to fill the silence.

Felix turned to her as they reached the summit to be greeted by a door. "...I'm sorry?"

"You know, the saying...? The 'wooden hill' is the staircase and 'Bedfordshire' is...well it's a county actually...but it's supposed to represent...*bed*..." she rambled.

Felix smiled. "I've lived in England for a long time but that saying seems to have passed me by."

"That's probably why you've never found you could fit in," she teased.

"You are so weird..." he grinned.

"It's a gift..." God she was scared; did he even know how much? He glanced at her momentarily, perhaps to assess if she was still up for this, and pulled a key out of his pocket to unlock it. The pair went inside and Felix closed the door behind them. Dee looked around the flat which was really very large and impressive – not to mention expensively furnished. She'd been expecting 'pokey'. The décor appeared to be in mainly white hues and the furniture was sparsely positioned. This could have been a show home.

"...You look so beautiful tonight. Even when I was up on stage, I couldn't stop staring at you," he said then. Dee didn't really know how to respond to that so was actually glad when he kissed her again, which was easier than talking feelings. Dee felt him slide his hands up her body and touch her breasts. She felt she ought to show some involvement and pushed his tux jacket off his shoulders. Then he moved his hands down to touch her behind and began to slide her dress up her thighs.

"...Wait," Dee gasped and stepped away.

"What's wrong?"

"...Nothing, I'm just really nervous," Dee admitted at last.

"I know, you're shaking," Felix noted.

"...I just never expected to be doing this again," Dee confided, "with somebody else..."

Felix sensed she hadn't quite psyched herself up for this yet. "Mm, come on, I'll make you a drink. What's your poison?" He took her through the mainly open-plan flat to the kitchen and he wandered over to open the fridge. Felix distractedly perused its contents. Dee looked about at the stainless steel room and noticed unwashed crockery lying about and a general sense that somebody had been here.

"...You've been living here, haven't you?"

"Well, I have been sometimes," he shrugged, pulling out yet another madly expensive bottle of champagne.

"You've been driven out of your own home because of me. I'm really sorry."

"...It's not your fault. It's just that we sold the Chelsea apartment when Milo gave us that house on Richmond Green - and I've felt uncomfortable living there ever since you split up with him. I'm always worried he'll drop over at a moment's notice to see Forrest or Ginny. I'm thinking of buying a new place soon but I'm not sure where. So I've been staying here now and then." He toyed with the foil at the bottleneck.

"...Felix, what are you actually expecting from this...?" Dee just had to ask.

Felix studied her for a moment. "...I don't think it's time for us to start shouting out how we feel about each other from the rooftops just yet...but we should just wait and see where this relationship takes us," he said and that was pretty much the right answer for tonight. "I don't actually know why I'm opening this bottle when you're already bombed. Shall we just have sex instead?" And virtually in an instant he was upon her again, pressing her up against the breakfast bar – so much so, she felt he may throw her down on it and make love to her right there and then. "How do you get into this dress? I want to see you naked." Chuckling, Felix caressed her throat ardently. Dee reminded herself that he was still making all the running here so she undid his belt buckle. Felix was still laughing as he searched for the dress zipper. Dee knew Felix was trying to keep this light and fun so as not to scare her off.

"...D-do you have a bed at all?" Dee stammered. She didn't think she could handle anything too kinky because this felt weird enough as it was.

Felix smirked. "Well yes, most apartments do. Come on." He took her through to the bedroom and immediately started to take off her dress. By the time they were down to their underwear, Dee was a bit of a nervous wreck. Felix pushed her down on the bed and she stalled again.

"...Do you have a condom? I'm not on the pill anymore," she gulped. Dee realised this was probably the most stop-start sexual experience she had ever had.

"...Um, yeah – of course...sorry, I should have asked." Felix reached over to the bedside table and rifled around in a draw until he found a packet of condoms. Dee was sitting up now and he crawled over to sit beside her. "Do you want to put it on for me?"

That was just a bridge too far for Dee. "No I don't!" she wailed as she leapt to her feet. "I can't put a condom on you! I don't think I can do this, Felix – it feels like I'm going to have sex with my brother!" Dee buried her face in her hands, absolutely mortified about the whole experience. He was going to be upset again; she just knew it.

Felix watched her with a vaguely amused confusion. "...Okay...we could just cut out the foreplay, I guess. I know you're nervous, so we could switch the lights off and just do it if you'd prefer..."

"No, I can't. This is too much too soon and I'm just not ready. I'm freaking myself out!" Dee grabbed her clothes and shoes from a white wooden chair near the bed. "I'm sorry if you think I led you on, Felix. I really thought I could go through with it but I can't. I'm going home – I'll get a cab," she jabbered quickly.

"Dee, please just calm down." Felix reached out his hands to clasp hers and sat her back on the bed beside him. "...If you don't want to do it, then we won't, okay? There's no pleasure in it for me if you're not really into it. But don't just run off into the night or I'll be worried sick about you. It's late and you're drunk. Stay the night," he suggested incredibly reasonably. "I promise we don't have to do anything. I can sleep on the sofa if you want but this is a huge bed and we could just be grown-ups and go to sleep in it. I won't lay a finger on you - I swear. Let's just talk and go to sleep. I don't want to fall out and never speak again over this," he told her gently. "I know what you're like."

"I don't want to fall out either…but you were so angry with me before…" she fretted.

Felix sighed guiltily. "…I know, and I'm sorry. I realise it's harder for you than it is for me," he assured her. "I hope that's not why you agreed to come up here – I wasn't browbeating you into sleeping with me tonight. I just wanted you to stop dismissing me as a possibility. If this is too much too soon, I understand…"

*

Dee could not help but feel she was a real simpleton for knocking back this utterly charming man. She had given him reason to believe she was ready for this, she had led him up the garden path so many times tonight, yet he was still being nice about it. But Dee just wasn't ready and she couldn't pretend to be something she wasn't.

"…I will stay the night if that's okay," Dee said gratefully, quite relieved now.

"Let me get you something to sleep in." Felix rose to his feet in only his boxers and searched a large wooden tallboy in the corner and pulled out a large white t-shirt. He threw it at his half-naked friend who extremely thankful to pull it over her head. She quickly got into bed. Felix found a t-shirt for himself to wear and climbed into bed beside his jittery pal. "You know, I never suspected you would turn out to be so prudish." He turned to her and smiled insolently.

"…People never do. They see I've had a troubled childhood and married twice – both times to rich guys, and they naturally assume that I'm some gold-digging-nymphomaniac," Dee sighed, feeling *so* much better now. She was almost calm.

"How many different men have you actually slept with?" he asked with interest.

"…Err, four…very nearly five if we'd gone ahead and-"

"God, and you married *two* of those. No wonder you're scared – you probably thought you'd have to marry me afterwards." He had slipped back into his old guise of comedian and Dee was glad; intense, brooding Felix was an unknown quantity.

Dee chuckled. "Oh alright, let's all have a laugh at the emotionally immature girl's expense." The tension had eased and Felix was relieved to see her laughing again.

"So Jerry and Cameron were the unlucky ones, huh? Not as unlucky as *me* of course..." Felix rubbed his tired eyes and turned to her again. "Every day I'm amazed by you."

"Since we're talking numbers, how many women have you slept with?" Dee fiddled with the hook of her bra before surreptitiously taking it off, threading it through the sleeve of her t-shirt. There was no way she could sleep in that. She decided it would be best to keep her pants on, though.

Felix actually had to think about that, staring into space. "...I'm really not sure. I'm not bragging, but I think it's up in the low-hundreds. I suppose that's not something to be proud of in today's climate. But when you're fairly famous and have money, some women tend to throw themselves at you. And when I was young and not particularly discriminating – well, you can guess the rest," he admitted. "I am surprised about *you*, though. I didn't for one minute think you were a slut or anything. It just seems that every man in my family has had a bit of a thing for you at one time or another, so I just imagined you'd had your fair share of lovers," he explained candidly. "...Dee, I'm sorry if you felt pressured into having sex with me tonight. Did I just misread the signs this evening? What I mean is - is this a '*no, not tonight*' or a '*no, not ever*' situation...?"

"...You didn't misread the signs, and if it were up to me-"

"It *is* up to you," he reminded her sagely.

"I do find you really attractive, Felix. What's more, I do want to move on...and I wish that could be with you. Because I'm so comfortable with you. You are so straightforward and uncomplicated and that's exactly the kind of man I need. Any woman in their right mind-" she stalled, "but I'm not in my right mind at the moment. My husband is seeing another woman, so I wish I could just..." Dee shook her head sadly. "I'm just not over Milo and I think it's going to take a long, long time before I am."

"...Do you think you'll want *me* when you are? In all likelihood, you'll be divorced in six or seven months. I would wait for you if you asked me to. Then we could just go on a normal date and see how it goes?"

"...Maybe. It's just...I wish you weren't related to him."

"That's not my fault," he reminded her sagely - *again*.

"No, but I wasn't fobbing you off when I said doing it with you felt like doing it with my brother. I've known you in a different light for so long that I'm not completely sure I can make the transition..." Dee confessed.

"So I'm confined to the ranks of friend forever, huh? It's just, I don't feel what we have is the same as what you have with say Bruce, Patrice or Evan..."

"No, you're right. It isn't. I admit I've got a bit of a thing for you but I just don't think I envisage you as my lover, not right now anyway," Dee explained carefully, so as not to offend him again.

Felix was pensive for a moment. "...Well, you're clearly not ready now. And it's probably for the best that you backed out. I wouldn't want you to resent me for pushing you into doing something you aren't comfortable with yet. Your friendship is very important to me."

Dee noticed how he said 'now' and 'yet' as though he was confident their relationship would still happen in the future. Dee didn't want to kill his hopes entirely - not just yet, not until she was sure... "Thanks Felix, you're incredibly important to me too." She reached over to hug him. Felix switched off the lamp, throwing them into darkness. Dee sighed. Maybe she had let a good opportunity and a good man slip by, but something had stopped her, so she had to go with her instincts. Dee wondered if she would actually manage to sleep but perhaps due to the alcohol or the overwhelming events of the day, she was soon out for the count.

*

It was still dark when Dee next came around but it must have been the twilight hours because the early morning sun of summer hadn't risen as yet. She would put the time at 4am if questioned - and her body clock was about right. As the moonlight filtered through the gaps in the blind, she noticed her sleeping partner's eyes were open. Felix was watching her thoughtfully with his cheek on his flat palm. He gave her a small smile.

"...Can't you sleep?" she whispered.

"...Just horny. I don't normally wake up to find such a beautiful woman in my bed," he said softly.

"...Where?" Dee sleepily tried to joke. He laughed with a quiet sniff.

"God, I wish you wanted me as much as I want you..."

Dee watched him carefully, a wave of need suddenly washing over her. She was only half awake but knew now what had woken her. Suddenly she wanted sexual gratification so badly that she prayed it would show on her face and he would take the hint. Felix noticed something very searching and urgent in her eyes – he just knew. Felix nestled a little closer. Still, he was so jumpy about her changing whims he had to ask, "...Is it alright...?"

Dee gave a little nod of her head. Once she had given him the go-ahead, his mouth was instantly covering hers. He kissed her so passionately and desperately, it took her breath away. He climbed on top of her, first removing her t-shirt, then his, peeling off her underwear before removing his own. The feel of his naked skin against hers seemed so unusual and the dimensions of his body were so different. The moon must have been hidden by clouds at that moment because it was so much darker, Dee could barely see him. This was Felix. This wasn't Milo. She could feel his hardness against her belly and knew it was imminently going to happen. Dee could actually sense his excitement coursing through his entire body and suddenly it frightened her. But it was too late to back out again. He was inside her. Dee could feel herself freezing up already. Felix held her hands down on the bed above her head, his fingers laced with hers. She let her chin rest on his shoulder, staring at the ceiling as he moved above her. Ashamed of her dreadful silence since he was clearly so aroused, Dee let out a small groan - a groan of pleasure that she didn't even feel. This only seemed to heighten his fervour; he whispered her name in her ear. Dee thought about how she had never *truly* imagined this happening before, not once. Maybe it was because this never really should have come to fruition. If she had let herself, she may actually have enjoyed it – enjoyed him. But she couldn't relax into their lovemaking due to the relentless guilt. The actual event probably didn't last terribly long, but to Dee it felt like an eternity before he reached a climax.

    Dee felt thoroughly sick with herself. She realised too late that yes, she had wanted sex, but not with him. With every pore of her body she cried out for Milo. But he was thousands of miles away with another woman. And Dee was lying here in bed with his cousin, hot and slick with his sweat covering her body and the dampness between her legs that belonged to him. This was Milo's cousin who she liked an awful lot and fancied a bit but not like this. Not like this.

    Felix gave her a brief, if slightly embarrassed, glance and rolled onto his back to catch his breath. He then planted a perfunctory kiss on her left temple, turned over and went to sleep. Dee, on the other hand, was wide awake. A single tear slid from her eye and ran down the side of her face to be buried in the pillowcase. She lay still, eyes open, accepting who she had become. A loathsome adulteress. No better than Milo. An odious creature, but with a fundamentally good person trapped inside, clambering to get out. Yet she would never be able to. Not after this.

    Dee remained like this for nearly an hour, wide awake, until the first light of morning flickered through the blinds. She got out of bed and scrambled around to find her clothes, shoes, jacket and clutch bag. She searched inside this to find her watch. It was almost five o'clock in the morning and that was late enough for her. She quickly dressed and quietly left the apartment, crept down the stairs. Out of Bedfordshire and down the wooden hill.

DEAL BREAKER

Ginny hurried along one of the leafy-green pathways in Richmond Park. As she walked, she felt the need to stop and appreciate how beautiful a day it was. But she couldn't stop, she had to be somewhere. Pulling her two daughters along behind her, the three made their way to the girls' gymnastic class that Saturday morning. As expected, up ahead she spotted her brother sitting outside the park café in the outdoor seating area. He perched on a glinting metal chair, nursing a cup of coffee and a croissant at the table. He looked up glumly as she and the children approached.

"Hi Felix, sorry – I haven't really got much more than fifteen minutes, I need to get the girls to gym class. That was an unexpectedly early text from you this morning..." Ginny seated herself beside him. "Did you guys have fun at the club last night?" She watched as the girls hurried off to an area where a couple of rabbits and guinea pigs were housed in two hutches. The girls began stuffing in the dandelion leaves they had been collecting especially along the way – like every weekend.

Felix pushed a latte he had ordered for her in her direction. "Um...yeah, it was great..."

"Did you come back to Richmond after the show?" Their house was so large, unless you actually went looking for a person, you could never be entirely sure if they were home or not.

He shook his head. "No, I stayed over at the club. I drove in just now..."

"Gosh, you were up early," she responded. "So, you don't often ask to meet up with me at 8:30 on a Saturday morning...is everything alright?"

"I don't know, Ginny. I called you because I need some advice and there isn't really anyone else I can talk to about this," he sighed.

"Then it must be about Dee. Because if it wasn't, you would be speaking to her about it, not me." Ginny pursed her lips.

Felix looked up, startled. "That's not fair – I pretty much tell you everything. You're my twin. But yes, this is about Dee..." he admitted and she arched an eyebrow as she settled down to listen. "I've done something that perhaps in the cold light of day I'm worried I shouldn't have..."

Ginny grimaced. "Do I really want to hear this...?"

"I'm afraid you don't have much choice. Dee stayed over with me at the flat after my set at the club last night. We slept together..."

"You had sex...?" She rubbed her temples anxiously, having to have this spelled out for her in 'dummy's terms' to be sure. Ginny had seen this coming, of course, but a part of her had always believed Dee and Milo would be reunited.

"Well, they're the same thing, yes."

"I don't know what I'm supposed to say to that. Um...was it all you were hoping for?"

"It was great – but that's not really the point," Felix gulped. His sister didn't seem to be overflowing with enthusiasm.

"God, I am having this awful image of you two doing it now, which is a picture of my brother that I would really rather not have in my head." Ginny let her head fall back listlessly.

"Well stop thinking about it then." Felix sipped his coffee and scratched his head, waiting for his sister to regroup.

"...So how was it between you this morning?" Ginny asked eventually.

"That's the thing, I don't know. She must have left at the crack of dawn – I was asleep. So I don't know what her reaction is because I haven't seen her."

Ginny began to steeple her fingers, trying to be pragmatic. "Well, leaving before you even woke up isn't the best indicator that she's okay with things. What do you want her reaction to be?"

"I don't know. I don't want to have ruined things between us. I don't want her to hate me and never talk to me again. Dee's like a sister to me."

"She is clearly NOT like a sister you!" Ginny snapped before managing to regain control of her temper. "...Did you-?" she floundered for a moment then began again. "You didn't cajole her into it, did you...?"

"Of course not! Why would you even say that? Dee was drunk, sure, we both were - but I asked her again and again if she was sure. She certainly had ample opportunity to back out," he insisted.

"And you didn't threaten to break friends with her if she didn't?"

"No! Well...maybe it might have come across like that at first but it was definitely consensual when it happened..." Felix explained. Ginny groaned and put her head in her hands. "What? I'm making it sound terrible – but it wasn't. I promise you, it was what we both wanted."

"How did this even come about? All Dee's friends were there and they don't even like you. Wasn't Joanna doing your set with you last night? How did she not notice anything?"

"I've no idea how I got away with it, and to be honest, I didn't even think about Joanna showing up at the flat. But she doesn't have a key so she couldn't have caught us or anything," he said. "I wasn't supposed to be closing the show so we just quietly slipped away."

"Who knows about this?"

"Nobody I think. None of Dee's friends knew she came up to the flat. And it's too early in the day for her to have told anyone..."

"Right, keep it that way – don't even tell Forrest. The less people that know about this, the better. I wish *I* didn't know..." Ginny was starting to appear more and more flustered. "Milo may be divorcing Dee at the end of the year, but if you think for one moment that he isn't going to care about what you've done, you're deluding yourself." She glanced over at the children to ensure they were still playing nicely with the animals. "If he finds out, he's going to kill you!" she hissed.

"Do you always have to be so melodramatic? Milo *already* thinks we slept together!"

"Forrest says Milo now has serious doubts about what he saw!"

Felix didn't know why but he was suddenly spooked. "Look, I asked you here for advice!"

"What advice? What advice could I possibly give but to hush it up? Dee left without even telling you she was going, didn't she? That speaks volumes. Whatever you have going on with her is doomed to failure – you do understand that, don't you? You need to go see Dee as soon as you can and just try to bury this thing; put it behind you as a one-off. If you want to continue any semblance of a friendship with her, my advice to you is to try to forget this ever happened," Ginny berated him, then checked herself. She smoothed her hands down her skirt and took a breath. "I have to go, Felix - or we will be late for gym. Forrest is out so we can speak alone tonight. I'll make us some dinner." She rose to her feet, completely ignored her untouched coffee and called the girls over. "...I love you Felix." She kissed the top of his head and hurried off with the twins to get to gymnastics on time. Felix finished his coffee in the morning sunshine. It wasn't the best reaction he could have hoped for.

*

Holding her infant son in an ungainly, under-the-arms manner (screaming like he was on fire), Dee opened the door to Evan later that morning. Evan smiled briefly before frowning at the little boy who was bright red in the face and covered in snot.

"What's wrong with Finn?" he said as he wandered through into the hall.

"Oh, he's not happy because I won't let him climb up the bookshelf to reach a rather lethal-looking letter opener. I don't know, I'm funny like that," Dee said, closing the door and finally letting the child down. Finn crawled away quicker than either of the adults could blink. The crying instantly stopped. "I might have to cancel his birthday trip to the knife-factory at this rate." She quickly ran after Finn who was just attempting to crawl through the open stair-gate and mount the stairs. He was at an exhausting age. All Dee wanted was to lie on the sofa and recover from the night before, and stare pensively up at the ceiling. Much like she had in the wee-small hours of the night. Dee locked the stair-gate and Finn crawled off like a paratrooper into the lounge. Both adults followed briskly.

"How are you feeling after last night?" Evan began and Dee turned her head to look at him tensely. What did he know? "You were really drunk and upset over your fight with Felix...and we just let you leave. I felt really bad about it," he admitted, lowering himself down in an armchair. "Hence why I'm here..." Evan straightened his glasses.

"Oh, don't worry - I was fine..." She stared at the half-empty pint glass of Berocca on the table and wondered how Finn hadn't managed to knock it over, he was in such a destructive mood. Finley was busily destroying a bunch of pretty orange gerberas in a vase in the log-less fireplace.

"Well, the coffee shop wasn't too busy so I left Bruce in charge and I thought I'd see if you were alright."

"Oh, thanks...but I'm okay - just really tired. I've hardly slept." Well that was true. Dee sat down on an adjacent sofa.

"So what happened last night? You had a big fight with Felix, you said?"

"...Yeah, but we made it up later," she murmured.

"Oh good...when did you get a chance to do that - on your way out of the club?" Evan screwed up his face.

She exhaled and surveyed him for a second. "...I have a confession to make but you have to promise you won't tell Bruce or anyone else. My life won't be worth living if you do." Dee engaged him in a meaningful stare. "...I did something *really* bad last night."

"...What did you do?" he groaned before he even knew what it was. Maybe because he subconsciously knew *exactly* what it was.

"I had sex with Felix," she grimaced.

"...I know I said I approved of you and him getting together, but I didn't say it had to be last night. You didn't do it because of what *I* said, did you...?" Evan gulped, feeling totally responsible.

"No, the me-and-Felix thing was going to come up last night no matter what," she replied pensively. But Evan had put the thought in her head and made the prospect sound attractive and maybe even feasible. Finley crawled over and pulled himself up at his mother's knee. She smiled at him and ran her fingers through his curly blonde locks. He was so like his dad.

"But I thought you quarrelled and left the club?"

"Well, I did argue with Felix and I was about to leave but I met him at the bar and we talked. Well, we did more than talk. Anyway, he took me upstairs to his flat he owns above the club and we...did the deed..." Dee rubbed her temples shamefacedly. There was a lot more to it than that but Evan didn't need to hear the grisly details.

"And was it...nice?" he asked, not really knowing how else to put it.

She rested her chin on top of Finley's head. "...Well, it was fine I suppose. He really wanted to and I really wanted to - at first. But as soon as it was actually happening...I just wanted Milo again. And now I completely regret it," Dee rambled. "...So at about five o'clock in the morning I got up and left without even saying goodbye. Evan, I feel so bad about what I've done." She let out a little whimper to prove the point.

"...Well, you haven't actually done anything *wrong*, as such. Your husband left you and shacked up with another woman," Evan reasoned kindly. "...So technically, is that even classed as cheating...?"

Dee mulled that over for a millisecond. "Oh, of course it's cheating! I'm still married and I slept with another man! I've committed adultery!" She shook her head ruefully. "I'm as guilty as Milo now..."

"I think you're being a bit hard on yourself. Maybe you should have waited a while for your own emotional state of mind, but you mustn't feel bad on Milo's account," Evan reasoned with his usual logic.

"Why do I keep doing these things? Why can't I just accept when I'm single like normal people? One man ditches me and I move right on to the next." Dee was just so sick of herself. "The trouble is...I don't think Felix is going to be the next Mr Right. I like him so much but I can't really visualise myself as his girlfriend. He's very intelligent and so funny and really cute, but does my heart skip a beat whenever he walks in the room? I don't know. He just isn't *Milo*. I suppose I'm never going to feel that way about anyone again."

"Maybe when you get to our age, love doesn't have to be like fireworks. Maybe it can grow gradually from a really deep friendship - like the one you have with Felix," he shrugged, mirroring something Dee had been trying to tell Felix about Joanna last night. Dee had heard and used that adage one too many times and it didn't quite seem to ring true in this case. "Time will tell I guess. God, you're having to beat men off with a stick at the moment."

"Oh yeah, all one of them," Dee sniffed satirically.

"Actually, two. My friend Oliver Brooke thinks you're adorable," he said advisedly.

"Oliver? The guy I met last night at the club?"

"Yeah, he's had a bit of a thing for you ever since you bought the coffee shop. I've known him for years. He's been coming into the store for as long as I can remember, but his visits have increased since *you* arrived on the scene." Evan eyed her over the top of his glasses. "He's a very genuine chap and only admired you from afar whilst you were with Milo, but now he knows about the divorce, he's already been asking me if it's a little premature to ask you out on a date."

"*Oliver?*" Dee repeated stupidly. "I barely knew who he was until last night. Why would he be interested in me? I'm a cockney girl from Bethnal Green with two kids by two different fathers and he's like, the poshest man I ever met. Well, the Starks are fairly posh, but not like Oliver. I bet he's got a title or something. I bet he's an aristocrat."

"Well, his father is. But he's a lovely, down-to-earth guy. You could-"

"*Puleeze* don't tell me I could do worse than Oliver…" Dee closed her eyes.

"Actually, I think you are far better suited to Felix, but the notion of you and Oliver isn't outside the realms of possibility. I mean, in the *distant future*," Evan was saying as the doorbell sounded. "I'll get it." He got up as he could see Dee had her hands full. Finley was climbing up on her lap and pulling at her hair.

"…Hi," said Felix, standing in her lounge doorway with Evan cringing at her from behind him. Dee looked up in surprise and realised she was totally unprepared for this meeting. Why hadn't she expected to see him sooner than later? Like only a few hours after *it* had happened?

"…Hi Felix," she answered in a tiny voice. Finn was distractingly kissing the side of his mother's face.

"Hey, thanks for last night, Felix. We all really enjoyed it," Evan piped up. "Well Dee, I have to be getting back to the shop – I'll see myself out," Evan said brightly. He gave Dee a secret shrug and hurried out of the house as fast as he could without actually running.

"Hello scamp." Felix ruffled Finley's hair as he wandered by. "Where's Angel?"

Dee watched him slump rather casually down in the chair where Evan had been seated. One of his legs was draped over the arm of the seat and he rakishly lit a cigarette. He always sat like that; like he had been dropped from a great height. "Val took her to gym class. It's the same club Paddy and Melody go to."

"…Oh." Felix feigned ignorance.

Dee gulped. "…Do you mind putting that fag out? I don't like cigarette smoke around the children..." she said in a faltering voice.

"Oh, of course. Sorry, I forgot what I was doing." Felix glanced around for somewhere to put it out and plumped for an empty coffee cup on the table. "...So how are you this morning, you raging drunk?"

"I'm alright...just crazy-tired..." Dee could not remember the last time she had felt quite so abashed. She could not bring herself to meet his eye. "You okay...?"

"Well, if you've been drunk as often as I have, you kind of get used to this morning-after feeling as your natural state of being," he replied with a wry grin. "I can take my booze better than most."

"That truly is a gift," Dee smiled but continued not to catch his eye. Finn climbed off her lap and Dee gave him a water-biscuit to gnaw on. That seemed to appease him for a while and he sat on the rug rather calmly (for him).

After a while, mostly due to the trivialness of his conversation and the way he was sitting so lazily, Dee began to get the impression that maybe the events of last night were not going to come up. Maybe it would be discreetly swept under the carpet. Well, that could work...

"...Anyway, since I was back in Richmond to grab a change of clothes, I just thought I'd pop by to check you'd made it home okay this morning," Felix informed her indolently. "I'd better go. I have to be in the West End in an hour to discuss a new production I've been asked to compose for," he explained. Dee raised an eyebrow. So he was just passing; popping by at ten in the morning having come all the way from Camden where he owned a flat (and certainly a change of clothes) and now he was on his way *back* to the West End for a meeting he needed to be at in an hour? *Really*?

"Okay cool..." Dee watched him apprehensively. He made to rise from his seat, shoving the box of cigarettes into his blazer pocket. Felix really wasn't going to mention it. Well, Dee decided since he was taking that line, she was quite happy to go along with it. Then he stalled and gave her a measured stare as though he were trying to predict what she was thinking. Felix slowly sank back down into his seat, sitting uncomfortably this time – anxiety written all over his face. Carefree Felix had gone.

"I suppose we really ought to talk about last night..." he began carefully and watched her face drop. "As great as it was...maybe it wasn't the best idea we ever had..."

"No, it really wasn't..." Dee agreed regretfully, thankful he felt the same way. She let her guilty, aching head fall into her hands. "Oh Felix, what the hell were we thinking?" she groaned, and he decided to come and sit beside her on the sofa because he feared she might cry. Dee wished he hadn't.

"The only thing I had to hold onto was my innocence. But we're just as guilty as him now. We're just adulterers...at least, I am..."

"This isn't the same as what Milo did to you. He left you and immediately hooked up with another woman!" Felix argued.

But she wasn't listening. "If he ever finds out, he's going to kill you. You remember what he did when you just *kissed* me?" Dee shook her head, inconsolable without yet crying.

Felix laughed scornfully. "Milo's not going to kill me! I don't think he even cares enough about you to do that. He's got someone else," he scoffed, rubbing her arm. She wished he would stop doing that too. "He's never going to find out unless we choose to tell him."

"Everything is spoiled..." Dee's head was still in her hands.

"What's spoiled? It's only sex," he reasoned.

"Oh don't...!" Dee blenched at the word. "And what about poor Joanna? I've slept with you behind her back! What did she ever do to me? I'm no better than Amber!"

"I wouldn't worry about Joanna, she and I have an arrangement. We're just not serious and she's fine with that."

"That doesn't make me feel any better!" Dee was a wicked person; she had put herself on trial and convicted herself.

"Look, you and me...there's been this *thing* between us for a while. Last night...we were drunk and lonely and that *thing* came up." Felix waited for her to look at him but she couldn't. "I admit I have...feelings for you, but whilst there was a chance Milo might come back, I tried not to act on it. Then I realised he wasn't coming back. So last night we just wanted to be together to console ourselves - we're only human..."

"But our friendship was so important to me. Your being around has kept me sane through the worst period of my life - and now it's all ruined! You said yourself last night, you've slept with more than a hundred women, but where are all those women now? Nowhere, that's where! You don't respect the women you sleep with; I know that - look at *Joanna*. You won't respect me; you won't see me as smart and funny and interesting anymore. I'll just be yet another notch on the bedpost." She was quite simply appalled with herself.

Felix shook his head. "You're my best friend, Dee," he said so sincerely she had to stop whining and look at him, *really* look at him for the first time today. She was his best friend? Dee had never heard him say that before. "Aside from Forrest, you really are. I refuse to let this friendship fizzle out because of one drunken shag." Felix was adamant. "I will always respect you, always. I for one am going to put last night down to experience

- a *really nice* experience." He rubbed her shoulder. "...By the way, when we...*did it*, about halfway through, you changed your mind, didn't you...?"

Actually, about thirty seconds in. This was truly the most hideous conversation of all time. "...Yes. But I really wanted to at first, I swear. It's just, when it was happening, I kind of froze..."

"...Yeah, I kind of...well at least I thought I felt something change...maybe I should have stopped but I was- man, this is really awkward..." Felix grimaced.

"You're the one still talking!"

"Did I make you do something you didn't want to do?" Felix just couldn't seem to let that go.

"No! Look, you asked me again and again if I was sure, and I *was* sure."

"I just don't want things being weird between us now we've had sex..."

"Jesus Felix, will you stop saying it?" she moaned, still shaking her head. "...God, what have we done?"

"Do you have to keep referring to it like it was the most awful experience of your life?" Felix began to lose confidence in his sexual prowess.

"It wasn't awful; it was lovely but-"

"I'm a red blooded male and I don't mind admitting that I had certain private fantasies about you and me doing- what we did. I'd like to be conceited enough to imagine you'd had those same kind of fantasies about *me*. I know we shouldn't have acted those fantasies out...but they do say to get over somebody, you need to get under somebody," he laughed (perhaps inappropriately). "It's only sex if we get down to basics. You said you needed a random guy last night and I think it was sensible that random guy was me..."

"I never said I needed a random guy! That was Bruce!"

"If it *had* been some random, it would all feel so sordid now. But I'm your best friend. If you were going to do it, then it was right that it was with someone you trust," he insisted, "...like me." Felix took the hand of his hungover friend. But during the close proximity between them, Dee began to remember vivid images of last night – Felix peeling off her clothes and passionately making love to her. She knew now things could never be quite the same between them. How could they possibly bounce back from that?

"I have slept with four men from the same family! This isn't my finest hour!" Dee rubbed her eyes again.

"We're going to remain friends, right...?" Felix suddenly wore a concerned expression. Her reaction the morning after was as he expected, but was still hurtful. "Look, the conversation we're having right now...we don't ever have to have this chat again. Let's just forget about last night as though it never happened."

"...Really?" She looked up. "Oh, that would be great, Felix. All I want is for our friendship to go back to the way it was - exactly the way it was." Dee suddenly felt hopeful. If he could just forget about it, she was more than prepared to try.

"...So, who else knows? I got the feeling Evan was acting all coy about something," Felix noted perceptively.

"I'm sorry, I had to talk to someone but he's the only one I've spoken to."

"Evan and Ginny then."

"Ginny?" Dee whined. What would Ginny, who had been so supportive, think of her now?

"Sorry, I needed to talk to somebody too. But that's it – nobody else needs to hear about our guilty secret. Not Forrest, not Bruce, not Patrice, not Cassie - and certainly not Milo. We can put it to rest now," Felix assured her and she agreed readily. "...So, now that I don't have to slink off into the annuls of history as one of Dee's hideous sexual mistakes...can I have a cup of coffee? Because you're like the worst host ever." It was the first time he had made her laugh today, and he was relieved when she did. That was one of the fundamentals of their relationship. Without that, they couldn't carry on. The West End meeting was completely forgotten.

BACK

'**Bookish**' was having a slow morning and maybe Dee ought to have been dwelling on that and her financial future. But she was dwelling on something else as she gazed listlessly into the street from the window seat. Evan and Bruce hung out there at the same table with her – being that it was so dull around here.

"God, I haven't served a customer in half an hour..." Evan grumbled.

"Yeah but that's because it's really hot outside and people don't want to be in a book-stroke-coffee-shop on a nice day." Bruce was happy to brush these things off, but then, he didn't own the store. Only Evan was concerned.

"It's fine, guys. It's just a one-off," Dee intoned distractedly.

"Well, I'll tell you which customer I'm not missing, Felix-Look-At-Me-I'm-Semi-Famous-Kellerman," Bruce sneered and Evan glanced at Dee. "I'm actually pleased you fell out at the club that night, I told you he was a dick," he informed her. Bruce had since assured that his parading Oliver Brooke in front of Felix at the club had nothing to do with their quarrel, so he had happily returned to his Felix-hate-campaign.

"Bruce, I've spoken to him since the club so don't get too excited..."

"Yeah, but he's not been in the store since. Clearly things are a bit frosty between you, so it's a win-win in my book," Bruce advised them and gave her a knowing smile. "What was the fight *really* about anyway?"

Dee's eyes flicked nervously to Evan again. "...Oh, nothing really. I was drunk and you know how blunt I can be with a drink in me. I just said something about his set being a bit...safe...and he took it the wrong way."

"Ha-ha-ha! Safe? Boring, you mean," Bruce grinned wickedly. He then leisurely rose to his feet to make more drinks, muttering as he went, "when failed boy-bands and reality-TV talent contests start doing *big-band* music, you know that it has no place in this world..."

"*Are* things a bit frosty between you and Felix...?" Evan asked under his breath. "You haven't told me what happened when he came over yesterday."

For the first time today, she seemed less disengaged and moved to sit beside him. "I couldn't say anything because of Bruce, could I?"

"Well?"

"Everything is fine, I suppose. He agreed it was a mistake and wants to be friends and we resolved never to talk about it again."

"...Oh...well that's not what I expected you to say but I guess that's what you wanted, right?" Evan sensed that Dee was not in the least bit relieved.

"Yes, I guess...I'm glad we're both on the same page." She *wanted* to be glad, but something didn't add up. "It's just he's done a complete one-eighty from his feelings at the club. We fought that night because he was upset about Bruce introducing Oliver as a potential suitor when he wanted me to see *him* as an option. And he even said he would leave Joanna and wait for me until after my divorce if I asked him to."

Evan grimaced and shrugged all at once. "Well...you ran out on him in the morning, maybe he's just trying to save face?" he suggested.

"I don't know...he *seemed* genuine yesterday. I mean, sweeping it under the carpet is really the best course of action because Milo can never know. Divorce or no divorce, he'd go bloody mental." Dee shifted uncomfortably in her seat. Why was this troubling her so greatly? She'd had a lucky escape, hadn't she? "The thing that sticks in my memory most about that night at the club was his intensity; how serious he seemed to be about me. And now he's all übercool again. Mind you, I did just freeze up and was barely involved when we *did it* – there's nothing like being crap in bed to put a guy off you..." Dee meandered around little pathways of her brain, speaking mostly to herself. Then she looked up to be greeted by a rather awkward looking Evan. "Sorry, I forgot I wasn't talking too Bruce - a little too much information?"

"Just a smidge." Evan broke into a smile. "I'm sure it wasn't that, Dee. The whole situation is just so messy. He's probably too scared to suggest taking things any further - what with Milo and the rest of your family breathing down your necks."

"I'm probably reading too much into this. Felix is probably cool with it like he says."

"So only I know about this?"

"And Ginny."

"Ginny?" he narrowed his eyes.

"Felix needed to speak to someone too," she reasoned.

"If he wanted to forget about it, I'm surprised he told his sister..."

"Well I told *you*, and I want to forget it," Dee reminded him.

"But that's typical of *you*; you have to dissect every little thing...but guys don't tend to," Evan sighed uneasily. "Dee, if Bruce works out what happened with Felix and then he discovers you told me and not him, he'd be crushed."

"I can't tell Bruce!" Dee hissed. "He detests Felix - he's never going to understand!"

"*I* understood."

"*You* wanted me to hook up with Felix permanently!"

"So you *are* saying it's my fault?"

"No!" Dee let her head fall into her hands, frustrated. "...I have a brain, I am in control of my choices, the only person who is at fault here is me."

"But I put the thought in your head," Evan reminded her guiltily.

"Trust me, with or without your intervention, it was going to come up," Dee assured him sadly. Felix had only one course of direction that night at the club, and Evan's intervention had little to do with the outcome. Well, maybe he was a *bit* responsible - but she wouldn't tell Evan that.

"...The thing Bruce hates most about Felix is that he feels Felix is your replacement for him. Which is why I don't know if it's a good idea to be secretive with Bruce. What do you need a coarsely witty best friend for when you have hilarious, talented and rich Felix Kellerman always on hand to whisk you off at a moment's notice?"

"He said that to you...?"

"Pretty much," Evan admitted with a twist of his mouth. "You're Bruce's best friend and since things are going down the toilet with Patrice, he needs you even more - but he feels redundant..."

"...Because I'm too preoccupied with my own crap? Nobody could replace Bruce for me. God I'm such a terrible friend!" Dee growled at her own insensitivity. "I ought to go and live alone in a mud-hut in some uninhabited, densely forested area of Papua New Guinea so I can stop fucking up everybody's life! I'm selfish, self-absorbed and I treat my friends like toys. My life is shit and it's all my own doing. I lead my male friends to believe I'm interested in them romantically when I'm not. I take and take and take and give nothing back. Maybe it *is* my fault my marriage ended. I spent so much time bleating about how hard done by I was, when maybe it's over because I led Felix on. I *kissed* another man. Milo had the right to be upset - I would have been upset if he'd done that to me." Perhaps it was time she started to point the finger at herself. How could anything ever change if she never took any responsibility?

Evan snorted derisively. "Are you done feeling sorry for yourself? D'you want my opinion? Your marriage is over because your husband has an insane jealousy problem – off the charts insane. He could have gone away and sulked for a while and then you should have been able to talk and patch things up. But instead he left you and slept with another woman because of *a kiss*. Are you at fault at all? A little bit, maybe – but your fault is your cripplingly blind naïvety," Evan advised bluntly. "And your naïvety stems from your broken childhood. You had nobody, so you spend your entire adult life trying to please everyone. We could all see Felix was getting too attached to you but you couldn't- *wouldn't* acknowledge it. Maybe that's our fault too because we, as your friends, know how immature you are about men. We should have intervened, not hinted at it." Evan made a fist and rested his chin on top. Dee swallowed. That hurt – but she deserved it. "I'm sorry - I don't mean to hurt your feelings…"

"No, it's fine…but next time, don't sugar-coat it…" she smiled tightly.

"For what it's worth, I think you had a lucky escape from Milo. I think he's toxic. But I happen to think Felix is a really solid, down-to-earth guy who could turn your life around. What you need is stability and I think Felix could offer you that. But it doesn't matter what I think; if Felix doesn't do it for you, you can't pretend he does." Evan rubbed her arm comfortingly.

"…Thank you for being so honest." Dee wiped a fleck of moisture from her eye. "But I'm done. I'm going to be single from now on," she said decisively (again).

"Dee, you're only thirty-two," Evan frowned.

Dee shook her head. "Thirty-two with two failed marriages under my belt and two children by two different fathers. No, it's better that I grow old alone than keep perpetuating this misery. Sometimes you have to accept your limitations, Evan, and men are clearly mine…"

*

Standing over the open bonnet of the metallic sky blue Ford Focus, Dee wondered what it was she was supposed to be looking at. The dirty engine stared back up at her and gave her no clues as to what was actually wrong with it. However, there was one thing she could safely say on that warm July morning, it didn't work.

"…What's your diagnosis?" said a warm, rich and familiar voice. Dee looked around to see a modest-sized black limo had pulled up beside her. Its passenger, Milo, was smiling out from behind a half-open tinted window. Dee was so surprised she couldn't speak for nearly five whole seconds.

"…You're back…" she gawped rather stupidly. Dee hadn't seen his face in weeks. He was wearing that heart-stopping smile and an expression that said he was pleased to see her. Milo climbed from the car, dressed in a familiar garb of jeans and a thin grey lamb's wool sweater over a white t-shirt, and just the aroma of him made her want to cry. "I thought you hated showing up in limos, you said it was crass." Dee quickly regained her composure, putting out of her head what she had done in his absence.

Milo sighed disappointedly – but what other reaction had he expected? "...Well yes, but I just flew in from the States and this was the easiest way of getting here." As much as Milo tried to be understated to impress this woman, sometimes he just couldn't help being rich. He turned away and quietly asked his driver to return for him later. The impressive car pulled away. "So why are you looking under the hood of this, frankly, ugly family hatchback?"

"It's Bruce's car. If you'll cast your mind back, mine was written off in an accident I had and I'm borrowing this until I can decide what to car to buy next. Anyway, after careful consideration of this particular automobile, I think that one of the mechanical or electrical parts isn't doing what it should be..." she said and Milo smirked.

"Are the kids here?" he asked.

"No, they're with Mrs Dawson until this evening. I had no idea you were coming back today. Anyway, I was just going food shopping, but the car won't start. The engine won't even turn over..." Dee glanced at the car again, hoping glaring at it might make it behave.

"I know quite a lot about cars. I'll have a look at it if you like."

"It's okay, I'll call out the AA," Dee said innocuously. After the initial shock and perhaps even pleasure at seeing him again, Dee remembered she should be feeling extremely angry.

"They'll take ages to come out. Why don't you make me a coffee and I'll see if it's something simple I can fix?" Milo gave her arm a friendly pat. Dee glanced at his hand on her arm then loitered for a moment, unsure whether to send him packing or accept his help.

"...Alright..." Dee murmured and wandered back up to the house.

Dee took her time over making the coffees because she needed a moment to mull over what tack she was supposed to take with her ex-husband. She was terribly upset with him, but she was also horribly ashamed of *herself* due to her very recent tryst with Felix. Before she could really construct some choice insults to batter him with, he was standing in the kitchen with oil-stained hands and a frown.

"I'm afraid it's a fairly serious problem. You're going to need a certain part which I can get for you, but not by today...not that it's your car," Milo reminded her. "I can call my driver back to take you where you need to go, if you like? I'm pretty certain I've diagnosed the problem, and I'd be surprised if *anybody* could get the part today, but I'm happy to call the rescue people for you to get a second opinion?" he said casually and came over to wash his hands in the kitchen sink. This only served to irritate her more so. He didn't even live here anymore and yet still he swept in and took over, took charge as though she were too inept or too female to cope.

"*Call the rescue people for me?* I was going to bloody well do that before you rocked up!" she snapped. "Well thank you, but I am quite capable of making a phone call. Anyway, I can't be bothered to go shopping anymore. I'm going for a walk," Dee told him sourly.

"...Well, shall we drink our coffee first? I haven't seen you in weeks and I thought we could talk..." Milo was clearly disheartened at her change of attitude.

"Actually Milo, the whole world doesn't revolve around you. Just because you happen to have flounced back from America, doesn't mean I have to drop everything just because you feel like a chat. The kids aren't here. If you want to see them in the near future, give me a call," Dee said archly, poured both freshly made cups of coffee down the sink and breezed by him with the final insult of, "if you care about them anymore, that is..."

"Hey!" Milo grabbed her arm. "That's not fair!"

And before Dee had time to keep her emotions in check, she found herself becoming overwrought.

"I'll tell you what's not fair, fooling a little three-year-old into believing she has a new daddy when really he doesn't give a crap! It's not fair that my daughter had to spend her third birthday without the man she's been tricked into believing is her father! It's not fair that you made such a big deal about adopting her when you barely even care about your *own* son!" she yelled and pushed by him, storming into the lounge. He quickly caught her up and grasped her wrist.

"You have no right to say that to me! I called you and I told you it was impossible to get back!"

"Impossible? Were you held hostage by terrorists? Were you trapped under something extremely heavy?" Dee enquired in her very best sarcastic tone. Milo was for it now. There was nothing he could say and nothing he could do to defend himself against Dee's nihilistic onslaught. She would make him wish he had never come back to England – wish he'd never been born. But her rage was about more than his apparent disregard for her daughter - he had made Dee an adulteress. Oh yes, she had been responsible too, but he broken her first. "So what was it that made it so impossible for the richest man in the world to hop on a plane and be at his daughter's birthday party?"

"I was in hospital and they wouldn't let me leave!"

Dee stood stock-still. "...Hospital? What was wrong with you...?" she said suspiciously, her eyes narrowed.

Milo disgustedly cast his eyes down to the floor. "...Carbon monoxide poisoning..."

"...What...? Carbon monoxide? How– how did that happen...?" Dee's mind was ablaze with crazy images. Carbon monoxide poisoning was from faulty gas fires or cooking in unventilated spaces or something – but none of that could possibly relate to *Milo*.

Milo continued not to meet her eyes. His voice was barely audible when he spoke again, "...I- I sat in my car in a locked garage," he mumbled. Some of the memory was just a blur, some was missing completely. But he remembered sitting in the driver's seat drinking gin from the bottle. "...and I ran the engine..."

CRYING FOR HELP

Dee's intense anger was instantly deflated. She had been psyching herself up for this very argument for weeks and was quite certain she had all the ammunition she needed to make him feel like the dirt on her shoe. This was to be the mother of all quarrels and one from which she would certainly have emerged victorious and triumphant. But Milo had pulled on the anchors and Dee was forced to pull up short.

"...What?" she muttered. "I don't understand..."

"...I think you do," Milo sighed and sat on the sofa dejectedly. "I've been in hospital for two weeks. I only got out yesterday..."

"...Is this some kind of joke?" Dee sat down beside him, her animosity still intact but the wind completely taken out of her sails.

"I wish it was. I've brought copies of medical letters...to my doctor. I brought them with me because I guessed I'd have to explain and I wasn't sure if you'd believe me," he said, placing the small attaché case on the sofa between them but not opening it. She hadn't even noticed him bringing it into the house. "First I was on a medical ward because of the carbon monoxide poisoning...and then they moved me to the psychiatric unit because...I was a risk. You'd call it 'sectioning' over here..."

"...You-" She could hardly make sense of it. "...You tried to commit suicide? Is that what you're telling me...?" Dee stammered breathlessly. Now she really looked at him and thought about it, Milo did not look his fit and healthy self. He was thinner than she remembered, and his colouring wasn't quite right. He was so pale and gaunt.

"Yes..." Milo kept his eyes on the carpet and refused to raise them.

"...Did you mean it? Did you really want to die...?"

"Yes, I really wanted to die."

"...Why?" Dee shook her head incredulously and then she was crying again, crying the way only Milo could make her cry.

"...Because of you," he said blankly. "Because I'd destroyed my marriage and drove away the only woman I'd ever loved..."

Dee shook her head to clear it. "...So you admit you were wrong about me?"

"...Yes." Milo gave a small nod of his head. "Since I've been getting the help, everything has become clear to me," he responded in a tiny voice. "You were innocent and I should have believed you...I'm so- sorry..."

So he had finally admitted it; said the words she had longed to hear for months on end. But even though he had grossly misjudged her character back then, he wasn't wrong anymore. Felix *had* happened. And all Dee felt was...fury. "How come you get to commit suicide when it was *you* who left *me*?!" she shouted angrily but that fury soon dissipated into sorrow - Dee was utterly crushed. "...Was it a cry for help or did you really want to end your life...?" she asked in a broken voice.

"If it was a cry for help - nobody heard..." Milo sort of smiled. "I know it was selfish and cruel but I *really* wasn't well; I wasn't in my right mind. I haven't been in my right mind for a long time. My psychiatrist says this probably started with me not dealing with Andrew's death properly – I was like a time bomb just waiting to go off. And Felix was the trigger," he said circumspectly. "I just wanted the pain to stop. I thought if I was dead-"

"...Do you still want to die now?"

"...Sometimes...but mostly I regret it."

"Why didn't anyone tell me? You tried to take your own life and were hospitalised and nobody told me." Dee shook her head again in disbelief.

"No Dee, don't think for a moment Forrest and Ginny kept it from you. They don't know. I didn't tell anyone," Milo said apologetically. "Well, my mother and father were aware, but I swore them to secrecy. I knew Forrest would go straight to you if he were told the truth," Milo explained mournfully.

Dee narrowed her eyes once more. "...But you had Amber with you?"

"Amber? No, I haven't seen Amber since I split up with her the day I found out she'd been pestering you with abusive calls," he explained blankly.

"But you went to America together..." Dee's blood had run cold. They'd split up?

"No we didn't. She may have flown back to the States but she certainly didn't go with me," Milo shrugged. "I told you I was going for business, but I really left England earlier than intended because I just couldn't take anymore. I needed to mourn our break-up by myself; I had to get some distance. I couldn't handle seeing you around all the time. But when I got back to The Hamptons, it got worse - everything got on top of me and I just cracked..."

"Why wouldn't you want me to know? I realise you don't want to be married to me anymore, but I still have the right to know if you're sick!" Dee shouted out of sheer frustration. "I don't want you to *die*! I still care for you! How could you keep that kind of thing from me?!" What had happened to this man she thought she knew, who she had pledged to spend the rest of her life with?

"You told me you wished I was dead - twice!"

"That's not fair, I was upset!"

"I wanted you to be there more than anything in the world! But I couldn't take the risk of letting you know…because I couldn't stomach the rejection if you didn't come!" he shouted back at her and she stalled for a moment, but only for a moment.

"What - like the rejection *I* felt when you didn't come visit me in hospital?"

"I did come!"

"I know I bruised my brain, Milo, but I think I might remember if you'd visited!"

Milo covered his face, exasperated. "I never actually *saw* you – but I tried three times to get there. I came on the evening of the accident, but I backed out when I saw Jerry and Elliott milling around the hospital entrance. I waited in the car for an hour but they just wouldn't leave. The morning after the accident, I was just about to bring the children when Amber returned from America and refused to let me see you. And the day after that, I finally managed to get into the hospital to see you about quarter of an hour after you were discharged. The nurse said you'd left with a man with black, curly hair and a five o'clock shadow," Milo said sadly. "I rang the ward countless times a day to check on you. I pretended I was your estranged father so the nurses wouldn't pass on that I'd called…"

"That only serves to prove that you're gutless!" Dee argued with a pointless, yet all-consuming anger.

"…I suppose I am," he admitted dully. "But I want you to know that when you were in that car accident, I was devastated. I thought about you every waking minute of every day. It killed me that I didn't get to be there with you…and instead *he* was there to hold your hand." Milo suddenly slipped his own hand into hers and Dee did not feel inclined to pull away. He had not touched her in so long that breaking away seemed petty and futile.

"…I know we can't be together anymore, Milo, but that doesn't mean I've been able to shut off my feelings for you. If I had known you were ill, I'd have grabbed the kids and flown to America like a shot – even after what you did to me. I'll always care for you…you're still my family…" Dee was still crying, and he felt compelled to comfort her.

"I didn't know that you still felt that way. You were always so aloof and off-hand, I thought you didn't care anymore. Every day I was in that hospital, I prayed you'd wake up one morning with a gut-instinct that something was wrong and fly out to see what had happened to me...but you didn't." He gently wiped the tears from her eyes with the pad of his thumb. "I have to come to terms with the fact that you won't be my wife anymore, but not to be in your life at all is unbearable. You were the best friend I ever had...you were the one person I could confide in. I'm intrinsically linked to you. That isn't just because we had a child together; you're a part of me," Milo said rather emotionally, his own eyes becoming misty. "When we first got together, I promised you I would be your family. But you were my family too. There's a bond between us that I can't break – and I know because I tried. I want you in my life. I *need* to be able to talk to you...and I don't want to be shut out anymore..." he professed genuinely. "It would be so much better for the children if their mommy and daddy were friends...and it would be so much better for *me*. I've done some pretty despicable things to you; Amber being the biggest of those - but Felix kissing you *literally* drove me insane. My breakdown and finally getting medical help...it's made me wake up to myself..."

So that was what had happened to him, a mental breakdown. "You have to promise me you will never do something like this again. You just admitted that you still sometimes wish you were dead. To put the children through that, to put me through that...it just isn't fair. How could we ever possibly get over it?"

"I swear I will never do something so selfish and stupid again. Just knowing you're prepared to talk to me makes me feel a thousand percent better. You won't shut me out again, will you...?" he asked warily.

"...Milo, I'm so thankful you didn't die and I'm relieved we're talking again. But some terrible, unforgivable things have happened," she reminded him. Mostly committed by him - one committed by her. "You left me for no good reason and took up with that woman..." Dee needed to point out his faults again for her own sanity. In that respect, nothing had changed.

"...I know what I did...but you've just told me you still care. I realise you don't *love* me anymore, and I can't expect you to want me as a best friend either," Milo began disconsolately, "but can't you bend a little? I'd do anything if you were just *nice* to me again." There was a slightly pleading edge to his voice, hidden beneath a half-smile. "I'd settle for that..."

Dee was still totally downcast, staring sorrowfully at the floor. Nice? This conversation right here was as nice as it was ever going to get. Once Milo found out what had happened with Felix, and he inevitably would, a cold war would break out again. "I thought I was being nice now..." she said in what wasn't much more than a whisper.

"...Nicer than usual – you're scary sometimes," Milo laughed softly. "Did you get my message on our anniversary?"

"...Message?" Dee looked up miserably.

"Yeah, I sent you an email from my phone in the hospital to wish you a happy anniversary."

Dee shook her head. "...No, I didn't get it. What did it say...?"

"Um..." Milo slid his phone from his pocket and pulled up the email, "oh...it's sitting in the outbox." He gave a deep sigh of regret. Milo put the phone in her hand so she could see for herself. Dee silently read, *'Two years ago today, I met my soulmate. That day remains the best day of my life. Maybe things haven't worked out as we'd hoped, but a lot of positives have come out of 'us'. We made a beautiful son, Angel has a new father and I found my kindred spirit. What we had is probably irrevocably fractured, but I'll always care for you. Please let's work towards being friends again. Happy Anniversary. x M'.*

Milo watched anxiously for a reaction. "The internet in the hospital was notoriously bad and sometimes...you see the message failed to send," he explained again. "I'm sorry Dee, I wasn't very well – they'd put me on this medication and I felt so vague. I just didn't realise..." he gulped piteously. Dee felt sick to her stomach. All those nails in the coffin of their relationship began to be figuratively pulled out with a claw hammer. The lines between what she knew and what she *thought* she knew became blurred and fuzzy at the edges. Milo had split up with Amber. He'd tried to take his own life and was sectioned, so couldn't come back for Angel's birthday. And he'd attempted to reach out to her on their anniversary. But the most heart-breaking realisation of all was, Milo was ill. Perhaps he had been ill all along – but she hadn't seen it. Dee couldn't help but feel if she had been privy to this information, perhaps that night with Felix would never have happened. In fact, she was sure of it.

"...Brilliant," she said numbly, handing back the phone. Events had conspired against them all along. Why should that single reconciliatory act on his part go according to plan? Nothing else had.

"Look, I know we can't turn back the clock. But at least we're *talking* now," he insisted as brightly as he could. "...So...would you like to make me a fresh cup of coffee?" Milo stroked her pale blonde hair from her wet eyes. "Oh, and this time, don't throw it down the kitchen sink. I'd quite like to drink it."

*

The morning cup of coffee had become lunch and an afternoon glass of wine and a classic movie in the cubbyhole. It was nice to stop talking for a while. He had even made himself at home enough to fall asleep halfway through the film. Milo was folded up as small as his long body would go on his usual side of the sofa, so exhausted was he after his hospital ordeal. During his nap, Dee had been pouring over copies of Milo's hospital discharge and psychiatrist letters to his GP. Milo had meant her to; he needed her to understand what was wrong with him. Her husband had now been diagnosed with severe depression with suicidal ideation after a nonfatal suicide attempt. He had been prescribed antidepressants which appeared to be alleviating his symptoms. Dee used to think him the strongest and most capable man in the world, it was odd to know he was so mentally fragile and vulnerable.

She could not help glancing over at her husband now and again as he slept. Dee had to reluctantly accept that he was the still the most beautiful man she had ever seen up close. To think she had been married to him. He was physically too perfect, too charismatic and always out of her league. Of course it hadn't worked out. Dee and Milo were totally mismatched as a couple, just like everyone had tried to warn them. But Dee had loved him. Who would have known this beautiful man was so broken inside?

"Sorry, I didn't mean to fall asleep," Milo said groggily as he came to, staring bleary-eyed at the black-and-white movie just ending on the TV. "God, I could just light up a cigarette now."

"I'd really rather you didn't," Dee said firmly. "...Um, would you like to stay for dinner? Angel and Finley will be home at about five and I think it would be really nice for them to see us sitting down to a meal again as a family..." she suggested hesitantly.

Milo sat up, pleasantly surprised. "I would love to...thank you. I can't wait to see them again...it's been so long. Can we do something as a belated birthday treat for Angel soon? I felt so awful not being here. Maybe we could do more things together as a family - that would be a healthy thing to do, right...?"

"I think that would be a good idea. I'm sorry you didn't get to see your children while you were sick in hospital..." Reading the letters had made it all more visceral to her. The diagnosis of mental illness brought his former problems into sharper focus. It was all so obvious now she knew.

"I wanted to see *you* most of all...and if you'd known, I realise now you would have come. But we're here building bridges, which is a huge milestone for me," Milo said softly, distractedly examining his bare feet.

"...I've been wanting to apologise for the whole *Amber* episode..." he began tentatively, steeling himself to continue. "She meant nothing to me, and I just...saw an opportunity to hurt you like I thought you'd hurt me..."

"Oh don't, Milo. I'm not ready to start dissecting the reasons why our marriage fell apart." Dee held her hand up as a blocking gesture. "But if we're going to look for faults, let's start by admitting we fell in love too hard and too fast. We didn't really know each other properly - just like everybody said."

"That's not why it all went wrong," he complained.

"No, that was you leaving me for Amber." But quickly relenting, Dee fought the urge to start another fight. "Anyway, we were always a bit too *'Romeo and Juliet'* to last, weren't we?" she murmured.

"...And what about Felix?" he said quietly.

"...What about him?" Dee froze. She had made a monumental mistake and had sex with him in the flat above his club a few days ago. Other than that, there wasn't much to say.

"Do you see much of him?"

"...Well, we weren't friends for a bit, but then we patched things up when you hooked up with Amber. I'd like to think one day you guys could be friends again too..." Dee said hopefully but wondered what would happen to this newly-forged friendship if Milo knew. Would this new gentler ex-husband be so affable?

Milo's eyes became glassy and his mouth set in a hard expression. "That's never going to happen," he asserted. "I asked him, as a friend, to take care of you whilst I was away, and he totally took advantage. Whatever you think of him, don't forget he's still a man who kissed his own *cousin's* wife." But it was now so much worse than that.

Dee decided not to push him on this point right now and left it at that. "You know, there was a lot of talk that you were never coming back to England when you went away."

"Well you shouldn't believe hearsay. I don't know why everyone thought I was off gallivanting with Amber, you all just assumed. And I can assure you I was completely alone. I would never want to live in a different country to my children. It's bad enough that I can't live *with them* anymore, let alone never be in the same Continent," he said balefully.

"You were prepared to leave them for good, Milo - by topping yourself," Dee reminded him. He looked away guiltily. "Look, I'm glad you're staying - the children need you close by. You will always be Finley and Angel's daddy," Dee promised him. "Shall I open another bottle of wine?"

His outlook seemed to brighten then. "Are you trying to get me drunk?"

Milo smirked.

"That was an open bottle and we've only had one glass," Dee declared.

"I'm joking. Okay, I don't have to drive home, someone else has to do that. I'd love another glass if that's alright."

Dee smiled. That was more than alright. She would never truly get over the loss of the greatest love of her life. But having him as a civil acquaintance – maybe one day even a friend - knowing he no longer despised her, made her feel a thousand percent better. Dee put out of her mind Felix and that night at the club. She was no guiltier than Milo; they were both adulterers now, but there was no way she could bring herself to tell him. Nor could she bring herself to consider the consequences if he ever found out.

*

Later that evening after dinner was over, Milo kissed and cuddled his children before he set out on his journey home. With Finley perched on his hip and Angel wrapped around him like a spider monkey, he felt surprisingly content and full of hope for a halfway decent future.

"Why didn't you call the driver? I hate to think of you walking home when you've just…been ill," Dee grimaced as the family loitered at the front door. Mrs Dawson stood in the kitchen doorway smiling knowingly. She had assisted Dee in preparing a meal and was overjoyed to see the couple on such good terms.

"It's a beautiful summer evening and I could do with some air to clear my head after all that wine," he said and handed Finley back to Dee, putting Angel down. "You didn't get the rescue people out for Bruce's car."

"It doesn't matter. I'll sort it out tomorrow." Dee silently thanked her lucky stars that the car had decided not to work this morning.

"I really enjoyed today…" he said in such a quiet voice that only Dee could have heard him.

"Yeah, I did too. I'm so glad you're feeling better." Dee felt it was safe to put her arms around him and give him a hug. She was grateful when he hugged her back. As hugs went, it felt amazing. "…Don't ever try to hurt yourself again," she warned him in a whisper.

"I won't," he said with rather moist eyes as Angel jumped up and down before him excitedly. "Maybe I'll drop in at the coffee shop tomorrow to say 'hello' if you're there." Milo kissed the kids again and placed a small kiss on Dee's cheek, waved to Mrs Dawson and walked to his car.

"I'll drop the kids off at yours on Saturday. Bye," Dee called and closed the door. She turned to look at Mrs Dawson who eyed her sagaciously. "What?" Dee asked.

"Oh nothing, it's just nice to see you two getting along so well again," she said innocently but her dark eyes twinkled with a wickedly mischievous glint.

IN HINDSIGHT

Evan was as surprised and interested in her news as Dee hoped he would be the next morning. He sat at his desk which was positioned adjacent to hers in the back office of the coffee shop. Dee was perched on the edge of her desk eating a small tub of strawberry cheesecake yogurt for her nutritious breakfast. She ate this whilst telling him the ins and outs of yesterday's events.

"So we spent the entire day together. He didn't leave until just before I put the children to bed and I have to say, for the first time in months, we got on really well," Dee concluded.

"I can't believe he tried to *kill* himself." Evan shook his head, trying to take in all he had heard.

"I know. It's terrible isn't it? If the gardener hadn't switched the days he works and Milo hadn't fallen unconscious on the horn of the car, nobody would have found him in time," Dee hated even to think of the consequences. Milo would be dead now. "I never thought I'd see the day when someone as strong and self-assured as him would turn out to be so fragile..." she sighed. "It's such a kick in the head. Everything I thought Milo was guilty of, everything I thought I knew that persuaded me that it was over with my husband – well a lot of it wasn't true. Milo *did* try to come and see me in the hospital, Milo wasn't in the States with Amber but in the psyche ward so he *couldn't* come back for Angel's birthday. And he *did* try to send me a message on our anniversary. If I'd known those things, Evan, I would never have slept with Felix. If Milo had just come back a few days earlier and told me the truth, I wouldn't have had an affair at all." Dee was so angry with herself, so angry with her lack of integrity that she could spit. "And now I'm just as guilty as Milo."

"No, now you're even," Evan shrugged.

"It's not a competition. I didn't do it to get my own back."

"Didn't you?" Evan arched his eyebrow.

"...I was lonely, I wanted affection...and I regret it," Dee said ruefully.

"Will you tell Milo what you did?" he asked.

"...No. I think that would just tip him over the edge. We've only just begun to be on good terms, I don't want to make him despise me again," Dee admitted. The total loss of Milo from her life had been like a permanent eclipse of the sun; dark and deathly cold.

"...Dee, surely you wouldn't think of taking him back if he asked you to? You may have got a couple of your facts wrong, but he still left you and slept with another woman. That hasn't changed."

Dee's hackles were immediately up. "He *hasn't* asked me to!" No, Milo hadn't asked, had he? He had said he was wrong, said he was sorry, said he just wanted her to be *nice* to him - but he hadn't asked to come home. Adversely, he hadn't really talked about the divorce either. "Milo just wants to be friends, which is the right thing to do for the children's sake."

"But if he did ask you...?"

"...I...no, no, of course I wouldn't. Too much has happened," Dee insisted quickly, covering up her hesitance.

"Hey Dee, there's some American I don't know wanting to see you," Bruce called into the office, making them both jump. It felt slightly wrong that Evan was now her confidante and not Bruce. But Evan knew about the fling with Felix and hence became privy to everything else. And Bruce could never know about Felix.

"Oh, alright," Dee replied, gave Evan a confused shrug and wandered out into the shop to find Milo's old friend Peter sitting on one of the sofas. Dee hadn't seen him since the wedding, and even then she had only managed to offer him a few drunken words on her circuit of the wedding reception. Dee remembered Peter mainly from the Christmas she and Milo had fallen in love. They had visited Peter in his lovely home in Bath, right before their spectacular falling out in the garden. Peter seemed to be a pleasant, genuine enough guy. He was more agreeable than his lecherous brother, Bob. Peter was reading a book and sipping from a grande coffee mug. "Hi Peter, how are you?" Dee put on her most gracious persona and he stood up to give her a hug.

"I'm fine, are you okay? I went to your house to see you and Milo but nobody was there. Milo isn't answering his phone so I came here to find out where he was...but your red-headed colleague has just told me you've split up," he said with the most stunned look on his face. Dee clutched his hand and they sat down together.

"Yes, I'm sorry you had to find out like that. I thought he might have told you."

"No. I understand he accused you having a fling with his cousin Felix and then he went off with Amber?" Peter was still holding her hand.

"Gosh, Bruce really has filled you in, hasn't he?" Dee eyed her co-worker standing behind the counter coldly. "There was honestly nothing going on with Felix; the kiss was just a foolish mistake on his part. But Milo didn't see it that way...so he moved out and started seeing Amber."

"God, this is madness! I can't tolerate that woman – she's been popping up in Milo's life for years. Even Milo used to admit that he only used her for– well, you can see where I'm going with this..." he cleared his throat. "She's just so conniving and controlling. I can't believe Milo left you and the kids to be with *her*. What on earth possessed him?"

"I think he wanted to punish me. Anyway, he's finally got rid of her now..." Dee shrugged. "So let me give you his new address and number. Oh and I'll give you his new office address too." She began jotting down the information for Peter on a napkin.

"Look, maybe I can talk some sense into Milo. You were the best thing that ever happened to him, Dee. I won't sit by and let a mistake like this happen. Maybe he'll listen to me."

"Peter, it's *over* between us. I'm flattered that you care, but Milo's whole family have sided with me and to be honest, he really hasn't got anyone to confide in anymore. Just go see him; he could do with a real friend right now. And let's face it, you were *his* friend first," Dee said pragmatically. "Anyway, Milo and I are getting on a lot better recently, and he hasn't been well so...don't rock the boat, huh?"

"...Well, alright...if you think that's best. God Dee, you're being really grown up about all this. I don't think I would be." Peter picked up the scrap of paper with Milo's addresses scribbled on it. After a while, Peter bid his goodbyes, hugged her again and left. Dee knew she had done the right thing. Milo had suffered too and needed a friend. She was not so shallow that she needed yet another person to take her side in the matter. It was no longer about sides anyway.

*

Some might call it a fairly disappointing July because the wilting heat and scorching sun just did not occur this year. June had been far better. But the weather was pleasant enough to sit outside in a light sweater or jacket. Peter and Milo had popped out for coffee and lunch at Benito's coffee house a day later. Peter had stayed overnight at Milo's place but would be driving home later that afternoon.

"Is this the place Dee calls Mussolini's?" Peter looked around whilst sipping his coffee and nibbling on a biscotti.

"Yeah," Milo smiled.

"She's kind of quirky, isn't she?"

"I suppose so," he shrugged with as much insouciance as he could muster.

"I have to say I never got the chance to know Dee very well, but every time I do meet her, I think she's such a great girl. I mean, I know Amber is stunningly beautiful, but she's really unpleasant and Dee is *sort of* pretty in her own way and has such a good heart..." Peter threw out the bait, wondering if Milo would bite.

"Hey, Dee *is* beautiful! She's timeless and natural, whereas Amber is like plastic," Milo said before checking himself. He wasn't supposed to be praising his ex. Peter smirked. "...Anyway, where are we going with this, Peter?"

"I just want you to really think about what you're doing, Milo. Dee still cares deeply for you. Do you know what she said when I dropped in at the coffee shop? She told me not to hassle you about leaving her and just to be a real friend to you. That was all she wanted. I mean, that's a really selfless thing to say," Peter stressed quite passionately.

Milo mulled that over. "...I'll always care for Dee. She's an amazing person and she's a good mother. She's never made it difficult for me to see the kids. I *know* Dee has a good heart and I know she's selfless, and we had a happy marriage once," he mused pensively. "...But I didn't trust her enough, and inadvertently, I made Felix happen. I don't deny it's my fault; I put him in her life. And him kissing her, it literally drove me mad. I've done some terrible things to her...and there's no coming back from that."

"So you admit there was no affair with Felix now?" Peter enquired with a sad shake of his head; all that pain and misery over what? A misunderstanding.

"...Since my breakdown...I've finally accepted that there wasn't actually anything physical going on. I honestly believe when I caught them kissing at the house, that was the first and last time. And I know now Felix instigated it and Dee played no part in it. But I made Felix an issue...created a problem that wasn't there before. They're close friends again now, and I've got this awful feeling he still wants her for himself. And I worry that, because of my behaviour, maybe she's developed secret feelings for him too-" Milo paused because thinking about it hurt so deeply - Felix was still very much a part of her life; the third person in their marriage. No, their marriage was over. Then he snapped out of his unhappy reverie and stared out onto the street. "I don't want to talk about it anymore, Peter. I'm all talked out. It's over, I realise that. But we've both been in hospital and that's made me certain I can't face losing her entirely. We're working towards being friends again now, and I've got to be grateful for that," Milo explained.

"Well that's something, at least. The Milo I used to know would never have tried to take his own life," Peter began - glad Milo had confided in him, "which is why I know just how damn low you must have been. You love her so much; you would rather have died than live without her. Maybe that should be telling you not to rule out a reconciliation," Peter jabbered on but stalled when he saw Dee, her red-headed friend and the two children bustling down the street. Dee and her party obviously did not see the two men as they came to seat themselves outside the same restaurant on the other side of a row of tall potted conifers.

"See? We *have* to get along in a small town like this. I bump into her all the time," Milo said very quietly.

"It's nice to see her looking so happy," Peter said in a hushed tone also, trying to peer through the plants.

Milo scratched his head. "I guess..." Yes, she did, didn't she? Happier without him.

Bruce was laughing and practically screeching as usual. "Oh Dee, I love your new kitten! You ought to let me keep her." The two friends and the two children had chosen the twelve-week-old kitten from a litter of five this morning; part of Dee's plan to restructure her life.

"No, Kirby is our family pet now and I would no sooner give you her than one of the children." Dee watched Angel seat herself on a chair and pull out her colouring things. Finley slept contentedly in his three-wheel buggy whilst Dee rocked him to and fro with her foot on the wheel. Bruce was already perusing the menu. "And I've always said, if you're going to have kids, you may as well have a pet."

"You have literally *never* said that."

"I have, I say it all the time," Dee insisted, not knowing how her husband frowned on the other side of the conifers. His wife was moving on; doing new things, making decisions that didn't involve him. "The days when I could just flit about and do whatever I want have long gone anyway." Although Dee was lucky enough to have a nanny, she still really believed that.

"Hey, that customer we served earlier was a complete toss-bag, wasn't he?" Bruce began.

"Oh yeah, he's so weird! He comes in all the time, and every time he tries to corner me and strike up a conversation. I can't believe you decided to take your break right at that moment and left me on my own with him in the store. He's the kind of guy who would follow you home from work and murder you," Dee assured him knowledgeably. "Since we're speaking of that, if they end up doing a reconstruction of my murder on 'Crimewatch', can you make sure they use a pretty stand in for me? And also, make sure they use one of my better photos, not one of these," she insisted, pulling a hideous face which successfully resembled one of her not-so-good snapshots. "That's my dying wish, Bruce, I'm entrusting you with that."

"What's 'Crimewatch'?" Peter whispered, grinning at Milo.

Milo laughed. "How long have you lived in this country, Peter? It's a monthly true-crime show where they try to solve recent murders, rapes and things...like 'America's Most Wanted'. I'm not sure it's even on anymore..." But *he* wouldn't know of its existence either if his wife didn't go on about how she wanted to be portrayed in it all the time. Milo couldn't help but be amused by the conversation he was eavesdropping on. Yet he did worry about his wife being in that coffee shop everyday on constant display to all the crazy people in the town.

"She's funny," Peter decided with a smile.

"...Yeah, I guess that's what drew me to her in the first place..." Milo begrudgingly agreed whilst Dee and Bruce hooted with laughter; displaying their horribly unattractive 'Crimewatch' photos. "That's her best friend, Bruce. Whenever they're together they are absolutely incorrigible. He doesn't think a great deal of me anymore, but he's a good guy – a loyal friend which is what she needs."

"Should you let her work in a store like that with all kinds of crazies coming in off the street?" Peter frowned then. "If it were *my* wife-"

"Even when I was married to her, I never had a say on what she did," Milo asserted.

"Oh no, my pants are on inside out!" Dee grumbled. "How did that happen? I must stop getting dressed in the dark." She and Bruce chuckled some more while their secret audience smiled at their little comedy show.

"Hello you two," said a terribly well-spoken voice and Dee and Bruce glanced up to see Oliver Brooke standing over their table. Dee almost groaned aloud as Oliver could not have failed to have overheard her last comment. Bruce was now doubled over with silent laughter.

"...Hello Oliver," Dee greeted him with a faltering voice.

"Who's he?" Peter said, virtually making no sound at all.

"...I don't know..." Milo's brow furrowed.

"Can I join you for a moment? I won't stop long because I'm already late back at the office - you know how it is, long lunch. So what happened to you at the club the other night? I didn't have a chance to say goodbye," Oliver stated as he sat down with them.

"...Oh, I left early. I wasn't feeling very well," Dee replied cautiously because even Bruce didn't know where she had disappeared off to that night.

"Yes, Evan said you'd had a rough day. I had actually been hoping to ask you something that night but once I realised you'd gone, it was too late," he continued affably.

"Oh...?" Dee gulped.

"Yes, I was wondering if you might possibly be free one evening this week. I thought perhaps you might like to go for a meal..." And then he began to look as nervous as Dee felt.

Dee had obviously known of this man's attraction to her, but only because Evan had tipped her off - and she hadn't honestly expected any action to be taken on the matter.

"...Err, oh, um..." Dee stammered gracelessly, highly embarrassed (if a smidgeon flattered too). "...Well, I suppose...yes that would be nice..." she said because that was the polite thing to do rather than because she felt any evident magnetism between them. In all honesty, she didn't know if she were coming or going as far as fancying a person was concerned anymore. She had been out of the dating game for such a long time that she had forgotten what she was supposed to do. Dee felt she had spent the majority of her adult life either married or heading *into* another marriage, and no in-betweens. Innocently dating a man before any physical action was apparent was simply beyond her experience.

"That's great," Oliver replied, more than pleasantly surprised. "I don't suppose you would be free tonight? There's a fabulous restaurant in town I'm sure you would love. Or would that just be a little too short notice?"

"...Um, well I guess I could be...my nanny is usually quite flexible – I could call her," Dee offered sweetly before cringing. *'My nanny'?* What had happened to her? This man was so terribly friendly that Dee felt an odd compunction not to let him down. "...I'll tell you what, let's just assume she can look after the children and I'll call you if she can't," she suggested and watched as he slapped the table once in agreement.

"Great, so shall I pop by your house about seven thirty to pick you up?"

"...Err, no. We'll meet in town. Let's meet outside the coffee shop and we can walk to the restaurant..." Dee rubbed the back of her neck because Bruce was still snickering and making this worse.

"Wonderful. You can reach me on any of these numbers." Oliver produced a business card and placed it gently in her hand.

"Thanks. Here's my card," Dee said, fumblingly fishing out *her* business card from her bag. She still hadn't got over the novelty of having one. Prior to purchasing the shop last year, she had never required a card in her life. "So, I'll see you at seven thirty then?"

"Yes, I'll look forward to it," he assured her and rose to his feet. "It was nice to see you again too, Bruce. Gosh, you are a pretty girl, aren't you?" Oliver told Angel, bid them all goodbye and left.

Dee let out a high-pitched whimper. "Ohhh, why did I say yes? I should have invented an excuse – I'm not ready for dates."

"*I've got my pants on inside out!*" Bruce laughed uncontrollably, he was now chortling so hard that tears were running down his cheeks.

"Oh, shut up!"

"He's a bit posh for you, isn't he?" Bruce was rubbing his stomach muscles which were beginning to ache from all the chuckling. Yes, he had paraded Oliver before her as a suitor option initially, but only to put Felix's back up.

"*You're* the one who introduced me to him at the club! And anyway, *I'm* posh," Dee protested and Bruce was nearly thrown from his chair due to the force of the next explosion of giggles. "Oh, alright!" She was beginning to feel a bit disgruntled. "Arghh! I shouldn't have agreed…" Dee growled again.

"Why?"

"Well, for one thing - he was wearing running trainers with jeans." It was as good an excuse as any.

"Oh yes…he was, wasn't he?" Bruce slapped the table once in imitation of Oliver, trying not to break into hysterics again because he was aware it was irritating her. "He probably owns a pair of red trousers too. You know what these posh people are like."

Dee stared at him with childishly wide eyes. "You don't think he really wears red trousers, do you?"

"Almost certainly, but his dress sense is just a tiny drawback; you can change a little thing like that," Bruce insisted. "Do you like him?" He wiped his streaming eyes.

"…I dunno'…I don't even know him," Dee shrugged. "…What do you think I should do? Should I cancel? Should I have put it off for a few days at least? I've got his card – I can call him and tell him Mrs D isn't available…"

Bruce scratched his head thoughtfully. "…Well, he always seems really nice when he comes in the shop. And you can't spend your life pining over Milo because he's a hopeless case."

"…I know," Dee said regretfully. "Why did I agree to *tonight,* though? I've got nothing to wear!"

"Let's hit the shops then." Bruce stood up.

"We haven't had lunch yet," Dee whined, she simply wasn't up for this.

"There's no time for that now, is there? We'll have to grab a take-away sarnie from the deli. We have to turn Dee of the Council Estates into Dee the Richmond Socialite." Bruce grabbed her wrist and forced her to her feet. Dee gathered together the children and their paraphernalia and trundled reluctantly after Bruce.

Peter turned to Milo and assessed his friend's reaction. It wasn't good. Milo's mouth had become a thin line, his brown eyes had narrowed to little slits and his brow was now so tightly knitted that Peter was worried he might be about to implode. Milo reached into his pocket for some cigarettes but found there were none.

"Well," Peter began brusquely, pushing his reading glasses up his nose rather importantly. "If you're happy for your wife to move on and start seeing other men, then that's your decision. But if it were me-"

"Well I'm *not* you!" Milo snapped and rose to his feet. "...I'm sorry Peter, but I have to get back to work." And forgetting this was supposed to be his goodbye lunch with Peter, he stalked off in a rage up the street towards his office building.

*

Dee was putting the finishing touches to her makeup in her en-suite bathroom that evening with Ella Fitzgerald blaring out from her bedroom. Her hair was sprayed to oblivion up in a chignon and she wore an above-knee, sleeveless, cotton shift dress and some mid-heeled ankle boots. She was nervous because she couldn't remember the last time she had been on an actual date. Dee was only used to unexpected affairs which turned into relationships. Jerry had been a drunken mistake at a party, Lance was more of an intense fling before they got serious, and Cameron was a slow-motion mistake she had drifted into. Milo, much Lance, was a tempestuous affair before they had fallen in love. Then of course there was Felix and there was no way on God's earth that could be classed as a date either. There was a very definite pattern forming. So maybe an ordinary first date would be a good thing.

Dee wandered from the bathroom into her bedroom where Kirby slept on her bed. Dee had taken the kitten back to her new home earlier this afternoon. It was a predominantly white bed on which Kirby was leaving copious amounts of black fir, but Dee didn't care. Dee sat on the bed with the kitten and told her how much she loved her a few times whilst studying herself in the mirror on the wardrobe. She wasn't entirely sure she was appropriately dressed for, what could be, a fancy restaurant - but she had been short-sighted enough to forget to ask where they would be dining. Dee could hear Mrs Dawson bustling around downstairs preparing to take the children for a sleepover at her house. Then Dee heard the doorbell chime and the sound of a man's voice in the hall. She sat up abruptly as someone mounted the stairs. Surely that wasn't Oliver totally flouting the plans, and surely Mrs Dawson hadn't allowed him to wander upstairs whilst she was dressing!

Dee jumped off the bed just as Felix opened the door to her room. Kirby skedaddled under the bed at the appearance of a stranger.

"Jesus, Felix, I could have been naked or something. Don't you ever knock?" Dee found herself barking out of sheer surprise more than anything. She hadn't seen him since the morning after *that night*.

"Is it true?" Felix snapped. His face was hard and his eyes were steely.

"...Well, that depends on what we're talking about." Dee naturally slipped into her indolent and glib repose, which she often did if she was nervous. "If you mean the lunar landings, then yes, the rumours are true. No human has ever been to the moon. I know, I know, it totally flies in the face of everything you've been led to believe but-"

"And you can forget about doing your little comedy routine, this is no joke. Are you going out on a fucking date or not?" he interrupted sternly.

"How the hell do you know? Who told you that?" Dee stamped her foot and balled up her fists in frustration much like her three-year-old daughter would. "Is nothing sacred anymore?"

"Evidently not! I bumped into Evan as he was locking up the shop - he let it slip," he gulped. "So, you *are* seeing that Oliver guy?"

"Yeah, so?" Dee shrugged. "I *am* single now and it's just a date. What are you in such a bad mood about?"

Felix made an angry growl and turned away. She thought he might kick something.

"Why him? Why not me?"

"...Felix," she sighed, finally getting it, "you and me – that was a mistake. You said so yourself." Dee's stance softened because she was beginning to glean he was in pain.

"I said that because I knew that was what you wanted me to say! I knew you'd be the one to back off and I didn't much feel like rejection. I knew the minute we got physical you would freeze me out!" he complained.

"...I'm not freezing you out. I really like you. You're sweet and funny and clever and attractive, and you are so important to me. But I can't *date* you."

Felix turned to face her. "But you said at the club that you wanted to move on – you said you wanted that to be with me..."

"We said a lot of things that night, Felix, things that in the cold light of day – we can't commit to..." she explained reticently. "I barely know this Oliver guy, I only said 'yes' tonight because I didn't know how to get out of it. But I'm so tired of secret flings – I just want to go out on a normal date and be a normal person for once."

"So you might end up with a guy you don't even have feelings for rather than be with me?"

"Felix, I have a thing for you, I admit it. But we can't end up together..."

"Why, just because I'm Milo's cousin?" Felix pressed.

"Well, yes. But also, *you* ended my marriage..." Dee reminded him gently.

"...Only because I love you." Felix's shoulders slumped and he looked just like a dejected little boy. Perhaps Dee ought to have expected this admission, but for some reason it came as a big shock to her. "...Haven't you realised that yet?"

"...You don't really love me, Felix." She attempted to keep the patronising note out of her voice, but completely and utterly failed.

"You have no right to tell me how I feel! You're not in my head so you don't know what I'm thinking!" he yelled in such an uncharacteristic way that Dee was forced to accept he must be serious. "...Why did you sleep with me if you didn't want me? I asked you again and again if it was what you wanted. You could have stopped it at any time but you didn't!"

"...I shouldn't have done it. I was totally in the wrong and I'm sorry...but if I'd known you were in so deep, I wouldn't have let it happen. I was drunk and lonely and you said it was safer to get it out of my system with you than some random guy. So I thought some no-strings affection would be okay." Dee sat down on the bed and he sadly came to sit beside her. "But I guess there are always strings. Someone always gets hurt..." she sighed and could palpably feel his misery emanating off him. "I honestly don't believe you're in love with me, it's just this infatuation is clouding your judgement-"

"I *do* love you." Felix didn't even seem to have the strength to shout anymore. Then he grabbed the phone from the nightstand and thrust it into her hand. "Call that Oliver guy, tell him you aren't coming. Stay here with me and we can talk things over. Call him and cancel," he pleaded and Dee felt so ghastly about herself and what she had reduced this confident young man to, she could have cried.

"...No, it's too late to cancel now; he'd have left the house. I promised to meet him." Dee shook her head, gently taking his hand. "I have feelings for you, Felix, but we can't be together..."

"You can't write me off just because Milo is my cousin..."

"You must see that I can't be involved with another Stark or Phillips...or Kellerman. Surely you see it would be too difficult for everyone; it would destroy your family. I can't have that on my conscience."

"People would get over it eventually..." he focused bravely on the carpet to stop himself becoming upset again.

"I don't think so...we would be ostracised. And I have my children to think about. You're their *uncle*. How could they ever be expected to understand?"

"Children are adaptable, they would just grow to accept it," he argued.

"Oh, and that's what you want, is it? To be a father-figure to my children?" Dee was beginning to lose her temper. "It's not just *me* you get involved with – its Lance's daughter and Milo's son, and I don't think you've even thought that through."

"I really like your children!" he protested vehemently.

"...You've barely had any interaction with them. When you're here, on the whole, you only have eyes for me. And that's perfectly okay; there's no reason you *should* love other people's kids. You don't even seem to have that great a fondness for Paddy and Melody, and they're your nieces."

"Have you met Paddy and Melody? They're monsters!" he retorted and both he and Dee couldn't help but laugh about that. Because it was true. The tension was eased a little. "...I like your kids a lot because they're fun and quirky, like you. And okay, I'm just their 'uncle' of sorts, but in time I'd grow to love them just through the very virtue of being around them," he said gently.

"That's not good enough for me. I'm not just some single girl you can take up with and walk away from when it doesn't work out. There are children involved who could get hurt *again* when we decide we aren't really suited," Dee groaned, desperately searching for the right words to make him understand.

"You're running away with this, Dee. I'm not asking you to marry me; I'm just asking you to give me a chance," he said quite reasonably, catching her eyes and slipping his milky-coffee-coloured hand in hers. "...But you're right, you and I probably are too much for people to get their heads around right now. Nobody has to know just yet until we're sure...I could be your secret..."

Mortified, Dee pulled her hand from his. "Oh my God! What have I done to you?"

"I don't mind, honestly," Felix reassured her mildly. "You have children and it's so much harder for you, I get that. You have more to lose than I do, so the least I can do is be patient and accept you can't acknowledge me yet..."

"This is nuts! Why couldn't we just leave things as they were? You were one of my best friends! How can I make you see without hurting you?" Dee could not believe what he was prepared to reduce himself to; to be her dirty little secret, hidden away in seedy hotel rooms, stealing the odd hour or so to be together, looking over their shoulders and living in fear of being caught. "...I don't see myself ending up with you. I don't see a future with you. I don't see myself growing old with you. Maybe that isn't an issue for most people starting out romantically, but that isn't an option for me - or for my children..." Dee relented and touched his arm. "You have to see that..."

"I don't have to see that! I am perfect for you!" Felix shook her off with tears pooling in his eyes. "Okay, maybe it wouldn't have been the fireworks and storms and dramas that you seem to be drawn to, but it would have been so easy. Me and you, we would have been happy...we would have laughed, we would have had fun. For the first time in your life, you would have been in a normal relationship." Felix shook his head in frustration and sheer disappointment in her. Then he calmly rose and left her bedroom, just like that. She listened to him hurry down the stairs and out of the house. Dee collapsed flat on the bed, clamped her shaking hands over her face and wept. She had done a terrible thing to a very good man and there was nobody to blame but herself. Dee longed to clamber under her duvet and cry herself to sleep, but she was due outside her coffee shop in an hour with a guy she barely knew and it was too late to cancel now. Eventually she got up, washed her face, reapplied her make-up, stole a cuddle of reassurance from the kitten who was standing by the bed now, and went downstairs to say goodbye to the children. Heartache had to take second place to an agreement.

PART OF THE PAST

Felix's visit had been such a sobering experience that no amount of alcohol could alleviate her deep-set misery. Oliver was very good company and did the lion's share of the talking at the restaurant while Dee nodded and laughed and feigned interest in all the right places. Not that Oliver wasn't interesting, he was. He was the son of an aristocrat (actually the son of a Lord) and owned a publishing house in the West End, but lived rather modestly in Richmond. His father owned a stately home in Surrey but spent every penny on its upkeep and restoration so, there was no family fortune. Oliver had married a very beautiful chef who had written a book which he had published, but a short time later they had divorced and she had taken half his money. So Oliver had no fortune to speak of either. He was handsome in a homely, English country-gent type way, terribly clever and ridiculously posh. Dee felt compelled to enlighten him on how she had acquired her wealth (her least favourite subject), but she had the feeling he was already aware of this information. Dee may even have enjoyed her evening because the shared histories and all these revelations were very interesting and were a great distraction from all her problems. If only she didn't have the prior knowledge that he fancied her and might expect a kiss or something, she could have relaxed.

The only painfully awkward moment was when Oliver had been musing aloud about how much he adored Scotland when spending time there, and how on his first visit, he 'couldn't get over the sheep'. Dee, at an ill-timed attempt at humour, had automatically responded, 'tall sheep, were they?', to which she had been greeted by a vacant stare. After this, Dee had been forced to explain the joke. And a joke that required explanation could never really hope to be funny. Dee decided to avoid making any more quips after that.

After the restaurant, Oliver took Dee to a bar a short walk from there and Dee was all for that. The goodnight kiss was put off for a little while, so that had to be a good thing. They had agreed Oliver would do the rest of the driving tonight, so Dee gratefully drank alcohol and chatted about life and love and ambition. He was good company and Dee liked him well enough, she couldn't imagine having any romantic inclinations towards him, but she liked him.

When closing time came, Oliver drove Dee home in a big blue Mercedes. Now that she knew he was a decent man who didn't murder young divorcees for kicks, she felt it was safe for him to know where she lived. He was so well bred and such a gentleman, he wouldn't allow her to open her own car door and walked right around the car to let her out. That was certainly a new one on Dee. She climbed from the car doing her best to keep her skirt down and hopped onto the pavement. It was raining rather heavily but Dee felt it only right she saw this evening through to the bitter end.

"Well, I've really enjoyed tonight," Oliver began again brightly as the rain turned his brown wavy hair into curls.

Dee gulped because she was afraid of what was coming. "Mm, I did too..."

"...So, um...I'd really like to see you again..." Oliver said, suddenly nervous and meaningful. He put a hand on the wet roof of his car as if to steady himself and leaned in to kiss her. Dee saw his face coming closer as if the slow-motion button had been pressed, and she was suddenly taking a step back. No more. No more perfectly nice men who desired something that she really didn't. No more. It was time to take charge; take responsibility for the events that transpired in her life.

"...Look, Oliver...I can't..." Dee stammered. "I'm sorry - I didn't mean to lead you on or anything. It's just I wanted to be over my husband so much, I thought it would be a good idea to start dating again," she jabbered. "But I think maybe it was too soon...I mean - I *know* it was too soon. You're an absolutely lovely man, and in a few months I'll be kicking myself that I let you slip through the net – but I just can't right now. I still love him, you see - even though he hurt me and I shouldn't. But you can't help how you feel. I'm sorry. I feel horrible."

Oliver gave a weak little smile. "...Don't feel horrible on my account. I've been through a divorce myself, and from experience, I can safely say it may take you years to get over it. For me at least, it was a little akin to a death. It's my fault. I should never have asked you on a date so soon after your separation from your husband," he said, then seemed to be deliberating over something. "...Was it because of the *sheep joke*...?"

"...The what?"

"The joke you made about the tall sheep – I suppose your husband would have got it," he floundered. "Honestly, I normally have a very good sense of humour but I was nervous tonight. And I only meant that the sheep in

Scotland have these big horns that-"

"Oh God, no it was nothing to do with the sheep joke." If one could die of awkwardness, Dee would be dead right now. And most probably Milo wouldn't have got it either; he'd have just laughed at how insanely childish his wife could be. *Felix* would have got it though... "It's nothing to do with your sense of humour, or your personality or anything about *you* at all. It's me, I'm just not in any fit state to start a relationship."

"Of course. I should have known better," Oliver smiled his adorably genuine smile.

"Now don't be nice. You're making me feel worse. Let's just agree that Dee is a horrible tease who deserves to spend the rest of her life alone," Dee grinned sheepishly, braving the rain collecting in her eyelashes because he was such a nice guy. "I'd suggest we be friends but that hasn't worked out well in the past for me either..."

"Well, if in six months or a year's time we are still both single and you are still kicking yourself, perhaps you will think about asking *me* on a date," Oliver suggested and Dee smiled, relieved he was being so normal about it. Maybe English men were easier going and didn't make such a big issue of every little thing. Then Dee remembered Jerry. And Lance. And Cameron.

"You're on," Dee agreed. Again he leaned in but this time he centred on her cheek and kissed it.

"Is that your house?" He gestured with his head and Dee nodded without looking, because he was gesticulating in the right direction. "Because there's a man sitting on your steps," Oliver told her blankly and then Dee was forced to look up.

Sopping wet, Milo Phillips sat dejectedly on the stone steps leading up to her house. He was watching them with his chin on his hand but with that malevolent look in his eyes. Dee knew this without really being able to pick out the features of his face because she knew his stance so well.

"...That's my husband," she stated, embarrassed and aghast all at once.

"I thought it might be. Would you like me to come in with you, I have the distinct feeling he isn't here to borrow a cup of sugar," Oliver grimaced.

"Oh God no, I can handle Milo. I'm sorry about this...but I'll see you in the shop no doubt. At least I hope so." Dee was already motioning towards the house. "If you stopped coming in, I would feel bad on many levels. Not just because you're a nice guy, but you're probably my best customer too. We'd go out of business. Thanks for a lovely evening, Oliver," she said with a look that expressed her reluctance to encounter what she was about to encounter. So as Oliver climbed back into his car, Dee was running up to the house to escape the rain.

*

Once she had splashed her way along the garden path, Dee stopped at the bottom step of the four that led up to her house where he was sitting at the top. Milo didn't even look up, his elbow resting in his lap and his chin resting on his fist. Dee sighed wearily - this was never going to go well. "...How long have you been sitting there?" she asked her husband as though he were three years old and she were rebuking him.

Milo glanced up sourly. "...Getting on for a couple of hours, I guess."

"But it's raining. Why didn't you sit in your car?" she asked with her usual logic.

"There is no car. I was pretty drunk when I left the pub so I walked here...and it wasn't raining for the first hour," he explained dully. Dee was already pushing the key in the lock and opening the door.

"Come inside, you're soaking wet," Dee told him in no uncertain terms. Milo hauled himself to his feet and followed her into the house. "So who told you?" she sighed, sloping into the kitchen and throwing her keys on the table. She was not looking forward to this.

"That doesn't matter. Who is he?" Milo stood in the kitchen doorway.

"Oliver."

"Oliver who?"

"Oliver Cromwell," Dee sulked. She filled the kettle with water because it was something to do while she awaited the interrogation.

"...Let me know if I get any of this wrong, then. His name is Oliver Brooke. He owns Brooke Publishing House and is the son of an aristocrat. I had him checked out," Milo informed her since she seemed in no mood to inform him.

"If you already know that, I'm not sure why you asked. Your stalker-like tendencies are not amongst your most attractive qualities, Milo. If I were you, I would keep that little quirk of yours a secret from your future girlfriends," Dee suggested indolently. If she had known from the start that he was so controlling and manipulative, she may have thought twice about getting involved with him. But Dee had fallen in love with Milo hook, line and sinker - and it was too late to change her feelings now. Right now, she was keeping a lid on things because she just couldn't stomach the inevitable shouting and tears.

"Trading up are we?" Milo glowered with those malicious eyes sparking to life again, leaning on the doorframe. "Moving up the social ladder?"

"Hardly," she said. "It isn't easy to trade up from the man who has more money than God. He just happens to be posh. Anyway, I think even *I'm* richer than he is," Dee stated matter-of-factly. It wasn't arrogance - it was just very probably true. She finished making two steaming mugs of tea. "I'll get some towels...you're drenched. I might even have some of your clothes that you haven't collected hanging around." Dee wandered off into the utility room and returned with a big white towel, a smaller hair towel, some of his old sweat-pants and a t-shirt. She handed these to Milo, picked up the tea and walked through into the lounge. "I'll light a fire so you don't catch cold."

Milo followed her, stopping by the sofa. He dried his hair and stripped off his wet jeans and sweater while watching her build a fire in the inglenook fireplace. It seemed a funny thing to be doing in July but it was such a miserable night, a fire was in order. She kept her eyes purposefully averted whilst he changed.

"Why didn't you invite him in for a nightcap?" Milo asked, rubbing the towel on his bare skin and slowly dressed in the clothes Dee had fetched for him. He sat on the sofa gingerly, never taking his eyes off her.

"Oh yeah, that would have been fabulous. *'Won't you come in for a coffee? My ex-husband will be joining us, you don't mind, do you?'* Ah, an evening to remember," she said sardonically, lighting the kindling and soon the fire engulfed the logs.

"...I'm not your ex-husband yet," he said darkly. "You made sure Mrs Dawson took the kids to her house, so you must have been expecting to bring him home."

"Mrs Dawson prefers to do sleepovers at her house. I had no intention of spending the night with him, if that's what you're driving at," she said flatly. He studied his wife who rose to her feet and brushed off her hands. Dee bit her upper lip circumspectly. She was a little wet herself in her shift dress and sandals, and she came over to where he sat. She reached down to pick up one of the towels beside him on the sofa, but Milo suddenly grasped her wrist rather desperately with one hand.

"Why are you doing this to me?" he finally snapped, and Dee was surprised even though she had been suspecting this would be the outcome from the get-go.

Dee didn't even attempt to break free but instead sunk down to her down to her knees before him. "Why do you even care, Milo? You had a relationship with Amber! Look, we're getting divorced so I can go on dates with whoever I want..."

The expected screaming and shouting didn't really materialise because he simply started crying. Perhaps he was still drunk, but he was crying so bitterly, Dee had no choice but to soften towards him. Milo had released her by now but she ventured to stroke his wet hair. "...Milo, please don't upset yourself. You've just got out of hospital, and you're sitting for hours in the pouring rain and making yourself anxious when you should be recuperating." She soon found that she too was crying. That was no big surprise these days.

"I don't care...I just need to know, why him and not Felix?"

Dee sighed. She had been asked that question twice tonight. "...Because I was never going to end up with Felix. He was just a misunderstanding...I told you that right from the start." Dee touched his face because it seemed like a natural thing to do. He was in such pain and she just wanted to comfort him. "But you left me for another woman and you wanted a divorce. So I decided I needed to move on too. I just wanted to be over you. I thought if I went on a date I would feel better. Oliver was just some really sweet guy I barely knew - and good company, but it's just too soon for me. I'm not ready for a new relationship and that's what I told him." Dee wiped his eyes. "I'll never love anyone as much as I loved you, but we need to accept that you and I are not going to be together. So you can't keep coming over here to frighten off prospective dates just because they might be *the one*."

Milo shook his head. "You never really fought for me. You barely ever asked me to come home. You just got on with your life and moved on. I see you around town with the kids or your friends and you look so happy without me...I feel like I was totally dispensable, totally replaceable," he told her just as Dee's new kitten tentatively wandered in as if on cue. The cat was another reminder that Dee's life hadn't stopped when Milo departed. Kirby must have been asleep somewhere in the house but she nervously approached the stranger and sniffed Milo's hand. Milo smiled through the tears. "Hello, you're cute. A tuxedo cat..."

"A what?"

"Black and white – the white part on chest is the tuxedo shirt," he advised dully.

"I've never heard that expression before; it must be an Americanism," Dee sniffed.

"Must be. You never mentioned you were getting a kitten..." Milo glanced up gingerly.

"I thought if I was going to grow old by myself, I might as well get a cat. She goes with my new 'spinster' lifestyle..." she smirked.

"You? A spinster? That's never going to happen," Milo smiled. "Somebody will snap you up...unfortunately for me."

Dee studied him thoughtfully. "Milo, I asked you to come home so many times; in person, in texts and emails...more times than I can count. In my heart, I actually believed you would one day. But when you took up with Amber, then I knew it was all over. I had to get on with my life. I had to pull it together for the kids. I couldn't sit around and cry all day and still be a good mother," she explained pragmatically. "I guess I've become very adept at picking up the pieces when things go wrong. People die, people hurt me, people leave...and although I might feel like I want to stop breathing, I can't. I continue to exist whether I want to or not."

"Amber was just a way to lash out and hurt you, you know that – right? I knew that my being with her would hurt more than anything. But even then, you just dusted yourself off and got on with your life. I just ended up hurting myself because it drove you even further away from me..." He stroked the kitten under its soft chin. Dee was still kneeling at his feet.

"...Felix wasn't even on my radar – but you wouldn't believe me. And when you hooked up with Amber, you broke my heart..."

"...I'm sorry...for everything," he said in a broken voice. Dee had to pinch herself that he had apologised to her twice in two days for his heartlessly cruel actions. And at last she could see it. Milo had finally snapped out of it, at last he was the old Milo she knew and loved - but it was far too late.

"...I'm sorry you had to walk in on me and Felix like that. I'm sorry I didn't pull away from him fast enough. I've been going over that day again and again in my brain and I don't know what happened. I didn't even suspect he was *going* to kiss me until he did. And I just froze. But you're right, I should have realised his feelings for me were inappropriate long before and put a stop to it – but I didn't. I'm sorry I'm so stupid and so gullible. You had every right to be upset and walk out for a couple of days to calm down. But you didn't have the right to drag it out and punish me for months like you did, and shack up with somebody else," Dee said with such heartfelt emotion that it brought tears to her eyes again. "I don't want to keep going over it because we've talked this to death. Too much has happened and we can't right those wrongs now. You said you wanted to be friends and we have to get over the resentment for the sake of that friendship, for our children..."

"I was sitting on the steps in the rain and I was thinking; I don't know if I can take anymore. I see you around town and you don't see me, and I think my chest is going to explode. You're going to meet new people and see different men, and one of those men is going to make you fall in love with him. I suppose there's a chance I might meet somebody...but I won't love her. I'll never fall in love again," he stressed fervently. "I love *you* and I will always love you," Milo assured her while stroking her hair from her eyes. "...I think I need to leave...go back to America for good."

"But Milo-" Dee began to protest.

"I know it's not fair on the children, but I can't live like this anymore. I can't get over you if I'm always around you. You're going to leave me behind and I don't want to be around to witness it..." Milo felt this was the only way. "You'll have to send the children over for their vacations - maybe you can come with them sometimes. We'll still be friends...we'll *always* be friends. But I need some distance or I'm going to make myself ill again."

"Milo, look what happened the last time you went back to the States all alone? You purposefully tried to poison yourself with carbon monoxide," she said harshly because it was the time for harsh words. "This break-up has been particularly awful because of all the animosity that's gone along with it. The worst thing for me was the complete absence of you from my life. I'm sure that if we were friends again, things would be better. And England is your home – you need to be around your family for your mental health. What if you start to feel low again? I won't be there to see you going downhill – I won't be there to stop you if you did something stupid..."

"I won't try that again, I promised you..."

"Please don't go. The children need a father and I need my best friend," Dee pleaded.

"...No, Dee. After tonight, I realise that I can't do this anymore." Milo let go of her hands and Dee knew he was going to leave her, perhaps for good this time. He stood up. "I'm going to fly out in the morning. I'll be back now and then to sort out the business, but after that you won't see a great deal of me. I'll call you and we can negotiate how often the children can come out to see me." He watched Dee clamber to her feet. Milo put his arms around her and they were both crying again now. "I love you," he cried.

"I love you too," she wept, holding him tight, racking her brains how to make him stay. But there was nothing she could say to change his mind. Milo broke free and turned away, heading for the hall and out of her life. She stared after him desperately as the biggest love of her life walked away from her – how could she just stand here and let this happen? But her brain was screaming, *'remember what he did to you. Remember what he did to you'*. "What if we made a pact...?" she blurted.

Milo stopped and turned back to face her. "...A what?"

"A pact - you know how I love pacts," Dee smirked and the corners of his mouth turned up a little too.

"Keep talking." He had raised an eyebrow in suspicion, but he evidently wanted to hear this *'pact'* idea of hers.

Dee cleared her throat, thinking on her feet. "What if I said tonight was the very last date I'd ever go on? What if I said I'd never date another guy again? If I told you I wouldn't see other people, would you stay in England then...?"

Milo frowned. "...Dee, you're only thirty-two years old. It would be unfair to expect you to commit to that."

"If it meant that my kids had a more-or-less full-time dad, I would." Right now she didn't care if she ever dated again. Men only ever seemed to cause her trouble anyway. "You said you couldn't stay in the U.K. because you didn't want to see me meet new guys and move on - so what if I don't meet somebody? I'd just stay single..."

"...You'd be celibate? Forever? You could do that?" Milo scratched his head uncertainly.

Dee shrugged. "I could if *you* could. A pact usually means *two* people committing to something..." Dee reminded him. Then it was her turn to test him, how much did Milo want to be in his family's life?

"...Alright," Milo said quite seriously.

"...Are you sure?"

"I wasn't planning on seeing anyone anyway." There was a definite glint of hope in his eyes now. He was almost smiling.

"Then it's a pact. Here, shake on it." Dee determinedly held out her hand. Milo slowly moved back into the room and took it, giving her hand a gentle shake. "Deal."

"...Deal," he repeated. Milo was staring at her as though completely confused and a little bit stunned. "Why would you care if I saw somebody new or not...?" he asked faintly.

Dee glanced at his hand still in hers. "...Because I don't particularly want to see you move on and meet somebody else either. And a stupid part of me still kind of thinks of you as...mine...even though you're not," she qualified quickly.

"...Actually, I kind of am." Milo let go of her hand very carefully. "And I think always will be..." he said and turned to leave again.

"Are you sure you don't just want to crash here? You've been drinking and I'm worried about you." This mad-cap scheme was crazy even for her. If they weren't going to see other people then they may as well- no, Milo had hurt her too badly. Dee must never forget that even though it was tempting to do so.

"I'm fine," he grinned. "I feel like I could do with some air to clear my head. I'll see you tomorrow, yeah? I could take you to breakfast and we can discuss this properly..."

"...Okay but maybe that ought to be brunch so you can sleep off some of that alcohol. Shall I call you a taxi? It's still pissing down out there and you've only just got dry…" She could hear the pattering of rain in the chimney breast.

"Honestly, I'm fine. I'll take the golfing-umbrella from the hall. I'll see you in the morning." Milo was back at his original position in the doorway of the hall again. "…Thank you…" he said with another small and hopeful smile. Milo grabbed the umbrella from under the stairs on his way out, opened the front door and left the house. He had a spring in his step as he gambled down the path and out of the gate. That spring hadn't been there for months. As he wandered down The Vineyard in the direction of his apartment (which he had actually come to loath no matter how expensive it was), Milo was filled with a nervous anticipation for new beginnings. Was this his wife's way of holding out an olive-branch? Was this the first seeds of forgiveness to be sewn? Milo smiled as he thought about Dee and her blessed pacts! Still, this might be a good one, especially if it grew into something else - something even better. He slowed a little as he passed a familiar-looking black Toyota. At least it appeared black in the dim yellow of the streetlights. It wasn't the car that was familiar so much as the number plate. Embedded within the registration was the word 'GUM'. But Milo's brain was so addled with drink, he couldn't place it. Oh well, it didn't matter - he had lived on this street for months, that was why he probably recognised it and it had become a subconscious memory. Milo ambled on, the large umbrella held high and keeping him almost shielded from the rain, his other hand stuffed in his track-pants pocket. He would have whistled a tune all the way home if he had been much good at whistling. But he wasn't.

THE LAST GENTLEMAN CALLER

Dee couldn't understand why she felt quite so happy. Nothing at all had been resolved. In fact, all she had succeeded in doing was committing herself to a life of singledom. But Dee didn't seem to mind at all. Because Milo was committing to the same thing too. And what was the big deal about relationships anyway? They only ever succeeded in bringing mistrust, deceit and misery. And Dee had had a bellyful of that. She was better off out of it. Kirby strolled back in from her basket in the kitchen and Dee picked her up, giving her a kiss on the top of her head. Kirby rubbed Dee's hand with the side of her face affectionately. Dee was tired now, but her mind was still buzzing with possibilities so she doubted that she would get a great deal of sleep. Still, she ought to try.

Dee turned to leave the lounge and found herself faced with Cameron standing in the hall doorway.

"JEEZUS Christ!" Dee gasped, nearly dropping the kitten from sheer fright. But in the presence of yet another stranger, Kirby leapt from Dee's arms and scampered from the room. "Cameron, you nearly gave me a heart attack! What are you doing here at this time of night?" Her heart pounded in her chest. It was nearly midnight and she had thought the house empty.

"...I thought he'd never leave..." Cameron answered simply.

Dee blinked. "...Did Milo leave the front door open? How did you get in...?" This was a bit odd to say the least.

"I have a key."

"No, I took that key back..."

"I'd had a spare copied."

It was then that the first prickles of concern began to nag at her. Cameron had been hanging on to a key he had secretly copied and now had used it to let himself into her house? "...Cameron, this is my home and you and I aren't friends anymore. You have no right to let yourself in here without my say-so. Do you realise how late it is? Do you realise how bad this looks...?" She chewed anxiously on her upper lip. Something was wrong with this scenario, something was wrong with *him*. It was his eyes, the way they roved about the room, over her. They looked almost...desperate.

Cameron scratched his head. "You took away my key and I felt it was safer that I had a spare because you're still my responsibility. You weren't here and it was raining, so I let myself in to wait."

"When? Milo has been sitting outside on my steps for two hours..."

"I must have arrived just before him," he shrugged indifferently.

Dee watched as the kitten came creeping anxiously back into the room and stood in the doorway, cats always seemed to need to be in sight of the possible danger; be it a hoover or hairdryer...or a stranger. Was Cameron a danger? "I should have bought a bloody guard-dog instead of a cat," Dee grumbled, just as a way of covering up a growing sense of unease in herself.

"It's a sweet kitten, I haven't been able to get it to come near me since I got here though..." he said. "It's a shame we aren't going to be able to keep it."

"...What...?" Dee gulped uncertainly. What did that mean? What was *wrong* with him? She then decided the best course of action was to deal with him calmly, by treading carefully. She didn't know why she knew that, but she just did. "...Cameron, why are you here?"

"I have to leave Richmond - England actually," he began. "You see...they know what I've done and they're closing in the net. I'm certain of it..." Cameron told her in an insisting voice. He ran a finger up the painted white rim of the doorframe, suddenly interested in it. "I'm leaving tonight and you need to come with me."

"Don't be ridiculous, I'm not leaving," Dee shook her head brusquely, perhaps too brusquely she then decided, softening her tone. "...What do you mean, *'they know what I've done'*?" That was never going to be a sentence with a pleasingly jolly explanation.

"The police..." Cameron replied flatly, but there was also a note of agitation about him. He came further into the room and sat on an armchair, sliding his hands under his upper legs to still them. "They've been asking questions up at the University - they've spoken to everyone; all the students, all the teachers." He was still looking around the room. Dee couldn't decide if he were drunk or on some kind of drug, but his eyes were alert and darting about, belying his mild tone.

Dee gulped. "...The police? Why were they up at the Uni? What were they asking questions about...?"

Cameron met her eyes properly at last. "About Kate Taylor, of course - Lance's secretary."

"...Kate-?" A vice-like grip of fear suddenly took hold of her heart. She had this dreadful sinking feeling, and even though Dee didn't know what he was going to say, she somehow had this instinct that she did. "What does anybody up at the Uni have to do with her? She has no connection to Kingston University...or with you, you didn't even know her." Something was wrong. Something was very wrong.

"Actually, that's not true. Kate had taken a part-time course in Business Studies. I probably wouldn't have crossed paths with her but for the fact that I met her at a student house-party," he confided dryly.

"...I didn't realise...you never said." Dee glanced at the door, she was now the one looking for a way out. How fast could she run if she had to? Could he catch her before she made it outside?

"Well no, I couldn't tell you that before now - you might have made the connection." Cameron distractedly twisted a ring on his finger. "I was sleeping with her - it was *before* my affair with you so needn't give me that look," he warned. What look? Dee hadn't given him any *look*. She had been concentrating on keeping her face impassive.

Every word, every one of his gestures made Dee's sense of fear deepen. "...*You* were the 'mystery boyfriend', weren't you?" Her mouth was completely dry. She was afraid. Why was she so afraid? This was Cameron and he wasn't dangerous - was he?

Cameron looked up. "Is that what they're calling me? Well then, yes I suppose I was..." He rest the side of his foot on his other knee, trying to appear casual but all the time his eyes were undermining that. "Kate knew I knew you. She knew I had a thing for you...and she had a plan to blackmail Lance so he would leave you. Did you know she loved him? It wasn't just about the money and the power. She was actually deeply in love with Lance - she wanted him to move to Australia with her so they could start a business or something. Of course I knew Kate was deluded, but I humoured her. So she let me in on the plan because she wanted my help." Cameron sat forward and fixed her with a stare, the lamplight glinting off his glasses. "At first I just laughed at her because it sounded so crazy...but after a while, I agreed to go along with it – see what would happen. I wanted you and Lance to split up as much as she did. Kate knew about Lance's embezzlement of course, but she wasn't sure that would be enough. Kate thought if there was something she had over *you* as well, Lance was bound to cave. She wanted me to get any extra *personal* information I could from you, which you willingly gave me. You were pretty low at the time, he made you so unhappy...you told me everything. And everything you told me, I passed it onto Kate."

Dee shook her head. "But there was nothing you could have told Kate about me that she didn't already know..."

"Perhaps, but the fact that she had first-hand insight into your personal life was enough to tip the scales. Once she felt she had enough ammo, she started blackmailing him. She threatened to destroy him, and destroy you along with him. Lance gave in instantly - the coward," he sniffed derisively. "He gave her money, bought her a flat, a new car - did whatever she asked of him. Which included sleeping with her, as you know," Cameron reminded her pointedly. "But Jerry and Elliott were getting suspicious - they'd noticed things; rapidly depleting accounts, missing funds. They hired a PI to look into it - I think they thought a staff member was stealing from them. Lance was getting more and more desperate to buy Kate off but was getting sloppier and sloppier about how he did it. I think he was getting sick by that point too...the headaches had started. When I saw things were getting out of control and the threat of police being called in, I told Kate I wanted no part of it anymore. But once a blackmailer, always a blackmailer...she said she'd take me down with her. Blackmail is a serious crime y'know, Dee. Kate would have done time for sure. I'm not sure what would have happened to me as an accomplice, but I'd lose my career and my reputation at the very least. Particularly since she'd given me some of that money extorted from Lance. I only took it because I wanted you to leave Lance for me, and you were so used to being rich that I didn't want you to feel you were living in reduced circumstances," he explained as though that were some kind of defence. "She bought two tickets to Australia - one for her and one for him. But Lance finally showed some backbone and said he would rather die. Which was ironic really as he *would* be dead within a couple of months. Kate was running out of time - she wanted me to take his ticket and come with her to Australia since we were '*in it together*'. I said 'no' of course, but she just kept on threatening me. I warned her to keep me out of it but she wouldn't let up. So I struck her - hard...and she fell down my stairs..." Cameron was staring at the rug beneath his feet, but his eyes were unseeing, he was reliving it. Dee closed her eyes, clenching her hands so tight, her nails bit into her palms. It couldn't be. It couldn't be. "I knew it was going to be a fatal injury before I reached the bottom of the stairs..." he murmured, "because there was something wrong with the shape of her head...like a boiled egg when you've beaten it with a teaspoon..."

Dee could hardly say the words. "...*You* killed her? At your house...?" She'd been in that house since – slept in it. *Angel* had slept in it. Kate Taylor had died there?

Cameron raised his eyes again to meet hers. "...Yes," he said eventually. *Keep him sweet, keep him sweet,* said the voice in her head. "...But it was manslaughter - an accident, right? I know you Cameron, you're not capable of murder..."

Cameron just watched her thoughtfully for a while. "...I wanted to believe that at first. But she was breathing for maybe one, two minutes? I didn't call an ambulance – not that it would have got there in time. I was so angry when I hit her - and I hit her *so* hard, I meant her to fall. And when I was certain she was dead, I was relieved. I waited until the early hours of the morning before I could bury her in the woods..." He licked his dry lips but managed to keep a dispassionate tone, and that frightened her the most. No, it was more the change in him; snivelling, pleading Cameron had gone - this Cameron was wary, yet in control. "I persuaded one of my other students who I'd been involved with to pose as Kate and fly to Australia. I asked her to use Kate's credit cards for a few days then disappear for a while before coming back on her own passport. She was hopelessly in love with me, so I knew she would do it."

Dee glanced at the door again. Could she make it outside before he did? Cameron would undoubtedly be faster. She had better keep talking. "No, I don't believe you meant any of this to happen - that's not the man you are. Let's go to the police station now and you can confess - I'll back you up. If you explain it was an accident but you buried her because you panicked, you might get off with a lighter sentence...especially if you're handing yourself in."

"That's not going to happen. I'm not going to prison." Cameron shook his head decisively and rose to his feet. "I'm going to Europe and you're coming with me. We'll drive to Dover tonight and get the first ferry to France in the morning. Where are the children...? With Mrs Dawson? We'll go and get them."

Dee's heart nearly stopped. Thank God the children were not here, thank God or whatever deity she believed in (she wasn't sure anymore). Dee had to keep them far, far away from him. "...No-" she lied. "They're with Jerry and Elliott tonight..." It was safer if Cameron thought the kids were with two men - that was Dee's thinking anyway.

Cameron chewed on his bottom lip distractedly. "...Oh, well that's no good. Jerry and Elliott will get suspicious if you turn up for your kids in the middle of the night." Cam appeared a little distressed at this disruption of his plans. "Then I'm afraid we won't be able to take the kids with us tonight...we'll have to find a way to come back for them when things have calmed down..."

"...Cameron, I don't want to go with you," Dee admitted, hoping a little honesty might work where soft-soaping hadn't. "If you want to do a runner, then that's okay...I won't report you. I didn't like Kate Taylor anyway, so you did me a favour. But I can't come with you. My life is here."

Cameron's eyes narrowed in a way she didn't like. "Now look, I've let you have your fun; you wanted to do things your way and marry that idiotic Milo - and I let you. But where did that get you? You've would up by yourself again. You needed to learn from your mistakes, and now that you have, you're coming back to me - where you belong. I need to leave England right now because the police are closing in on me. One of the students, one of the teachers will have said something that links me to Kate - so I've got to go before they arrest me. And you're coming with me."

Dee chewed on the inside of her mouth. "...This isn't about Milo. You and I aren't in a relationship and you can't expect this of me. I'm staying in England...this is my home..."

A steely glint flickered across his eyes and he deftly stepped towards Dee. Before she even had time to register he was bearing down on her, he was grabbing her by the fabric at the front of her dress. "Why? Because you want to stay for *Felix*?!"

Dee cringed as his face came within centimetres of hers. She had made him mad now, and she just *knew* it was critical she didn't make him mad. "...What has this got to do with Felix?"

"You know I was at the club that night!" Cameron growled. "Maybe you thought you'd got away with it unnoticed, but I saw him kissing you at the table and then at the bar! I saw you disappear upstairs with him! Did you fuck him that night? Did you?!"

"No!" she cried out, but no sooner had the word left her mouth than she felt the grip on her dress transfer to her throat, tighter this time.

"If you lie to me again...!" he hissed in her face, she felt his spit land on her lip. Was this some kind of nightmare? Could this really be happening? As Dee's confused mind came back into focus, she realised this was a dangerous and desperate man. A killer by his own admission. She had to appease him, just until she was sure he meant her no harm. Surely he couldn't mean her any harm? "Now for the last time, did you or did you not fuck him?!"

"Yes!" Dee cowered away from him again; lying to him again when he was quite clearly unhinged just seemed like a terrible plan. "Just once, just that night at the club – it's over now, I swear..."

Cameron watched her silently, breathing heavily. "...Right...don't ever lie to me again. I'm just upset because I'm supposed to protect you from people like him...but just don't lie to me." He licked the spittle from his lips.

"I won't," Dee promised.

"I'm sorry if I frightened you." Cameron kissed her briefly on the mouth. Dee froze, but forced herself not to react. "I love you Dee, and you're safe with me, but you've been left to your own devices for too long. I've been waiting here for you for hours, but you were out with *yet another guy* this evening. You're out of control. This behaviour has to stop." Cameron watched for the curt little nod of her head. "I know what's best for you – better than you do," he insisted, almost smiling now as he ran a hand through her hair, his anger subsiding.

Was this really the desperately needy Cameron she had known and befriended all those years ago? Had he secreted this current psychotic nature or had he been driven mad by the foul deeds he had committed? Dee had proven herself a poor judge of people already, but this? "Now, we don't have any more time to talk - you know everything you need to know. I've packed you a small holdall whilst I was upstairs and I've got your passport. We need to hit the road."

"...Okay...but why do we have to go tonight? If there aren't any ferries until morning-" Dee began again but she could see that hard edge creeping back across his face. But Dee *had* to stall him. If he managed to get her into that car in the middle of the night, her chances of escape were greatly reduced.

"Dee, if you're trying to think of a way to trick me-"

"No, I swear I'm just..." Dee gulped, wracking her brain for ways to delay his plans. "I'm on your side and I want to help you, but I don't want you to have to live the rest of your life looking over your shoulder. There has to be a better way, I can buy you the best legal representation and-"

"I can't take that risk and I won't go to jail. There's no other way," he glowered irritably.

"I just don't see the point in this midnight dash when we could be sitting down and forming a plan. What's the rush? If the police were going to arrest you, they'd have done it by now..." Dee took his hands, however revolting an act that was, just for emphasis. Please God he wouldn't try to kiss her again and expect something more. Because to have to refuse him could spark him off again. "If you must leave tonight, then I get that. You'd get away easier alone anyway. Get the first ferry out like you planned and find yourself somewhere to stay in France or Spain – wherever. Then send me a message to let me know where you are and I can follow you out with the children."

"No."

But Dee kept on, she had no other option. "Cameron, it will be impossible for us to sneak back into England to fetch the kids if the police are looking for us by then-"

"I said NO!" Cameron bellowed, his fiery eyes flashed and this time Dee could not help but flinch. "I'm not letting you out of my sight until I'm sure I can trust you!" Or before he could break her. He grasped her wrists and Dee involuntarily closed her eyes. "You're coming with me *tonight*!"

"Take your hands off my wife," said a soft, yet unyielding voice. Taking a risk, Dee opened her eyes for a peek only to be greeted by the amazingly welcome sight of Milo standing menacingly in the lounge doorway. He was sweating and breathing heavily as though he had run a very long way and very fast. How long had Milo been there? How much had he heard? Did he realise that Cameron was a dangerously unhinged man? A murderer? Did he realise the peril he had walked into?

Cameron seemed to be wracked with confusion and indecision for a second. "*You*," he said balefully, *hatefully,* to a man he detested more than any being on this earth. "You have ruined everything. Everything I've done, everything I've been through just so that Dee and I could be together...and there you were at the funeral, from nowhere, and you took her from me. You who could never be good enough, never be deserving of her...and yet you still took her from me."

"Well, you're right about that at least. It turned out I *wasn't* good enough and I didn't deserve her," Milo agreed steadily. "But even if I'd never been at that funeral, even if she'd never met me - Dee still wouldn't be with you now. I mean, *I* was bad enough, but do you honestly believe Dee could ever love a guy as completely fucking insane as you?"

Cameron leered at him momentarily, and with a yell of rage, lunged at Milo howling, "I'm going to kill you!!" Dee felt herself scream involuntarily but Milo deftly sidestepped this attack, cracked him across the jaw with sharp left jab, manoeuvred the already staggering Cameron in such a way that he lost his balance, and forced him down to the floor. Then he leapt onto the now prone and punch-drunk Cameron Quinn to pin him down on his back.

"Quickly, Dee!" Milo shouted without looking back at her. "Call the police before he comes to his senses!"

With a wave of relief rushing over her, Dee even found time to smile fondly at him before she began to cry, she had never been so glad to see anyone in her entire life. "...You came back..."

HERO

It was just turning three in the morning when Dee and Milo finally climbed out of the police car, returning wearily back her house after Dee had given her statement at the police station. It had been the Devil's own job to keep Milo from angrily berating the Detective Inspector to such an extent that he too may have got himself arrested. After being given a warning, Milo had finally simmered down and kept his mouth shut so Dee could get on with the arduous business of explaining the night's events.

"And to think, they took *Cameron* to the hospital and not you!" Milo was still cursing as Dee unlocked the front door and let him into the hallway.

"Why would they take me to the hospital?" Dee said absently. She still vividly recalled how two uniformed officers had skilfully manhandled a struggling and handcuffed Cameron. He had given her one final baleful glance as he was hauled outside to the police car to seek medical attention before his arrest. "He barely touched me..."

"Because you're clearly in shock!" Milo marched through into the lounge as though he still lived here.

"I'm not in shock..." Dee frowned, following him. "I'm surprisingly okay." And she was, Dee couldn't understand why she was taking it so well. Perhaps the enormity of what had happened here tonight would hit her later.

"I wish you'd stop playing it down, Dee. To think that *monster* could have murdered or raped you, or kidnapped you and be halfway to fucking Dover by now while the cops dragged their feet!" Milo was simply irate that something like this could have been allowed to happen.

"...I really don't think Cameron would have hurt me physically – he *loved* me," Dee offered a little uncertainly. Yes, he loved her – in the unhealthiest way imaginable. "And if we're thinking logically, what could the police do before tonight? They said he had been on their radar for months, but they hadn't enough evidence to take him in for questioning again. They didn't want to spook him until they did. I guess they have to follow procedure to secure a conviction that will stand," she pretty much parrot-fashion repeated the Detective Inspector's excuses.

"Oh right, and in the meantime, you could have been abducted!" Milo knew he ought to try to be more calming and protective of Dee's fragile nerves, but he was simply livid that Cameron was free to walk into her house tonight with such sinister intensions.

"Milo, everything worked out!"

"Why aren't you angry? Why aren't you upset? You keep putting this positive spin on it but something terrible happened to you tonight!"

"Look, I'm just about holding it together here, so will you stop telling me how close I came to death or whatever!" Tears sprang into her eyes for only the second time since 'the Cameron incident'. "And it doesn't help that you're so aggravated that you nearly got yourself arrested for abusing the Detective Inspector!" she advised him reproachfully.

Milo rolled his eyes with a derisive sniff but soon came over and enveloped her in his arms. "...I'm sorry...I was just so afraid for you."

"...For a while there, I was too," Dee admitted.

Milo kissed the top of her head, not knowing if he were overstepping the mark or not, but choosing to ignore that. "This is all my fault. Cameron would never have come here tonight if I hadn't left my family, he knew you were alone and unprotected," he muttered.

"I'm alright..." Dee told him with just the hint of a smile, clutched tight to his chest.

"So you keep saying, but *I'm* not." Milo ignored her independent streak and let her go to stare at her worriedly. "Come and sit down, you must be exhausted," he insisted. Dee seated herself awkwardly and watched as he sat down beside her.

"...You saved me..." Dee advised him again as she had at least twice before tonight, but softly this time.

Milo shrugged that off. "You're a resourceful girl; you'd have found a way to escape given a bit of time..." He didn't seem to want to take credit for anything he had done. "Maybe I should have got the squad car to take us somewhere else. It must be difficult for you to come back here tonight."

"I *wanted* to come home." Dee just wanted to stare at him wonderingly, drink him in. No matter what he said, he had saved her tonight and she saw him in a new light (or an old light). Milo was her protector; the one who kept her safe – mostly. Milo met her eyes properly, noticing the adoration in hers - he pushed a strand of hair from her forehead.

"...Dee, I know I'm not going to be your husband for much longer, but I want to protect my family. If it would make you feel safer here, I could buy a house just up the street. I could check in on you and the kids every evening. And you could call me up if ever you were worried - I'd be just a few hundred feet away," he offered a little anxiously, afraid of a rebuff.

Dee scratched her head doubtfully. "So you're definitely not leaving London then...?"

"After tonight? Never," he asserted with an adamant shake of his head.

"You don't have to do that for me. Anyway, there aren't any houses for sale on The Vineyard..."

"Do you even know me at all? As if I'd let a little detail like that get in the way," Milo scoffed but his eyes then seemed to light up with mischief. "...Dee, I'm sorry to be the one to have to advise you of this, but your taste in men is fucking awful." They both had a little chuckle about that, even Milo saw the irony.

"I know! Still...one of them was so amazing that, in spite of all the pain, I don't regret a single moment of that short time we had. Cameron was just the perfect guy," she continued jocularly and they both laughed again, Milo was just glad she still could. Dee was world-class at gallows humour. "...No, seriously - being with you, it was the happiest time of my life while it lasted," she said softly and Milo stopped laughing. Dee was still observing him closely. "...How did you know to come back?" She had wanted to ask him this for hours but so much had been going on.

"...I noticed his car up the street," Milo explained. "What I mean is, I recognised the number plate. To be honest, it rang a bell because I'd followed Cameron on a couple of occasions when I was in the U.K. in January just to make sure he wasn't hassling you. Aren't you lucky your husband has *stalker-like tendencies*?" He smirked and Dee couldn't help but join him. "...But I couldn't place where I knew the plate from at first so I just kept on walking. I was halfway home before I realised why I knew that registration. And it was like my heart stopped...because I just knew. I ran all the way back, I'm so sorry I didn't get here sooner..." he said shamefacedly.

"You don't owe me any apologies, Milo," Dee insisted. "In fact, I owe *you* one..."

"Me?"

"Yes, you kept telling me Cameron was unbalanced and I just wouldn't believe you. I thought you were just jealous...but you knew..."

"Well, I knew he wasn't quite right...but I could never have imagined-" Milo shook his head in disgust. "It was *him* who killed that secretary...and all the while I was convinced poor Lance had done it. And the only one who believed in my late brother was *you*..."

Dee sighed. "...Even I doubted Lance's innocence at times. I would never have guessed that Cameron was involved. I didn't even realise he *knew* Kate..." Dee was still shell-shocked. "...But I still don't understand how you knew to come back. I mean, Cam might just have been parked in my road for another reason - to see somebody else," she said.

Milo scratched his head. "...I don't know...when it struck me that I knew where I'd seen that car before...it was like my blood ran cold. I can't explain it. I just knew I had to turn back and run as fast as I could. Thank God I still have my key."

Two spare keys had been used in that door tonight; Cameron ought never to have had one in the first place to copy. But Dee knew she would never even think of asking Milo to return his now. True, he didn't live here anymore, but he had earned the right to freely walk into his family's home again.

"...Yes...thank God. Before you showed up, for a moment there I thought-" Dee stated thickly but had to stop speaking.

"...If anything had happened to you-"

Dee seemed to instantly regret her lack of composure. "But I'm fine now Milo, because you cared enough to come back..."

Milo was giving her the strangest look; considering, contemplating - but he seemed to snap out of it. "...So I'd better call somebody; you can't be left here alone after the ordeal you've been through. Would you like me to call Jerry or Elliott maybe? You need a guy here to make you feel safe."

Dee eyed him sadly. "...You're a guy...*you* make me feel safe. I feel safer with you than with anybody else..." Why did he want to leave so badly? Couldn't he forgive her even now?

Milo looked away, his eyes misting over. "How can you possibly feel safe with me after all I've done to you?" His eyes had begun to pool with tears. "I've ruined your life, Angel's and Finn's – my *own* life...I'll never forgive myself..."

Dee wiped a tear from his eye before it escaped down his cheek. She watched as he shook his head ruefully. "Milo, you saved me from God-knows-what tonight, and I will never forget that," Dee said firmly but kindly.

Milo met her eyes again with a sheepish smile. "...Right place, right time." He had so needed to hear some form of forgiveness from her. Milo brushed the last of the tears from his eyes and quickly rose to his feet. "So are any of the spare rooms made up?"

"...Um...I don't know. Mrs D keeps an eye on that sort of thing. I'll have a look-"

"No, I can do it," Milo grinned at her, so much happier now. "Where do we keep bedding these days?"

"In the airing cupboard..." Dee said reticently. Would he really stay? She hoped so.

"I'll go check it out. And while I'm doing that I'd better call Jerry and Elliott...and Forrest-" he stalled as Dee opened her mouth. It was *three* in the morning. "Don't worry, I won't let any of them come over. But my brothers need to know that Lance was innocent and they're in the clear - they've suffered for long enough. And my *other* brother will need to know I'm here. Forrest won't have gone to sleep because he always calls me at night and I haven't replied - he worries about me lately," Milo explained. So he *was* staying? Thank God.

*

Dee sat alone in the lounge as Milo busied himself upstairs. She could hear his voice on the phone, placating at times, trying to convince the recipient that everything was fine now. To still her mind, Dee set to work rebuilding the fire which had by now burned down to only embers. It easily began to burn again. Kirby slunk back into the room gingerly and Dee brushed off her hands, scooping her up onto her lap as she seated herself again. She had forgotten about her for a while. She must have been cowering somewhere in the kitchen whilst all the commotion went on. Poor little cat. Dee's mind was whirring. Tonight's incident had brought everything into such stark clarity. An unspeakable thing could have happened to her; a life-changing event – but Milo had stopped it in its tracks. She knew exactly what she wanted her future to look like now, but didn't quite know how to put that thing into practice.

Soon enough Milo returned, jamming his phone into the back pocket of his jeans. "Everything is sorted. *All three* of them completely freaked-out, but I calmed them down before anybody could rush over here and make a fuss. I promised we'd see them tomorrow," he advised importantly. "One of the spare rooms was already made up so I'll sleep in there...unless you're worried about being alone. If you want, I could sleep in the chair in our...I mean *your* bedroom - so you'd feel safe," Milo offered helpfully.

"Milo, I'm not going to make you spend an uncomfortable night in a chair!" Dee rolled her eyes. She rose to her feet, still clutching the cat to her chest.

"Jesus Dee, it's not far off morning - I'm not going to be able to sleep anyway!" Milo complained. "What's a few crappy hours in a chair compared to your peace of mind? Come on, you need some rest..." He brusquely turned away towards the hall again.

Dee chewed on her lip, her heart hammering in her ears, words screaming around her brain - desperate to get out. "...Are you seriously going to wait for *me* to ask you back...?" Dee tentatively called after him as the shape of his body was disappearing out into the darkness of the hallway.

Milo stopped dead in his tracks and turned around. "...What?"

Her heart was pounding so hard now, she felt a bit ill. "...You said you were wrong about me - over Felix. You said you were sorry...and that you still loved me - but you've never asked to come home..." Certain rejection. Again. Dee had to take a risk. This could be their last chance, and she couldn't envisage a better opportunity ever coming up.

"I didn't think you'd *take* me..." Milo was back in the doorway again, studying her quizzically. "...Am I hearing this right? You want me back after everything I did?"

Dee said nothing, she had said enough. Her chest rose and fell, her breath laboured – afraid now.

"Dee...would you-?" he stammered, pacing slowly closer. "...Please take me back...I'll never hurt you again – I swear. Please give me another chance..."

Dee swallowed, her mouth so dry that she could hardly speak. "...I s'pose," she shrugged.

Milo broke into a diffident smile. "...You *s'pose*? I guess that's better than I deserve..." He was still nearing Dee until he stopped in front of her – now standing so unbelievably close. Closer than he had been in months. Dee could barely breathe. Milo cautiously reached up to run his fingers through her hair, studying her eyes – leaning slowly in, brushing his lips so lightly on hers. Dee closed her eyes, even now – not daring to hope. Then he cupped her face in his hands and kissed her so earnestly, she thought she might topple over. The next few minutes seemed fuzzy and somewhat dreamlike - frenzied even. He pushed her down on the sofa so feverishly that Kirby went tearing from the room again, skittering off across the floor. He was soon climbing on top of her, straddling her hips. Milo kissed her with such ferocity that he bruised her lips. He stripped off her dress so wildly that he tore it. Dee couldn't quite get her head around this. This was Milo. *Her* Milo. And he was home. Four men had been here tonight, and Milo was the very last of those she had expected to be staying the night.

Both were down to their underwear before Dee suddenly froze and held him at arm's length. "...Wait...can we just- wait...?" She pulled herself to a sitting position abruptly, rubbing her face. He sheepishly climbed off her lap, awaiting some kind of signal from her so he knew what to do next. Milo *still* didn't know about Felix. And when he found out...

Milo seemed a bit shell-shocked as he settled himself beside her. "...You can't forgive me, can you?" he surmised. The let-down was unbearable. But he had brought this on himself. "...I can't blame you, but I thought-"

"No, honey, it's not that..." Dee attempted to explain. She *had* to tell him. Dee knew full well she was no guiltier than he was, but she also knew her husband. Or at least, she did now. Milo would wildly overreact – just like last time. He would accuse her of a long-term affair or say she had *always* wanted Felix or-

"...So, do you just want to slow this down, then? Because I can do that..." he said, not knowing whether it was too premature to be relieved or not.

"Yes," Dee said quickly, needing an excuse. "I just want to slow this down..." She realised she couldn't do it. She couldn't bring herself to tell him. If she told him, he would leave. No question. And Dee couldn't bear that. But could she really lie to him forever and expect three other people to keep their mouths shut too?

Milo pursed his lips stoically. "It's probably for the best that we do. I've been imagining this moment for months, and I think I've built it up too much in my mind. I'd hate to be a disappointment to you."

"Don't be stupid. You could never be a disappointment to me," she assured him. Dee stroked his bare back and caressed his hair with her fingers. Sometimes, she wished she didn't love him this much.

"I'm still taking the antidepressants. They say they can depress your libido, and I don't know if-"

"...Oh," Dee said. She had forgotten that. At least she understood *his* reticence now.

"I mean, I'm quite certain that I *want* to - you literally have no idea," he grimaced. "But perhaps it's good that we slow this down or I'll ruin it, and you'll realise I wasn't worth waiting for..."

"Oh honey, I could never feel like that. Why don't we just hold each other until we fall asleep? The fact that you want to come home and that you still love me is enough." Great, she could stall for a while, give herself time to think. "So, I'll get a duvet and we can just fall asleep in front of the fire – shame to waste it." Dee stood up in nothing but her underwear and dimmed the lamps as she went off to find some bedding.

When she returned, they climbed under the duvet, stretched out on the sofa and were content to hold each other whilst listening to the rain beating down outside. Just his being so close *really was* enough. Well, sort of. Sensing the wild behaviour had calmed down, Kirby wandered back in the room and snuggled up by their feet. Milo said, "sorry I ripped your dress..."

"Oh yeah, you did, didn't you? Well, you can replace that," Dee smiled,

her head on his bare chest.

"I'll buy fifty new dresses," he replied. "I can't believe I'm actually here with you. I'm really home...not having sex with my wife." He gave a silent laugh that she felt beneath her cheek.

"...We can make up for lost time when we're ready," Dee assured him mildly.

"I'll stop taking the antidepressants tomorrow..."

She looked up. "No, I don't think you're supposed to stop abruptly like that - you're meant to wean yourself off. We'll speak to your GP in the morning," Dee insisted. "You could move your things back in tomorrow too - put your apartment on the market?" she said hopefully. There was so much to do *tomorrow* that Dee didn't know how they'd fit it all in.

"I don't care if I never see that place again." Although beautiful, that apartment now only smacked of miserable days and miserable nights.

"Get some sleep, babe. You look so pale and drawn. I think you need some serious looking after, you know; proper female attention." She listened to the sound of his heart beating steadily beneath her ear. "I'll make sure you're so happy that you'll be yourself again in no time," Dee promised. He could have *died*. He could have stopped breathing in that carbon-monoxide-filled car and she wouldn't even have known until days later. But if she could just work out a way to solve this 'Felix' problem chiselling away at her conscience, she could focus on Milo; how to fix the broken pieces of his troubled mind. Maybe he didn't need to know, was she really prepared to be the one to tip him over the precipice on which he teetered?

*

At nearly five in the morning, Dee opened her eyes to find that her peacefully sleeping husband was still beside her. She was so grateful that the whole thing hadn't been a very vivid dream. But Dee had been having disturbed and unsettling dreams of her own; dreams that had obviously featured Cameron heavily. He could have killed her or raped her or kidnapped her, and the only reason she was still lying here more-or-less unharmed was because of Milo. Dee sat up, wide awake now. It was so nearly morning she would never get back to sleep. She had put on a brave face last night, but a dreadful thing had happened, and it might take some time to get over it. Since the sun had risen, Dee felt she may as well too. She carefully disengaged herself from Milo so as not to wake him and stood up. Kirby, at the bottom of the sofa, rose to her feet too and followed Dee into the kitchen - she was ever hopeful of the chance of food. The kitten was a bit like a dog, the way she trailed after her owner.

Once in the kitchen, standing in her white camisole and hot-pants, Dee opened the fridge. She pulled out a sachet of cat food for Kirby who stood hopefully at her feet. Dee crouched down and popped a portion in her bowl and the kitten forced Dee's hand out of the way so she could wolf it down. Dee then fished out half a chocolate cheesecake; but something other than nightmares about Cameron had woken her. She was suffering from horribly insistent pangs of guilt again – her husband *still* didn't know the truth. Milo had finally come to his senses, but he had done so whilst in possession of only half the facts. Dee feared if he was given this information, he would leave her again. She *could* choose never to disclose it. But Felix, Evan and Ginny were all in on the secret (not to mention Cameron), and the truth always had a way of coming out. And if Felix loved her the way he said he did, he wasn't likely to be able to hide it. But if she told Milo of her own volition, he was *sure* to walk away. The dilemma was just too awful; the decision just too hard.

"You know Kirby, you haven't even been living with us for twenty-four hours, but I think I love you," Dee told her, nuzzling her soft ears, and running the silky points repeatedly between her fingers.

"...But you still have room in your affections for me, right?" Milo was standing at the kitchen doorway. Dee looked up and smiled.

"...Always." Dee loitered there, not quite knowing what to do with the plate of cheesecake in her hands.

"Don't you like sleeping?" He padded barefoot further into the room.

"Sleep is for wimps," Dee replied. "I don't know about you, but I think cheesecake is underrated as a breakfast choice. Want some?" She watched as he came to stand very close to her, an unreadable look on his face. They were both dressed only in their underwear.

"I find I can only eat cheesecake at five o'clock in the morning if I'm licking it off your body," he said in virtually a whisper and moved in to kiss her neck sensuously. Dee closed her eyes and blindly placed the cheesecake on the work surface behind her. His nerves must have dissipated and his ardency was infectious. How she wanted him.

"...D'you think you can-?" she groaned, pushing her guilt to the back of her mind. Cameron had instilled a fear in her that had never existed before. Milo offered warmth; he offered protection and safety. Only Milo could make this fear go away. Why shouldn't she let him?

"I'm positive." He ran his fingers down her belly, slipping them into her pants. The longing within her was fit to burst. But the incessant chiselling away at her conscience suddenly caused a great big crack. Dee grabbed his wrist sharply before he could take things any further. "...What?" He broke away. "I *really* want to-"

"Wait Milo, we can't have sex - we can't do anything until I've told you something." Dee's subconscious had made the decision for her. She could not live a lie. "And once I've told you, you might not want to anymore..."

"...Maybe I don't want to hear it then." Milo looked away stubbornly.

Dee was confused by that response. "If we're going to get back together, then we have to be honest with each other. I don't want to start out on a lie because it will only come back to haunt us," she exhaled very slowly. He was still keeping his face turned from hers, as though there was something exceedingly interesting to see outside the window. "...When you accused me of cheating with Felix, it wasn't true. It wasn't true *then,* but that doesn't mean to say it isn't true now..."

"...Don't say anymore..." Milo was shaking his head adamantly.

"Listen to me, Milo. I *have* slept with Felix – but only once and only very recently..." Dee realised she was shaking. The fear she felt at the prospect of losing him again was so overwhelming that she could barely form a sentence. And he was silent, so deathly silent, that she wasn't sure he had even heard her.

"I know..."

THE TRUTH WILL OUT

A solitary tear had begun to trickle down Milo's face. The teardrop ran down to his lips where it got caught and he licked it away. He continued to keep his eyes averted. He stood so rigidly that Dee wasn't sure if he were even breathing.
"You know…?"
Milo shifted his feet a little but kept his eyes on the window. "…When I let myself in the house tonight and I realised there was a commotion going on in the lounge, I waited out in the hall for a moment. I couldn't work out what was happening. I heard you admit it to Cameron. I'd hoped you said it out of fear – but I knew…"
"You overheard that and you weren't going to say anything?" Dee had broken into a cold sweat. Milo had known when he rescued her from Cameron, he had known when she was interrogated at the police station, and he had known when he came back to the house…and asked to come home.
"I just wanted to forget it." Milo chewed on his lip, always keeping his focus elsewhere.
"…Please let me explain how it happened," Dee began cautiously, watching for the infinitesimal nod of his head which he eventually gave. "After you left, I hardly spoke to Felix at first. But on your birthday…when you told me you were sleeping with Amber…I gave up on you," she gulped. "Felix and I decided to be friends again. I think deep down I knew he still fancied me but I ignored it. Everything came to a head a few days ago…on the two-year anniversary of the day you and I had met. I was really low; it was the anniversary of Lance's funeral too, and you hadn't shown up for Angel's birthday a few days before. I thought you'd gone off to America with Amber for good. I thought you had given up on all of us," Dee said in almost a whisper.
"…I explained all that…I'd dumped Amber, and I was sick, so I couldn't-"
"Yes, but what I know now, I didn't know then," she replied. "Felix took me out that evening to cheer me up. He invited me and my friends to his

club in Camden....and he admitted his feelings hadn't changed. We were both very drunk and very lonely. So he suggested we sleep together to help me get over you..." Dee ploughed on, feeling more and more sickened. "...We were in the flat above the club. The whole thing was a bit of a farce and I didn't think I could go through with it. So we decided just to go to sleep. But later...it happened..." She didn't mean to be so blunt or cruel, but there seemed to be no way of sugar-coating it. Dee was painfully aware that her admissions were suicidal, but to lie and lie for the remainder of their married lives was just not something she was prepared to do.

"...Were you attracted to him?" he asked without really wanting to know the answer.

Dee stalled. Yes. Not before, but now...yes. But that sort of confession would crucify Milo. "...No, I was just lonely," she murmured. "I'm as responsible as Felix for what happened; he didn't push me into it or anything like that..." Dee confided though it pained her to say these things, because she knew with every word she was driving him away. "But I want you to know that I regret what I did. I've regretted it from the moment it happened." Dee too was crying now for the millionth time – over Milo.

"Was it...*better* with Felix than with me...?" Milo said in a small voice.

For some reason, Dee had not expected that question, although perhaps she should have.

"No," she replied honestly. "I did it to get my own back...so I didn't take any pleasure in it. I felt sick afterwards at what I'd done. I told him the next day I didn't want to repeat it. And he agreed. I thought we'd get past it and we could just be friends, but as of yesterday evening, we've fallen out again..." She watched her husband staring fixedly into space.

"...Does he love you?"

"...I don't think so." More lies. Felix had admitted it himself yesterday, but what good would the truth do? "When you came back from the States...you were nice to me for the first time in months and you explained away all the things I was mad at you about. So you can imagine how disgusted I felt when I found out that everything I thought I knew – everything that made me sleep with Felix - I didn't actually know at all."

"...If I'd come back a couple of days earlier, nothing would have happened with Felix?" Finally, he met her eyes again.

"Of course," Dee retorted mildly. "Look, if you're going to leave me again, can we just decide that now? I've got my hopes up too much already..." Dee wiped her eyes and waited for him to speak.

Eventually he did. "...Who says I'm leaving?"

Dee stared at him, dumbstruck. "...You left me over an unrequited kiss and now I'm actually guilty, you really believe you could forgive that...?" She shook her head disbelievingly.

"...Well, it's all my fault, isn't it?" Milo gave a bit of a hopeless shrug. "*I put Felix in your life, I forced you together. Then I freaked out over nothing and left my entire family for months and got involved with another woman, so how can I possibly *not* forgive you?"

Dee was still shaking her head, totally unprepared to let herself have faith when the rug was going to be pulled out from under her feet later on. "What happened with Felix *happened.* It can't be undone. If you're totally honest with yourself, you must know you'll never be able to come to terms with this..."

"...You forget I was prepared to die because I couldn't have you..."

Dee mulled that over quietly. "Milo, I want you to stay more than anything, but maybe you need to sleep on this. I mean, I know we've *both* been unfaithful now – but I've had longer to get my head around it."

"I'm staying, there's nothing to think about," Milo said brusquely.

Dee narrowed her eyes. Was he for real? "...Is there any point in me asking how many times you slept with Amber?" In all those months, Dee realised it would be too many times to have kept count.

Milo almost laughed but sheepishly slipped his hand into hers instead. "...If I tell you, you won't believe me," he assured her.

Dee gulped. What did *that* mean? "...How many times?"

"...None." Milo gave a bit of a nervous wince, as though she might strike him.

"Oh please, Milo! You guys were together for months so don't insult my intelligence!" Dee pulled her hand from his. But Milo forced his hand right back into hers and she had no choice but to face him.

"I'm telling you the truth, Dee. Amber only ever crashed at mine when she was in England - she wasn't *living* with me. She used to pester me and I used to put her off because...she repulsed me..." Milo said terribly earnestly.

"But you told me at the Dorchester that you *had!*" Dee was filled with a feeling of complete dread; if he hadn't been unfaithful and she had...

Milo sighed. "I lied." He tried to conceal his intense shame with another shrug. "You showed up at my house-party...and you were so beautiful and so sweet. I felt so utterly miserable, I just wanted to go off and be alone with you somewhere to talk. But Amber spoiled everything and draped herself over me...and you left. I insisted on following you to The Dorchester because it was my birthday and I wanted to be near you. But Amber kissed me at the bar...and you were *so* upset. I felt awful. But when you asked me if I'd slept with her...that same old rage came over me, so I said I did. Just to hurt you. Then you told me you wished I was dead. And *I* wished I was dead too..." Milo wiped his tearful eyes on the back of his hand at the memory of that horrible night.

"Are you serious? Why would you lie about a thing like that? Don't you realise that was the end of us?" Dee glowered, he had robbed her of even the chance of feeling relieved that he hadn't committed adultery. So he was faithful. And she wasn't.

"I wasn't in my right mind." Milo raised his eyes to the heavens, exasperated – but only with himself.

"And are you in your right mind now? Will you be in your right mind when you come off the medication?" Dee was very nearly shouting.

"Dee, I wasn't well. But I'm getting help now, I'll keep seeing the psychiatrist and I'll wean off the meds – whatever the doctor tells me to do," he said mournfully. "I'm not the man I was in February; I swear I'll never be that man again..."

"So the only adulterer in this room is *me*...?" Dee was so angry she could have punched him. But instead, she burst into floods of tears again, her hands over her face.

Milo tentatively put his arms around her and pulled her into his chest. "Baby, this is all my fault – I'm not denying that. I forced you into that relationship with Felix. *I* did this to us."

"You'll never let me hear the end of it. It'll be hanging over my head for the rest of our lives!" Dee was so irate, she wanted to shake him off but was too deflated to muster enough energy.

"I want to forget it as much as you do," Milo insisted so vehemently that Dee was forced to stop crying and look up at him. "Nothing has changed. You asked me to come home – or you asked me to ask *you*, whatever. But don't forget I *already knew* about Felix...and I still gratefully accepted. We never have to bring up what happened with Felix ever again, I swear. I want to spend the rest of my life with you," he stressed. "Dee, I'm all in. Are you...?" Milo asked with hopeful determination.

"I *do* want you back," Dee admitted, wiping her streaming eyes and nose on the inside of her wrist.

"Then that's all that matters, isn't it? Would it honestly make you feel any better if I *had* been unfaithful too?" he implored her. Dee thought about that. Well...maybe. "...I couldn't do it, you've ruined me for anyone else," Milo explained truthfully. "Can't we just agree to be together and stop talking about who did what?"

"...I was hoping you would stop talking ten minutes ago..." she snivelled.

Milo grinned at last, still holding one of her hands. "...Maybe we should go back to sleep for a bit - I'm just so tired," she sighed wearily.

"Sleep is for wimps..." Milo's lips neared hers again.

Just before his mouth was on hers, Dee said, "are you sure you don't still want to take things slow...? I mean, the medication-"

"Do I look like a man who wants to take things slow?"

Dee felt his lips finally close in on hers. She shut her eyes and at last allowed herself to surrender to this. She kissed him back harder, wound her fingers in his hair which had curled up from the rain. Milo pushed her back against the work surface, lifting her gently to sit on it. She freed him from his boxers as he peeled off the last of her underwear. Dee needed to pinch herself that this was going to happen; she *had* given up on him, she had never expected to experience any kind of intimacy with him ever again. Milo groaned and she could tell by the hardness on her leg that his libido hadn't been affected.

"...Milo," she moaned as soon as he was inside her. He pressed his forehead against hers and stared into her eyes while they made love. Dee ran her hands up his back, up to the nape of his neck; feeling the curve of his body, the shape of his muscular arms and torso, the familiarity of his form entwined with hers. It all felt so right – as though those months and months apart hadn't happened. Milo called her name, losing his inhibitions, losing control. The feeling heightened for them both – too much to take now. Dee was fighting not to climax. She had waited so long for this moment, she wanted to make it last.

But somehow he knew that. "Don't wait for me..."

"...But I want *you* to-" she began breathlessly. Amber could not even tempt him but Dee needed to know that she still could.

"Let it happen..."

Dee realised she couldn't hold out any longer if she tried. "...*Milo!*" she cried out, gripping his hair tight enough to hurt and his body tensed up at almost exactly the same time in what was a shared climax - which didn't happen terribly often. Dee held him in her arms, his head buried in her chest - at his most vulnerable and fragile. Her body taught, over-sensitised now – Dee held him tight to her. When he finally looked up, Milo gently kissed the remnants of tears from her eyes, tasting the salty water on his lips, whispering over and over, *'What was I thinking? What was I thinking?"* He would never know why he had reacted so unbelievably badly and walked away from the one and only love of his life.

*

Milo, insistent that the fire hadn't *quite* gone out and that he could get it going again, placed another log on the embers. He prodded it with a poker to reignite it. Dee lay back down on the sofa and huddled under the duvet, watching her naked husband deftly fixing the fire. Milo had a beautiful body. He was lean, toned and lithe - thinner than he ought to be due to loss of appetite during his depression. Still, he was hers again and she would fatten him up. Soon he came to join her under the duvet, lacing his fingers with Dee's. "That was amazing," he told her. "I missed having sex with you..."

"...Same for me," she confided. "I feel like I belong to you again..."

"That you do. And I belong to you."

"Do you think we need to go for marriage counselling?"

Milo groaned. "Uggh! I'm already seeing a shrink; I don't think I can stomach even more therapy that only serves to remind me what a terrible person I am."

Dee stroked his arm. "Not *terrible*...but you *are* the most jealous man I ever met. The way you engineer situations to get what you want isn't normal, Milo. But I love you and if there's anybody on earth who's prepared to stick by you, it's me. I realise I'm not perfect either. I latch on to the men who come into my life and maybe I give off the wrong signals – and I just think marriage counselling would be good for us both," Dee reasoned.

"...Can I think about it? I'm determined not to screw this marriage up again," Milo declared. "...When we first got together, you had a list of provisos I had to agree to before you would be with me...and now I have one proviso for you," he said carefully. Dee listened with bated breath. "I don't want you to ever speak to Felix again."

Dee sighed. "...Felix made a mistake; he wanted your forgiveness so badly for such a long time. But then I had the car accident and you didn't come...and he gave up on you like I did..."

Milo's mouth set in a hard line. "Felix has got to be out of our lives...it's non-negotiable. It's the only thing I'm asking of you."

"...Alright," Dee agreed sadly. These terms were fair. She would hardly be happy if he continued a friendship with Amber. And although Felix Kellerman had come to mean far too much to her, Dee had to be prepared to sacrifice him for Milo.

"There is one other thing I *do* want, it's not a proviso - I would just like it if you agreed. I'm going to be in England pretty much full time now, but when I do have to go back to the States, will you come with me? I don't want to spend any more time apart. I can't handle it," he admitted wearily.

"Of course." Dee wanted to spend every day of the rest of her life with him from now on. "...To think of spending just one night here in this house alone without you now that-"

"Dee..." Milo rolled on his front to look her in the eye. "I've been so looking forward to moving back in here with you guys, but if you can't feel comfortable here, then we can move wherever you like. You can choose the place," he assured her. "But you can't let Cameron make you afraid when you used to be so strong, because then he wins. It's going to take some time to get over what happened last night, but you will." Milo placed a kiss on her mouth and Dee gulped down a huge lump of emotion. "...I wish I'd killed him so you didn't have to feel like this...but he'll get life, I promise you. He's a murderer," he asserted. Dee nod her head, trying to wear her brave face again. Milo noticed how tired and drawn she looked. "...We should get a little sleep before Mrs Dawson brings back the children." It was six now and Mrs D would be here about nine so that allowed them at least two hours, factoring in showers and dressing. Dee smiled her assent – too tired to argue and feeling safer now, safe enough to sleep.

*

By the time morning had arrived, the atmosphere around the house was so different that it felt as though Milo had never been away. Mrs Dawson opened the front door with her key and ushered Angel in and carried Finley in her arms. She expertly kicked the door shut with her foot but she stopped short because the sound of soft voices upstairs reached her ears. Mrs Dawson sighed, in her heart she had hoped nothing would materialise between Dee and last night's date. Change was difficult for anyone and Mrs Dawson had an uneasy feeling that this was the beginning of the end of a working environment she had thoroughly enjoyed. This had been more than employment to her; she had grown to love these children, Dee, and had even become fond of the misunderstood Milo. And his disappearance from their lives bothered her greatly.

Mrs Dawson was staring at the empty stairway which suddenly contained the enigmatic figure of Milo Phillips descending the steps. She transferred her gormless stare to Dee who followed Milo whilst wearing a smug little smirk. It was only nine in the morning and this was an odd time for Dee's ex to visit. "...Are you-?" Val began reticently, hardly daring to believe it.

"Yes!" Dee's smirk broke into an all-out beam.

"But I don't-" Val only just managed to stop herself blurting the obvious about Dee's date with Oliver. And Felix Kellerman had been here too, but she had never expected Milo to be gliding down the stairs.

"I know. It was a mental night – you'll never believe *how* mental...but Milo saved me." Dee ran a thankful hand across his back as they reached the bottom to greet Mrs Dawson.

"Dee," Milo groaned with a roll of his eyes.

"What? You did." Dee glanced at Mrs Dawson who was peering at them confusedly.

"Hey you guys!" Milo turned his attentions on his two children. Angel happily leaped into his arms and Val handed him his son. "How ya' doing?" He held his three-year-old daughter and ten-month old son on either hip and felt more content than he had felt in months.

"I think we'd better sit down Val and I'll explain what happened last night," Dee decided, gingerly leading Val into the kitchen but then she turned back to the occupants of the hall briefly. "...Oh Angel, your daddy has something to tell you."

"What?" Angel finally stopped jabbering.

"Honey, I'm coming back home to live with you guys for good," he informed her and Angel seemed strangely lost for words for a moment.

"Here? With Mummy, Finley and me?" she gasped and as he nodded his head, she threw her arms around his neck. Finley obviously did not know what was going on but he did seem to be smiling at seeing his mother and father around him with big grins on their faces. That hadn't been the case in months. Dee placed a kiss on her husband's lips, kissed her children and wandered into the kitchen. Milo took the children into the lounge to play with them just like a father should. She then sat Val down at the table and proceeded to explain the dramas of last night. Only Mrs Dawson's eyes could be seen after a while as her nose and mouth were covered by her hands in horror.

"Thank God he came back..." Val gulped. "...And you and Mr Phillips...you're really back together...?"

"Yes," Dee replied proudly and Mrs Dawson spontaneously threw her arms around her. It took Dee a moment to realise Mrs Dawson was crying.

Soon Milo returned to the kitchen, placing Finn in his highchair and grinned as Angel bounded into her seat. Val stood up and placed an unexpected kiss on Milo's cheek then she hurried over to the hob, wrapping her apron around her waist and mopping her eyes.

"I'll make a start on breakfast!" she chirped with a wavering yet cheery voice.

"She looks pleased," Milo said softly to his wife as he sat down beside her at the table. "How do you think everyone else will take the news?"

"...I think reactions will be mixed," Dee told him honestly and turned her attention to Angel who was happily babbling away about something to her parents that they had missed the gist of entirely. But the child was happy, that was the main thing.

Mrs Dawson turned to look at Dee while standing at the stove. "You don't know how glad I am. In my heart I always prayed that you and Mr Phillips would patch up your differences but I didn't believe you really would."

"…Well, we love each other…so we decided to try again," Dee explained, slipping her hand into Milo's, as though the process had been the easiest in the world. Milo smiled at her fondly. "…Val, thanks for being there for me while I was down and probably not being the best mother."

"Don't be ridiculous," Mrs Dawson huffed. "Now, the children are washed and just need breakfast which will be ready in a few minutes. But don't forget I can't stop for long this morning as I've got to get to my hair appointment."

"No worries," Dee said, still staring lovingly into her husband's eyes. He was sitting right there at the breakfast table, just like in happier times.

"I expect you'll want to move some of your things back home today, Mr Phillips? And you'll have to break the news to a lot of people when you go to Ginny's birthday party this evening," she reminded them and both Dee and Milo's faces fell. They had clean forgotten. "Now some may question your judgement, but I've spent a lot of time around you two and I know you were meant for each other," she insisted. Dee wasn't looking forward to tonight, but breaking the news had to be done. She was feeling rather tired in all honesty, after a night with precious little sleep, but this was alleviated by the sheer elation of Milo's return.

Dee hadn't wanted to discuss Felix again, but now she had no choice. She lowered her voice. "I'd completely forgotten Ginny's birthday party this evening. Jerry's throwing the bash at the hotel, isn't he? And if it's Ginny's birthday then it's-"

"Felix's birthday, yes I know." Milo glanced away disdainfully. "I presume Jerry has to throw the party for both of them – not that Jerry even likes him."

"Then should we go? I really don't want to have the conversation with him that I need to have on his birthday…" How could she have forgotten Felix's birthday? He had been pretty much one of the most prominent people in her life for months.

Milo was still keeping his eyes averted. "Well, we can't avoid him forever…so you may as well tell him tonight." And then he seemed to dismiss that part of the conversation to angle it towards something more to his liking. "Do you have a present for Ginny?"

"Yes," Dee murmured. She had a gift for Felix too. She had found a rare book about music through the ages, and bought it for him weeks ago.

Giving it in secret was going to be the problem.

"You can help me choose something for her today," Milo mused. "Let's see tonight as a good opportunity to let everyone know we're back together. Ginny and Forrest are going to be pleased, but I don't know about anyone else," he sighed.

"...I'm not sure what Bruce, Patrice, Evan and Cassie's reactions will be." Dee could not really call it. Bruce was understandably angry with Milo, but presumably should be relieved Felix was out of the picture. Patrice had always tried to stay firmly on the fence. But Evan's loyalties had changed recently and Cassie was incredibly upset with the way Milo had behaved.

"We'll see." He gave her an awkward grimace. Milo proceeded to speak in an even quieter voice. "...After breakfast I'm going to shoot off to see my doctor about weaning off this medication. Then I've got to drop into the office. Oh, and then I'll go up to the apartment and pick up some of my things. I can meet you in town early this afternoon for coffee and you can help me choose something for Ginny."

Dee's eyes suddenly widened to the size of saucers and she had the appearance of somebody who was about to cry. "...Oh...so am I going to be on my own in the house with the kids?"

"...What? Oh God, sorry - I didn't think..." Milo gripped her hand tighter. His wife was afraid, afraid to be on her own in the house; scared about the prospect of protecting two small children all by herself. "...*I knew* you weren't fine..." he said gravely.

"I am, I am- I was just thinking aloud, that's all." Dee looked away, but Milo turned her jaw so she was forced to face him again.

"You're strong, Dee - you're the strongest person I know..."

"But I'm not strong, am I? Physically - I couldn't have defended myself last night...or my children." That was the hardest part. She felt Cameron had stolen that strength of will and character from her. Maybe she could have escaped him last night, but maybe she couldn't. If he had used any kind of force, could she have stopped him? Dee was physically weak in comparison, and any man could hurt her if they had a mind to do so. If Milo hadn't come to rescue her, there was no knowing what would have happened.

"Dee..." Mrs Dawson ventured over worriedly, overhearing their whispered conversation. "I can cancel my appointment and stay with you; it's just a silly haircut."

"No-no, I'm being stupid. They're going to lock him up and I need to get used to being alone in my own home," Dee asserted weakly.

"I could call Bruce and ask him to come over. Or I can cancel my engagements," Milo offered. "I can just put them off for another day."

Dee shook her head. "No. I've got to be on my own sooner or later." She steeled herself to be brave. It was daytime for-crying-out-loud! But nighttime; being alone here in this house in the dark, that would be a whole different battle. Dee was just going to have to find a way to come to terms with this.

"I'll come pick you up myself. I'll be gone a couple of hours max," Milo promised. "You're safe here, Dee. Cameron had a *key*...and now he's locked up. But even so, when I come back, I will bring my security guy and he can fit new locks and burglar alarms and CCTV. You'll feel safe then. If you decide you can't live here anymore, we'll find somewhere else. But don't forget how much you loved this house, it would be a shame to let Cameron spoil that."

Dee smiled a watery smile. "Thank you for coming home." She pressed her forehead against his.

Milo snaked an arm around her. "Thank you for asking me...or asking me to ask you..."

IT'S A GIFT

It was still light when Dee and Milo pulled into the gravel drive of the hotel up on Richmond Hill that summer evening. Milo thrust his hand firmly in hers the moment they stepped from the car. It remained there as they wandered gingerly up the driveway and through the open glass doors into the lobby. Dee knew Milo was determined to display their reunion right from the get-go. But she was oddly nervous; nervous about her friends' reactions. Dee and Milo eventually made their way past reception and all too soon immersed themselves in the throngs of people bustling about one of the hotel reception rooms. Live lounge music was skilfully played by a pianist in the corner. Dee's head jerked involuntarily in this direction – but the musician wasn't Felix. She breathed a sigh of relief, knowing she would have to face him soon, but glad it wasn't now. The guests were all milling around with champagne flutes and nibbles as Dee picked out faces she recognised in the crowd. Ginny stood with Jerry's arms about her waist and Dee spotted other faces such as Forrest, Cassie, Bruce, Patrice, Evan, and Elliott. She and Milo were still invisible for the moment but her nerves increased because any moment now...

Cassie and Forrest were loitering near the bar but she was the first to spot Dee standing sheepishly with her ex. "Oh my God, she's here!" Cassie literally ran across the room, throwing her arms around her cousin and dissolving into tears. "Thank God you're okay," she sobbed as Dee staggered under the weight of her. Soon enough Forrest had wheeled himself over.

"Dee, we've all been so worried...Milo wouldn't let me come over..." Forrest said plaintively.

"...Does *everybody* know?" Dee groaned. She glanced at Milo. She had been so preoccupied with her newly rejuvenated marriage (and sleeping), she hadn't checked her phone which was full of messages.

"Yes, Jerry and Elliott and Forrest have been telling everyone before you got here. Forrest didn't think to tell me before tonight because he said he didn't want to upset me!" Cassie gave him an accusatory glare. "And to think you could have been-" she stalled, and then her eyes roved slowly over to Milo. "...Thank you...for saving my cousin..."

"I'm just as pleased as you are," Milo shrugged as though he hadn't much to do with it. "Cassie, I'm so sorry about Gordon – and that I didn't get to know him properly. I wanted to pay you a visit but, I didn't think under the circumstances-"

"...It's okay. I got your card and flowers – I'm sorry, I've been feeling too fragile to respond," Cassie said in a subdued voice. "...After losing my dad, if anything had happened to Dee...but it didn't, because of *you*."

"Seriously, I just got lucky," he insisted.

Dee smiled at her husband proudly. "Stop being so casual about it, you were amazing. You should have seen how your brother handled himself, Forrest," she bragged for him.

"Nobody is more proud of him than me," Forrest grinned. However, he stopped when Milo gave Dee a discreet little peck on the lips; somehow the linked hands had gone unnoticed in the adoration of all things Milo. "...Good grief. Are you-?"

"...You haven't bloody got back together, have you?" Cassie's eyes widened, this expression unnerving Dee.

"...We bloody have," Milo said, baffled at all the fuss the simple act of a kiss had caused. "And you don't have to worry, Cassie. I've been a complete fool but I'm going to look after your cousin properly this time."

She stalled for a moment, studying him intently. "...You'd better...but if this is what you both want...then I'm happy for you," Cassie said rather emotionally and threw her arms around Dee again.

Forrest shook his brother's hand. "Milo, that's wonderful...and it's about time too!"

"Thanks, Forrest." Milo knew he had taken an astonishingly long time to do what everyone else knew he should do, but he just hadn't been ready to swallow his pride before. He just hadn't been *himself* before.

Very soon, Ginny was on her way over with Jerry in tow. Dee wished she and Milo weren't attracting so much attention. Dee shuffled slightly closer to Milo for emotional support.

"Happy Birthday, Ginny," Dee said before anyone else could speak.

"Never mind about that, you must have been terrified!" Ginny too burst into tears and hugged Dee tight. "And you!" She dragged Milo into the hug. "All is forgiven. You're my hero!"

"And mine," Dee laughed as she was finally released.

Jerry eyed Milo darkly then stuck out a tentative hand. "...Thank you Milo, for saving my sister..." He evidently found that fairly painful to say but Milo shook the hand that was offered.

"I was just in the right place at the right time," Milo said something he had been saying repeatedly since last night.

"He was *not*; he ran halfway across Richmond to *be* in the right place!" Dee frowned at Milo, making certain he got his due. "Milo had no fear for his own safety, he just-" she was interrupted by Jerry giving her yet another emotional hug.

"...Now did I notice some kind of a *kiss* before I got over here?" Ginny was wearing half a smile. "Are you two getting back together?"

"Of course we are," Milo replied, almost beginning to be amused this this.

"That's the best news I've heard in months!" Ginny yelped.

"Well, I hope you know what you're doing, Dee..." Jerry sighed. "I'm very grateful for what you did Milo, don't get me wrong - but this doesn't change the appalling way in which you treated Dee for the last few months."

"I realise that. You've every reason to dislike me more than you ever did. But I made a mistake...a terrible mistake. Still, Dee is prepared to forgive me and we want to give our marriage another chance." Milo's hand had found its way back into hers.

"This is what we both want, Jerry," Dee told him in her most placating tone.

"You can't just get back together out of gratitude, Dee," he continued with a pragmatic rather than a condescending voice.

Milo sighed. "Jerry, can we have a word in private?" he asked wearily and took his suspicious brother aside to explain himself. Dee grimaced at the others.

"...Jerry has a point. You *do* need to be sure, Dee. We all saw how he treated you. Milo broke your heart," Cassie reminded her.

"I know. But he's different now...what I mean is, he's turned back into the man he was before this all blew up. Everybody deserves a second chance, don't they? I couldn't turn down perhaps our last hope of resolving our differences out of pride," Dee reasoned.

"...But he *did* cheat on you..." Ginny stressed. She would be pleased for Dee if this was what she truly wanted. It was important Dee was doing this for the right reasons.

Dee gnawed on the inside of her mouth. "...Well, actually he *didn't*...but he made it look like he did. That's a long story we need to chat about over a coffee one day." She tried to ignore the way Cassie, Forrest and Ginny all glanced at each other quizzically. "But he's disgusted with himself over the way he behaved. Milo wants to make it up to me...and I can forgive him." Dee looked across the room where Milo who was being sternly spoken to by his brother Jerry. Jerry was waggling a finger at him so Dee was pretty certain Milo was receiving a ticking-off. But judging by his nonchalant pose, this was not affecting Milo too greatly. Elliott joined them and appeared to be placating the situation, and Dee decided Milo was big enough to deal with it without her help. "This isn't just misplaced gratitude over Milo saving me from Cameron; I wanted him back, and now he is."

"Well, if it's what you really want, then I'm pleased for you," Ginny asserted. The three women hugged again and Forrest wheeled himself in the direction of his berated brother to see if he could be of any help in his defence. Cassie's curiosity soon got the better of her and she wandered over to give Milo any backup that was required. She owed him that at least, and Jerry *was* a tool.

Ginny gave a small smile now they were alone. "...I don't think Felix is going to take this news very well..."

Dee opened her mouth to feign ignorance but remembered Ginny knew everything. "...No, I don't expect he will. I'm sorry to do this on his birthday..." Judging by the reaction last night, Felix wouldn't like this *at all*.

"I guess it can't be helped. Felix was terribly upset when he heard about Cameron breaking into your house – and him being a...a murderer and all-" Ginny found it hard to even let herself imagine what might have happened, let alone talk about it.

"I'm pretty upset myself," Dee retorted. "...Look, Milo knows...about Felix."

"...Oh," Ginny gulped. "...Well, I don't suppose it was wise to try and conceal a secret like that. Evan and I know for starters, and secrets always tend to get out. How did he take it...?"

"Milo was hurt, but he says he still wants to get back together."

"And Milo *didn't* cheat on you...?"

Dee gulped. "He lied at The Dorchester that night...to hurt me..." She recognised the same look of bafflement on Ginny's face that she had worn at five o'clock this morning. "Look, I'm sorry I dragged your brother into this mess. I was at a seriously low point in my life that night at his nightclub, and I knew I should have stopped it but-"

"You don't need to apologise to me, I know my brother. He gave you an ultimatum, you tried to turn him down and then he threatened to break off your friendship. Felix is a very decent person really, but when it comes to you, I don't think he can see straight," Ginny sighed.

"...What?" Dee sputtered. "Oh no, it wasn't like *that*. Well, technically I guess...but no, you're making him sound conniving and that's not Felix at all. Is that what he told you...?"

"I guessed, but he didn't deny it," Ginny shrugged. "So, what's going to happen between Milo and Felix now?"

"I won't lie to you - Milo is very upset. I've explained Felix and I were both at fault...and neither of us was in possession of all the facts back then..."

"Yes, what *did* happen in the States after Amber left those threatening messages and he left the country? Forrest seems to know something but wouldn't divulge anything at all."

"I'm not really at liberty to say either, but if you ask Milo personally, I'm sure he'll tell you," Dee assured her gently. "Anyway, I'd better find Felix and get this over with."

Ginny rubbed her arm. "For what it's worth...not everybody will agree with me, but I think you're doing the right thing."

Dee smiled weakly and wandered off to face the music. She soon bumped into Bruce, Patrice and Evan. Before she had time to explain herself, Bruce threw his arms around her, he *too* bursting into tears.

"Thank God you're safe!!" he bawled. Patrice put his arms around them both, he was *also* on the verge of tears.

And this time, Dee felt like crying too. "...I'm so sorry I didn't listen to you, Bruce. I owe you a big apology..."

"Me?" He broke off, wiping his nose with his shirt sleeve.

"You always said there was something wrong with Cameron, but I refused to take any notice of you." Yes, there had been more than *something wrong* with that man; he was a murderer. Cameron Quinn killed that secretary in cold blood, it was unthinkable.

"But I can't believe *he* killed Kate Taylor, I would never have thought of him in a million years." Bruce shook his head, mortified. "...You don't have to worry, if he ever gets out of prison, I swear I will-"

"It's alright, Bruce. Cameron will never be released," Patrice said quite seriously. When the two men had let her go, Evan gave her a smaller hug of his own.

"...God, it's good to see you in one piece," he said rather thickly. "...So am I right in thinking you and Milo are back together...? Are you sure this is what you really want?" Evan asked knowingly. "You mustn't forget how much he hurt you before..."

"Evan, I know things now that I didn't know before that explain his behaviour," she replied. "And everyone deserves a second chance," Dee heard herself say again.

"I'm just as angry with him as you Evan, but...maybe Milo *does* deserve this second chance," Bruce agreed sagely. "Dee probably wouldn't be here tonight talking to us if it wasn't for Milo. I'm going to go over there and speak to him, and after I slap him very hard across the face for being such a dick, I'm going to shake his hand!" he stomped off emotionally and Patrice followed after him with a roll of his eyes.

Evan put his hands in his pockets. "Dee, we all owe Milo a great debt of gratitude, we *really* do. But I'm not sure you're making the right decision..."

"...The vows say, 'in sickness and in health', and he *was* sick-"

"But they don't say anything about forgiving somebody who destroyed your life, who nearly broke you."

"I love him, Evan."

"Yes, but sometimes love isn't enou-"

Dee cut him off. "Evan, I'm going to do this," she said resolutely.

He sighed and gave a resigned shrug. "...Well, it's your choice...but two strikes and he's out, Dee. This has *got* to be his last chance. Promise me that, at least," Evan said and Dee gave a reluctant nod of her head. Evan gave her his hug of semi-approval. Dee advised him she could not be present at this party much longer. She had come here to break the news to their friends and family, even if it meant breaking Felix's heart. It was now long overdue time to find Felix, because she just couldn't stomach leaving it any longer.

*

It can't have taken much longer than two or three minutes to find Felix amongst the throngs of people, but to Dee, it felt like an age before she came across him standing at the bar. He was nursing a whiskey with a brooding expression on his face. Gosh, he was handsome, wasn't he? Dee wondered why she hadn't always thought so. When he first set eyes on her, his eyes glittered with a kind of suppressed anger but this completely dissipated when he seemed to remind himself of what could have happened to her last night.

"God, are you okay-?" Felix raised a hand involuntarily to touch her face, but there was just the merest flinch from Dee that stopped him and made him lower his hand. "...I wasn't going to *kiss* you..."

"No-no, I didn't think that," Dee was suddenly flustered. "It's just Milo-"

"I was *worried* about you, if that's okay? I freaked out when I heard what happened to you last night. How the hell did Cameron get in the house?" Felix shook his head.

"...He had a key. I'd taken his key back but I didn't realise he'd made a copy," Dee said sheepishly.

"Why on earth would you give a man like that a key? You've never given *me* a key and I wouldn't harm a hair on your head! How many other psychotic exes have access to your house? This is London, y'know!"

Dee blanched. "*Richmond*, actually. I know I was careless...but by the time I get home, my house will be like Fort Knox; new locks, a key-code, a burglar alarm and there's even going to be a camera outside - Milo insisted. I don't think *I'll* even know how to get in," she said. "Anyway, I paid for my lack of security-consciousness..." Dee chewed on her thumbnail and wondered what steps she was going to have to take to get over what had happened last night.

Felix thought better of his attitude. "I'm sorry, of course it's not your fault - it's just the thought of anything bad happening to you..."

Dee lowered her gaze. "...So, Happy Birthday..." She could hardly look at him as she rummaged in her bag and fished out the wrapped hardback book she had secreted in there earlier. "Open it later if that's alright..."

He eyed her darkly. "Like in a broom closet where I can't be seen by Milo, you mean?" Felix cocked his head to one side. "Did you buy me the restoration of your common sense at all? Because that's the only gift I could do with right now - seeing as the world has gone completely mad."

"...So, judging by the sarcasm, I gather you don't need me to tell you Milo and I ended up getting back together last night?" Dee sighed with a heavy heart.

"...No, but thanks for the horribly belated heads-up. I obviously have so much charisma that I can drive women back into the arms of their obsessively controlling estranged husbands. First you're dating some obscure customer from your shop and later that same night, in between nearly getting abducted by another insane ex, you're back with the man who made the last few months of your life a misery – *made my life a misery*. When the obvious thing to do would have been to choose *me*!" Felix fixed her with a cold glare.

Dee gulped. "...Felix, you and I were never going to be together. I have deeper feelings for you than I should, but what we did was a mistake. I'm sorry if I led you on, I didn't mean to. But all these miserable months, I just wanted Milo to come home. Now we're finally getting another chance. I'm really happy about it. So I realise you're angry now and you have every right to be...but if you could try to forgive me one day, that would mean a lot," she said.

Dee and Felix stood in silence for a moment, catching a glimpse of Milo through the crowds with a mobile phone stuck to his face, deep in conversation. He hadn't spotted them. Felix was glaring at her with his glass firmly grasped in his fist.

"...You want my approval?" he replied sourly. "Are you fucking insane? You're getting back together with that conniving control-freak when you were so close to being out of that marriage!" Felix said rather viscously.

"Felix, you know this is the best outcome for everyone," Dee groaned.

"Really? Is it the best outcome for me? You know how I feel about you!"

"Don't Felix...I don't think you really- *love* me...and one day you'll realise that-"

"Is that what you're telling yourself?" He was being horribly cynical again and it was beginning to dawn on Dee that nothing would ever be quite the same. "How could you be so stupid after everything he did to you?"

"Some of the things we assumed about Milo...well, we assumed wrong," Dee sighed, she was not at liberty to tell Felix about the suicide attempt. "He didn't ever sleep with Amber, he lied and said he had just to upset me..."

"What? What kind of manipulative monster would lie about having an affair?" Felix shook his head incredulously. "And how do you know he isn't lying about *lying*?"

Dee scratched her head uneasily. "He's telling the truth, Felix."

"Then, don't you see he drove us to do what we did?" He threw up his arms. "Because saying you did a thing, making people believe you did, well that's tantamount to actually doing it!"

"...Well, Milo admits he forced you into my life and he realises lying about Amber had a big impact on...my relationship with you." Dee cleared her throat. "...Because you see, he knows...I told Milo...about us..."

"...You did what? What would possess you to do a thing like that?" Felix gawped, stupefied at her lack of confidentiality. "You do realise that if it's actually true that he's innocent of infidelity and you're not, Milo will never let you live it down? He will use it against you for the rest of your life! Not to mention how he's going to use it against *me*!"

"What else could I do? I had to tell Milo! We couldn't base a fresh start on lies. He's taken it really well and he just wants to put the past behind us. But he's asked that I don't speak to you anymore, and of course that isn't what I want," Dee mumbled nervously, "...but I had to agree to it..."

Felix's frosty demeanour suddenly dissolved again. "...We can't speak anymore? We can't be friends?"

"How could I refuse him this? I cheated on him with *you*! How would I feel if he insisted on keeping Amber in his life?" Dee finally touched his arm but the physical contact was too big of a reminder of that fateful night they had shared together in the flat above the club. She removed her hand rapidly, as though she had touched something too hot.

"...So you ratted on me and now you've sold me out? You're as guilty as I am!"

"I know that! I'm not trying to place all the blame on you, but Milo wants me back and I really want things to work between us. So that means I have to cut you out of my life...at least for now," Dee apologised, fighting back more tears. "Maybe he'll get over what happened given time, maybe he'll forgive you..."

"Forgive me for fucking his wife? Yeah right, the man who couldn't forgive a stupid kiss – I can see that happening," Felix hissed acidly, ignoring how his harsh words made Dee flinch. "So I like how you get off scot free whilst he's going to make my life a living hell!"

Dee threw back her head, exasperated. "All I did was tell the truth! Milo knows that you and I were both at fault and I didn't get cajoled into anything. But he has the right to ask this of me. Milo just wants you to leave us alone," she ignored the look of disgust on his face.

"Did you sleep with him - last night...?"

Dee blinked in surprise. "...Well, yes." This conversation wasn't going to plan; it wasn't brief or to the point or being met with disinterest like she'd hoped. "Look, I'm sorry that I have to do this on your birthday. I came over here because I had to explain my position to you - but after tonight, I can't speak to you anymore. I am so sorry for hurting you..." She scrubbed at her eyes and turned. "I have to go now..."

"Dee..." Felix caught her wrist and she was forced to face him again, the pain in his eyes was unmistakable. All his fury had now vanished and he began again softly, "...just a week ago, I was *inside* you. I wasn't your husband's cousin, and I wasn't your friend - I was your *lover*. I've shared with you the most intimate thing we could possibly have done together..."

Dee bristled. "Yes I remember, thank you."

"You can't just consign me to being some nobody after that – we slept together..."

"So what? Didn't you keep saying the next morning it was *only sex*? You've shared that most *intimate thing* with a hundred-odd other women, you told me that yourself..."

"But I'm in love with you..." he said in a tiny voice and Dee searched his face for some trace of a fabrication but there was only honesty...and pain. Dee was so thoroughly ashamed of herself, ashamed of how she had selfishly broken him. "...If- if *I* had saved you last night, would it be me and you walking in here hand-in-hand? Would you have chosen me then?"

"What...? No, no Felix - it's not about who saved me..."

"Because it *could* have been me, if I'd just come back..." How he wished he had, if only he'd had some inkling something was wrong last night.

Dee was pensive momentarily. "...No, only Milo would have doubled back like that. Maybe because he's weird and complicated and overly-paranoid, but it would only *ever* have occurred to Milo to run across town late at night in the pouring rain on a gut-feeling." Dee suddenly knew that with complete certainty. Only her enigmatic, illogical and difficult husband could have suspected such unlikely danger.

"Offering your congratulations?" Milo had suddenly joined them and both Dee and Felix jumped; Felix instantly dropping her wrist from his hand.

"...I-I was just explaining to Felix what we discussed..."

"I know, honey." Milo briefly kissed her lips and Dee was slightly knocked off balance. She had the feeling the display was entirely for Felix. "Could I speak to Felix alone for a moment?"

"...Oh...um, okay..." Dee gave Felix a final worrisome glance and gingerly walked away.

Felix shoved his hands in his pockets. "So, are we going to start with the threats now?"

"You fucked my wife, did you think I was going to come over here and kiss you?" Milo said coldly.

"...Nothing physical ever would have happened if you hadn't been such an asshole!"

"It's that goddamn self-preserving attitude that you've always had about the whole thing that makes me sure that I could never forgive you! It's never your fault, is it? You've never apologised, you've never been remotely sorry for what you did!" Milo glowered, angry yes, but there was an element of hurt in his voice that Felix hadn't witnessed before now. "...You were like a brother to me, I was closer to you than I was even to Forrest. What kind of man does that to family? You knew what Dee meant to me..."

Felix licked his dry lips. "...I knew the moment it happened I should never have kissed Dee. I fucked up and I fully accepted that. I swear it would never have been repeated if you hadn't gone off the rails like you did. I wanted you and Dee to get back together just as much as anyone else did," Felix explained resentfully. "But you immediately hooked up with Amber, and you didn't even have the decency to come visit Dee in the hospital after her car accident. I thought she was going to *die*. It was then I- I realised how much I really cared about her...and that I didn't care about you anymore. I knew I could treat Dee far better than you ever could..."

"Whatever helps you sleep at night," Milo muttered disparagingly.

"I tried to apologise a million times but you wouldn't see me, you wouldn't take any of my calls or answer my texts!" Felix snapped. "And how dare you place the entire blame on me after the unforgivable way you treated your own wife!"

"You know nothing! You have no idea what I was going through!" Milo very nearly exploded right there at the bar, but calmed himself. "If you were anyone else -" he began again with a kind of malevolent calmness which was far worse than his anger. "But because you're my family and I did care about you once, I'm going to let the fact that you seduced my wife go. Dee wants me to be less controlling and I'm going to be whatever she wants me to be. But don't come near her again. That means you don't come to my house, you don't set foot in the store, if you see her in the street - you cross the road. At family gatherings, you don't speak to her, smile at her, or even catch her eye. Is that clear?"

"If that's what she wants..."

"That's what she wants. Stay out of our lives," Milo said and turned to walk away.

"Hey..." Felix said and Milo looked back. "...Thank you...for rescuing her last night..."

Milo arched his eyebrows in bemusement and walked away. Felix watched him go and wondered how he had turned out to be the only loser in this whole fiasco.

WHAT BECOMES OF THE BROKENHEARTED?

Dee was standing at the far end of the bar, polishing off her second glass of champagne in five minutes. Felix had been so upset; it was his birthday and *she* had done that to him. Dee found the thought simply suffocating. Felix had been so kind to her, he had been there for her when the man who should have been...wasn't. Milo touched her waist and Dee spun around edgily.

"...You know I was just explaining, don't you? I needed to let him know we couldn't be friends anymore," she began immediately.

"I know that."

"It had to come from me or he wouldn't have understood."

"I know, I know. Calm down." Milo gently touched her face and, before she could quash it, she was crying.

She buried her head in his chest. "I'm just scared you're going to leave again if I so much as look at Felix in the wrong way."

"...I didn't leave because I caught you looking at each other-" Milo blurted before he had time to check himself and was instantly greeted by the mortified look on her face.

Dee took a step away from him. "Felix was right...you're going to be forever throwing what happened with him in my face. What you did to me was far worse than what I did to you."

"Was it? I let you think something was going on with Amber to get even with you. But you hooked up with Felix because...I don't know why - do you love him? You seem to have genuine feelings for him!" It seemed both had been working so hard to be forgiving last night and this morning, that they had forgotten to air their resentments.

"Of course I don't love him! Nor do I have feelings for him!" Actually, she did. But although she wanted to be honest with Milo, telling him this would simply be too destructive to their fragile relationship. "You started this! You admitted that!"

"...I-I'm sorry, I didn't mean it. I love you so much, and it just hurts seeing you with him..." Milo pulled her closer to him again. Dee was in two minds about pushing him away, but decided to let him hold her. "Why is Felix taking this so hard if it was just a fling? He wants you to *be* with him, doesn't he...?" Milo wiped a tear from her cheek with his thumb.

Dee didn't know how to respond at first, whatever she said just put Felix in a worse light and she didn't want to do that to him. "...No, I think it's just upset him that we can't be friends anymore..."

"...No, you can't," Milo said softly. It wasn't what she wanted to hear, but it just had to be this way. "You belong to me...and I belong to you," he repeated something he'd said this morning.

"I hope you know how much I love you, Milo, and how glad I am we're back together," Dee professed tearfully as he held her close. "But promise me you won't make his life difficult. Felix is no more to blame than I am, and you forgave me. Promise me you'll just leave him alone..."

"What do you take me for? I have the right to be angry...but of course I'll leave him alone." Milo shook his head, letting her go; injured by that. Why did she feel the need to protect Felix?

"Thank you. And I swear I'll have nothing to do with him – he's out of my life," Dee pledged. Milo so needed to believe that, but he could not help but feel totally despondent. Felix - his cousin, his *friend*; a man who had never been a problem before – was certainly a problem now. Circumstantially, Felix had no real option but to remain in Milo and Dee's lives. And Milo had brought that problem about all by himself. "...Now please give me a hug," she entreated him weakly. Slowly and tentatively he replaced his arms about her. Dee climbed up on her tiptoes to plant a kiss on his mouth. He responded gently at first, then with a rather passionate kiss of his own, cupping her face in his hands. Milo, by the skin of his teeth, had secured his place in her life again - and he wasn't about to allow Felix any room to muscle him back out.

*

The reunited pair did not feel Felix's stare still fixed upon them through the crowds. Painfully, he witnessed their rejuvenated adoration for each other. He stood jostled and bumped by other party goers, and pondered how he had managed to misjudge that woman's feelings so badly. He wondered how he had allowed his own feelings to become so raw and unchecked. Felix shook his aching head and decided to leave the party.

As he turned to go he found Evan blocking his exit path. Felix eyed him warily, and mentally prepared himself for yet another confrontation. "You're not leaving, are you?" Evan asked.

"Yep – this party has suddenly begun to suck very badly."

"But it's *your* birthday. From what I understand, Dee and Milo are just ducking in to show their faces and then they'll be off again."

"I think I'm done." Felix motioned to wander off but Evan stopped him with a knowing look.

"She's making a mistake," he assured him sagely.

"...Did you tell her that?" Felix scratched his head, not really expecting an ally from the Campbell camp.

"It's not my place, but she knows I'm concerned..." Evan swirled the remnants of the wine around his glass pensively. "Nobody would blame you if you decided to exit stage left at this point, and I'm really not sure if you're prepared to wait it out - because things will probably get worse before they get better. But if you did decide to stick around, I have this feeling that your time will come..." For some reason, Evan knew he just had to come over here and give Felix that piece of advice. Because he felt as sure as he had ever felt about anything that it was true.

"Are you living in some alternate universe to the rest of us? Because I've been told in no uncertain terms by Milo that I'm not to come within twenty feet of her again. And he appears to have brainwashed Dee into agreeing with those terms."

Evan sighed. "Look, Dee invested so much into that marriage that I think she feels she has no choice but to give it another shot. She has two children and to all intents and purposes – they're Milo's. So if you look at it from her position – she *has* to try again. But I'm telling you – that marriage isn't going to work out. I never had a problem with Milo before all this blew up, but I see now that he isn't quite right. And I think you're a completely sound guy who also just happens to be perfect for her. The problem is, Dee hasn't quite figured that out yet – but I think she will..."

"Are you serious? Milo just did a marathon-man last night and ran across town to save her from Cameron. I can't compete with that, Evan." Felix almost laughed at the futility of it all.

"Maybe, but you can't base a marriage on gratitude alone," Evan shrugged.

Felix eyed him apprehensively. "Look, I appreciate the support and all, but I've had about as much as I can take tonight. It's time to bail..."

"You can't just go, it's *your* birthday party," Evan reasoned again.

"Actually it's Ginny's party thrown by Jerry. I was just tacked-on because I'm her twin. Anyway, I've had worse birthdays...no, actually I haven't. Still, I think I'll go and drink myself into oblivion somewhere else." He patted Evan's arm and took another step to go.

"Then I'll come with you." Evan put his drink down on a nearby table.

"Look, you really don't need to be charitable – all your friends are here..."

He gave a dismissive sniff. "They won't miss me when I'm gone. And I'm your friend too – sort of. Come on, nobody wants to drink alone on their birthday," Evan smiled. Felix puffed up his cheeks, blowing a slightly baffled sigh out of his lips.

"Well, if you insist – The Grapes?"

"The Grapes it is," Evan agreed with a rub of his hands.

Felix nodded. "Let's bounce."

Evan winced. "Really...? *Bounce*? Didn't you just turn thirty-eight?"

Felix laughed for the first time today. "Thirty-eight isn't old!" he assured Evan as they wandered to the room exit.

"Face it, it's very nearly forty..."

*

Dee and Milo would not be far behind. Although they were happy to be together after five months of torturous separation, their feelings were more of relief and tonight was not a night for celebrating. It was a night for reflecting on past mistakes and being utterly grateful for second chances. Milo sat up on a barstool and Dee nestled between his knees, her back to him and her eyes on the room. Felix had left his own birthday party because of her. Dee hadn't seen him go but he wasn't here, she just knew it.

"I don't know about you, but I don't really want to be here anymore," Dee said, fiddling with the bracelet on her wrist that he had once bought her. "I'm so relieved we're back together but I don't feel like partying. This has possibly been the worst year of my life; you leaving me, Gordon dying, and Cameron-"

Milo kissed the top of her head. "I know...but we're only halfway through the year. I swear I'll make the second half better."

"...What I *really* want is to go home, and after an hour or so of trying to work out how to get into our house, I'd like to spend some more time alone with my husband..." Dee grinned sheepishly to herself. Even though she couldn't see his face, his feelings were expressed as his arms tightened around her waist.

Even Milo could not help a little smile creep onto his mouth. "...Your husband thought you'd never ask." Encouraged at last, Milo jumped off the barstool, took her hand and led her off to the exit of the reception room.

"Do you think we need to say goodbye to the others?" Dee wondered.

"That could take an hour in itself," Milo assured her. "Let's just creep off quietly. Everybody knows that we only came to break the news."

"And it went as well as could be expected - you being a hero helped," Dee decided.

"I do hope you're going to stop calling me that one day soon," Milo rolled his eyes.

"Why would I do that when I know how much it winds you up?" she teased. "And think of the opportunities for role-play during foreplay. I think I'd make a great damsel in distress."

"You? Don't make me laugh." Milo shook his head. "And I see your propensity for being weird hasn't gone away."

Dee pondered over that. "It was lying dormant for a while, but I'm afraid it's flared up again."

"Good," he said gruffly, giving her that good-natured glare. "I think I might have missed that most of all."

They discreetly left the Georgian reception room, heading off to their new (or rather, their old but recently upholstered) life. Every step would be a baby step but Dee determined to put things right. Milo had his problems, that couldn't be dismissed to the back of her mind anymore, but he was *her* problem. He had too much potential for her to give up on him now. She knew his true gentle nature and he realised there was nobody more accepting, tolerant and forgiving than her. Dee saw something worthwhile in him that perhaps other people couldn't see, but then she always had. And Milo would never allow the only person in this world prepared to understand his nature be taken from him again. Not without a fight, anyway.

THE END

A NOTE ABOUT THE AUTHOR

Adele Archer was born in Bethnal Green, East London in the 1970's, the second youngest of six children. Growing up in a council flat in not the most salubrious part of town, she was always a dreamer - and her imagination was the best escape of all. Adele was writing books from the age of eleven - but inventing stories in her head long before that.

Adele spent the majority of her working life as a trained nurse but it was in 2011, after the death of her beloved sister, that she decided it was time that writing novels could no longer just be a secret hobby. Because, in her bitter experience, life was too short for *'if onlys'*.

'American Cousins' is the second in the series of the three-book 'International Relations' saga. Book three coming soon. She also writes an amusing weekly blog, 'Adele Archer Writes'.

Adele now resides in the West Country with her wonderful husband and two amazing daughters. In her spare time, she writes songs and sings, reads voraciously and crams in as many period/costume drama shows as her long-suffering family will allow. She would wear a bustle and a bonnet on a daily basis if she could...

Printed in Great Britain
by Amazon